Praise for Ellen Datlow's
INFERNO

"Award-winning SF/fantasy editor Datlow's first non-themed collection includes twenty stories by British and Australian writers that run the gamut from the grotesque to family-security worries. . . . All of the stories are wisely chosen and deserve the attention and comment."

—*Library Journal*

"When you see [Datlow's] name attached to a book, you know you're in for a rich literary meal. And what a feast it is! The writing on display in *Inferno* is exquisite, and the concepts even more so. You won't find any tired old clichés here, only fiercely original stories told with some of the best prose I've read all year. *Inferno* is a monument to all that horror fiction is capable of."

—*Fearzone*

"There was no absence of high-quality writing in this far above the average original selection."

—Don D'Ammassa, *SF Chronicle*

"*Inferno* delivers in full on its awaited premise, and Ellen Datlow stands on the same plinth as Dante, if only in fright-coordinating echo. More anthologies like *Inferno,* and its predecessor of a few years ago, *The Dark,* should be urgent priorities. It's very clear that horror at short length is poised for a major revival."

—Nick Gevers, *Locus*

"Ellen Datlow is the queen of anthology editors in America. She has great taste, an amazing talent for finding good new writers, and many, many enduring friendships in the community of SF/fantasy/horror writers, which means she can always call upon the cream of the crop. *Inferno* isn't just good, it is astonishingly good, the product of an editor who really knows what she is doing."

—Peter Straub, *New York Times* bestselling author of
In the Night Room

Turn the page to see more raves for *Inferno*.

"Fans of horror fiction owe it to themselves to pick up this creepy, stylish anthology." —*SciFi.com*

"*Inferno* promised twenty original tales of terror, and it wasn't kidding. Killer stories by Gallagher, Cadigan, Ford, and Jeter make it worth the price alone. But the others are no slouch in the terror department either; they're jacked-up and creeped down, perfect for late-night reading when you want to get your chill on. An excellent anthology."
—Joe R. Lansdale, author of *Lost Echoes*

"This is a smorgasbord for any horror reader, regardless of where his or her interests may lie; horror, terror, or gross out. This book serves up excellent, high-quality creep." —*The Green Man Review*

"The literary writers have their Nobel Literary Prizes and Oprah. The mystery writers have the *New York Times* bestseller lists. The science fiction writers have guest of honor appearances, and the horror writers have Ellen Datlow. We have many horror editors churning out multiauthor collections, but few are even close to being as competent and talented as Ellen Datlow." —*Whispers of Wickedness*

"A great horror anthology that features a nice mix of established and newer writers. Nathan Ballingrud's 'The Monsters of Heaven' is particularly ferocious, but stories by Lucius Shepard, Jeffrey Ford, Conrad Williams, and many others are also very effective." —Jeff VanderMeer, *Locus Online*

"Ellen Datlow is a lover of short horror fiction, and her work as one of the best-known and most-loved editors in the field of fantastic literature is unparalleled. . . . [She] is to be commended for her body of work, and this latest collection of hers deserves to be widely read." —*Dayton City Paper*

"Datlow's *Inferno* is a legend-in-the-making anthology that should find a home on your bookshelf between *Prime Evil* and *The Descent of Horror*. This is the real deal, folks." —J. L. Comeau, *Countgore.com*

"This must for fans of horror is a strange and motley array of stories. While there is no theme per se, there is a pervasive sense of loss, vengeance, and horror that fans will enjoy—if one can call being completely creeped out enjoyable."
                                                            —*Romantic Times BOOKreviews*

. . . And for *The Dark*

"Datlow has cast her net beyond the horror genre's usual names and pulled in contributors whose stories are the equal of their best work, as well as mystery, fantasy, and SF writers whose tales seem to be the ghost story they've always wanted to tell. This book is sure to provide a yardstick by which future ghost fiction will be measured."
                                                    —*Publishers Weekly* (starred review)

"Crack genre editor Datlow draws top-notch talent. *The Dark* is one of those must-buy anthologies for anyone who enjoys well-written ghost stories that will have readers starting at shadows and turning on night-lights."
                                                            —*St. Louis Post-Dispatch*

"Datlow remains one of the surest anthologists in the business, with catholic tastes, impeccable discernment, and access to top talent. *The Dark* offers a wide range of specters and approaches to them, from Jamesian subtlety to outright, no-bones-about-it horror shows. It's a good selection to dip into on long winter nights."
                                                            —*San Francisco Chronicle*

"Datlow again proves she's one of the top editors in the horror field, collecting sixteen memorable ghost stories together in a single volume, proving that there's plenty of life left in this subgenre. Highly recommended."
                                                            —Hank Wagner, *Hellnotes*

"Any anthology of stories edited by Ellen Datlow is a volume to savor. Datlow's *The Dark* proves there is quite a gamut to run when it comes to the modern ghost and there are still chills to be found in spectral stories."
                                                            —*Cemetery Dance*

INFERNO

New Tales of Terror
and the Supernatural

EDITED BY

Ellen Datlow

A Tom Doherty Associates Book
New York

INFERNO

Copyright © 2007 by Ellen Datlow

A Tor Book
Published by Tom Doherty Associates, LLC
175 Fifth Avenue
New York, NY 10010

www.tor-forge.com

Tor® is a registered trademark of Tom Doherty Associates, LLC.

Library of Congress Cataloging-in-Publication Data

Inferno : new tales of terror and the supernatural / edited by Ellen Datlow.
        p. cm.
    "A Tor book."
    ISBN-13: 978-0-7653-1559-5
    ISBN-10: 0-7653-1559-9
  1. Horror tales, American. 2. Horror tales, English. 3. Short stories, American.
4. Short stories, English. 5. American fiction—21st century. 6. English fiction—
21st century. I. Datlow, Ellen.
    PS648.H6I56 2007
    823'.0873808—dc22

                                                                    2007026073

First Hardcover Edition: December 2007
First Trade Paperback Edition: April 2009

Printed in the United States of America

0 9 8 7 6 5 4 3 2 1

Copyright Acknowledgments

I would like to dedicate this book to the memory of
CHARLES L. GRANT,
master storyteller, editor of the Shadows *series,*
and lovable curmudgeon (even when he was young).
We'll never forget you.

1942–2006

Acknowledgments

I'd like to thank Gordon Van Gelder, who came up with the title several years ago at a dinner party. During the discussion of a good title for a non-theme horror anthology that I wanted to edit, he said, "How about 'Datlow's Inferno'?" We all laughed and I thought, how silly . . . yet when I actually wrote up the proposal, "Inferno" as a title didn't seem so bad. And, of course, when anyone asks for it, I hope they'll request "Datlow's Inferno."

I'd also like to thank my editor, James Frenkel, who fought hard to buy the book, and who has been supportive all along the way to the anthology's completion.

Contents

Introduction

ELLEN DATLOW

I love the horror short story and novella. To me, they're the most powerful and important forms in the field. For at least two hundred years the short form has proven to be enormously fertile ground for dark literature that plumbs the depths of fear and the evil that may reside in the human soul.

Undeniably, the novels of Stephen King and such other dark novels as *The Monk* by Matthew Gregory Lewis, *Dracula* by Bram Stoker, *Frankenstein* by Mary Shelley, as well as those by H. P. Lovecraft, have been enormously popular. Nonetheless, throughout the history of British and American horror, the short story has been the most celebrated form of the genre. Edgar Allan Poe, Nathaniel Hawthorne, M. R. James, Robert Bloch, Robert Aickman, Ray Bradbury, Shirley Jackson, Charles Beaumont, Richard Matheson, Ramsey Campbell, and Dennis Etchison, to name but a small number of great practitioners of the genre, are some of the authors who come to mind when we think of those who have crafted many of our favorite horror and terror tales.

I think that fiction of the supernatural works better in the shorter forms for the simple reason that the short form lends itself with great ease and flexibility to an enormous variety of narrative styles and strategies. Novels, while they can be quite chillingly effective, are an entirely different matter. Very few longer works truly carry the power to force the reader to sustain the suspension of disbelief necessary for the kind of stunning, chilling, or flat-out terrifying effect of a great short work.

Over the course of my career as an editor thus far, I have edited a number of anthologies that focus on stories with a common theme, the subjects ranging from sexual horror to cat horror stories; from stories of vengeance and revenge to ghost stories. I've enjoyed editing them all, but have always wanted to edit an all-original, non-themed horror anthology—to showcase the range of subjects imagined by a number of my favorite writers inside and outside the horror field.

The non-themed horror anthology is a rich part of the horror tradition: Series such as *The Pan Book of Horror* (taken over for several years by Gollancz and retitled *Dark Terrors*), edited by Stephen Jones and David Sutton;

Shadows, edited by the late Charles L. Grant; *Masques,* edited by the late J. N. Williamson; and *Borderlands,* edited by Thomas F. Monteleone are all fine examples of series that have published outstanding original short fiction.

There have also been major one-shots of reprinted material such as *The Playboy Book of Horror* (an anthology that strongly influenced me as a reader and editor); *The Arbor House Treasury of Horror and the Supernatural,* edited by Bill Pronzini; *Great Tales of Terror and the Supernatural,* edited by Phyllis Wagner and Herbert Wise; *The Dodd, Mead Gallery of Horror,* edited by Charles L. Grant; *Modern Masters of Horror,* edited by Frank Coffey; *The Dark Descent,* edited by David G. Hartwell; and *The Mammoth Book of Terror,* edited by Stephen Jones. And the past thirty years have witnessed the publication of one-shot anthologies of original material. I think especially of the enormously successful *Dark Forces,* edited by Kirby McCauley; and others like *The Cutting Edge* and *Metahorror,* edited by Dennis Etchison; *Prime Evil* and *Revelations,* edited by Douglas E. Winter; and *999,* edited by Al Sarrantonio.

When I've edited non-themed reprint anthologies (two OMNI series and twenty volumes of the horror half of *The Year's Best Fantasy and Horror*), I've usually been surprised to discover that certain ideas or, if you will, themes recur anyway, and it's not until the contents are chosen and I look at the stories as a group that the stories' commonality reveals itself to me. However, the themes that I discover in those anthologies are the product of the work of authors writing for other editors, in a wide variety of venues ranging from slick magazines to semiprofessional 'zines, from single-author story collections to themed anthologies edited by any number of different editors.

In the present volume, though, I present for the first time stories all of which I've chosen and edited. And all of them had to succeed on my terms: to provide the reader with a frisson of shock, or a moment of dread so powerful it might cause the reader outright physical discomfort; or a sensation of fear so palpable that the reader feels impelled to turn up the lights very bright and play music or seek the company of others to dispel the fear; or to linger in the reader's consciousness for a long, long time after the final word is read. Such stories are my passion. For fear is a part of life, and horrific or frightening stories have always been the surest way humanity has found to deal with the very tangible terrors of the real world. It's been that way since people first sat around a fire, surrounded by the darkness and dangers of the wild beyond their circle of light. Listening to stories of the terrifying beasts and other natural threats, our ancestors used narratives to help conquer their fears, by putting them into tales that they themselves wrought, stories in which they dealt with fears by naming them, thus rendering them known, less powerful for being told, the stories handed down from generation to generation, a tool that has never lost its power and usefulness.

My editor at Tor Books, Jim Frenkel, told me, when we first discussed *Inferno,* that he still remembers with utter clarity the sensation of being terrified by a story he read when he was twelve years old. The details had blurred for him over the decades, but the actual feelings—of fear, of disquietude, of dread—remain vivid for him to this day. So vivid, in fact, that merely bringing up the subject caused him to experience immediately a flood of sensations which brought him a shiver that he couldn't suppress. I have memories like this as well as do, I know, many other people who enjoy horror.

But there are those who don't read horror, short form or long, and there's no arguing with personal tastes in reading, or anything else. Such people don't seem to understand that being scared by the act of reading a work of fiction is not necessarily a trivial pursuit; at its best, it can be an act of catharsis. A cheap one, perhaps, but nonetheless quite real. When we are taken from the real world to a place only available through a story, we are free to be as frightened, as helpless as we can bear.

When the story is over and we emerge back in the real world, we've survived a test of courage, or of endurance, or whatever other tests the skilled author has posed to challenge us—or our imaginary avatar, as created within the narrative. And back in the real world, we are once again whole—and often, as readers have experienced in the most effective tales, we are more whole than before. A gifted storyteller's craft can uplift, transform, and challenge us in ways that are either unlikely or downright impossible in the real world.

Vicarious adventures in terror are a lot easier to survive than some of the terrors we face in life. Violence, violation, loss, revulsion; mental, emotional, or physical suffering . . . all are trials that in life may bow us and break our spirit. In fiction, though, we survive them and are strengthened by our survival.

And that is the beauty of short horror. In its shorter lengths, horror fiction, as evidenced in an enormous number of effective, memorable works, continues to be a literary form that speaks to us powerfully. If one needs confirmation of this assertion, one needs look no further than film and television, which have been mining short fiction for almost a century. Television series such as *The Twilight Zone, Alfred Hitchcock Presents,* and others, as well as films too numerous to mention, have successfully adapted short horror fiction to the shivery delight of generations of viewers.

So here are twenty stories I hope you'll enjoy. After editing as many books and magazines as I have, I'm not so naïve as to believe you'll agree with every single story I've chosen. But if even one of these tales does for you what they have all done for me, perhaps you will have one of those great memories that will stay with you always, a memory of something dark, dangerous, and brooding. One that will bring you a momentary thrill when you recall it.

So . . . what have I discovered in putting together *Inferno*? Although there are no demonic children, there are missing children, abused and/or orphaned children who have experienced unspeakable horrors; angry adult children, children who inadvertently cause pain to their loved ones. The relationship between parent and child is primal and powerful, and its influence is lifelong.

In addition, you'll find psychological and supernatural stories of madmen and -women; of the powerless and of those with too much power; tales of revenge and vengeance and loss.

To my mild surprise, I noticed there are no war stories here. Perhaps authors have realized that there is enough horror in the real wars we've been fighting for years. Nor are there zombies, vampires, witches (well, maybe one, if you stretch it), evil children, or werewolves. Their absence is not intentional, but I don't think readers will be disappointed by the absence of these staples of horror fiction. There are plenty of other monsters within these pages.

I hope you'll enjoy encountering them as I've enjoyed presenting them.

ELLEN DATLOW
New York City
November 2006

INFERNO

Riding Bitch

K. W. JETER

K. W. Jeter has written some very edgy novels, including Dr. Adder, The Glass Hammer, *and* Infernal Devices. *He has also had a number of short stories published. His work defies classification.*

A lot was still going to happen.

He would stand at the bar, he knew, locked in the embrace of his old girlfriend.

"Probably wasn't your smartest move." Ernie the bartender would run his damp rag along the wood, polished smooth by the elbows of generations of losers. "Sounds like fun at the beginning, but it always ends in tears. Trust me, I know."

He wouldn't care whether Ernie knew or not. The beer wouldn't do anything to numb the pain. Not the pain of having a dead girl, whom once he'd loved, draped across his shoulders. Her left arm would circle under his left arm. When she'd been alive, whenever she'd conked out after too many Jäger's and everything else, she'd always wrapped herself around him just like that, from the back. Up on tiptoes in her partying boots, just blurrily awake enough to clasp her hands over his heart.

He would knock back the rest of the beer in front of him, remembering how he'd carried her, plenty of nights, when there'd still been partying left in him. He'd shot racks of pool like this, leaning over the cue with her negligible weight curled on top of his spine like a drowsy cat, her face dropping close beside his, exhaling alcohol as he took his shot, skimming past the eight ball. . . .

Her breath wouldn't smell of anything other than the formaldehyde or whatever it was that Edwin had pumped her full of, back at the funeral parlor. And it wouldn't really be her breath, anyway, her not having any in that condition. He would gaze at the flickering Oly Gold neon in the bar's bunker-like window, and swish another pull of beer around in his mouth, as though it could Listerine away the faint smell in his nostrils. The dead didn't sweat, he would discover, but just exuded—if you got that close to them—an odor half the stuff hospital floors were mopped with, half Barbie-doll plastic.

"Those look like they chafe."

Ernie the bartender would catch him tugging at the handcuffs, right where the sharp edge of metal would be digging through his t-shirt and into the skin over his ribs.

"Yeah," he'd say, "they do a bit." *Should've thought of that before you let 'em strap her on.* "I wasn't thinking too clearly then."

"Hm?" Ernie wouldn't look over at him, but would go on peering into the beer mug he'd just wiped with the bar towel.

"I blame it on Hallowe'en," he would explain.

"Hallowe'en, huh?" Ernie would glance at the Hamm's clock over the bar's entrance. "That was over three hours ago." Ernie would lick a thumb and use it to smear out a grease spot inside the mug. "Over and done with, pal."

"Couldn't prove it around here." The bar would be all orange-'n'-blacked out with the crap that the beer distributors unloaded every year: cheap cardboard stand-ups of long-legged witches with squeezed cleavage, grinning drunk pumpkins Scotch-taped to the wall over by the men's room, bar coasters with black cats arched like croquet wickets, Day-Glo spiderwebs, dancing articulated skeletons with hollow eyes that would've lit up if the batteries hadn't already run flat by the thirtieth, everything with logos and trademarks and brand names.

"Why do you let them put all that up, Ernie?"

"All what up?" The bartender would start on another mug, scraping away a half-moon of lipstick with his thumbnail. "What're you talking about?"

He'd give up then. There'd be no point. What difference would it make? He'd shift the dead girl a little higher on his shoulder, balancing her against the tidal pull of the beers he would put away. The combination of low-percentage alcohol with whatever the EMTs would huff him up with, when they scraped him off the road and into their van, would wobble his knees. Hanging onto the edge of the bar, instead of trying to walk, might be the only good idea he'd have that night.

And not all the ideas, the weird ones, would be his. There would still be that whole trip the other guys in the bar would come up with, about the reason Superman flies in circles.

But everything else—that would still be Hallowe'en's fault. Or what Hallowe'en had become. That was what he had told the motorheads, back when the night had started.

No—Cold lips would nuzzle his ear. *You've got it all wrong.*

He'd close his eyes and listen to her whisper.

It's what you became. What we became. That's what did it.

"Yeah . . ." He'd whisper to himself, and to her as well, so no one else could hear. "You're right."

"I blame it all on Hallowe'en."

"That so?" The motorhead with the buzz cut didn't even look up from the skinny little sport bike's exhaust. "What's Hallowe'en got to do with your sorry-ass life?"

He hadn't wanted to tell someone else exactly what. He hadn't wanted to tell himself, to step through the precise calculus of regret, even though he already knew the final sum.

"It's not me, specifically," he lied. "It's what it did to everything else. It's frickin' satanic."

That remark drew a worried glance from Buzz Cut. "Uhh . . . you're not one of those hyper-Christian types, are you?" He fitted a metric wrench onto a frame bolt. "This isn't going to be some big rant, is it? If it is, I gotta go get another beer."

"Don't worry." Something he'd thought about for a long time, and he still couldn't say what it was. Like humping some humongous antique chest of drawers out through a doorway too small for it, and getting it stuck halfway. He could wrestle it around into some different position, with the knobs wedged against the left side of the doorjamb rather than the right, but it would still be stuck there. "It's just . . ."

"Just what?"

He tried. "You remember how it was when you were a kid?"

"Vaguely." Buzz Cut shrugged. "Been a while."

"Regardless. But when we were kids, Hallowe'en was, you know, for kids. And the kids got dressed up, like little ghosts and witches and stuff. The adults didn't get all tarted up. They stayed home and handed out the candy."

"True. So?"

"So you've got three hundred and sixty-four other days, including Christmas, to act like a cheap bimbo, or to prove that you're a beer-soaked trashbag. Why screw around with Hallowe'en?"

"Dude, you have got to stop thinking about stuff like this." Buzz Cut went back to wrenching on the bike. "It's messing up your head."

He couldn't stop thinking about it, if pictures counted as thought. Didn't even have to close his eyes to see the raggedy pilgrimage, the snaking lines of pirates and bedsheeted ghosts and fairy princesses, and the kids you felt sorry for because they had those cheap store-bought costumes instead of ones their mothers made for them. All of them trooping with their brown paper grocery bags or dragging old pillowcases, already heavy with sugar loot, from the sidewalk up to the doorbell and back out to the sidewalk and the next house, so many of them right after each other, that it didn't even make sense to close the door, just keep handing out the candy from the big Tupperware bowl on the folding TV tray. And if you were some older kid—too old to do that stuff anymore, practically a sneering teenager already—standing behind your dad and looking past him, out through the front door and across the chill, velvety-black night streets of suburbia, looking with a strange-crazy clench in your stomach, like you were first realizing how big and fast Time was picking you up and rolling and tumbling you like an ocean wave, head over heels away from the shore of some world from which you were now forever banished—looking out as though your front porch were now miles up in the starry-icy air and you could see all the little kids of Earth winding from door to door, coast to coast, pole to pole, stations of a spinning cross . . .

No wonder these guys think I'm messed up. He had managed to freak himself, without even trying. *Like falling down a hole*. He tilted his head back, downing the rest of the beer, as though he could wash away that world on its bitter tide.

"So how's the nitrous setup working for you?"

Blinking, he pulled himself back up into the garage. Around him, the bare, unpainted walls clicked into place, the two-by-four shelves slid across them as though on invisible tracks, the cans of thirty-weight and brake fluid lining up where they had been before.

He looked over toward the garage door and saw the other motorhead, the red-haired one, already sauntered in from the house, picking through the butt-ends of a Burger King french fries bag in one hand.

"The nitrous?" It took him a couple seconds to remember which world that was a part of. At the back of his skull, a line of little ghosts marched away. An even littler door closed, shutting off a lost October moon. "Yeah, the nitrous . . ." He shrugged. "Fine. I guess."

"You guess," said Buzz Cut. "Jesus Christ, you pussy. We didn't put it on there so you could *guess* whether it works or not. We put it on so you'd use it. Least once in a while."

"Hey, it's okay." They'd both ragged him about it before. "It's enough to know I got it. Right there under my thumb."

Which was true. Even back when he and the motorheads had been installing the nitrous oxide kit on the 'Busa, he hadn't been thinking about ever using it. The whole time that the motorheads had been mounting the pressurized gas canister on the right flank of the bike—"Serious can of whup-ass," Buzz Cut had called it—and routing the feeder line to the engine, all 1298 cubic centimeters of it, they'd been chortling about how much fun would ensue.

"There's that dude with the silver Maserati Quattroporte, you see all the time over around Flamingo and Decatur. Thinks he's bad 'cause his machine can keep up with a liter bike."

"Hell." A big sneer creased Red's face. "I've smoked the sonuvabitch plenty of times."

"Not by much. That thing can haul ass when it's in tune and he's not too loaded to run it through the gears." Buzz Cut had tapped an ominous finger on the little nitrous can, *tink tink tink*, like a bomb. "But when this shit kicks in, Mister Hotshot Cager ain't gonna see anything except boosser taillight fading in the distance." He had looked away from the bike and smiled evilly. "Won't that be a gas? For real?"

He had supposed so, out loud, just to shut the two of them up. Neither motorhead, Buzz Cut or Red, had a clue about potentialities. How something could be real—realer than real—if it just hung there in a cloud of *still could happen*. Right now, the only way that he even knew the rig worked was that the motorheads had put the 'Busa on the Piper T & M dynamometer at the back of their garage and cranked it. Stock, they'd gotten a baseline pull of 155 point nine horsepower. Tweaking the nitrous setup with a number 43 jet, they'd wound up at 216 and a half, with more to go. "Now that's *serious* kick," Buzz Cut had judged with satisfaction.

It didn't matter to him, though. He sat in his usual perch on the greasy workbench, where he always sat when he came by the motorhead house, adding empty beer cans to the litter of tools and shop catalogues, and thought about the way their heads worked.

They didn't work the way his did. That was the problem, he knew. Nobody's did. *Or maybe mine doesn't work at all.* He had to admit that was a possibility. There'd been a time when it had—he could remember it. When it hadn't gone wheeling around in diminishing circles, like a bike whose rider had been scraped off in the last corner of the track. Gassing on about Hallowe'en and nitrous oxide buttons that never got punched, and somehow that made it all even realer than the little ghost kids had been—

Inside his jacket, his cell phone purred. He could have burst into tears, from sheer relief. He dug the phone out and flipped it open.

Edwin calling, from the funeral parlor. He didn't have to answer, to know; he recognized the number that came up on the postage-stamp screen. And he didn't have to answer, to know what Edwin was calling about. Edwin only ever called about one thing. Which was fine by him, since he needed the job and the money.

"I'll see you guys later." He pocketed the phone and slid down from the workbench. "Much later."

"Yeah, maybe." Buzz Cut had finished with his customer's bike, standing back from it and wiping his hands on a shop rag. "Maybe next Hallowe'en."

"So what is the big deal?" Behind Edwin, the grandfather clocks lining the hallway ticked like ratcheting crickets. "You take it *from* here, you take it *to* there. You drop it off. And you get paid." Edwin's manicured hand drew out an eelskin wallet; a finger with a trimmed, glistening nail flicked through the bills inside. "So why are you making it so hard on yourself?"

The tall clocks—taller than him, way taller than Edwin—were part of the funeral parlor decor. They had been Edwin's father's clocks, back when the old guy had run the place, and Edwin's grandfather's, who had started it all. Edwin had inherited the family business, right down to the caskets in the display room. You could hear the clocks all over the place, in the flower-choked foyer and past the softly murmuring, endlessly repeating organ music in the viewing rooms. Maybe they reminded the customers in the folding chairs of eternity, or the countdown to when they'd be lying in a similar velvet-lined box. So they had better talk to the funeral director on the way out and make arrangements.

"I don't know . . ." He looked down the hallway. Past Edwin's office was the prep room, where the public didn't go, where it was all stainless steel and fluorescent bright inside, and smelled chemical-funny. Edwin had taken him in there one time, when it had been empty, and shown him around. Including the canvas-strapped electrical hoist mounted on the ceiling, that Edwin's father had installed when his back had gone out from flipping over too much cold dead weight. "This is kinda different . . ."

"What's different?" Edwin's face was all puffy and shiny, as though he hadn't actually swallowed anything he drank—the glass with the melting ice cubes was still in his hand—and now the alcohol was leaking out through his skin. "It's the same as before."

"Well . . . no, actually." It puzzled him, that he had to explain this. "Before; there was like a van. Your van. And all I had to do was help you load it up, and then drive it over there."

"The van's in the shop."

That didn't surprise him. Everything about the funeral parlor was falling apart, gradually, including Edwin. Things stopped working, or something else happened to them, and then they were supposedly getting fixed but that never happened, either. Which was the main reason that all the funeral business now went over to the newer place over on the west side of town. With a nice big sweep of manicured lawn and a circular driveway for the mourners' cars, and an overhang jutting out from the glass-walled low building, so the casket could get loaded in the hearse without the flowers getting beaten up on a rainy day. All Edwin got was the occasional cremation, because the oven his father had installed was right there on the premises, in a windowless extension behind the prep room.

Or used to get—Edwin had managed to screw that up as well. To keep the money from dwindling away quite so fast, what he'd gotten after his dad died, he'd taken on a contract from the local animal shelter, to take care of the gassed dogs and cats, the ones too ugly or old or mean to get adopted out in ninety days. An easy gig, and reliable—the world never seemed to run out of stiff, dead little corpses—but Edwin hadn't been picky enough about raking out the ashes and the crumbly charred bits from the cooling racks. Edwin had still gotten some human-type jobs, family leftovers from his father and grandfather running the place, and some old widow had opened up the canister that nothing but her husband's remains was supposed to be in, and had found the top half of a blackened kitten skull looking back all hollow-eyed at her. Things like that were bad for business, word-of-mouth-wise. Even the animal shelter had unplugged itself from Edwin, and then the state had revoked the cremation license, and now the oven also wasn't working, or Edwin hadn't paid the gas bill or something like that. Edwin had told him what the deal was, but he hadn't really paid attention.

"I don't get it." He pointed down the ticking hallway, toward the prep room. "Why do they keep dropping jobs off here, anyway?"

"Hey." Edwin was sensitive about some things. "This is still an ongoing business, you know. Mortenson's gets booked up sometimes. They're not *that* big." That was the name of the other place, the nicer one. "So I can take in jobs, get 'em ready, then send 'em over there. Split the fees. Works for them, works for us. This is how you get paid, right?"

Barely, he thought. Hard to figure that the other funeral parlor did a fifty-fifty with Edwin, since they would do all the flowers and the setting up of the casket in the viewing room, the hearse and the graveside services, all of that. The actual getting the body into the ground. What would they pay Edwin for providing a slab-tabled waiting room? Not much. So no wonder that the most he got from Edwin, for driving the van back and forth, was a ten-dollar bill or a couple of fives. Only this time, there was no van.

"Actually," he mused aloud, "you should pay me more for this one. If I were to do it at all. Since I'd be providing the wheels."

"How do you figure that?" Impatience lit Edwin's pudgy face even brighter and shinier. "Gas is cheaper for a motorcycle than a van. Even a hopped-up monster like yours."

If he hadn't finished off the six-pack, back at the motorheads' place, he might have been able to come up with an argument. *It's my gas*, he thought. *I paid for it*. But Edwin had already steered him down the hallway, past the clocks, and right outside the prep room door.

"Just do it, okay?" Edwin pushed the door open and reached in to fumble for the light switch. "We'll work out the details later."

Edwin had another sideline to get by with, dealing cigarettes dipped in formaldehyde, that being something he had gallon jugs of. The customers at the funeral parlor's back door were all would-be hoody teenagers, slouching and mumbling. Their preferred brands seemed to be Marlboros and those cheesy American Spirits from the 7-Eleven. Edwin fired one up, puffed, then handed it to him. "Just to calm you down."

It had the opposite effect, as usual. The chemical smoke clenched his jaw vise-tight, the edges of the contracting world burnt red. He exhaled and followed Edwin inside the prep room.

"This better not be a bag job." He handed the dip back to Edwin. "Like that one that got hit by the train. That sucked." He'd hated everything about that particular gig, including hosing out the van afterwards.

"All in one piece." Edwin pulled the sheet off. "Looks like she's sleeping."

He looked down at what lay on the table, then shook his head. "You sonuvabitch." His fist was ready to pop Edwin. "This is not right."

"For Christ's sake. Now what's the matter?"

"What's the matter? Are you kidding?" The table's cold stainless-steel edge was right at his hip as he gestured. "I dated her."

"How long?"

He thought about it. "Four years. Practically."

Edwin took another hit, then snuffed the dip between his thumb and forefinger. "Not exactly being married, is it?"

"We lived together. A little while, at least."

"Like I said. Come on, let's not make a big production about this. Let's get her over to Mortenson's, let's get paid, let's get you paid. Done deal."

He turned back toward the table. At least she was dressed; that much was a comfort. She had on her usual faded jeans, with a rip across the right knee, and a sweatshirt he remembered buying her, back when they'd been an item. The sweatshirt said UNLV across her breasts. For some reason, she'd had a thing about college basketball, even though they'd never gone to a game. There was a cardboard box full of other Rebels junk, sweats and t-shirts and caps, that she'd left when she moved out of his apartment. Plenty of times, he'd come home drunk and lonely and horny, and he'd pull the box out of the closet, kneel down, and bury his face in its fleecy contents, lifting out the tangled sweatshirts and inhaling the faded, mingled scent of her sweat and Nordstrom's cosmetics counter perfumes, more stuff that he'd bought, usually around Christmastime. He still kept in his wallet the list she'd written out for him, the stuff she wore. Which meant that now, every time he opened it up to pay for a drink, he'd catch a glimpse of the little folded scrap of paper tucked in there, and his equally frayed heart would step hesitantly through its next couple of beats, until the wallet was safely tucked in his back pocket again and he was recovered enough to continue drinking. Which helped. Most of the time.

He didn't have to ask how she'd wound up here. She'd had bad habits, mainly the drinking also, back when they'd been hooked up. But he'd heard they had gotten worse after the split-up. He had mixed feelings about that. On one hand, there was a certain satisfaction in knowing that she was as screwed up about him as he was about her. On the other, a certain pang that came with the thought of her heart wheezing to a stop under the load of some cheap street crap.

Which was apparently what had happened. He could tell. Whatever prep work Edwin had done, it wasn't enough to hide the blue flush under her jaw-line. He'd had buddies go that way, and they'd all had that delicate Easter egg color beneath the skin.

"So you're gonna do it, right? Don't be a schmuck. Think about her. For once. If you don't take her over to Mortenson's, I'll have to dump her in a wheelbarrow and take her over there myself."

"Yeah, like that's gonna happen." He knew it wouldn't; Edwin got winded just heading upstairs to get another drink. "This is gonna be double."

"Fine. You got me in a jam. Just do it, okay?"

It struck him that maybe this was some elaborate joke on Edwin's part. What would the punchline be? Her sitting up on the table, opening her eyes and flashing her old wicked smile at him?

I wish. That was something else that wasn't going to happen.

"Exactly how do you propose I'm gonna get this done?" He knew from previous jobs that she wouldn't be stiff anymore. She didn't even smell stiff. "Maybe I could sling her over the back of the bike and bungee her down. Or maybe across the front fender, like those guys who go out deer hunting with their pickup trucks." He nodded. "Yeah, just strap her right on there. Who'll notice?" The dip load in his brain talked for him. "Maybe we could make a set of antlers for her out of some coat hangers."

"Look," said Edwin, "you don't have to get all pissy about this. I'm the one doing you a favor, remember? I thought of you because you're always going on about how you need the money."

Which was true. He nodded again, deflated. "All right. So what exactly did you have in mind?"

Edwin had already thought it through. He pulled the handcuffs out of his jacket pocket and held them up. "These'll do the trick. We just sit her on the bike behind you, throw her arms around your chest, clip these on her wrists and you're all set. Anybody sees you, just another couple cruising along. Young love."

"No way. She never liked to ride bitch." He'd found that out after he'd already pulled the stock seat off the 'Busa and put on a Corbin pillion for her.

"She always wanted her own scoot. Remember, I was gonna buy her that Sportster? The powder blue one."

"Yeah, yeah, yeah." Edwin gave him a wearied look. "It's not as if she's in a position to complain about it, is she?"

The guy had a point there.

Took a lot of wrestling—for which Edwin was no frickin' use—but he finally got on the road. With her.

He rolled on the throttle, in the dark, kicking it up from fifth to sixth gear as the single lane straightened out. The chill of her bloodless hands, icy as the links of the handcuffs, seeped through his leather jacket and into his heart.

He stayed off Boulder Highway and the bigger, brighter main streets, even though it meant racking up extra miles. There was a helmet law in this state, though he'd never heard of the cops enforcing it. Or anything else for that matter—you'd have to shoot the mayor to get pulled over in this town.

Still, just his luck, the one time some black 'n' white woke up, to get nailed with a corpse on back of the 'Busa. Cruel bastards to do it, though. He could see, without looking back over his shoulder, how her hair would be streaming in the wind, a tangling flag the color of night. With her pale cheek against his neck, she'd look as though she were dreaming of pure velocity, the destination that rushed just as fast to meet you, always right at the head-light's limit.

And if he closed his own eyes, as if he were sharing the same furious pillow of air with her . . .

Not a good idea. He didn't even see the patch of gravel, dropped on the asphalt by some construction truck. His eyes snapped open when the rear wheel started to skid out from beneath him. He yanked the 'Busa straight from the curve he'd banked into. The bike felt awkward and top-heavy with her weight perched a couple inches higher than his own. He steered into the skid, wrestling the bike back under control, his knee clearing the guardrail as he trod down on the rear brake.

That all took about one second. But that was enough to have shifted his cold passenger around on the seat behind him. The handcuffs rode up under his armpit, her face with its closed, sleeping eyes no longer close to his ear but now pushed into the opposite sleeve of his jacket, down below his shoulder. One of the boots that Edwin had worked back onto her ivory, blue-nailed feet had popped loose from the rear peg. Her denim-clad leg trailed behind the bike, the boot's stacked heel skittering on the road. The body slewed around even more as he squeezed the front brake tight. By the time he brought the 'Busa to a halt, she was almost perpendicular on the seat behind him, her hair dangerously close to snagging in the wheel's hub.

"God damn." Edwin and his stupid ideas—this whole job was becoming more of an annoyance than it was worth. He levered the kickstand down and leaned the bike's weight onto it. Her hair swept a circle in the roadside debris. He was annoyed at her as well. If she had still been alive, he would have figured she was doing it on purpose. Drunk and screwing around again. Her weight toppled him over as he swung his own leg off the bike.

Now she was underneath him. As though she had brought him down in a wrestling hold—back when they had lived together, he had taught her a couple of moves he remembered from the junior varsity squad. Above him, the stars of the desert sky spun, wobbled, then held in place. If he rolled his eyes back, he could just see her face, somewhere by his ribs. If she had opened her eyes, she could've seen the stars, too.

His thin gloves scuffed on the sharp-edged rocks as he rolled onto his hands and knees, pulling her up on top of himself. That much effort winded him. It wasn't that she was so heavy, but every part of her seemed to have cooked up its own escape plan, as though none of her wanted to get dumped off at another funeral parlor. Her legs sprawled on his other side, the boots twisting at the ankles.

The handcuffs had been an even dumber idea. Edwin probably got some thrill out of the notion. It would've worked better if they had dug up a roll of duct tape and strapped her tight to his body. This way, she had just enough of a hold on him to be a nuisance. In that, not much had changed from when she had been alive. He rooted around in his jacket pocket for the key; couldn't find it. It must've popped out, somewhere on the ground.

He tried standing up, and couldn't make it. He toppled forward and grabbed the bike to keep his balance. The near-vertical angle rolled her weight forward, the handcuffs sliding onto his shoulderblade, her head lolling in front of him. The bike gave way, the kickstand scything through the loose dirt. The hot engine burned through his trouser knee as he fell.

The three of them—corpse, motorcycle, and its rider—hit the side of the road hard. He could smell gasoline leaking from the tank's filler cap. The links of the handcuffs gouged the middle of his spine. She was sandwiched between him and the toppled bike, her face upturned toward him, as though waiting for a kiss, one denimed leg wedged into his groin.

He pushed himself away from the bike, dragging her up with him. The handcuffs slithered down to the small of his back as he managed to stand upright at last. That brought her face down to his belt level.

Well, that's sweet. He stroked her tangled, dusty hair back from her brow.

Just like old times. Memory tripped through his head, strong enough to screw him up worse.

"Come on," he spoke aloud. "Nice and all, but we gotta get going."

He reached down, grabbed her above the elbows and lifted. She only came up a few inches before he realized he was pulling up his trousers as well, the frayed denim cuffs sliding above the tops of his own boots.

"What the—" He looked down. His eyes had adjusted enough to the slivered moonlight, that he could see her hair had snagged in the trousers' zip.

It must've happened while he and the corpse had been wrestling on top of the fallen motorcycle. Every stupid, annoying thing was happening tonight. That brought back memories as well.

Her cold face was caught so close to him, he couldn't even slide his hands down between her cheek and the front of the trousers. Not without undoing his buckle first; the loose ends of his belt flapped down beside her shoulders. He sucked in his gut and managed—barely—to pinch the zipper's metal tag. "Damn," he muttered. "Come on, you bastard." Half-inch by reluctant half-inch, he worked the zipper open, his knuckles chilled against her brow. Loosened, the trousers slid partway down his hips.

The world lit up. Headlight beams raked across him, a car rounding the road's curve. He shielded his eyes from the probing glare. His shadow, and hers, spilled back across the empty landscape.

He could see the silhouettes of the people inside. The driver, his wife beside him, a couple of little kids in the backseat, their faces pugnosing against the side windows as they got a better look. He glanced down and saw how perfectly the white, shifting light caught her profile. Or at least the part of it that wasn't shadowed by his open fly.

Then the headlight beams swung away from him and down the length of road farther on. The car was right next to him; he could have let go of her arm and rubbed his hand across the car's flank as it sped past. Close enough that the people in the car didn't need the headlights to see what was going on, or think they saw. There was enough moonlight to glisten on the handcuffs' links as the driver looked up to his rearview mirror, the wife and kids gaping through the rear window.

My life's complete now. He had been there when some tourist yokels from Idaho or some other numb-nut locale had caught a glimpse of another world, where other stuff happened. Like the tightly rolled-up windows of their rental car had been the inch-thick glass of some darkened aquarium that you could push your nose up hard against and witness sharks copulating with jellyfish, all blurry and wet. It would give them something to talk about when they got back to Boise, especially the bit about the poor ravaged girl being handcuffed around the guy's waist.

Two streaks of red pulsed down the asphalt. The car had hit its brakes. Worse; he turned, looked over his shoulder and saw another red light come on, above the car. It flashed and wavered, with blue-white strobes on either side. They weren't tourists from out of state; he saw that now. He watched as a Metro patrol car threw a U-turn, one front wheel crunching across the gravel, then bouncing the suspension as it climbed back onto the road.

"Shit." The headlights pinned him again. He looked down and saw, as if for the first time, how luminous pale her skin was. *They could tell*, he thought in dismay. One thing to be spotted getting skulled on the side of the road, even with the handcuffs involved—that was probably happening all over this town at any given moment, not worth the police's attention. But with a corpse—was that a felony or just a misdemeanor? It didn't matter, what with him still being on parole for things he couldn't even remember when he was straight.

He lifted harder this time, his hands clamped to her ribcage, hard enough to snap free a lock of her hair and leave it tangled in his zipper. Her arms still encircled him; that actually made it easier to sling her against one hip, his other hand tugging his trousers back in place. The difficult part was getting the bike upright again, but somehow he managed, even as the patrol car's siren wailed closer. Red flashes bounced off the tank and the inside of the windscreen, as he lugged her onto the seat behind him, the cuffs slipping across the front of his jacket once more.

The 'Busa coughed to life. As he kicked it down to first and let off the clutch, the cop car slewed a yard in front of him, spattering road grit against the front fender. He yanked the bike hard to the right, bootsole scraping the asphalt, then wrenched it straight again, pouring on the throttle. Something loose—maybe her boot?—clipped the patrol car's taillight as he jammed past.

He was already into fourth, redlining the tach, by the time he heard the siren coming up behind him. Fifth, and the yowl faded for a moment, then just as loud again as the driver cop stood on the accelerator pedal. Hitting the nitrous button wouldn't do him any good. The road was too straight; if they had been up in the mountains with some tight twisties to slalom through, he could've left the cops way behind. Out here in the flat desert, though, they could just keep hammering on top of him, long after the nitrous canister was exhausted, until he either gave up or sliced a curve's guardrail too close. The first would leave him on the ground, but alive at least, with a tactical boot on his throat and a two-handed forty-four pointed between his eyes. The second would probably leave two corpses on the ground, one freshly bleeding from the impact.

Just as he hit sixth, the 'Busa screaming into triple digits, the siren and the flashing red light jumped in front of him. *How'd that happen?* He didn't have time to wonder. A shining white wall reared before him. The 'Busa's head-light painted a big red X in the middle of it. That was all he saw as the brakes grabbed hold, too late to keep the bike from hitting broadside, even as it fell.

"You with us, pal? How many fingers?"

He wasn't sure. "Two?"

"Close enough."

He tried to turn over on his side, but couldn't. She was still hooked up to him, arms encircling him on the cot where they lay.

The paramedic van was like the inside of his head. Eye-achingly lit up, smelling of chemicals, and filled with mysterious objects that he didn't rec-ognize.

"You hit us a good one." One of the EMTs had a knotted ponytail. He pointed to a spot near the van's floor. "You can see the dent from in here."

"I can pay for it." He pushed himself up on his elbow. "Not right now, but—"

"Forget that." The other EMT, looking back from the driver's seat, had tattoos and smoke-reddened eyes. The whole van reeked of party atmos-phere. "This is not good."

"Yeah, yeah, I know." He tugged at the handcuffs but they stayed locked. "Look, just don't hand me over to the cops—"

"Cops? What cops?" The EMTs glanced at each other, above him. "We didn't see any cops."

A small comfort, that he was just screwed up and not pursued. *I must've made 'em up.* Another good reason for not riding in that kind of condition—all that beer and the hit off the dip that Edwin had given him.

"I'll just be on my way." The van's interior swam and tilted as he sat up, dragging her with him. "You don't have to report this—"

"Report it? Are you kidding? This is a frickin' fatality situation."

"What?" Then he realized what the tattooed one was talking about. "Uhh . . . actually, she was this way before."

They weren't listening to him. "I'm not calling it in," said Ponytail. "*You* call it in."

"Screw that. I'm not filling in all that paperwork again. I did the last one we had. Remember? The coronary?"

"Guys—"

"Well, we can't just let him walk."

"Why not?"

They both looked at him, then at each other, then back to him. Ponytail slowly nodded. "Maybe . . ."

He put his weight on his left foot. The resulting bolt through his spine nearly took the top of his skull off. He collapsed backward, propped up by the dead girl.

"You're not going anywhere in that condition, pal."

He looked down at himself and saw how ripped-up his trousers were. The whole long seam along the left leg had been torn open, the skin beneath bruised and chewed red by a skid over asphalt. God knew what condition the bike was in.

"I don't care." He gripped the edge of the cot with sweating hands, trying to keep from passing out. "I gotta get out of here. I got a delivery to make."

"Her?" Ponytail nodded toward the shackled weight, with the long dark hair and dreaming face.

"Give him something," said the driver. "Just get him on the road. Long as I don't have to fill out any paperwork, it's cool."

"Right—" Ponytail nodded as he fumbled around with the equipment shelved on either side. He spun a valve on a chrome canister, then tethered the plastic mask to his own face. He inhaled deeply, then held it out. "Here, try this."

The van expanded and dissolved with the first hit. The blood throb in his battered leg faded, along with any other sensation of having a body. All he could feel was her pulseless hug around his chest. He pushed the mask away. The paramedic van slowly coalesced, now formed of sheets of vaguely transparent gelatin, warping beneath him and yielding to a poke of his finger.

"Off you go, pal." Ponytail maneuvered him toward the van's open doors, like a parade balloon. "You have a good night. Try and stay out of trouble, okay?"

He found himself standing in the middle of an empty road, his wavering legs straddling a long scrape mark gouged out of the pavement. At its end, the 'Busa leaned on its kickstand. The EMTs must have picked it up after he T-boned their van. He wanted to thank them, but they were already gone.

He pulled his passenger along with himself, over toward the bike. She seemed weightless as well, the handcuffs the only thing keeping her from floating away into the glittering night sky. The toes of her boots seemed to barely trail across the earth's surface.

"That was nice of them." He laid his hands on the tank. He could smell gasoline, but the bike didn't seem in too bad of a shape. The left fairing was a total write-off; that must have been the side he laid it down on. The pegs and bits of engine on that flank were scraped gleaming and raw. It could probably be ridden, if he could figure a way of holding on to it without getting blown away by the wind, like roadside scrap paper.

Whatever the EMTs had given him, he was still way slammed by it. The chemical tides in his bloodstream would have to roll out a bit—or a lot—before he'd be able to climb on the 'Busa again. *Sleep it off*, he told himself. Maybe he could just curl up at the side of the road, wrap her tighter around himself, spooning like old times. . . .

Better not. A soft voice whispered at his ear. *I can't keep you warm anymore. Not like this*.

That was when he knew exactly how screwed up he was. And not by whatever was still percolating in his brain. That you could get over. The past, you never did.

He looked around and spotted, if not refuge, at least a waiting room. One that both of them were familiar with. How had he wound up in this part of town?

It didn't matter. He gripped her arms and brought her up higher on his back, her cheek close beside his, and stumbled toward the bar's sputtering neon.

"The problem's not Hallowe'en," said Ernie. "It's you."

Don't listen to this guy.

He didn't know if the bartender could hear what she said. Maybe the dead spoke only in private whispers. Like lovers. He knocked back the latest beer that had been placed in front of him. "Why is it me?"

Like I said. Her voice again. *This one was always full of crap*.

"You really want to know why?"

He shrugged. "Do I have a choice?"

"You don't even want one." Ernie wiped his sodden towel across the bar. "Here's the deal. You're blaming the world for what happened to you. That's all backwards."

Right now, the world consisted of this bar and its tacky, orange 'n' black decorations, courtesy of the beer distributors. He looked around at the dangling pasteboard junk, then back to Ernie. "I didn't do this." He pointed to the grinning, long-legged witches. "You can't blame me."

Yes, he can. You just wait.

The bar had emptied. He was the only one left inside, after Ernie the bartender had switched off the outside neon. While he had nursed one of the string of beers, Ernie had started stacking the chairs up on the tables. Then he had come back behind the bar to finish sorting out the world's problems.

"Just hear me out," said Ernie. "I mean, it's cool that you came here with your iced old lady cuffed to you. That shows some effort on your part." ·

"Hey. We broke up, remember?"

Did we?

He ignored her whisper. "Long time ago," he told the bartender.

Not long enough.

"Whatever." Ernie seemed not to have heard anything she said. "But that doesn't suffice. You gotta look inside yourself. It's not what Hallowe'en did to you. It's what you did to Hallowe'en."

He wished Ernie hadn't said that. Not because the bartender was wrong. But because he knew—standing at the edge of a vast, lightless abyss inside himself, looking down into it—he knew that the bartender might be right. About too much.

"You can't expect things to stay the same," said Ernie, "and you just get to change all you want. Like there's no connection between the two." Ernie uncapped another beer and set it on the bar. "But there is."

"He knows that," said another voice. "But he's got it backward. Like usual with him."

He turned and saw, a little farther down the bar, Buzz Cut taking a pull at a half-empty bottle. The other motorhead, the one with the red hair, sat on the next stool over, drinking and nodding slowly in agreement.

"You should've heard him before," continued Buzz Cut. "With his whole Hallowe'en rap. Boo hoo hoo. It's all so frickin' sad."

He had thought the bar had all cleared out. Where'd these guys come from?

"Sad, all right." Red set his own bottle down. "Just listening to him."

"He's got this whole thing, you see." Buzz Cut tried to explain it to Ernie the bartender. "About how Hallowe'en has changed. It's like really important to him. The poor sad bastard."

"Yeah, right. I've heard it." Ernie pointed around at the decorations. "He goes off about all this stuff, too."

"Wait a minute." It ticked him off, the way they were talking about him. In the third person, like he wasn't even there. When he wasn't even sure that they were there, or were just drug vapors. "Just because you guys—"

Set me as a seal upon your heart.

The whole bar went silent. As though they all could hear her now.

For a moment, she wasn't draped across his back, her pale hands cuffed in front of his chest. She sat right next to him, leaning forward, those hands wrapped around her own beer. She turned and looked at him, beautiful and unsmiling, her dark hair a veil.

As a seal upon your arm, she whispered. *For love is strong as death, passion fierce as the grave*. She took a sip, then continued. *Its flashes are flashes of fire, a raging flame . . .*

"Okay, now I'm totally spooked." He gripped the edge of the bar, forcing it to become real and solid. "Give me a break."

She leaned over and kissed him. *If all the wealth of our house were offered for love*, she said, *it would be utterly scorned.* When he opened his eyes, she wasn't sitting there anymore. Her hands pressed against his heart once more, her cold arms wrapped around him.

Still full of surprises, even dead; he had to give her that. Though not totally a surprise; she'd come up with stuff like that when they'd been together the first time. Pentecostalist childhood, for both of them. He recognized it: Song of Solomon, chapter eight, verses six and seven. There were some hot bits in that Bible book, favorites of hers. Though he couldn't recall her spouting that one before.

"You gotta go back." Ernie's voice penetrated his meditations. "That's what she's trying to tell you."

Maybe they had heard her. He didn't know what that might mean. "Go back where? I already been all over town."

"Not where. When. You gotta go back to when you went wrong. The two of you. And then do it right."

"He'll never make it." Another voice came from the end of the bar. He looked and saw Edwin down there, stubbing out a cigarette butt in a drained highball glass. "He's too screwed up."

"Up yours." The motorheads came to his defense. Buzz Cut nodded along with Red. "He can do it. We gave him all he needs. In this world, at least."

"I'm not following this. . . ."

"Pay attention." Ernie leaned over the bar, bringing his face close to his and the dead girl's, as if they were in a football huddle. "I heard you out before. I know where you're coming from. Believe me, I've heard it from other guys like you. You think the world changed out from under you, and that's why things are all wrong." Ernie tapped him on the brow. "But it's the other way around. *You* changed. You gave up the old faith. You thought you could mess around all you wanted, and the world would still be the way it was, the way it's supposed to be, when you got done. It doesn't work that way."

"Listen to the man." Somebody shouted that from one of the tables in the corner of the bar. He glanced over his shoulder and saw the EMTs sitting there, empty bottles soldiered in front of them. And outside the bar—he could sense both the Metro patrol car and the tourist family from Idaho, slowly circling around. Except that he had made them up. So they at least were gone.

"Is this one of those *Twilight Zone* bits?" He felt even creepier than before. "You know, like where the guy is dead, only he thinks he's still alive?"

"You should be so lucky," said Ernie. "Don't change the subject. Don't try to get yourself off the hook. You want the world to be the way it should be? Then you need to go back and be the way you should've been. You and her." Ernie reached out and stroked her dark hair, tenderly. "You should've been different. All this screwing around, and being trashy and wild—yeah, that's fun and I'm happy to help you do it, but it doesn't get the job done."

"What job?"

"Come on. You and her, you were supposed to be the people handing out the candy. To the kids. On Hallowe'en. You were supposed to have a house, with a front door, and the bowlful of candy beside it. That's what you were supposed to do. That was your job. Instead, you screwed around. All of you." Ernie gestured toward the bar's walls. "You think all this crap isn't here for a reason? It's because of you. People like you. Not doing your job. That's how it got here."

"Yeah, well, that's real great. Telling me where—or when—I need to go, and all. Only problem is, there's no way of getting there. It's gone."

"Strictly a technical problem." Buzz Cut shrugged. "Just need to know how. That's why you have friends like us."

"What's the matter?" Edwin had the kind of sneer that revealed a line of yellow teeth. "Didn't you read *Superman* comics when you were a kid? You weren't one of those Marvel faggots, were you?"

"What's Superman got to do with it?"

"Don't you remember?" Buzz Cut regarded him with pity. "Jeez, what a wasted childhood you must've had. No wonder you turned out this way."

"When Superman needed to go back," said Ernie, "remember how he did it?"

"Uh, that was a comic book."

"Regardless. Remember how?"

"He went real fast." A page full of bright yellows and reds and blues surfaced in his memory. "In a circle. Spinning, like."

"Going in a circle doesn't cut it. If you think about this." Buzz Cut might have been explaining the difference between Keihin carbs and direct fuel injection. "It's the going fast that does the trick. Obviously. Go fast enough, you can get anywhere. Or when. The spinning around in a circle, that was just so Superman would still be where he started out. Right? Otherwise, he would've gone back, but he would've been out around Neptune. Or Alpha Centauri or some other rat-ass place like that."

"Going fast, huh?"

"That's why people like to do it. Go fast, I mean. Even when they have no place to get to. Even when they're just going around in circles. They know what they're doing. They're trying to get back. And you know what?" Buzz Cut leaned toward him, imparting a secret, but loud enough that everyone in the bar could hear. "Sometimes they do."

Some of it made sense, some of it didn't. "Don't you have to go as fast as Superman? To make it work. Super fast?"

"Hell, no. That was just because Superman had to go back to ancient Egypt, or go fight dinosaurs or something. *You* don't have that far to go."

Red chimed in. "You just have to get back to where you went wrong. And start over. The two of you. That's just not that far back."

It's not. Her whisper. *Let's go for it.*

"And no circles?"

"I told you already. Head down, full tuck, and accelerate." Buzz Cut got nods of agreement from the others along the bar. "Strictly straight line."

"Kinda hard to tuck down behind the windscreen, with . . ." He tilted his head toward hers. "You know . . ."

"Do the best you can," said Buzz Cut. "Do it right, you won't even be outside the city limits. When you make it there."

He knew what they were all going on about. "You mean the nitrous."

"Well, of course. We put it on there for a reason. Now you know."

Go for it.

They all watched him. Their gaze weighed heavier on him than she ever had.

They were right. Buzz Cut and the others, Ernie the bartender, even Edwin. They were right.

"I'm not paying you, though." Edwin had pointed that out. "This is some other deal you got going."

Once he got himself and her on the 'Busa again, and started it up, he realized how right they were. He didn't make it to the city limits. Out in empty desert again, sawtooth mountain silhouettes against the night sky—but if he had looked over his shoulder, he would still have been able to see the city's clustered neon, a single blue-white beam bending its trajectory above him.

He didn't need to look back. Her face was right next to his, her eyes closed, dreaming into the wind.

Straight shot, up into sixth gear, the road a knife's edge in front of them, throttle rolled to the max. Nothing left but the red button on the handlebars, his leathered thumb already resting upon it.

Now's the time.

Her whisper a kiss at his ear; he turned his cheek closer against the brush of her cold lips. He could barely breathe, she held him so tight. If his heart beat any stronger, it would break the links of the little chain.

Come on . . .

Or maybe the handcuffs had snapped apart already—he couldn't feel them—and it was her own locked grip binding her to him. The way it had before, her eyes closed, velocity and dreamless. His hand at the center of a small world, trembling with both their pulses, every small motion a new possibility.

The button rose to meet his thumb. He pushed as hard as she did.

Then he knew why he had waited so long.

First to go was the 'Busa's fairing, where it had cracked in the spill before. As the nitrous oxide poured into the engine and ignited, the stars blurred horizontal. A wall of air hit him, almost peeling him off the bike. In the rush that enveloped him, he could see but not hear the crack along the left side widen bigger than his gloved fist. It spidered into a jigsaw cobweb for only an instant, then shattered, the razor fragments swirling around him, then gone in the bike's streaming wake.

Pinned, the tach and speedometer were useless now. He couldn't even see them, unable to bring his sight down from the black horizon racing toward him.

Do it, she whispered somewhere. *Harder.*

The wind tore his jacket into tatters, stripped it from his chest. Her hands held tight, cupping his heart.

The front wheel came up from the road, spun free in hurtling air. The distant mountains tilted as he rolled in her embrace, face full against hers. He let go of the handlebars and pulled her tighter to himself, her knees crushing his hips. Beneath them, the motorcycle broke apart, into fire as meteors do, a matchflame struck against the earth's atmosphere. Fiery bits of metal skittered along the road, white heat dying to red sparks.

"We're not going back." He turned and kissed her. "We're here already."

Lies and stories. There'd never been any going back. That'd all been crap they'd told him, that he'd told himself, to get to this point.

The old faith would have to do without them. If the children out at night looked up at the incendiary wound bleeding across the dark, they could take it as a sign.

Just before they struck the earth, she opened her eyes and looked into his. The road would strip their flesh away, their entwined bones charring to ash.

"Fierce." She smiled. "As the grave."

Misadventure

STEPHEN GALLAGHER

Stephen Gallagher was born in Salford, England, in 1954. He is the author of over a dozen novels including Nightmare, with Angel, Red, Red Robin, and The Spirit Box. He has numerous screenplay credits and in 1997 wrote and directed a TV adaptation of his novel Oktober. His short stories have been published in various magazines and anthologies including The Magazine of Fantasy & Science Fiction, Asimov's Science Fiction, Weird Tales, Shadows, and The Dark; his collection Out of His Mind won a British Fantasy Award in 2004.

His latest novel is The Painted Bride and a new story collection will be published by Subterranean Press in 2007. His recently completed historical novel, The Kingdom of Bones, is to be published by Random House under the imprint of senior editor Shaye Areheart.

F our of us waited in the van, parked under a streetlamp on the bridge. Below us ran the motorway, a river of light in a valley of steel, a steady flow of people with somewhere to be. Beside the motorway stood the gym and the parking lot that served it. Well-lit, but almost deserted now.

Outside the van, our foreman paced up and down. He had his phone in his hand. Every now and again he'd glance at it, checking the signal.

"They call him the Sheriff," Peter the Painter said.

No one else responded, so I did.

"Why?"

Peter had his little finger stuck in his ear. He waggled it with a crackling sound and then inspected the result.

"You'll find out," he said, and wiped off on his overalls.

To look at us, you'd think we were a gang getting ready to rob the place. We were a rough-enough set of characters and nobody was in a mood for conversation. There was Peter the Painter, who I knew, and a couple of others who I didn't. Miserable-looking types, both. Disappointed men who'd reckoned themselves cut out for something better. We all sat as far away from each other as it was possible to get. One of them lay across the back seat with his hand over his eyes, shading them from the lights.

"What's going on down there?" Peter said, so I took a look.

"I think the boss is coming out," I said.

The gym's parking lot was floodlit but close to empty. The last of the customers had left about fifteen minutes before, and staff had been drifting out steadily ever since.

Two figures were now emerging through the glass doors. Outside the van, our foreman stopped his pacing and shaded his eyes for a better view. Way down below, the two appeared to be bidding each other good night. They were so far off that you'd need a sniper's eyesight to be sure.

The last man waited until the other had driven away, and then he started to make a call. Almost immediately, our foreman's phone played a tune.

It was a conversation that was over in just a few seconds.

"We're on," our foreman said as he got behind the wheel.

It took us no more than a couple of minutes to get down there. A gym doesn't really describe it. You'd think you were looking at a factory unit, an immense low-rise building with no visible windows and all its air ducting on the outside. Inside were tennis courts, squash courts, swimming pool, sauna, and a weights room the size of a zeppelin hangar. On the outside, a second swimming pool and a barbecue terrace.

By the time we arrived, two more vans were on-site. Unlike ours, these were clean and had all their original doors and didn't look as if gypsies had been keeping dogs in them. They had ladders on their roofs and the name of a building maintenance company on their sides. When we went into the club's foyer to be briefed, the two men who'd arrived with them stayed apart from the rest of us.

Outside the doors, our foreman exchanged a few words with the gym's manager and then the manager got into his car and drove away.

Then the foreman came inside.

"Right," he said. "Here's how it's going to be. We've until the end of the week to get everything done. We can only work when the place is closed, which means from ten at night until seven in the morning."

He winced, hitched up and scratched his nuts through his pants, and carried on. "Tonight we mask off all the switches and skirting boards. There's some filling and sanding to be done. We need to drain the pool and clean it out—it's a two-day job just to empty it, so there are waders in the van. Once it's empty we need to recaulk the expansion joints and fill it up again. There are tiles to replace in the steam room, and locker doors to rehang in the changing areas. I'll do a walk-around and show you where the work needs doing. Any questions?"

I said, "What about cameras?"

"The manager's switched them off."

And one of the men I didn't know said to no one in particular, "I suppose that means he's in on the deal."

"Enough of that," the foreman said. "You don't care."

It was about ten-thirty.

I wondered why they called him the Sheriff.

Don't ever let anyone tell you that a modern building with all its lights on can't feel spooky. Only the tennis courts were dark, separated from the main walk-through by hanging nets. Also, the grille was down on the sports shop and they'd locked up the crèche. Otherwise everything was wide open and ablaze, and as we walked around it was like one of those movies where you wake up and you're the last person on earth and you can go anywhere. The world's your playground but it still feels as if you're being daring. Someone had been through ahead of our arrival, spray-marking each of the job sites with a white arrow or otherwise pointing them up with colored tape or a note.

It was just snagging work, really. The building had been up for five years and the faults were no more than routine wear and tear. They were superficial but they made the place look bad. If the place looked bad then the members would complain. The membership would be families, mostly—so this wasn't like a boxing gym or a back street hangout for bodybuilders, where a bit of exposed brick or a leaking roof only added to the ambience. This was pastels on the walls and ciabatta in the restaurant, and you'd better believe it.

The Sheriff assigned me to help Peter. The two newcomers, who he called Geordie and Jacko, were to work around the pool. They had to chisel out broken tiles in the steam room until the pool's water level had dropped low enough for them to put on the waders and start scrubbing. All four of us stood there and watched as the Sheriff flipped back a cover and opened the sluice, and while he was doing it I heard the one called Geordie say, "Hey. What was that?"

He was looking out at the pool. After an hour without use it had settled to almost complete tranquillity, and its surface was like a vast blue gel. We were at the deep end, where it seemed to go on down for ever and ever.

"What was what?" I said.

He seemed about to answer, but then he changed his mind.

Peter the Painter lowered his voice to me as we were all walking along the side of the pool toward the exit.

"This is going to be fun," he said. "Not even got started yet, and already he's seeing ghosts."

I saw Geordie looking back again as we filed out of the door to go back to the foyer. I was last out, and I lingered.

Maybe I saw what he saw, I don't know. But I saw something. A dark shape in the deep end, like a big fish making a fast turn. But only the turn, and then there was nothing.

Which only made sense when you considered that the main drain was down in the deepest part of the pool and that as the sluice opened and the pump started, it would create eddies right down at the bottom. All right, so for a moment it had looked like something black and muscular, limbless and featureless and turning on itself like an eel, vanishing as quickly as it had been called into creation. But an eddy in any great weight of still water would bend the light in exactly such a way.

And if anybody ought to know a ghost when they saw one, it was me.

When I was thirteen, I had a bad fall. I hit my head and they tell me that my brain swelled up and it almost killed me, and I suppose that's the reason I started to see things. It ended when I finally got better. But while it lasted, it was quite something.

It happened when I was playing with some friends in the ruins of Feniscowles Hall. It was a building that had been around as a ruin for almost as long as it had stood as a house. Pollution from the river had driven the family out of it, and for the same reason no one had done anything with the land since. Back in the 'thirties they'd ripped all the timbers out and left the walls to fall in on themselves. Everything had become overgrown, the formal gardens had turned to jungle, and the surrounding woodland had grown dense and blocked off any access. The estate was surrounded by a barbed wire fence, but no one seemed to maintain it. It was a great and secret place to play. But the worst possible place to have an accident.

When I came to I was lying on my back and in pain, and my friends had all disappeared. I imagined that they'd gone to get help, but I later found that they'd all run home and quickly tried to establish alibis.

But I wasn't alone, that was the thing. When I managed to sit up I could see people moving through rooms and doorways that weren't even there. And I knew they had to be ghosts because there were too many of them in the same place at the same time—they were overlapping and passing through each other, as if I was seeing events that had been separated by years but were now replaying themselves all at once. The entire building was like a transparent shell before me, the broken walls of the ruin merging seamlessly up into the frozen smoke of the original lines.

I watched for a while, convinced that if I tried to rise then the spell would be broken. And then I tried to rise, and it wasn't. Everything lurched and changed a bit but the basic picture stayed the same. Maybe there were fewer of the layers now, but that was all.

I didn't know what to do. I knew that I'd been hurt, but your thirteen-year-old self doesn't think in terms of damage—you just want it to stop, and then you'll be back as you were. I just stood there with this great silent doll's house of activity going on before me, in a kind of stupor. After a while I saw someone coming out toward me.

She was a couple of years older than me. I don't remember what she was wearing. She was quite pretty but her teeth were bad. She looked straight at me and then she started to walk away. Not back to the house, but toward the woodland beyond it. I watched her go, and when she'd covered a few yards she came back and stood looking at me again. The way a dog does. It was then that I realized that, like Lassie, she meant for me to follow her.

She took me to a cobbled track ascending through the woods. It led up from some kind of a yard at the back of the house and I imagine it was the way they would have brought goods and supplies in. It was so overgrown that in places you'd hardly know it was there, and there were whole stretches where it had disintegrated into a rockery.

Despite the pain, it didn't seem to be taking me much effort to climb. I'd a sense that there were other figures amongst the trees, watching as I passed, but all my attention was on my guide. I don't think she looked back at me once.

I know it sounds strange as I'm telling you this. You're probably thinking that I was delirious or having a dream. All I can say is that it's what I saw. If I close my eyes I can see it almost as clearly now.

At the top end of the old driveway was a farm gate with a KEEP OUT notice that I was on the wrong side of. The gateway led into a posh close of big houses; nothing as grand as the ruined hall down in the wooded valley, but big enough for driveways and tennis courts and all that Agatha Christie stuff. The gate was chained and padlocked and I don't know how I got over it, but I did.

The next thing I recall was walking up one of the driveways with my ghost guide no longer in sight. A teenaged girl in riding gear came out of the house looking as if she was about to order me off the property, and I saw hostility turn to horror when she got a good look at me. She fled back into the house and I sank down to the gravel. It bit into my knees and then into my hands and finally into my cheek as I laid my face on the ground.

The earth seemed to hum, as if I was hearing its entire secret machinery for the first time.

I slept, then.

When we got back to the foyer, it was to find that the two regular building company employees had stacked the ladders, sheets, paint, and all the other equipment in the middle of the space and then gone. It was unlikely that we'd be seeing them again. They'd get a cut of the money but it would be us, the casuals, who did all the work.

That was the arrangement. On paper it was a full-price company job, but in practice they were fielding a second team of cut-rate unskilled labor at a fraction of the cost. We took cash, we paid no tax, we got no benefits. No insurance, no security, no rights of any kind. I'd done two years of a college course that I didn't finish and three in the army, and now this was all I could get. In principle I was doing it until something better came along but in truth, I'd stopped looking.

I won't say I was happy with the station I'd reached in life, but I didn't openly resent it the way that Geordie and Jacko obviously did. Jacko more than Geordie, if I read them right. As we laid the dust sheets and put up ladders in the squash court corridor, Peter told me about them.

"A right pair of wheeler-dealers," he called them, "in their dreams."

They'd gone into business together but it wasn't a real business, more of a franchise deal where they interposed themselves as middlemen between some company with an overpriced product and a group of buyers spending someone else's money.

Peter said, "You know there's got to be something wrong with the world when a box of office widgets that cost pennies to make comes all the way from America and gets hand-delivered out of the boot of a BMW with a gimmick number plate. Blokes like them dream big but it's always on the never-never. It never lasts and they never see the end coming."

The end came when the supplying company stopped taking calls and the latest widget shipment failed to materialize. Geordie and Jacko had mortgaged their houses to buy the franchise, and now lost their shirts. They tried to get into the air-conditioning business and attended a couple of recruitment seminars for the pyramid-selling of kitchen products, but the end was already written. First the cars with the personalized plates had gone, and then the suits. Geordie had grown surly and sarcastic. Jacko had grown a beard.

It was at this point that the Sheriff came by to check on our progress. He saw us talking as he came down the corridor.

"Come on, lads," he said. "What's the hold-up?"

And Peter looked at me with one eyebrow raised.

"Nothing, boss," he said.

Then the Sheriff said to Peter, "I'll give a hand with this. You nip down and straighten that Jacko out. He won't go in the steam room. Find out what he's moaning about and get him sorted."

"I'm not the foreman," Peter said. "Why aren't you doing it?"

"'Cause I'm so sick of his fucking whining," he said. "I'm seriously worried that if he starts it up again, I'll deck him."

"Hey," I said. "I'll do it."

Well, it was nothing to me, so down I went.

I followed signs marked HYDROUS, through the empty restaurant and down to the pool area. There wasn't just the pool and a steam room, there was the sauna and the cancer beds and both sets of changing rooms. I cut through the women's, just because I could.

Jacko and Geordie were arguing at the poolside when I got there. There was a whirlpool over the drain in the deep end and the water level had already begun to drop.

"What's the problem?" I said, and Jacko fell silent.

"He says he saw someone in there," Geordie said, and Jacko flared up again.

"I didn't say anything about that," he said. "I didn't say anything about *anything*."

"Well," I said, "let's have a look."

The steam room's door was a single sheet of toughened frosted glass, and the steam room itself was about eight feet by twelve with a tiled bench around three of its walls. The steam had been off for ages now but the starlight effect in the ceiling was on, tiny points of light that changed pattern every few seconds.

I came out and looked at the two of them.

"There's no one in there and nowhere to hide," I said. "So what exactly was it you didn't see?"

Neither spoke, and then Geordie said, "Tell him, you daft get."

"Nothing," Jacko said.

"Someone through the glass, just standing inside?"

The way his eyes widened was answer enough.

"This is what's probably doing it," I said, and I stuck my hand in through the open doorway and showed the effect when the lights played on it. It looked nothing like a person standing there, and he didn't seem impressed.

I said, "There's not enough light in there to work by, anyway. Nip up to the foyer and get a lamp with an extension lead. Nobody's going to get paid for arguing about it."

Jacko went off. As well as the beard he'd let his hair grow, and it made him look like a bony hermit type. When he was gone, Geordie said, "That's not what he told me."

"What did he tell you?"

"He said he could see a little lad in there."

"A little lad?" I said. "Can't you see when someone's trying to wind you up?"

When I came to in the hospital, I was in a room on my own just off the medical assessment ward. My head was bandaged and I was on a drip to reduce the swelling, and loads of painkillers as well. I'm not saying I felt good, but I suppose I was mostly insulated from my injuries.

My parents came, and my aunts came, and in amongst the relief and concern there was dark talk of the police turning up as well. But I don't think anybody had the heart to give me a hard time. Back in those days they wouldn't let parents stay in hospital with a child, so I spent that night in the side ward on my own.

I don't know what hour it would have been, but I woke in the night with the certainty that there was someone in the room with me. What little light there was seemed gray and grainy and my eyes were almost gummed shut with sleep crystals, so it was hard to get a focus. But he was there. I could see him against the Venetian blind. Sitting. Half-turned away. Gray like a stone, or like some kind of a golem. A jaw like a shovel and, when he turned toward me, eyes that were just fissures.

I closed my eyes to make him go away and, when I felt as if I'd waited long enough, cautiously opened them again. It was then that I found that he'd crossed the room and was inspecting me closely. I quickly screwed my eyes shut and I didn't open them again, or relax or find sleep, until dawn came a couple of hours later. They had to change my sheets that morning.

In the course of the day my best friend Malcolm was brought in for a visit and my memory is of him holding onto his mother's hand at the end of my bed looking green and unsteady, a state which she put down to empathy but which I knew was terror at the prospect of being challenged or exposed. Malcolm was the one that I'd have least expected to run off and leave me there, but he had. We'd continue as friends, but I'd never forgive him. I hadn't thought it all the way through at that stage, but it seems to me that it was only the dead who'd shown any concern for me. The living had thought only of themselves, and left me to struggle.

Everyone seemed pleased with my progress that day and I was told that in the morning I'd be moved onto an open ward with all the other children, as if that was something I ought to look forward to.

I was feeling stronger, and I spent most of the day sitting up. So when the shovel-jawed figure came again that night I found the strength to get out of bed and flee.

I hadn't seen outside the room before, so I'd no idea where I was or which way to go. I ran blindly, convinced that he'd be right behind me. I just wasn't ready for the hospital. It was like the haunted doll's house all over again, but this time it went on and on.

Hundreds of them. More than a thousand, maybe.

Everywhere I looked, there were more of them. Many were very old, and most were just standing. The entire building, which had been on this spot for more than a hundred years, was like a refugee station filled with the lingering images of those who'd died there. I saw people with terrible injuries, and those wasted by their suffering. I saw children, bald and bloated with drugs. Babies the size of my fist floated like bubbles through the air before me, trailing their bloody cords like the tails of kites.

When a hand fell on my shoulder from behind, I screamed out loud.

But it was only someone from the nursing staff, catching up with me to take me back to my room.

Jacko never came back. Geordie said he'd go to look for him and he didn't come back, either. It seemed to me that for men without options, they scared off far too easily.

But they were also men in a low state, and I had a theory that it took a troubled mind to see what they might have seen. I went and stood at the poolside and looked into the vortex that swirled over the drain pump. All I saw was water, twisting around and looking like something alive. I turned and looked toward the steam room, but nothing moved behind the frosted glass. Once I might have seen more, but these days I was healed. I saw no more than most other people.

When I told the Sheriff that we appeared to have a couple of deserters, he put his hands to his head and cursed them loud and long, and then got out his phone and disappeared for a while in search of a signal. Peter and I carried on with the preparation work until he returned.

"We're on our own for tonight," he said. "We need to get as much done as we can."

Over the next few hours the three of us pitched in and got as many of the jobs started as we could manage. Tomorrow there'd be some new faces brought in, but on our tight schedule we needed to grab all the ground we were able. Peter carried on with his preparation, the Sheriff started breaking tiles out with a cold chisel, and I got a bucket of filler and a ladder and started patching the cracks where plaster had shrunk away from joints.

A couple of odd things happened. Like when I threw the wrong switch in the cardio suite and all the empty running machines started up together, and Peter nearly crapped himself on the spot. I found a couple of excuses to visit the pool area again, but the Sheriff started looking at me suspiciously and so I just went back to my work.

I might not be able to see my ghosts anymore, but that didn't mean they weren't there. So I took an interest when others did.

They kept me on the open ward for a couple of days and then they let me go home, with strict instructions that I was to stay in bed and take no exercise.

Little did they know that they were setting a lifestyle choice that was to see me all the way through my teenaged years.

My bedroom was at the top of the stairs and my grandmother's was across the landing. She'd lived with us for two years and she'd died there the previous summer while I was away on a school trip. She'd been a widow for almost as long as I could remember, but toward the end she'd grown vague and forgetful and developed some odd ideas that meant she couldn't be trusted to look after herself. She couldn't be trusted not to empty the occasional pot of her pee into our kitchen sink, either.

For three days and nights after the ambulance brought me home, I saw nothing unusual. I had books from the library and the radio in my room, but the hours were endless and if there had been anything there to see, there's no way I would have missed it. I wondered if my so-called gift had been a short-lived one, and then after a while I began to wonder whether I'd really experienced it at all. What's memory, after all? Just certainty in retrospect. And mere certainty's no actual proof of anything.

On the fourth day, when my mother went out for an hour, I went and took a look in Grandma's old room.

The bed was still in there but the mattress was gone and the carpet had been taken up, and now it was mainly used to store empty suitcases and broken furniture that my father had ideas of someday repairing. My dad could never pass up a useful-looking piece of wood. He might never be quite sure what he wanted it for, but he always knew it had to be handy for something. He held onto one piece of driftwood for at least twenty years, moving house three times and taking it with him. After he died and I had to clear everything out, I put it in with other stuff from the garage and took it all to the local recycling point. Three or four old guys watched me dropping it into the skip, and before I left I saw one of them carrying it back to his car.

Grandma was by the bed. I'd half-expected her. What I hadn't been prepared for was the massive blow to the heart it gave me to see her again. All the other ghosts had been strangers and, naïvely, I'd expected this one to feel the same. I don't know if she saw me or if she knew me. I don't think she did. She moved about the room, her hand outstretched, touching for things that were no longer there. For some time afterwards I tried to think what her action reminded me of, until it struck me. She was like a lone fish in a bowl, circling, the days all the same and the scenery never changing.

I'd noticed back in the hospital how all these people seemed to be hanging around near the spot where they'd died. As if they were anchored to it somehow, and unable to leave. Repeating actions that they'd once performed in the places where they'd once performed them, never straying too far.

Did this mean that they were just mindless after-images? Photographs of past actions, fading slowly with time?

No, seemed to be the answer to that one. Otherwise that girl would never have come over and led me to safety. The dead were aware. Of the living, if not of themselves.

Grandma saw me and smiled. Then seemed to forget me again, and moved on.

I stood at the edge of the pool and looked into the deep end. The level had fallen, but with a pumping-out rate of more than eighty gallons a minute, it should have fallen more.

The waders were a size too large for me, but no matter. I'd manage. I took the long boat hook from the wall and climbed down the steps with it. The pole was about fifteen feet long and the double hook on the end was a small one, meant for snagging the cord on a life preserver to pull it over to safety. I moved gingerly down the sloping tile, and when I reached the water's edge I went in up to my waist and then extended the hook down toward the drain cover.

It shouldn't have lifted as easily as it did. It should have been bolted down, but it wasn't. I lost my purchase on it and the water pressure sucked it back into place again, but when I got the hook in for the second time I was able to pull it completely clear. The grille spun around in the water and settled with a muffled clank. I advanced a little farther and probed with the hook, down into the darkness of the uncovered drain.

I've a theory, of sorts. I don't think that ghosts are the people they were. They're more like the husks of people, the stuff left behind that the dead don't need. Shedding the earthly form like a reptile with its skin. It just doesn't make sense to me that we move on into any kind of afterlife with every scrap of material baggage that this life has thrown our way. We all have that experience of looking at the body of someone we love and knowing in an instant that they're no longer there. That they've dumped the body and flown.

And yet with ghosts, an image of the physical body is exactly what we see. Even down to clothing. Where's the sense in that? Where do you draw the line? Jewelry? Dandruff?

My dad's collection of useful-seeming timber?

Down there in the drain, my hook met resistance. I pushed a bit harder and felt it yield. It was like pushing into soft wax. I turned the pole in my hands and tried to work the hook around, looking to see if I could get any purchase.

So my theory is this: There's a condition where you can see things that aren't there to be seen, but which you've picked up with other senses. It's called synaesthesia. You taste words, you feel colors as texture. It's real to one sense, but manifests as another.

I reckon there has to be an equivalent condition where we pick up on the presence of those shed husks with whatever primitive antenna we've forgotten we have, and something makes us render it as a visual experience. The presence is real. And we really see it. But we're summoning the picture out of more subtle information.

I heard the steam room door. Out came the Sheriff, spitting dust and cursing. "Bloody thing."

I didn't look up. "What?"

"Got a piece of shit in my eye."

"Should have worn the goggles."

I'm guessing it must be a brain thing. I had it in spades for a while, and as my injuries got better I lost it. Some people reckon they're born with it. But usually you get it when your head's in a state. You don't have to fall off a wall like I did. Fear, loss, grief—anything that makes you susceptible will do it.

The invisible, made visible. For as long as it lasts.

I could feel something against the hook, so I renewed my grip on the pole and pulled. Nothing happened at first, but I kept up the pressure and then, slowly, I felt something beginning to slide. It was like drawing a cork. Steady pressure, steady pressure, and then out it came.

It erupted out of the drain in a cloud of matter, which immediately swirled around and was sucked back into the hole like a genie into its bottle. I walked backwards out of the water, pulling the cargo on my hook like a sack of mussels up the beach.

The Sheriff gawped, and forgot the splinter in his eye.

"What the fuck is *that*?" he said.

"I think it *used* to be a little lad," I told him.

And I was glad that I was out of the water by then, because he puked in it.

They linger close to where they died.

That was something I understood from very early on. I don't know how long for and I don't know why, but it's what I'd observed.

His name was Johnny Jaggs and he'd been missing for almost a year. They'd looked all over for him, but they hadn't looked here. Why would they? Only members used the pool.

But Jaggs and a couple of others had climbed over the fence on the barbecue terrace on a crowded summer's day and once they were in, they hadn't been challenged. Jaggs was the youngest, and the smallest. The others had brought him along because they thought he'd be small enough to get into the swimming pool drain and pick up the loose change they'd convinced themselves would be down there.

They were wrong about the change, right about his size. Small enough to get in, but not strong enough to fight the current and get out again. Instead of raising the alarm when he didn't resurface, they'd reacted in a way I recognized only too well.

They'd run home and established alibis, and kept their silence as the search began.

In the end it took a couple of child psychologists to get the full story out of them. As concerns had risen, the price of confession had quickly become too high until, after a while, they'd begun to believe in the tale as they told it.

I'd pulled only a part of him out of the drain. The chlorinated water had done things to the flesh and they took the rest of him out in pieces, like a late abortion. He'd only partially blocked the pipe. The efficiency of the pumps had been reduced, but not enough to make anyone act. There's a high turnover of staff in these places and it's hard to get anyone to care.

Our bosses took a hammering over our black-economy working setup, but not as much as they deserved. There was talk of nailing me and Peter for benefit fraud. I don't know about Peter but I'm still waiting to hear.

I didn't tell anyone what had led me to the blockage. I let them think it was the slow rate at which the pool had been draining, and left it at that.

Whatever haunts the pool and the steam room, I don't believe that it's little Johnny Jaggs himself. It's something he left behind at the moment of his passing, the pattern of the form in which he walked in this world, a coat that he shucked off and let fall. It's the same with all of them. Incomplete, discarded, abandoned. Left to hover, to wander, and eventually to fade. To be sensed and, when conditions are right, to be seen.

But whatever they might be, whether or not they remember what they were, I do know that they see us too. They know when something's not right, and they'll try to get our attention. It seems to worry them. If there's anything I can do to ease that worry, I won't hesitate. I don't care if it costs me a job, or gets me into trouble.

When others ran or looked away, one of them was there for me.

So what if they're only the dead? I still owe them my life.

The Forest

LAIRD BARRON

Laird Barron was born in Alaska, where he raised and trained huskies for many years. He migrated to the Pacific Northwest in the mid nineties and began to concentrate on writing poetry and fiction.

His award-nominated work has appeared in SCI FICTION *and* The Magazine of Fantasy & Science Fiction, *and has been reprinted in* The Year's Best Fantasy and Horror, Year's Best Fantasy 6, *and* Horror: The Best of the Year, 2006 Edition.

Barron currently resides in Olympia, Washington, where he is working on a number of projects.

After the drive had grown long and monotonous, Partridge shut his eyes and the woman was waiting. She wore a cold white mask similar to the mask Bengali woodcutters donned when they ventured into the mangrove forests along the coast. The tigers of the forest were stealthy. The tigers hated to be watched; they preferred to sneak up on prey from behind, so natives wore the masks on the backs of their heads as they gathered wood. Sometimes this kept the tigers from dragging them away.

The woman in the cold white mask reached into a wooden box. She lifted a tarantula from the box and held it to her breast like a black carnation. The contrast was as magnificent as a stark Monet if Monet had painted watercolors of emaciated patricians and their pet spiders.

Partridge sat on his high wooden chair and whimpered in animal terror. In the daydream, he was always very young and powerless. The woman tilted her head. She came near and extended the tarantula in her long gray hand. "For you," she said. Sometimes she carried herself more like Father and said in a voice of gravel, "Here is the end of fear." Sometimes the tarantula was a hissing cockroach of prehistoric girth, or a horned beetle. Sometimes it was a strange, dark flower. Sometimes it was an embryo uncurling to form a miniature adult human that grinned a monkey's hateful grin.

The woman offered him a black phone. The woman said, "Come say good-bye and good luck. Come quick!" Except the woman did not speak. Toshi's breathless voice bled through the receiver. The woman in the cold white mask brightened then dimmed like a dying coal or a piece of metal coiling into itself.

Partridge opened his eyes and rested his brow against window glass. He was alone with the driver. The bus trawled through a night forest. Black trees dripped with fog. The narrow black road crumbled from decades of neglect. Sometimes poor houses and fences stood among the weeds and the ferns and mutely suggested many more were lost in the dark. Wilderness had arisen to reclaim its possessions.

Royals hunted in woods like these. He snapped on the overhead lamp and then opened his briefcase. *Stags, wild boar, witches. Convicts.* The briefcase was nearly empty. He had tossed in some traveler's checks, a paperback novel, and his address book. No cell phone, although he left a note for his lawyer and a recorded message at Kyla's place in Malibu warning them it might be a few days, perhaps a week; that there probably was not even phone service where he was going. Carry on, carry on. He had hopped a redeye jet to Boston and once there eschewed the convenience of renting a car or hiring a chauffeur and limo. He chose instead the relative anonymity of mass transit. The appeal of traveling incognito overwhelmed his normally staid sensibilities. Here was the first adventure he had undertaken in ages. The solitude presented an opportunity to compose his thoughts—his excuses, more likely.

He'd cheerfully abandoned the usual host of unresolved items and potential brushfires that went with the territory—a possible trip to the Andes if a certain Famous Director's film got green-lighted and if the Famous Director's drunken assertion to assorted executive producers and hangers-on over barbecued ribs and flaming daiquiris at the Monarch Grille that Richard Jefferson Partridge was the only man for the job meant a blessed thing. There were several smaller opportunities, namely an L.A. documentary about a powerhouse high school basketball team that recently graced the cover of *Sports Illustrated*, unless the documentary guy, a Cannes Film Festival sweetheart, decided to try to bring down the Governor of California instead, as he had threatened to do time and again, a pet crusade of his with the elections coming that fall, and then the director would surely use his politically savvy compatriot, the cinematographer from France. He'd also been approached regarding a proposed documentary about prisoners and guards at San Quentin. Certainly there were other, lesser engagements he'd lost track of, these doubtless scribbled on memo pads in his home office.

He knew he should hire a reliable secretary. He promised himself to do just that every year. It was hard. He missed Jean. She'd had a lazy eye and a droll wit; made bad coffee and kept sand-filled frogs and fake petunias on her desk. Jean left him for Universal Studios and then slammed into a reef in Maui learning to surf with her new boss. The idea of writing the want ad, of sorting the applications and conducting the interviews and finally letting the new person, the stranger, sit where Jean had sat and handle his papers, summoned a mosquito's thrum in the bones behind Partridge's ear.

These details would surely keep despite what hysterics might come in the meanwhile. Better, much better, not to endure the buzzing and whining and the imprecations and demands that he return at once on pain of immediate career death, over a dicey relay.

He had not packed a camera, either. He was on vacation. His mind would store what his eye could catch and that was all.

The light was poor. Partridge held the address book close to his face. He had scribbled the directions from margin to margin and drawn a crude map with arrows and lopsided boxes and jotted the initials of the principals: Dr. Toshi Ryoko, Dr. Howard Campbell, Beasley, and Nadine. Of course, Nadine—she snapped her fingers and here he came at a loyal trot. There were no mileposts on the road to confirm the impression that his destination was near. The weight in his belly sufficed. It was a fat stone grown from a pebble.

Partridge's instincts did not fail him. A few minutes before dawn, the forest receded and they entered Warrenburgh. Warrenburgh was a loveless hamlet of crabbed New England shop fronts and angular plank and shingle houses with tall, thin doors and oily windows. Streetlights glowed along Main Street with black gaps like a broken pearl necklace. The street itself was buckled and rutted by poorly tarred cracks that caused sections to cohere as uneasily as interleaved ice floes. The sea loomed near and heavy and palpable beneath a layer of rolling gloom.

Partridge did not like what little he glimpsed of the surroundings. Long ago, his friend Toshi had resided in New Mexico and Southern California, did his best work in Polynesia and the jungles of Central America. The doctor was a creature of warmth and light. *Rolling Stone* had characterized him as "a rock star among zoologists" and as the "Jacques Cousteau of the jungle," the kind of man who hired mercenaries to guard him, performers to entertain his sun-drenched villa, and filmmakers to document his exploits. This temperate landscape, so cool and provincial, so removed from Partridge's experience of all things Toshi, seemed to herald a host of unwelcome revelations.

Beasley, longstanding attendant of the eccentric researcher, waited at the station. "Rich! At least you don't look like the big asshole *Variety* says you are." He nodded soberly and scooped Partridge up for a brief hug in his powerful arms. This was like being embraced by an earthmover. Beasley had played Australian rules football for a while after he left the Army and before he came to work for Toshi. His nose was squashed and his ears were cauliflowers. He was magnetic and striking as any character actor, nonetheless. "Hey, let me get that." He set Partridge aside and grabbed the luggage the driver had dragged from the innards of the bus. He hoisted the suitcases into the bed of a '56 Ford farm truck. The truck was museum quality. It was fire engine red with a dinky American flag on the antenna.

They rumbled inland. Rusty light gradually exposed counterchanged shelves of empty fields and canted telephone poles strung together with thick dipping old-fashioned cables. Ducks pelted from a hollow in the road. The ducks spread themselves in a wavering pattern against the sky.

"Been shooting?" Partridge indicated the .20 gauge softly clattering in the rack behind their heads.

"When T isn't looking. Yeah, I roam the marshes a bit. You?"

"No."

"Yah?"

"Not in ages. Things get in the way. Life, you know?"

"Oh, well, we'll go out one day this week. Bag a mallard or two. Raise the dust."

Partridge stared at the moving scenery. Toshi was disinterested in hunting and thought it generally a waste of energy. Nadine detested the sport without reserve. He tasted brackish water, metallic from the canteen. The odor of gun oil and cigarette smoke was strong in the cab. The smell reminded him of hip waders, muddy clay banks, and gnats in their biting millions among the reeds. "Okay. Thanks."

"Forget it, man."

They drove in silence until Beasley hooked left onto a dirt road that followed a ridge of brambles and oak trees. On the passenger side overgrown pastures dwindled into moiling vapors. The road was secured by a heavy iron gate with the usual complement of grimy warning signs. Beasley climbed out and unlocked the gate and swung it aside. Partridge realized that somehow this was the same ruggedly charismatic Beasley, plus a streak of gray in the beard and minus the springloaded tension and the whiskey musk. Beasley at peace was an enigma. Maybe he had quit the bottle for good this time around. The thought was not as comforting as it should have been. If this elemental truth—Beasley the chronic drunk, the lovable, but damaged brute—had ceased to hold, then what else lurked in the wings?

When they had begun to jounce along the washboard lane, Partridge said, "Did T get sick? Somebody—think Frank Ledbetter—told me T had some heart problems. Angina."

"Frankie . . . I haven't seen him since forever. He still working for Boeing?"

"Lockheed Martin."

"Yah? Good ol' L&M. Well, no business like war business," Beasley said. "The old boy's fine. Sure, things were in the shitter for a bit after New Guinea, but we all got over it. Water down the sluice." Again, the knowing, sidelong glance. "Don't worry so much. He misses you. Everybody does, man."

Toshi's farm was more of a compound lumped in the torso of a great, irregular field. The road terminated in a hardpack lot bordered by a sprawl of sheds and shacks, gutted chicken coops, and labyrinthine hog pens fallen to ruin. The main house, a Queen Anne, dominated. The house was a full three stories of spires, gables, spinning iron weathercocks, and acres of slate tiles. A monster of a house, yet somehow hunched upon itself. It was brooding and squat and low as a brick and timber mausoleum. The detached garage seemed new. So too the tarp and plastic-sheeted nurseries, the electric fence that partitioned the back forty into quadrants, and the military drab short-wave antenna array crowning the A-frame barn. No private security forces were in evidence, no British mercenaries with submachine guns on shoulder slings, nor packs of sleek, bullet-headed attack dogs cruising the property. The golden age had obviously passed into twilight.

"Behold the Moorehead Estate," Beasley said as he parked by slamming the brakes so the truck skidded sideways and its tires sent up a geyser of dirt. "Howard and Toshi bought it from the county about fifteen years ago—guess the original family died out, changed their names, whatever. Been here in one form or another since 1762. The original burned to the foundation in 1886, which is roughly when the town—Orren Towne, 'bout two miles west of here—dried up and blew away. As you can see, they made some progress fixing this place since then."

Partridge whistled as he eyed the setup. "Really, ah, cozy."

There were other cars scattered in the lot: a Bentley, a Nixon-era Cadillac, an archaic Land Rover that might have done a tour in the Sahara, a couple of battered pickup trucks, and an Army surplus jeep. These told Partridge a thing or two, but not enough to surmise the number of guests or the nature of Toshi's interest in them. He had spotted the tail rotor of a helicopter poking from behind the barn.

Partridge did not recognize any of the half-a-dozen grizzled men loitering near the bunkhouse. Those would be the roustabouts and the techs. The men passed around steaming thermoses of coffee. They pretended not to watch him and Beasley unload the luggage.

"For God's sake, boy, why didn't you catch a plane?" Toshi called down from a perilously decrepit veranda. He was wiry and sallow and vitally ancient. He was dressed in a bland short sleeve button-up shirt, a couple of neck sizes too large, and his omnipresent gypsy kerchief. He leaned way over the precarious railing and smoked a cigarette. His cigarettes were invariably Russian and came in tin boxes blazoned with hyperbolic full color logos and garbled English mottos and blurbs such as, "Prince of Peace!" and "Yankee Flavor!"

"The Lear's in the shop." Partridge waved and headed for the porch.

"You don't drive, either, eh?" Toshi flicked his hand impatiently. "Come on, then. Beasley—the Garden Room, please."

Beasley escorted Partridge through the gloomy maze of cramped halls and groaning stairs. Everything was dark: from the cryptic hangings and oil paintings of Mooreheads long returned to dust, to the shiny walnut planks that squeaked and shifted everywhere underfoot.

Partridge was presented a key by the new housekeeper, Mrs. Grant. She

"That's the absolute truth. I'm busier than a one-armed paper hanger."

"I'm sure. Anyway, I said you'd duck us once again. A big movie deal, fucking a B-list starlet in the South of France. It'd be something."

"—and then Beasley said something on the order of—"

"Hell yeah, my boy will be here!—"

"—come hell or high water!"

"Pretty much, yeah. He believes in you."

Partridge tried not to squirm even as her pitiless gaze bore into him. "Well, it was close. I canceled some things. Broke an engagement or two."

"Mmm. It's okay, Rich. You've been promising yourself a vacation, haven't you? This makes a handy excuse; do a little R&R, get some *you* time in for a change. It's for your mental health. Bet you can write it off."

"Since this is going so well . . . how's Coop?" He had noticed she was not wearing the ring. Handsome hubby Dan Cooper was doubtless a sore subject, he being the hapless CEO of an obscure defense contractor that got caught up in a Federal dragnet. He would not be racing his classic Jaguar along hairpin coastal highways for the next five to seven years, even assuming time off for good behavior. Poor Coop was another victim of Nadine's gothic curse. "Condolences, naturally. If I didn't send a card. . . ."

"He *loves* Federal prison. It's a country club, really. How's that bitch you introduced me to? I forget her name."

"Rachel."

"Yep, that's it. The makeup lady. She pancaked Thurman like a corpse on that flick you shot for Coppola."

"Ha, yeah. She's around. We're friends."

"Always nice to have friends."

Partridge forced a smile. "I'm seeing someone else."

"Kyla Sherwood—the Peroxide Puppet. Tabloids know all, my dear."

"But it's not serious."

"News to her, hey?"

He was boiling alive in his Aspen-chic sweater and charcoal slacks. Sweat trickled down his neck and the hairs on his thighs prickled and chorused their disquiet. He wondered if that was a massive pimple pinching the flesh between his eyes. That was where he had always gotten the worst of them in high school. His face swelled so majestically people thought he had broken his nose playing softball. What could he say with this unbearable pressure building in his lungs? Their history had grown to epic dimensions. The kitchen was too small to contain such a thing. He said, "Toshi said it was important. That I come to this . . . what? Party? Reunion? Whatever it is. God knows I love a mystery."

Nadine stared the stare that gave away nothing. She finally glanced at her watch and stood. She leaned over him so that her hot breath brushed his ear. "Mmm. Look at the time. Lovely seeing you, Rich. Maybe later we can do lunch."

He watched her walk away. As his pulse slowed and his breathing loosened, he waited for his erection to subside and tried to pinpoint what it was that nagged him, what it was that tripped the machinery beneath the liquid surface of his guilt-crazed, testosterone-glutted brain. Nadine had always reminded him of a duskier, more ferocious Bettie Page. She was thinner now, probably going gray if not for the wonders of modern cosmetics. Her prominent cheekbones, the fragile symmetry of her scapulae through the open-back blouse, registered with him as he sat recovering his wits with the numb intensity of a soldier who had just clambered from a trench following a mortar barrage.

Gertz slunk out of hiding and poured more coffee into Partridge's cup. He dumped in some schnapps from a hip flask. "Hang in there, my friend," he said drolly.

"I just got my head beaten in," Partridge said.

"Round one," Gertz said. He took a hefty pull from the flask. "Pace yourself, champ."

Partridge wandered the grounds until he found Toshi in D-Lab. Toshi was surveying a breeding colony of cockroaches: *Periplaneta americana*, he proclaimed them with a mixture of pride and annoyance. The lab was actually a big tool shed with the windows painted over. Industrial-sized aquariums occupied most of the floor space. The air had acquired a peculiar, spicy odor reminiscent of hazelnuts and fermented bananas. The chamber was illuminated by infrared lamps. Partridge could not observe much activity within the aquariums unless he stood next to the glass. That was not going to happen. He contented himself to lurk at Toshi's elbow while a pair of men in coveralls and rubber gloves performed maintenance on an empty pen. The men scraped substrate into garbage bags and hosed the container and applied copious swathes of petroleum jelly to the rim where the mesh lid attached. Cockroaches were escape artists extraordinaire, according to Toshi.

"Most folks are trying to figure the best pesticide to squirt on these little fellas. Here you are a cockroach rancher," Partridge said.

"Cockroaches . . . I care nothing for cockroaches. This is scarcely more than a side effect, the obligatory nod to cladistics, if you will. Cockroaches . . . beetles . . . there are superficial similarities. These animals crawl and burrow, they predate us humans by hundreds of millions of years. But . . . beetles are infinitely more interesting. The naturalist's best friend. Museums and taxidermists love them, you see. Great for cleansing skeletal structures, antlers, and the like."

"Nature's efficiency experts. What's the latest venture?"

"A-Lab—I will show you." Toshi became slightly animated. He straightened his crunched shoulders to gesticulate. His hand glimmered like a glow tube at a rock concert. "I keep a dozen colonies of dermestid beetles in operation. Have to house them in glass or stainless steel—they nibble through anything."

This house of creepy-crawlies was not good for Partridge's nerves. He thought of the chair and the woman and her tarantula. He was sickly aware that if he closed his eyes at that very moment the stranger would remove the mask and reveal Nadine's face. Thinking of Nadine's face and its feverish luminescence, he said, "She's dying."

Toshi shrugged. "Johns Hopkins . . . my friends at Fred Hutch . . . nobody can do anything. This is the very bad stuff; very quick."

"How long has she got." The floor threatened to slide from under Partridge's feet. Cockroaches milled in their shavings and hidey-holes; their tick-tack impacts burrowed under his skin.

"Not long. Probably three or four months."

"Okay." Partridge tasted breakfast returned as acid in his mouth.

The technicians finished their task and began sweeping. Toshi gave some orders. He said to Partridge, "Let's go see the beetles."

A-Lab was identical to D-Lab except for the wave of charnel rot that met Partridge as he entered. The dermestid colonies were housed in corrugated metal canisters. Toshi raised the lid to show Partridge how industriously a particular group of larvae were stripping the greasy flesh of a small mixed-breed dog. Clean white bone peeked through coagulated muscle fibers and patches of coarse, blond fur.

Partridge managed to stagger the fifteen or so feet and vomit into a plastic sink. Toshi shut the lid and nodded wisely. "Some fresh air, then."

Toshi conducted a perfunctory tour, complete with a wheezing narrative regarding matters coleopteran and teuthological, the latter being one of his comrade Howard Campbell's manifold specialties. Campbell had held since the early seventies that One Day Soon the snail cone or some species of jellyfish was going to revolutionize neurology. Partridge nodded politely and dwelt on his erupting misery. His stomach felt as if a brawler had used it for a speed bag. He trembled and dripped with cold sweats.

Then, as they ambled along a fence holding back the wasteland beyond the barn, he spotted a cluster of three satellite dishes. The dishes' antennas were angled downward at a sizable oblong depression like aardvark snouts poised to siphon musty earth. These were lightweight models, each no more than four meters across and positioned as to be hidden from casual view from the main house. Their trapezoidal shapes didn't jibe with photos Partridge had seen of similar devices. These objects gleamed the yellow-gray gleam of rotting teeth. His skin crawled as he studied them and the area of crushed soil. The depression was over a foot deep and shaped not unlike a kiddy wading pool. This presence in the field was incongruous and somehow sinister. He immediately regretted discarding his trusty Canon. He stopped and pointed. "What are those?"

"Radio telescopes, obviously."

"Yeah, what kind of metal is that? Don't they work better if you point them at the sky?"

"The sky. Ah, well, perhaps later. You note the unique design, eh? Campbell and I . . . invented them. Basically."

"Really? Interesting segue from entomological investigation, doc."

"See what happens when you roll in the mud with NASA? The notion of first contact is so glamorous, it begins to rub off. Worse than drugs. I'm in recovery."

Partridge stared at the radio dishes. "UFOs and whatnot, huh. You stargazer, you. When did you get into that field?" It bemused him how Toshi Ryoko hopscotched from discipline to discipline with a breezy facility that unnerved even the mavericks among his colleagues.

"I most assuredly haven't migrated to that field—however, I will admit to grazing as the occasion warrants. The dishes are a link in the chain. We've got miles of conductive coil buried around here. All part of a comprehensive surveillance plexus. We monitor everything that crawls, swims, or flies. Howard and I have become enamored of astrobiology, cryptozoology, the occulted world. Do you recall when we closed shop in California? That was roughly concomitant with our lamentably overpublicized misadventures in New Guinea."

"Umm." Partridge had heard that Campbell and Toshi disappeared into the back country for three weeks after they lost a dozen porters and two graduate students in a river accident. Maybe alcohol and drugs were involved. There was an investigation and all charges were waived. The students' families had sued and sued, of course. Partridge knew he should have called to offer moral support. Unfortunately, associating with Toshi in that time of crisis might have been an unwise career move and he let it slide. *But nothing slides forever, does it?*

"New Guinea wasn't really a disaster. Indeed, it served to crystallize the focus of our research, to open new doors. . . ."

Partridge was not thrilled to discuss New Guinea. "Intriguing. I'm glad you're going great guns. It's over my head, but I'm glad. Sincerely." Several crows described broad, looping circles near the unwholesome machines. Near, but not too near.

"Ah, but that's not important. I imagine I shall die before any of this work comes to fruition." Toshi smiled fondly and evasively. He gave Partridge an avuncular pat on the arm. "You're here for Nadine's grand farewell. She will leave the farm after the weekend. Everything is settled. You see now why I called."

Partridge was not convinced. Nadine seemed to resent his presence— she'd always been hot and cold when it came to him. What did Toshi want him to do? "Absolutely," he said.

They walked back to the house and sat on the porch in rocking chairs. Gertz brought them a pitcher of iced tea and frosted glasses on trays. Campbell emerged in his trademark double-breasted steel blue suit and horn-rim glasses. For the better part of three decades he had played the mild, urbane foil to Toshi's megalomaniacal iconoclast. In private, Campbell was easily the dominant of the pair. He leaned against a post and held out his hand until Toshi passed him a smoldering cigarette. "I'm glad you know," he said, fastening his murky eyes on Partridge. "I didn't have the nerve to tell you myself."

Partridge felt raw, exhausted, and bruised. He changed the subject. "So . . . those guys in the suits. Montague and Phillips. How do you know them? Financiers, I presume?"

"Patrons," Campbell said. "As you can see, we've scaled back the operation. It's difficult to run things off the cuff." Lolling against the post, a peculiar hybrid of William Burroughs and Walter Cronkite, he radiated folksy charm that mostly diluted underlying hints of decadence. This charm often won the hearts of flabby dilettante crones looking for a cause to champion. "Fortunately, there are always interested parties with deep pockets."

Partridge chuckled to cover his unease. His stomach was getting worse. "Toshi promised to get me up to speed on your latest and greatest contribution to the world of science. Or do I want to know?"

"You showed him the telescopes? Anything else?" Campbell glanced to Toshi and arched his brow.

Toshi's grin was equal portions condescension and mania. He rubbed his spindly hands together like a spider combing its pedipalps. "Howard . . . I haven't, he hasn't been to the site. He has visited with our pets, however. Mind your shoes if you fancy them, by the way."

"Toshi has developed a knack for beetles," Campbell said. "I don't know what he sees in them, frankly. Boring, boring. Pardon the pun—I'm stone knackered on Dewar's. My bloody joints are positively gigantic in this climate. Oh—have you seen reports of the impending Yellow Disaster? China will have the whole of Asia Minor deforested in the next decade. I imagine you haven't—you don't film horror movies, right? At least not reality horror." He laughed as if to say, *You realize I'm kidding, don't you, lad? We're all friends here*. "Mankind is definitely eating himself out of house and home. The beetles and cockroaches are in the direct line of succession."

"Scary," Partridge said. He waited doggedly for the punch line. Although, free association was another grace note of Campbell's and Toshi's. The punch line might not even exist. Give them thirty seconds and they would be nattering about engineering *E. coli* to perform microscopic stupid pet tricks or how much they missed those good old Bangkok whores.

Toshi lighted another cigarette and waved it carelessly. "The boy probably hasn't the foggiest notion as to the utility of our naturalistic endeavors. Look, after dinner, we'll give a demonstration. We'll hold a séance."

"Oh, horseshit, Toshi!" Campbell scowled fearsomely. This was always a remarkable transformation for those not accustomed to his moods. "Considering the circumstances, that's extremely tasteless."

"Not to mention premature," Partridge said through a grim smile. He rose, upsetting his drink in a clatter of softened ice cubes and limpid orange rinds, and strode from the porch. He averted his face. He was not certain if Campbell called after him because of the blood beating in his ears. Toshi did clearly say, "Let him go, let him be, Howard. . . . She'll talk to him. . . ."

He stumbled to his room and crashed into his too-short bed and fell unconscious.

Partridge owed much of his success to Toshi. Even that debt might not have been sufficient to justify the New England odyssey. The real reason, the motive force under the hood of Partridge's lamentable midlife crisis, and the magnetic compulsion to heed that bizarre late-night call, was certainly his sense of unfinished business with Nadine. Arguably, he had Toshi to thank for that, too.

Toshi Ryoko immigrated to Britain, and later the U.S., from Okinawa in the latter sixties. This occurred a few years after he had begun to attract attention from the international scientific community for his brilliant work in behavioral ecology and prior to his stratospheric rise to popular fame due to daredevil eccentricities and an Academy Award-nominated documentary of his harrowing expedition into the depths of a Bengali wildlife preserve. The name of the preserve loosely translated into English as, "The Forest that Eats Men." Partridge had been the twenty-three-year-old cinematographer brought aboard at the last possible moment to photograph the expedition. No more qualified person could be found on the ridiculously short notice that Toshi announced for departure. The director/producer was none other than Toshi himself. It was his first and last film. There were, of course, myriad subsequent independent features, newspaper and radio accounts—the major slicks covered Toshi's controversial exploits—but he lost interest in filmmaking after the initial hubbub and eventually faded from the public eye. Possibly his increasing affiliation with clandestine U.S. government projects was to blame. The cause was immaterial. Toshi's fascinations were mercurial and stardom proved incidental to his mission of untangling the enigmas of evolutionary origins and ultimate destination.

Partridge profited greatly from that tumultuous voyage into the watery hell of man-eating tigers and killer bees. He emerged from the crucible as a legend fully formed. His genesis was as Minerva's, that warrior-daughter sprung whole from Jupiter's aching skull. All the great directors wanted him. His name was gold—it was nothing but Beluga caviar and box seats at the Rose Bowl, a string of "where are they now" actresses on his arm, an executive membership in the Ferrari Club and posh homes in Malibu and Ireland. Someday they would hang his portrait in the American Society of Cinematography archives and blazon his star on Hollywood Boulevard.

There was just one glitch in his happily-ever-after: Nadine. Nadine Thompson was the whip-smart Stanford physiologist who had gone along for the ride to Bangladesh as Toshi's chief disciple. She was not Hollywood sultry, yet the camera found her to be eerily riveting in a way that was simultaneously erotic and repellant. The audience never saw a *scientist* when the camera tracked Nadine across the rancid deck of that river barge. They saw a woman-child—ripe, lithe, and lethally carnal.

She was doomed. Jobs came and went. Some were comparative plums, yes. None of them led to prominence indicative of her formal education and nascent talent. None of them opened the way to the marquee projects, postings, or commissions. She eventually settled for a staff position at a museum in Buffalo. An eighty-seven-minute film shot on super-sixteen millimeter consigned her to professional purgatory. Maybe a touch of that taint had rubbed off on Partridge. Nadine was the youthful excess that Hollywood could not supply, despite its excess of youth, the one he still longed for during the long, blank Malibu nights. He carried a load of guilt about the whole affair as well.

Occasionally, in the strange, hollow years after the hoopla, the groundswell of acclaim and infamy, she would corner Partridge in a remote getaway bungalow, or a honeymoon seaside cottage, for a weekend of gin and bitters and savage lovemaking. In the languorous aftermath, she often

confided how his magic Panaflex had destroyed her career. She would forever be "the woman in that movie." She was branded a real-life scream queen
and the sexpot with the so-so face and magnificent ass.

Nadine was right, as usual. "The Forest that Eats Men" never let go once
it sank its teeth.

He dreamed of poling a raft on a warm, muddy river. Mangroves hemmed
them in corridors of convoluted blacks and greens. Creepers and vines
strung the winding waterway. Pale sunlight sifted down through the screen
of vegetation; a dim, smoky light full of shadows and shifting clouds of
gnats and mosquitoes. Birds warbled and screeched. He crouched in the
stern of the raft and stared at the person directly before him. That person's
wooden mask with its dead eyes and wooden smile gaped at him, fitted as it
was to the back of the man's head. The wooden mouth whispered, "You forgot your mask." Partridge reached back and found, with burgeoning horror,
that his skull was indeed naked and defenseless.

"They're coming. They're coming." The mask grinned soullessly.

He inhaled to scream and jerked awake, twisted in the sheets and sweating. Red light poured through the thin curtains. Nadine sat in the shadows at
the foot of his bed. Her hair was loose and her skin reflected the ruddy light.
He thought of the goddess Kali shrunk to mortal dimensions.

"You don't sleep well either, huh," she said.

"Nope. Not since Bangladesh."

"That long. Huh."

He propped himself on his elbow and studied her. "I've been considering
my options lately. I'm thinking it might be time to hang up my spurs. Go live
in the Bahamas."

She said, "You're too young to go." That was her mocking tone.

"You too."

She didn't say anything for a while. Then, "Rich, you ever get the feeling
you're being watched?"

"Like when you snuck in here while I was sleeping? Funny you should
mention it. . . ."

"Rich."

He saw that she was serious. "Sometimes, yeah."

"Well you are. Always. I want you to keep that in mind."

"Okay. Will it help?"

"Good question."

The room darkened, bit by bit. He said, "You think you would've made
it back to the barge?" He couldn't distance himself from her cry as she flailed

overboard and hit the water like a stone. There were crocodiles everywhere. No one moved. The whole crew was frozen in that moment between disbelief and action. He had shoved the camera at, who? Beasley. He had done that and then gone in and gotten her. Blood warm water, brown with mud. He did not remember much of the rest. The camera caught it all.

"No," she said. "Not even close."

He climbed over the bed and hugged her. She was warm. He pressed his face into her hair. Her hair trapped the faint, cloying odor of sickness. "I'm so fucking sorry," he said.

She didn't say anything. She rubbed his shoulder.

That night was quiet at the Moorehead Estate. There was a subdued dinner and afterward some drinks. Everybody chatted about the good old days. The real ones and the imaginary ones too. Phillips and Montague disappeared early on and took their men-at-arms with them. Nadine sat aloof. She held onto a hardback—one of Toshi's long out-of-print treatises on insect behavior and ecological patterns. Partridge could tell she was only pretending to look at it.

Later, after lights out, Partridge roused from a dream of drowning in something that wasn't quite water. His name was whispered from the foot of the bed. He fumbled upright in the smothering dark. "Nadine?" He clicked on the lamp and saw he was alone.

It rained in the morning. Toshi was undeterred. He put on a slicker and took a drive in the Land Rover to move the radio telescopes and other equipment into more remote fields. A truckload of the burly, grim laborers followed. The technicians trudged about their daily routine, indifferent to the weather. Campbell disappeared with Phillips and Montague. Nadine remained in her room. Partridge spent the morning playing poker with Beasley and Gertz on the rear porch. They drank whiskey—coffee for Beasley—and watched water drip from the eaves and thunderheads roll across the horizon trailing occasional whip-cracks of lightning. Then it stopped raining and the sun transformed the landscape into a mass of illuminated rust and glass.

Partridge went for a long walk around the property to clear his head and savor the clean air. The sun was melting toward the horizon when Beasley found him dozing in the shade of an oak. It was a huge tree with yellowing leaves and exposed roots. The roots crawled with pill bugs. Between yawns Partridge observed the insects go about their tiny business.

"C'mon. You gotta see the ghost town before it gets dark," Beasley said. Partridge didn't bother to protest. Nadine waited in the jeep. She wore tortoiseshell sunglasses and a red scarf in her hair. He decided she looked better in a scarf than Toshi ever had, no question. Partridge opened his mouth and Beasley gave him a friendly shove into the front passenger seat.

"Sulk, sulk, sulk!" Nadine laughed at him. "In the garden, eating worms?"

"Close enough," Partridge said and hung on as Beasley gunned the jeep through a break in the fence line and zoomed along an overgrown track that was invisible until they were right on top of it. The farm became a picture on a stamp and then they passed through a belt of paper birches and red maples. They crossed a ramshackle bridge that spanned an ebon stream and drove into a clearing. Beasley ground gears until they gained the crown of a long tabletop hill. He killed the engine and coasted to a halt amid tangled grass and wildflowers and said, "Orren Towne. Died circa 1890s."

Below their vantage, remnants of a village occupied the banks of a shallow valley. If Orren Towne was dead its death was the living kind. A score of saltbox houses and the brooding hulk of a Second Empire church waited somberly. Petrified roofs were dappled by the shadows of moving clouds. Facades were brim with the ephemeral light of the magic hour. Beasley's walkie-talkie crackled and he stepped aside to answer the call.

Nadine walked partway down the slope and stretched her arms. Her muscles stood forth in cords of sinew and gristle. She looked over her shoulder at Partridge. Her smile was alien. "Don't you wish you'd brought your camera?"

The brain is a camera. What Partridge really wished was that he had gone to his room and slept. His emotions were on the verge of running amok. The animal fear from his daydreams had sneaked up again. He smelled the musk of his own adrenaline and sweat. *The brain is a camera and once it sees what it sees there's no taking it back*. He noticed another of Toshi's bizarre radio dishes perched on a bluff. The antenna was focused upon the deserted buildings. "I don't like this place," he said. But she kept walking and he trailed along. It was cooler among the houses. The earth was trampled into concrete and veined with minerals. Nothing organic grew and no birds sang. The subtly deformed structures were encased in a transparent resin that lent the town the aspect of a waxworks. He thought it might be shellac.

Shadows fell across Partridge's path. Open doorways and sugar-spun windows fronted darkness. These doors and windows were as unwelcoming as the throats of ancient wells, the mouths of caves. He breathed heavily. "How did Toshi do this? *Why* did he do this?"

Nadine laughed and took his hand playfully. Hers was dry and too warm, like a leather wallet left in direct sunlight. "Toshi only discovered it. Do you seriously think he and Howard are capable of devising something this extraordinary?"

"No."

"Quite a few people spent their lives in this valley. Decent farming and hunting in these parts. The Mooreheads owned about everything. They owned a brewery and a mill down the road, near their estate. All those busy little worker bees going about their jobs, going to church on Sunday. I'm sure it was a classic Hallmark. Then it got cold. One of those long winters that never ends. Nothing wanted to grow and the game disappeared. The house burned. Sad for the Mooreheads. Sadder for the people who depended on them. The family circled its wagons to rebuild the mansion, but the community proper never fully recovered. Orren Towne was here today, gone tomorrow. At least that's the story we hear told by the old-timers at the Mad Rooster over cribbage and a pint of stout." Nadine stood in the shade of the church, gazing up, up at the crucifix. "This is how it will all be someday. Empty buildings. Empty skies. The grass will come and eat everything we ever made. The waters will swallow it. It puts my situation into perspective, lemme tell you."

"These buildings should've fallen down. Somebody's gone through a lot of trouble to keep this like—"

"A museum. Yeah, somebody has. This isn't the only place it's been done, either."

"Places like this? Where?" Partridge said. He edged closer to the bright center of the village square.

"I don't know. They're all over if you know what to look for."

"Nadine, maybe . . . Jesus!" He jerked his head around to peer at a doorway. The darkness inside the house seemed fuller and more complete. "Are there people here?" His mind jumped to an image of the masks that the natives wore to ward off tigers. He swallowed hard.

"Just us chickens, love."

A stiff breeze rushed from the northwest and whipped the outlying grass. Early autumn leaves skated across the glassy rooftops and swirled in barren yards. Leaves fell dead and dry. Night was coming hard.

"I'm twitchy—jet lag, probably. What do those weird-looking rigs do?" He pointed at the dish on the hill. "Toshi said they're radio telescopes he invented."

"He said he invented them? Oh my. I dearly love that man, but sometimes he's such an asshole."

"Yeah. How do they work?"

Nadine shrugged. "They read frequencies on the electromagnetic spectrum."

"Radio signals from underground. Why does that sound totally backwards to me?"

"I didn't say anything about radio signals."

"Then what did you say?"

"When we get back, ask Toshi about the node."

"What are you talking about?" Partridge's attention was divided between her and the beautifully grotesque houses and the blackness inside them.

"You'll see. Get him to show you the node. That'll clear some of this stuff up, pronto."

Beasley called to them. He and the jeep were a merged silhouette against the failing sky. He swung his arm overhead until Nadine yelled that they would start back in a minute. She removed her shades and met Partridge's eyes. "You okay, Rich?" She refused to relinquish her grip on his hand.

"You're asking *me*?"

She gave him another of her inscrutable looks. She reached up and pushed an unkempt lock from his forehead. "I'm not pissed, in case you're still wondering. I wanted you to see me off. Not like there're any more weekend rendezvous in the stars for us."

"That's no way to talk," he said.

"Just sayin'." She dropped his hand and walked away. In a moment he followed. By the time they made the summit, darkness had covered the valley. Beasley had to use the headlights to find the way home.

Gertz served prawns for dinner. They ate at the long mahogany table in the formal dining room. Jackson Phillips begged off due to an urgent matter in the city. Beasley packed him and one of the musclebound bodyguards into the helicopter and flew away. That left six: Toshi, Campbell, Nadine, Carrey Montague and the other bodyguard, and Partridge. The men wore suits and ties. Nadine wore a cream-colored silk chiffon evening gown. There were candles and elaborate floral arrangements and dusty bottles of wine from the Moorehead cellar and magnums of top dollar French champagne from a Boston importer who catered to those with exclusive tastes and affiliations. Toshi proposed a toast and said a few words in Japanese and then the assembly began to eat and drink.

Somewhere in the middle of the third or fourth course, Partridge realized he was cataclysmically drunk. They kept setting them up and he kept knocking them down. Toshi or Campbell frequently clapped his back and clinked his glass and shouted "*Sic itur ad astra!*" and another round would magically appear. His head was swollen and empty as an echo chamber. The winking silverware and sloshing wineglasses, the bared teeth and hearty laughter came to him from a seashell. Nadine abruptly rose and fled, weeping.

Dinner blurred into a collage of sense and chaos, of light and dark, and he gripped his glass and blinked dumbly against the shattering flare of the low slung chandelier and laughed uproariously. Without transition, dinner was concluded and the men had repaired to the den to relax over snifters of Hennessy. They lounged in wing-backed leather chairs and upon opulent leather divans. Partridge admired the vaulted ceiling, the library of towering lacquered oak bookcases, and the impressive collection of antique British rifles and British cavalry sabers cached in rearing cabinets of chocolate wood and softly warped glass. Everything was so huge and shiny and far away. When the cigar and pipe smoke hung thick and the men's cheeks were glazed and rosy as the cheeks of Russian dolls, he managed, "I'm supposed to ask you about the node."

Campbell smiled a broad and genial smile. "The node, yes. The node, of course, is the very reason Mr. Phillips and Mr. Montague have come to pay their respects. They hope to buy their way into Heaven."

"He's right, he's right," Mr. Carrey Montague said with an air of merry indulgence. "Jack had his shot. Didn't he though. Couldn't hack it and off he flew."

"I was getting to this," Toshi said. "In a roundabout fashion."

"Exceedingly so," Campbell said.

"Didn't want to frighten him. It's a delicate matter."

"Yes," Campbell said dryly. He puffed on his pipe and his eyes were red around the edges and in the center of his pupils.

"Shall I. Or do you want a go?" Toshi shrugged his indifference.

"The node is a communication device," Campbell said through a mouthful of smoke. "Crude, really. Danforth Moorehead, the Moorehead patriarch, developed the current model. Ahem, the schematic was delivered to him and he effected the necessary modifications, at any rate. Admittedly, it's superior to the primitive methods—scrying, séances, psychedelic drugs, that nonsense. Not to mention some of the more gruesome customs we've observed in the provincial regions. Compared to that, the node is state of the art. It is a reservoir that filters and translates frequency imaging captured by our clever, clever radio telescopes. It permits us to exchange information with our . . . neighbors."

Partridge dimly perceived that the others were watching him with something like fascination. Their eyes glittered through the haze. "With who? I don't—"

"Our neighbors," Campbell said.

"Oh, the things they show you." Carrey Montague sucked on his oxygen mask until he resembled a ghoul.

Partridge swung his head to look from face to face. The men were drunk. The men seethed with restrained glee. No one appeared to be joking. "Well, go on then," he said dreamily. His face was made of plaster. Black spots revolved before him like ashen snowflakes.

"I told you, Richard. Mankind can't go on like this."

"Like what?"

Toshi chuckled. "Assuming we don't obliterate ourselves, or that a mete-orite doesn't smack us back to the Cambrian, if not the Cryptozoic, this planet will succumb to the exhaustion of Sol. First the mammals, then the reptiles, right down the line until all that's left of any complexity are the arthropods: beetles and cockroaches and their oceanic cousins, practically speaking. Evolution is a circle—we're sliding back to that endless sea of pro-toplasmic goop."

"I'm betting on the nuclear holocaust," Campbell said.

Partridge slopped more brandy into his mouth. He was far beyond tast-ing it. "Mmm hmm," he said intelligently and cast about for a place to in-conspicuously ditch his glass.

"NASA and its holy grail—First Contact, the quest for intelligent life in the universe . . . all hogwash, all lies." Toshi gently took the snifter away and handed him a fresh drink in a ceramic mug. This was not brandy; it was rich and dark as honey in moonlight. "Private stock, my boy. Drink up!" Par-tridge drank and his eyes flooded and he choked a little. Toshi nodded in sat-isfaction. "We know now what we've always suspected. Man is completely and utterly alone in a sea of dust and smoke. Alone and inevitably slipping into extinction."

"Not quite alone," Campbell said. "There are an estimated five to eight million species of insects as of yet unknown and unclassified. Hell of a lot of insects, hmm? But why stop at bugs? Only a damned fool would suppose that was anything but the tip of the iceberg. When the time of Man comes to an end *their* time will begin. And be certain this is not an invasion or a hostile occupation. We'll be dead as Dodos a goodly period before they emerge to claim the surface. They won't rule forever. The planet will eventually become cold and inhospitable to any mortal organism. But trust that their rule will make the reign of the terrible lizards seem a flicker of an eyelash."

"You're talking about cockroaches," Partridge said in triumph. "Fucking cockroaches." That was too amusing and so he snorted on his pungent liquor and had a coughing fit.

"No, we are not," Campbell said.

"We aren't talking about spiders or beetles, either," Toshi said. He gave Partridge's knee an earnest squeeze. "To even compare them with the citizens of the *Great Kingdom* . . . I shudder. However, if I *were* to make that com-parison, I'd say this intelligence is the Ur-progenitor of those insects scrab-bling in the muck. The mother race of idiot stepchildren."

Campbell knelt before him so they were eye to eye. The older man's face was radiant and distant as the moon. "This is a momentous discovery. We've established contact. Not us, actually. It's been going on forever. We are the latest . . . emissaries, if you will. Trustees to the grandest secret of them all."

"Hoo boy. You guys. You fucking guys. Is Nadine in on this?"

"Best that you see firsthand. Would you like that, Rich?"

"Uhmm-wha?" Partridge did not know what he wanted except that he wanted the carousel to stop.

Campbell and Toshi stood. They took his arms and the next thing he knew they were outside in the humid country night with darkness all around. He tried to walk, but his legs wouldn't cooperate much. They half dragged him to a dim metal door and there was a lamp bulb spinning in space and then steep, winding concrete stairs and cracked concrete walls ribbed with mold. They went down and down and a strong, earthy smell overcame Partridge's senses. People spoke to him in rumbling nonsense phrases. Someone ruffled his hair and laughed. His vision fractured. He glimpsed hands and feet, a piece of jaw illumed by a quivering fluorescent glow. When the hands stopped supporting him, he slid to his knees. He had the impression of kneeling in a cellar. Water dripped and a pale overhead lamp hummed like a wasp in a jar. From the corner of his eye he got the sense of table legs and cables and he smelled an acrid smell like cleaning solvents. He thought it might be a laboratory.

—Crawl forward just a bit.

It was strange whatever lay before him. Something curved, spiral-shaped, and darkly wet. A horn, a giant conch shell—it was impossible to be certain. There was an opening, as the *external os* of a cervix, large enough to accommodate him in all his lanky height. Inside it was moist and muffled and black.

—There's a lad. Curl up inside. Don't fight. There, there. That's my boy. Won't be long. Not long. Don't be afraid. This is only a window, not a doorway.

Then nothing and nothing and nothing; only his heart, his breathing, and a whispery static thrum that might've been the electromagnetic current tracing its circuit through his nerves.

Nothingness grew very dense.

Partridge tried to shriek when water, or something thicker than water, flowed over his head and into his sinuses and throat. Low static built in his ears and the abject blackness was replaced by flashes of white imagery. He fell from an impossible height. He saw only high velocity jump-cuts of the world and each caromed from him and into the gulf almost instantly. Fire and blood and moving tides of unleashed water. Bones of men and women and cities. Dead, mummified cities gone so long without inhabitants they had become cold and brittle and smooth as mighty forests of stone. There loomed over everything a silence that held to its sterile bosom countless screams and the sibilant chafe of swirling dust. Nadine stood naked as ebony in the heart of a ruined square. She wore a white mask, but he knew her with the immediacy of a nightmare. She lifted her mask and looked at him. She smiled and raised her hand. Men and women emerged from the broken sky-scrapers and collapsed bunkers. They were naked and pallid and smiling. In the distance the sun heaved up, slow and red. Its deathly light cascaded upon the lines and curves of cyclopean structures. These were colossal, inhuman edifices of fossil bone and obsidian and anthracite that glittered not unlike behemoth carapaces. He thrashed and fell and fell and drowned.

Nadine said in his ear, *Come down. We love you.*

The cellar floor was cool upon his cheek. He was paralyzed and choking. The men spoke to him in soothing voices. Someone pressed a damp cloth to his brow.

—Take it easy, son. The first ride or two is a bitch and a half. Get his head.

Partridge groaned as gravity crushed him into the moldy concrete.

Someone murmured to him.

—They are interested in preserving aspects of our culture. Thus Orren Towne and places, hidden places most white men will never tread. Of course, it's a multifaceted project. Preserving artifacts, buildings, that's hardly enough to satisfy such an advanced intellect. . . .

Partridge tired to speak. His jaw worked spastically. No sound emerged. The concrete went soft and everyone fell silent at once.

Partridge stirred and sat up. He tried to piece together how he ended up on the back porch sprawled in a wooden folding chair. He was still in his suit and it was damp and clung to him the way clothes do after they have been slept in. The world teetered on the cusp of night. Parts of the sky were or-ange as fire and other parts were covered by purple-tinted rain clouds like a pall of cannon smoke. Partridge's hair stood in gummy spikes. His mouth was swollen and cottony. He had drooled in his long sleep. His body was stiff as an old plank.

Beasley came out of the house and handed him a glass of seltzer water. "Can't hold your liquor anymore?"

Partridge took the glass in both hands and drank greedily. "Oh you're back. Must've been a hell of a party," he said at last. He had slept for at least sixteen hours according to his watch. His memory was a smooth and fric-tionless void.

"Yeah," Beasley said. "You okay?"

Partridge was not sure. "Uh," he said. He rolled his head to survey the twilight vista. "Beasley."

"Yeah?"

"All this." Partridge swept his hand to encompass the swamped gardens and the decrepit outbuildings. "They're letting it fall down. Nobody left from the old days."

"You and me. And Nadine."

"And when we're gone?"

"We're all gonna be gone sooner or later. The docs . . . they just do what they can. There's nothing else, pal." Beasley gave him a searching look. He shook his shaggy head and chuckled. "Don't get morbid on me, Hollywood. Been a good run if you ask me. Hell, we may get a few more years before the plug gets pulled."

"Is Montague still here?"

"Why do you ask?"

"I heard someone yelling, cursing. Earlier, while I slept."

"Huh. Yeah, there was a little fight. The old fella didn't get his golden ticket. He wasn't wanted. Few are. He shipped out. Won't be coming back."

"I guess not. What was he after?"

"Same thing as everybody else, I suppose. People think Toshi is the Devil, that he can give them their heart's desire if they sign on the dotted line. It ain't so simple."

Partridge had a wry chuckle at that. "Damned right it's not simple, partner. I'm still selling my soul to Tinsel Town. No such luck as to unload the whole shebang at once." Partridge shook with a sudden chill. His memory shucked and jittered; it spun off the reel in his brain and he could not gather it fast enough to make sense of what he had seen in the disjointed frames. "Lord, I hate the country. Always have. I really should get out of here, soon."

"My advice—when you get on that bus, don't look back," Beasley said. "And keep your light on at night. You done with that?"

"Um-hmm." He could not summon the energy to say more right then. The strength and the will had run out of him. He put his hand over his eyes and tried to concentrate.

Beasley took the empty glass and went back into the house. Darkness came and the yard lamps sizzled to life. Moths fluttered near his face, battened at the windows, and Partridge wondered why that panicked him, why his heart surged and his fingernails dug into the arm rests. In the misty fields, the drone of night insects began.

He eventually heaved to his feet and went inside and walked the dim, ugly corridors for an interminable period. He stumbled aimlessly as if he were yet drunk. His thoughts buzzed and muttered and were incoherent. He found Toshi and Campbell in the den crouched like grave robbers over a stack of shrunken, musty ledgers with hand-sewn covers and other stacks of photographic plates like the kind shot from the air or a doctor's X-ray machine. The den was tomb-dark except for a single flimsy desk lamp. He swayed in the doorway, clinging to the jamb as if he were in a cabin on a ship. He said, "Where is Nadine?"

The old men glanced up from their documents and squinted at him. Toshi shook his head and sucked his teeth. Campbell pointed at the ceiling. "She's in her room. Packing. It's Sunday night," he said. "You should go see her."

"She has to leave," Toshi said.

Partridge turned and left. He made his way up the great central staircase and tried a number of doors that let into dusty rooms with painter's cloth draping the furniture. Light leaked from the jamb of one door and he went in without knocking.

"I've been waiting," Nadine said. Her room was smaller and more feminine than the Garden Room. She sat lotus on a poster bed. She wore a simple yellow sun dress and her hair in a knot. Her face was dented with exhaustion. "I got scared you might not come to say good-bye."

Partridge did not see any suitcases. A mostly empty bottle of pain medication sat on the nightstand beside her wedding ring and a silver locket she had inherited from her great-grandmother. He picked up the locket and let it spill through his fingers, back and forth between his hands.

"It's very late," she said. Her voice was not tired like her face. Her voice was steady and full of conviction. "Take me for a walk."

"Where?" he said.

"In the fields. One more walk in the fields."

He was afraid as he had been afraid when the moths came over him and against the windows. He was afraid as he had been when he pulled her from the water all those years ago and then lay in his hammock bunk dreaming and dreaming of the crocodiles and the bottomless depths warm as the recesses of his own body and she had shuddered against him, entwined with him and inextricably linked with him. He did not wish to leave the house, not at night. He said, "Sure. If you want to."

She climbed from the bed and took his hand. They walked down the stairs and through the quiet house. They left the house and the spectral yard and walked through a gate into the field and then farther into heavier and heavier shadows.

Partridge let Nadine lead. He stepped gingerly. He was mostly night blind and his head ached. Wet grass rubbed his thighs. He was soaked right away. A chipped edge of the ivory moon bit through the moving clouds. There were a few stars. They came to a shallow depression where the grass had been trampled or had sunk beneath the surface. Something in his memory twitched and a terrible cold knot formed in his stomach. He whined in his throat, uncomprehendingly, like a dog.

She hesitated in the depression and pulled her pale dress over her head. She tossed the dress away and stood naked and half hidden in the fog and darkness. He did not need to see her, he had memorized everything. She slipped into the circle of his arms and he embraced her without thinking. She leaned up and kissed him. Her mouth was dry and hot. "Come on," she muttered against his lips. "Come on." Her hands were sinewy as talons and very strong. She grasped his hair and drew him against her and they slowly folded into the moist earth. The soft earth was disfigured with their writhing and a deep, resonant vibration traveled through it and into them where it yammered through their blood and bones. She kissed him fiercely, viciously, and locked her thighs over his hips and squeezed until he gasped and kissed her back. She did not relinquish her fistful of his hair and she did not close her eyes. He stared into them and saw a ghost of a girl he knew and his own gaunt reflection, which he did not know at all. They were sinking.

Nadine stopped sucking at him and turned her head against the black dirt and toward the high, shivering grass. There was no breeze and the night lay dead and still. The grass sighed and muffled an approaching sound that struck Partridge as the thrum of fluorescent lights or high voltage current through a wire or, as it came swiftly closer, the clatter of pebbles rolling over slate. Nadine tightened her grip and looked at him with a sublime combination of glassy terror and exultation. She said, "Rich—"

The grass shook violently beneath a vast, invisible hand and a tide of chirring and burring and click-clacking blackness poured into the depression from far flung expanses of lost pasture and haunted wilderness, from the moist abyssal womb that opens beneath everything, everywhere. The cacophony was a murderous tectonic snarl out of Pandemonium, Gehenna, and Hell; the slaughterhouse gnash and whicker and serrated wail of legion bloodthirsty drills and meat-hungry saw teeth. The ebony breaker crashed over them and buried them and swallowed their screams before their screams began.

After the blackness ebbed and receded and was finally gone, it became quiet. At last the frogs tentatively groaned and the crickets warmed by degrees to their songs of loneliness and sorrow. The moon slipped into the moat around the Earth.

He rose alone, black on black, from the muck and walked back in shambling steps to the house.

Partridge sat rigid and upright at the scarred table in the blue-gray gloom of the kitchen. Through the one grimy window above the sink, the predawn sky glowed the hue of gun metal. His eyes glistened and caught that feeble light and held it fast like the eyes of a carp in its market bed of ice. His black face dripped onto his white shirt, which was also black. His black hands lay motionless on the table. He stank of copper and urine and shit. Water leaked in fat drops from the stainless steel gooseneck tap. A grandfather clock ticked and tocked from the hall and counted down the seconds of the revolutions of the Earth. The house settled and groaned fitfully, a guilty pensioner caught fast in dreams.

Toshi materialized in the crooked shadows near the stove. His face was masked by the shadows. He said in a low, hoarse voice that suggested a quantity of alcohol and tears, "Occasionally one of us, a volunteer, is permitted to cross over, to relinquish his or her flesh to the appetites of the colony and exist among them in a state of pure consciousness. That's how it's always been. These volunteers become the interpreters, the facilitators of communication between our species. They become undying repositories of our civilization . . . a civilization that shall become ancient history one day very soon."

Partridge said nothing.

Toshi said in his hoarse, mournful voice, "She'll never truly die. She'll be with them until this place is a frozen graveyard orbiting a cinder. It is an honor. Yet she waited. She wanted to say good-bye in person."

Partridge said nothing. The sun floated to the black rim of the horizon. The sun hung crimson and boiling and a shaft of bloody light passed through the window and bathed his hand.

"Oh!" Toshi said, and his mouth was invisible, but his eyes were bright and wet in the gathering light. "Can you *imagine* gazing upon constellations a hundred million years from this dawn? Can you imagine the wonder of gazing upon those constellations from a hundred million eyes? Oh, imagine it, my boy. . . ."

Partridge stood and went wordlessly, ponderously, to the window and lingered there a moment, his mud-caked face afire with the bloody radiance of a dying star. He drank in the slumbering fields, the distant fog-wreathed forests, as if he might never look upon any of it again. He reached up and pulled the shade down tight against the sill and it was dark.

The Monsters of Heaven

NATHAN BALLINGRUD

Nathan Ballingrud was born in 1970 in Massachusetts but grew up in the American South. He's worked as a cook on offshore oil rigs, a bartender in New Orleans, and a freelance writer wherever he can find it. Currently he lives just outside of Asheville, North Carolina, with his daughter.

Ballingrud has only published a handful of stories since his work's first appearance in 1994, but his most recent fiction has appeared in SCI FICTION, The 3rd Alternative, The Magazine of Fantasy & Science Fiction, *and* The Year's Best Fantasy and Horror, Seventeenth Annual Collection.

Who invented the human heart, I wonder? Tell me, then show me the place where he was hanged.

—Lawrence Durrell, *Justine*

For a long time, Brian imagined reunions with his son. In the early days, these fantasies were defined by spectacular violence. He would find the man who stole him and open his head with a claw hammer. The more blood he spilled, the further removed he became from his own guilt. The location would often change: a roach-haunted tenement building; an abandoned warehouse along the Tchoupitoulas wharf; a pre-fab bungalow with an American flag out front and a two-door hatchback parked in the driveway.

Sometimes the man lived alone, sometimes he had his own family. On these latter occasions Brian would cast himself as a moral executioner, spraying the walls with the kidnapper's blood but sparing his wife and child—freeing them, he imagined, from his tyranny. No matter the scenario, Toby was always there, always intact; Brian would feel his face pressed into his shoulders as he carried him away, feel the heat of his tears bleed into his shirt. You're safe now, he would say. Daddy's got you. Daddy's here.

After some months passed, he deferred the heroics to the police. This marked his first concession to reality. He spent his time beached in the living room, drinking more, working less, until the owner of the auto shop told him to take time off, a lot of time off, as much as he needed. Brian barely noticed. He waited for the red and blue disco lights of a police cruiser to illuminate the darkness outside, to give some shape and measure to the night. He waited for the phone to ring with a glad summons to the station. He played out scenarios, tried on different outcomes, guessed at his own reactions. He gained weight and lost time.

Sometimes he would get out of bed in the middle of the night, careful not to wake his wife, and get into the car. He would drive at dangerous speeds through the city, staring into the empty sockets of unlighted windows. He would get out of the car and stand in front of some of these houses, looking and listening for signs. Often, the police were called. When the officers realized who he was, they were usually as courteous as they were adamant. He'd wonder if it had been the kidnapper who called the police. He would imagine returning to those houses with a gun.

This was in the early days of what became known as the Lamentation. At this stage, most people did not know anything unusual was happening. What they heard, if they heard anything, was larded with rumor and embellishment. Fogs of gossip in the barrooms and churches. This was before the bloodshed. Before their pleas to Christ clotted in their throats.

Amy never told Brian that she blamed him. She elected, rather, to avoid the topic of the actual abduction, and any question of her husband's negligence. Once the police abandoned them as suspects, the matter of their own involvement ceased to be a subject of discussion. Brian was unconsciously grateful, because it allowed him to focus instead on the maintenance of grief. Silence spread between them like a glacier. In a few months, entire days passed with nothing said between them.

It was on such a night that Amy rolled up against him and kissed the back of his neck. It froze Brian, filling him with a blast of terror and bewilderment; he felt the guilt move inside of him, huge but seemingly distant, like a whale passing beneath a boat. Her lips felt hot against his skin, sending warm waves rolling from his neck and shoulders all the way down to his legs, as though she had injected something lovely into him. She grew more ardent, nipping him with her teeth, breaking through his reservations. He turned and kissed her. He experienced a leaping arc of energy, a terrifying, violent impulse; he threw his weight onto her and crushed his mouth into hers, scraping his teeth against hers. But there immediately followed a cascade of unwelcome thought: Toby whimpering somewhere in the dark, waiting for his father to save him; Amy, dressed in her bedclothes in the middle of the day, staring like a corpse into the sunlight coming through the windows; the playground, and the receding line of kindergarteners. When she reached under the sheets she found him limp and unready. He opened his mouth to apologize but she shoved her tongue into it, her hand working at him with a rough urgency, as though more depended on this than he knew. Later he would learn that it did. Her teeth sliced his lip and blood eeled into his mouth. She was pulling at him too hard, and it was starting to hurt. He wrenched himself away.

"Jesus," he said, wiping his lip. The blood felt like an oil slick in the back of his throat.

She turned her back to him and put her face into the pillow. For a moment he thought she was crying. But only for a moment.

"Honey," he said. "Hey." He put his fingers on her shoulder; she rolled it away from him.

"Go to sleep," she said.

He stared at the landscape of her naked back, pale in the streetlight leaking through the blinds, feeling furious and ruined.

The next morning, when he came into the kitchen, Amy was already up. Coffee was made, filling the room with a fine toasted smell, and she was leaning against the counter with a cup in her hand, wearing her pink terrycloth robe. Her dark hair was still wet from the shower. She smiled and said, "Good morning."

"Hey," he said, feeling for a sense of her mood.

Dodger, Toby's dog, cast him a devastated glance from his customary place beneath the kitchen table. Amy had wanted to get rid of him—she couldn't bear the sight of him anymore, she'd said—but Brian wouldn't allow it. When Toby comes back, he reasoned, he'll wonder why we did it. What awful thing guided us. So Dodger remained, and his slumping, sorrowful presence tore into them both like a hungry animal.

"Hey boy," Brian said, and rubbed his neck with his toe.

"I'm going out today," Amy said.

"Okay. Where to?"

She shrugged. "I don't know. The hardware store. Maybe a nursery. I want to find myself a project."

Brian looked at her. The sunlight made a corona around her body. This new resolve, coupled with her overture of the night before, struck him as a positive sign. "Okay," he said.

He seated himself at the table. The newspaper had been placed there for him, still bound by a rubber band. He snapped it off and unfurled the front page. Already he felt the gravitational pull of the Jack Daniel's in the cabinet, but when Amy leaned over his shoulder and placed a coffee cup in front of him, he managed to resist the whiskey's call with an ease that surprised and gratified him. He ran his hand up her forearm, pushing back the soft pink sleeve, and he kissed the inside of her wrist. He felt a wild and incomprehensible hope. He breathed in the clean, scented smell of her. She stayed there for a moment, and then gently pulled away.

They remained that way in silence for some time—maybe fifteen minutes or more—until Brian found something in the paper he wanted to share with her. Something being described as "angelic"—"apparently not quite a human man," as the writer put it—had been found down by the Gulf Coast, in Morgan City; it had been shedding a faint light from under two feet of water; whatever it was had died shortly after being taken into custody, under confusing circumstances. He turned in his chair to speak, a word already gathering on his tongue, and he caught her staring at him. She wore a cadaverous, empty look, as though she had seen the worst thing in the world and died in the act. It occurred to him that she had been looking at him that way for whole minutes. He turned back to the table, his insides sliding, and stared at the suddenly indecipherable glyphs of the newspaper. After a moment he felt her hand on the back of his neck, rubbing him gently. She left the kitchen without a word.

This is how it happened:

They were taking Dodger for a walk. Toby liked to hold the leash—he was four years old, and gravely occupied with establishing his independence—and more often than not Brian would sort of half-trot behind them, one hand held indecisively aloft should Dodger suddenly decide to break into a run, dragging his boy behind him like a string of tin cans. He probably bit off more profanities during those walks than he ever did changing a tire. He carried, as was their custom on Mondays, a blanket and a picnic lunch. He would lie back in the sun while Toby and the dog played, and enjoy not being hunched over an engine block. At some point they would have lunch. Brian believed these afternoons of easy camaraderie would be remembered by them both for years to come. They'd done it a hundred times.

A hundred times.

On that day a kindergarten class arrived shortly after they did. Toby ran up to his father and wrapped his arms around his neck, frightened by the sudden bright surge of humanity; the kids were a loud, brawling tumult, crashing over the swings and monkey bars in a gabbling surf. Brian pried Toby's arms free and pointed at them.

"Look, screwball, they're just kids. See? They're just like you. Go on and play. Have some fun."

Dodger galloped out to greet them and was received as a hero, with joyful cries and grasping fingers. Toby observed this gambit for his dog's affections and at last decided to intervene. He ran toward them, shouting, "That's my dog! That's my dog!" Brian watched him go, made eye contact with the teacher and nodded hello. She smiled at him—he remembered thinking she was kind of cute, wondering how old she was—and she returned her attention to her kids, gamboling like lunatics all over the park. Brian reclined on the blanket and watched the clouds skim the atmosphere, listened to the sound of children. It was a hot, windless day.

He didn't realize he had dozed until the kindergarteners had been rounded up and were halfway down the block, taking their noise with them. The silence stirred him.

He sat up abruptly and looked around. The playground was empty. "Toby? Hey, Toby?"

Dodger stood out in the middle of the road, his leash spooled at his feet. He watched Brian eagerly, offered a tentative wag.

"Where's Toby?" he asked the dog, and climbed to his feet. He felt a sudden sickening lurch in his gut. He turned in a quick circle, a half-smile on his face, utterly sure that this was an impossible situation, that children didn't disappear in broad daylight while their parents were *right fucking there*. So he was still here. Of course he was still here. Dodger trotted up to him and sat down at his feet, waiting for him to produce the boy, as though he were a hidden tennis ball.

"Toby?"

The park was empty. He jogged after the receding line of kids. "Hey. *Hey!* Is my son with you? *Where's my son?*"

One morning, about a week after the experience in the kitchen, Brian was awakened by the phone. Every time this happened he felt a thrill of hope, though by now it had become muted, even dreadful in its predictability. He hauled himself up from the couch, nearly overturning a bottle of Jack Daniels stationed on the floor. He crossed the living room and picked up the phone.

"Yes?" he said.

"Let me talk to Amy." It was not a voice he recognized. A male voice, with a thick rural accent. It was the kind of voice that inspired immediate prejudice: the voice of an idiot, of a man without any right to make demands of him.

"Who is this?"

"Just let me talk to Amy."

"How about you go fuck yourself."

There was a pause as the man on the phone seemed to assess the obstacle. Then he said, with a trace of amusement in his voice, "Are you Brian?"

"That's right."

"Look, dude. Go get your wife. Put her on the phone. Do it now, and I won't have to come down there and break your fucking face."

Brian slammed down the receiver. Feeling suddenly lightheaded, he put his hand on the wall to steady himself, to reassure himself that it was still solid, and that he was still real. From somewhere outside, through an open window, came the distant sound of children shouting.

It was obvious that Amy was sleeping with another man. When confronted with the call, she did not admit to anything, but made no special effort to explain it away, either. His name was Tommy, she said. She'd met him once when she was out. He sounded rough, but he wasn't a bad guy. She chose not to elaborate, and Brian, to his amazement, found a kind of forlorn comfort in his wife's affair. He'd lost his son; why not lose it all?

On television the news was filling with the creatures, more of which were being discovered all the time. The press had taken to calling them angels. Some were being found alive, though all of them appeared to have suffered from some violent experience. At least one family had become notorious by refusing to let anyone see the angel they'd found, or even let it out of their home. They boarded their windows and warned away visitors with a shotgun.

Brian was stationed on the couch, staring at the television with the sound turned down to barely a murmur. He listened to the familiar muted clatter from the medicine cabinet as Amy applied her makeup in the bathroom. A news program was on, and a handheld camera followed a street reporter into someone's house. The JD bottle was empty at his feet, and the knowledge that he had no more in the house smoldered in him.

Amy emerged from the kitchen with her purse slung over her arm and made her way to the door. "I'm going out," she said.

"Where?"

She paused, one hand on the doorknob. She wavered there, in her careful makeup and her push-up bra. He tried to remember the last time he'd seen her look like this and failed dismally. Something inside her seemed to collapse—a force of will, perhaps, or a habit of deception. Maybe she was just too tired to invent another lie.

"I'm going to see Tommy," she said.

"The redneck."

"Sure. The redneck, if that's how you want it."

"Does it matter how I want it?"

She paused. "No," she said. "I guess not."

"Well well. The truth. Look out."

She left the door, walked into the living room. Brian felt a sudden trepidation; this is not what he imagined would happen. He wanted to get a few weak barbs in before she walked out, that was all. He did not actually want to talk.

She sat on the rocking chair across from the couch. Beside her, on the television, the camera focused on an obese man wearing overalls smiling triumphantly and holding aloft an angel's severed head.

Amy shut it off.

"Do you want to know about him?" she said.

"Let's see. He's stupid and violent. He called my home and threatened me. He's sleeping with my wife. What else is there to know?"

She appraised him for a moment, weighing consequences. "There's a little more to know," she said. "For example, he's very kind to me. He thinks I'm beautiful." He must have made some sort of sound then, because she said, "I know it must be very hard for you to believe, but some men still find me attractive. And that's important to me, Brian. Can you understand that?"

He turned away from her, shielding his eyes with a hand, although without the TV on there was very little light in the room. Each breath was laced with pain.

"When I go to see him, he talks to me. Actually talks. I know he might not be very smart, according to your standards, but you'd be surprised how much he and I have to talk about. You'd be surprised how much more there is to life—to my life—than your car magazines, and your TV, and your bottles of booze."

"Stop it," Brian said.

"He's also a very considerate lover. He paces himself. For my sake. For me. Did you *ever* do that, Brian? In all the times we made love?"

He felt tears crawling down his face. Christ. When did that start?

"I can forget things when I sleep with him. I can forget about . . . I can forget about everything. He lets me do that."

"You cold bitch," he rasped.

"You passive little shit," she bit back, with a venom that surprised him. "You let it happen, do you know that? You let it all happen. Every awful thing."

She stood abruptly and walked out the door, slamming it behind her. The force of it rattled the windows. After a while—he had no idea how long—he picked up the remote and turned the TV back on. A girl pointed to moving clouds on a map.

Eventually Dodger came by and curled up at his feet. Brian slid off the couch and lay down beside him, hugging him close. Dodger smelled the way dogs do, musky and of the earth, and he sighed with the abiding patience of his kind.

Violence filled his dreams. In them he rent bodies, spilled blood, painted the walls using severed limbs as gruesome brushes. In them he went back to the park and ate the children while the teacher looked on. Once he awoke after these dreams with blood filling his mouth; he realized he had chewed his tongue during the night. It was raw and painful for days afterward. A rage was building inside him and he could not find an outlet for it. One night Amy told him she thought she was falling in love with Tommy. He only nodded stupidly and watched her walk out the door again. That same night he kicked Dodger out of the house. He just opened the door to the night and told him to go. When he wouldn't—trying instead to slink around his legs and go back inside—he planted his foot on the dog's chest and physically pushed him back outside, sliding him backwards on his butt. *"Go find him!"* he yelled. *"Go find him! Go and find him!"* He shut the door and listened to Dodger whimper and scratch at it for nearly an hour. At some point he gave up and Brian fell asleep. When he awoke it was raining. He opened the door and called for him. The rain swallowed his voice.

"Oh no," he said quietly, his voice a whimper. "Come back! I'm sorry! Please, I'm so sorry!"

When Dodger did eventually return, wet and miserable, Brian hugged him tight, buried his face in his fur, and wept for joy.

Brian liked to do his drinking alone. When he drank in public, especially at his old bar, people tried to talk to him. They saw his presence as an invitation to share sympathy, or a request for a friendly ear. It got to be too much. But to-night he made his way back there, endured the stares and the weird silence, took the beers sent his way, although he wanted none of it. What he wanted tonight was Fire Engine, and she didn't disappoint.

Everybody knew Fire Engine, of course; if she thought you didn't know her, she'd introduce herself to you posthaste, one hand on your shoulder, the other on your thigh. Where her hands went after that depended on a quick negotiation. She was a redhead with an easy personality, and was popular with the regular clientele, including the ones that would never buy her ser-vices. She claimed to be twenty-eight but looked closer to forty. At some un-fortunate juncture in her life she had contrived to lose most of her front teeth, either to decay or to someone's balled fist; either way common wis-dom held she gave the best blowjob in downtown New Orleans.

Brian used to be amused by that kind of talk. Although he'd never had an interest in her he'd certainly enjoyed listening to her sales pitch; she'd become a sort of bar pet, and the unselfconscious way she went about her life was both endearing and appalling. Her lack of teeth was too perfect, and too ridiculous. Now, however, the information had acquired a new kind of value to him. He pressed his gaze onto her until she finally felt it and looked back. She smiled coquettishly, with gruesome effect. He told the bartender to send her a drink.

"You sure? She ain't gonna leave you alone all night."

"Fuck yeah, I'm sure."

All night didn't concern him. What concerned him were the next ten minutes, which was what he figured ten dollars would buy him. After the necessary negotiations and bullshit they left the bar together, trailing catcalls; she took his hand and led him around back, into the alley.

The smell of rotting garbage came at him like an attack, like a pillowcase thrown over his head. She steered him into the alley's dark mouth, with its grime-smeared pavement and furtive skittering sounds, and its Dumpster so stuffed with straining garbage bags that it looked like some fearsome monster choking on its dinner. "Now you know I'm a lady," she said, "but sometimes you just got to make do with what's available."

That she could laugh at herself this way touched Brian, and he felt a wash of sympathy for her. He considered what it would be like to run away with her, to rescue her from the wet pull of her life; to save her.

She unzipped his pants and pulled his dick out. "There we go, honey, that's what I'm talking about. Ain't you something."

After a couple of minutes she released him and stood up. He tucked himself back in and zipped his pants, afraid to make eye contact with her.

"Maybe you just had too much to drink," she said.

"Yeah."

"It ain't nothing."

"I know it isn't," he said harshly.

When she made no move to leave, he said, "Will you just get the fuck away from me? Please?"

Her voice lost its sympathy. "Honey, I still got to get paid."

He opened his wallet and fished out a ten-dollar bill. She plucked it from his fingers and walked out of the alley, back toward the bar. "Don't get all bent out of shape about it," she called. "Shit happens, you know?"

He slid down the wall until his ass hit the ground. He brought his hand to his mouth and choked out a sob, his eyes squeezed shut. He banged his head once against the brick wall behind him and then thought better of it. Down here the stench was a steaming blanket, almost soothing in its awfulness. He felt like he deserved to be there, that it was right that he should sleep in shit and grime. He listened to the gentle ticking of the roaches in the dark. He wondered if Toby was in a place like this.

Something glinted farther down the alley.

He strained to see it. It was too bright to be merely a reflection.

It moved.

"Son of a—" he said, and pushed himself to his feet.

It lay mostly hidden; it had pulled some stray garbage bags atop itself in an effort to remain concealed, but its dim luminescence worked against it. Brian loped over to it, wrenched the bags away; its clawed hands clutched at them and tore them open, spilling a clatter of beer and liquor bottles all over the ground. They caromed with hollow music through the alley, coming at last to silent rest, until all Brian could hear was the thin, high-pitched noise the creature made through the tiny O-shaped orifice he supposed passed for a mouth. Its eyes were black little stones. The creature—*angel*, he thought, *they're calling these things angels*—was tall and thin, abundantly male, and it shed a thin light that illuminated exactly nothing around it. *If you put some clothes on it,* Brian thought, *hide its face, gave it some gloves, it might pass for a human.*

Exposed, it held up a long-fingered hand, as if to ward him off. It had clearly been hurt: its legs looked badly broken, and it breathed in short, shallow gasps. A dark bruise spread like a mold over the right side of its chest.

"Look at you, huh? You're all messed up." He felt a strange glee as he said this; he could not justify the feeling and quickly buried it. "Yeah, yeah, somebody worked you over pretty good."

It managed to roll onto its belly and it scrabbled along the pavement in a pathetic attempt at escape. It loosed that thin, reedy cry. Calling for help? Begging for its life?

The sight of it trying to flee from him catalyzed some deep predatory impulse, and he pressed his foot onto the angel's ankle, holding it easily in place. "No you don't." He hooked the thing beneath its shoulders and lifted it from the ground; it was astonishingly light. It mewled weakly at him. "Shut up, I'm trying to help you." He adjusted it in his arms so that he held it like a lover, or a fainted woman. He carried it back to his car, listening for the sound of the barroom door opening behind him, of laughter or a challenge chasing him down the sidewalk. But the door stayed shut. He walked in silence.

Amy was awake when he got home, silhouetted in the doorway. Brian pulled the angel from the passenger seat, cradled it against his chest. He watched her face alter subtly, watched as some dark hope crawled across it like an insect, and he squashed it before it could do any real harm.

"It's not him," he said. "It's something else."

She stood away from the door and let him come in.

Dodger, who had been dozing in the hallway, lurched to his feet with a sliding and skittering of claws and growled fiercely at it, his lips curled away from his teeth.

"Get away, you," Brian said. He eased past him, bearing his load down the hall.

He laid it in Toby's bed. Together he and Amy stood over it, watching as it stared back at them with dark flat eyes, its body twisting away from them as if it could fold itself into another place altogether. Its fingers plucked at the train-spangled bedsheets, wrapping them around its nakedness. Amy leaned over and helped to tuck the sheets around it.

"He's hurt," she said.

"I know. I guess a lot of them are found that way."

"Should we call somebody?"

"You want camera crews in here? Fuck no."

"Well. He's really hurt. We need to do something."

"Yeah. I don't know. We can at least clean him up I guess."

Amy sat on the mattress beside it; it stared at her with its expressionless face. Brian couldn't tell if there were thoughts passing behind those eyes, or just a series of brute reflex arcs. After a moment it reached out with one long dark fingernail and brushed her arm. She jumped as though shocked.

"Jesus! Be careful," said Brian.

"What if it's him?"

"What?" It took him a moment to understand her. "Oh my god. Amy. It's not him, okay? It's *not him*."

"But what if it is?"

"It's *not*. We've seen them on the news, okay? It's a, it's a *thing*."

"You shouldn't call it an 'it.'"

"How do I know what the fuck to call it?"

She touched her fingers to its cheek. It pressed its face into them, making some small sound.

"Why did you leave me?" she said. "You were everything I had."

Brian swooned beneath a tide of vertigo. Something was moving inside him, something too large to stay where it was. "It's an angel," he said. "Nothing more. Just an angel. It's probably going to die on us, since that's what they seem to do." He put his hand against the wall until the dizziness passed. It was replaced by a low, percolating anger. "Instead of thinking of it as Toby, why don't you ask it where Toby *is*. Why don't you make it explain to us why it happened."

She looked at him. "It happened because you let it," she said.

Dodger asked to be let outside. Brian opened the door for him to let him run around the front yard. There was a leash law here, but Dodger was well known by the neighbors and generally tolerated. He walked out of the house with considerably less than his usual enthusiasm. He lifted his leg desultorily against a shrub, then walked down to the road and followed the sidewalk farther into the neighborhood. He did not come back.

Over the next few days it put its hooks into them, and drew them in tight. They found it difficult to leave it alone. Its flesh seemed to pump out some kind of soporific, like an invisible spoor, and it was better than the booze—better than anything they'd previously known. Its pull seemed to grow stronger as the days passed. For Amy, especially. She stopped going out, and for all practical purposes moved into Toby's room with it. When Brian joined her in there, she seemed to barely tolerate his presence. If he sat beside it she watched him with naked trepidation, as though she feared he might damage it somehow.

It was not, he realized, an unfounded fear. Something inside him became turbulent in its presence, something he couldn't identify but which sparked flashes of violent thought of the kind he had not had since just after Toby vanished. This feeling came in sharp relief to the easy lethargy the angel normally inspired, and he was reminded of a time when he was younger, sniffing heroin laced with cocaine. So he did not object to Amy's efforts at excluding him.

Finally, though, her vigilance slipped. He went into the bathroom and found her sleeping on the toilet, her robe hiked up around her waist, her head resting against the sink. He left her there and crept into the angel's room.

It was awake, and its eyes tracked him as he crossed the room and sat beside it on the bed. Its breath wheezed lightly as it drew air through its puckered mouth. Its body was still bruised and bent, though it did seem to be improving.

Brian touched its chest where the bruise seemed to be diminishing. *Why does it bruise?* he wondered. *Why does it bleed the same way I do? Shouldn't it be made of something better?* Also, it didn't have wings. Not even vestigial ones. Why were they called angels? Because of how they made people feel? It looked more like an alien than a divine being. *It has a cock, for Christ's sake. What's that all about? Do angels fuck?*

He leaned over it, so his face was inches away, almost touching its nose. He stared into its black, irisless eyes, searching for some sign of intelligence, some evidence of intent or emotion. From this distance he could smell its breath; he drew it into his own lungs, and it warmed him like a shot of whiskey. The angel lifted its head and pressed its face into his. Brian jerked back and felt something brush his elbow. He looked behind him and discovered the angel had an erection.

He lurched out of bed, tripping over himself as he rushed to the door, dashed through it, and slammed it shut. His blood sang. It rose in him like the sea and filled him with tumultuous music. He dropped to his knees and vomited all over the carpet.

Later, he stepped into its doorway, watching Amy trace her hands down its face. Through the window he could see that night was gathering in little pockets outside, lifting itself toward the sky. At the sight of the angel his heart jumped in his chest as though it had come unmoored. "Amy, I have to talk to you," he said. He had some difficulty making his voice sound calm.

She didn't look at him. "I know it's not really him," she said. "Not really."

"No."

"But don't you think he is, kind of? In a way?"

"No."

She laid her head on the pillow beside it, staring into its face. Brian was left looking at the back of her head, the unwashed hair, tangled and brittle. He remembered cupping the back of her head in his hand, its weight and its warmth. He remembered her body.

"Amy. Where does he live?"

"Who."

"Tommy. Where does he live?"

She turned and looked at him, a little crease of worry on her brow. "Why do you want to know?"

"Just tell me. Please."

"Brian, don't."

He slammed his fist into the wall, startling himself. He screamed at her. *"Tell me where he lives! God damn it!"*

Tommy opened the door of his shotgun house, clad only in boxer shorts, and Brian greeted him with a blow to the face. Tommy staggered back into his house, due more to surprise than the force of the punch; his foot slipped on a throw rug and he crashed to the floor. The small house reverberated with the impact. Brian had a moment to take in Tommy's hard physique and imagine his wife's hands moving over it. He stepped forward and kicked him in the groin.

Tommy grunted and seemed to absorb it. He rolled over and pushed himself quickly to his feet. Tommy's fist swung at him and he had time to experience a quick flaring terror before his head exploded with pain. He found himself on his knees, staring at the dust collecting in the crevices of the hardwood floor. Somewhere in the background a television chattered urgently.

A kick to the ribs sent Brian down again. Tommy straddled him, grabbed a fistful of hair, and slammed Brian's face into the floor several times. Brian felt something in his face break and blood poured onto the floor. He wanted to cry but it was impossible, he couldn't get enough air. *I'm going to die*, he thought. He felt himself hauled up and thrown against a wall. Darkness crowded his vision; he began to lose his purchase on events.

Someone was yelling at him. There was a face in front of him, skin peeled back from its teeth in a smile or a grimace of rage. It looked like something from hell.

He awoke to the feel of cold grass, cold night air. The right side of his face burned like a signal flare, his left eye refused to open. It hurt to breathe. He pushed himself to his elbows and spit blood from his mouth; it immediately filled again. Something wrong in there. He rolled onto his back and lay there for a while, waiting for the pain to subside to a tolerable level. The night was high and dark. At one point he felt sure that he was rising from the ground, that something up there was pulling him into its empty hollows.

Somehow he managed the drive home. He remembered nothing of it except occasional stabs of pain as opposing headlights washed across his windshield; he would later consider his safe arrival a kind of miracle. He pulled into the driveway and honked the horn a few times until Amy came out and found him there. She looked at him with horror, and with something else.

"Oh, baby. What did you do. What did you do."

She steered him toward the angel's room. He stopped himself in the doorway, his heart pounding again, and he tried to catch his breath. It occurred to him, on a dim level, that his nose was broken. She tugged at his hand, but he resisted. Her face was limned by moonlight, streaming through the window like some mystical tide, and by the faint luminescence of the angel tucked into their son's bed. She'd grown heavy over the years, and the past year had taken a harsh toll: the flesh on her face sagged, and was scored by grief. And yet he was stunned by her beauty.

Had she always looked like this?

"Come on," she said. "Please."

The left side of his face pulsed with hard beats of pain; it sang like a war drum. His working eye settled on the thing in the bed: its flat black eyes, its wickedly curved talons. Amy sat beside it and put her hand on its chest. It arched its back, seeming to coil beneath her.

"Come lay down," she said. "He's here for us. He's come home for us."

Brian took a step into Toby's room, and then another. He knew she was wrong; that the angel was not home, that it had wandered here from somewhere far away.

Is heaven a dark place?

The angel extended a hand, its talons flexing. The sheets over its belly stirred as Brian drew closer. Amy took her husband's hands, easing him onto the bed. He gripped her shoulders, squeezing them too tightly. "I'm sorry," he said suddenly, surprising himself. "I'm sorry! I'm sorry!" Once he began he couldn't stop. He said it over and over again, so many times it just became a sound, a sobbing plaint, and Amy pressed her hand against his mouth, entwined her fingers into his hair, saying, "Shhhh, shhhhh," and finally she silenced him with a kiss. As they embraced each other the angel played its hands over their faces and their shoulders, its strange reedy breath and its narcotic musk drawing them down to it. They caressed each other, and they caressed the angel, and when they touched their lips to its skin the taste of it shot spikes of joy through their bodies. Brian felt her teeth on his neck and he bit into the angel, the sudden dark spurt of blood filling his mouth, the soft pale flesh tearing easily, sliding down his throat. He kissed his wife furiously and when she tasted the blood she nearly tore his tongue out; he pushed her face toward the angel's body, and watched the blood blossom from beneath her. The angel's eyes were frozen, staring at the ceiling; it extended a shaking hand toward a wall decorated with a Spider-Man poster, its fingers twisted and bent.

They ate until they were full.

That night, heavy with the sludge of bliss, Brian and Amy made love again for the first time in nearly a year. It was wordless and slow, a synchronicity of pressures and tender familiarities. They were like rare creatures of a dying species, amazed by the sight of each other.

Brian drifts in and out of sleep. He has what will be the last dream about his son. It is morning in this dream, by the side of a small country road. It must have rained during the night, because the world shines with a wet glow. Droplets of water cling, dazzling, to the muzzle of a dog as it rests beside the road, unmenaced by traffic, languorous and dull-witted in the rising heat. It might even be Dodger. His snout is heavy with blood. Some distance away from him Toby rests on the street, a small pile of bones and torn flesh, glittering with dew, catching and throwing sunlight like a scattered pile of rubies and diamonds.

By the time he wakes, he has already forgotten it.

Inelastic Collisions

ELIZABETH BEAR

Elizabeth Bear was born on the same day as Frodo and Bilbo Baggins, and very nearly named after Peregrine Took. She is the recipient of the John W. Campbell and Locus Awards, and she currently lives in southern New England, where she is engaged in murdering inoffensive potted plants and writing science fiction and fantasy.

Her most recent books are a science-fiction novel, Carnival, from Bantam Spectra; an urban fantasy, Whiskey and Water, forthcoming from Roc; and—with Sarah Monette—a Norse heroic fantasy called A Companion to Wolves, forthcoming from Tor.

Too easy by half, but a girl had to eat.

Tamara genuflected before the glistening white sphere, a black one peeking over its top. She bent over the felted slate table like a sacrifice—a metaphor more ironic than prophetic—letting her shirt hike up her nubby spine. The balls were round, outside her domain, but that was a detail too insignificant to affect Tamara's understanding of the geometry involved.

All that mattered were the vectors.

bored, Gretchen murmured, as the cue stick slipped curveless through Tamara's fingers. **bored bored bored bored bored.**

The cue stick struck the cue ball. The cue ball jolted forward, skipping into the eight ball and stopping precisely as its momentum was transferred. An inelastic collision. *Thump. Click.* The eight ball glided into the corner pocket, and Tamara lifted her head away from the table, shaking razor-cut hair from her neck. She showed her teeth. To her sister, not to the human she'd beaten.

Gretchen leaned her elbows on the pool table, pale bones stretching her skin gorgeously. Tendons popped as she flexed her fingers. The shape she wore was dough pale, sticky and soft, but hunger made it leaner. Not enough leaner.

"You lose," Gretchen said to Tamara's prey.

The male put a gold ring on the edge of the table, still slick inside with fat from his greasy human skin. Gretchen slipped a fingernail through the loop and scraped it up, handling it by the edges. She was dirty herself, of course, dirty in a dirty human body. It didn't make human grease any nicer to touch.

Gretchen tucked the ring into her pocket. She nagged. **hungry.**

Tamara, reaching for the chalk, stopped—and sighed, though she could not get used to the noises made by the meat—and let the blunt end of her cue stick bump the floor. "Play again?" the human asked. "I'd like a chance to win that back." He pointed with his chin at Gretchen's pocket.

He was dark-haired, his meat firm and muscular under the greasy toffee-colored skin. Disgusting, and looking at him didn't help Tamara forget that she too was trapped in an oleaginous human carcass, with a greasy human tongue and greasy human bones and a greasy human name.

But a girl had to eat.

"Actually," she said—and showed her teeth to the human, willing him to snarl back. No. *Smile* back—"how do you feel about dinner?"

Gretchen was furious. Tamara felt it as from twitching tail-tip to shivering pricked ears. Her human cage had neither, but *she* still remembered what it was to be a Hound. Gretchen's flesh-clotted legs scissored to crisp ninety degree angles. Her razor-cut hair snapped in separate tendrils behind her.

you're angry, Tamara said, finally, desperately. It was wrong to have to ask why, wrong to have to *ask* anything. Between sisters, between terrible angels, there should be consensus.

Gretchen did not answer.

The May night was balmy. Tamara wrapped her fingers around her shoulders and pressed them against the ridge of bone she could feel through cloying meat. She set her heels.

Gretchen stalked ten steps further and halted as sharply as if someone had popped her leash. An inelastic collision. Her heeled shoes skittered on parking lot gravel.

Tamara waited.

you knew I was hungry, Gretchen said. **you let him get away.**

i didn't!

But Gretchen turned toward her, luminous green-brown eyes unblinking above the angles of her cheekbones, and Tamara looked down. Wrong, *wrong,* that she could not hear what her sister was thinking. **i didn't,** she insisted.

you showed your teeth.

i smiled at him.

sister, Gretchen said sadly, **they can tell the difference.**

They sold the ring at a pawnshop and took the money to another bar. While Gretchen thumbed quarters into the pool table, Tamara worried. Worry was a new thing, like distance from her sister. Exile on this round spinning world in its round spinning orbit was changing them; Tamara had learned to count its revolutions and orbits, as the humans did, and call them *time* now that she could no longer sense the real time, the Master's time, inexorable consumption and entropy.

She had been its warden, once. The warden of the real time, immaculate and perfect, as unlike the messy, improvisational sidereal time of the meat puppets as a diamond crystal was unlike a blown glass bauble. But she and her sister had failed to bring to justice a sorcerer who had upset the true time, and unless they could regain the Master's favor, they would not rejoin their sisters in Heaven.

All the painful curves of this world—the filthy, rotting, organic bodies that stayed fleshy and slack no matter how thin the sisters starved them; the knotted curves of roots and veins and flower petals—were slow poison.

Tamara had lost her home. Exile was costing her her sister, as well.

She hunched on the barstool—her gin and tonic cradled in her right hand, gnawing the rind of the lime—and watched Gretchen rack the balls. The second bar was a smoky little place with canned music and not much of a crowd. Some male humans sat at the bar nursing beers or boilermakers, and a female whose male companion wasn't drinking fiddled with a plate of hot wings and a cosmopolitan in a booth on the wall. Gretchen rattled the rack one last time and lifted it with her fingertips. A human female's hands would have trembled slightly. Gretchen's stayed steady as if carved.

She turned away to hang the rack up, and when she looked back, she bared her teeth.

She didn't care what Gretchen said; Tamara *couldn't* tell the difference. She shredded the rind of the lime between her teeth and washed its bitterness down with the different bitterness of the gin and tonic. When she got up to go to Gretchen, she left her glass on the bar so somebody might offer to buy her another one.

It was hard, playing badly. Hard to miss once in a while. Hard to look like she was really trying, poking a sharp triangle of tongue between taut lips, narrowed eyes wrinkling the bridge of her nose. Gretchen, walking past, patted her on the haunches.

Tamara sucked her tongue back into her mouth, smiled against the cue stick, and broke.

She had to let Gretchen win two games before they attracted any interest. The squeak of rubber on the wood floor caught her ear, but she didn't raise her head until the human cleared his throat. She straightened and turned, already alerted by her sister's posture that something unusual was happening.

The male paused before her sat in a wheelchair, his hands folded across his lap. He was ugly even by human standards, bald and bristly and scalded-looking, with heavy jowls and watery eyes that squinted through thick thumbprint glasses. He pointed to the rack of cues over Gretchen's shoulder and said, "There's only one table. Mind if I play the winner?"

His voice was everything his body wasn't. So rich and comforting, full of shadowy resonances like the echoes off of hard close planes. Tamara recognized him: he was the male who had been with the dark-haired female eating the chicken wings. Tamara glanced toward the door, but his companion seemed to have left. He smelled of salt water and beer, not grease and rotten meat the way most humans did. "I'm Pinky Gilman," he said, as if Tamara had answered, and extended his hand.

crippled, Gretchen murmured. **weak.** Tamara made sure to keep her teeth covered when she smiled. **prey,** she answered, and felt Gretchen laugh, tongue lolling, though her human cage remained impassive. "Tamara," Tamara said. She reached out and gingerly squeezed thick human fingers. "Gretchen is my sister."

"I see the resemblance," he said. "Am I interrupting?"

"No." Gretchen turned to reach another stick down. "I was going to take a break."

Tamara disentangled her fingers from the meat-puppet's, and stepped back. Her tongue adhered to the roof of her weird blunt-toothed mouth. "Can you? . . ."

"Well enough," he said, and accepted the cue stick Gretchen extended across the table at arm's length.

Gretchen patted Tamara on the arm as she went by. "Do either of you want a beer?"

Tamara was learning so many new emotions in her cage, and so many nuances on the old ones. Worry, discontent, and now another: surprise.

Because she didn't have to try not to beat Pinky Gilman too easily. Rather, he was making her work.

The first game, she let him break, and never chalked her stick. In fact, Tamara handled Pinky's cue more than her own, because he passed it to her to hold while he manipulated the wheelchair.

He sank three balls on the break, chose solids, and proceeded to clear the table with efficiency and a series of small flourishes, mostly demonstrated when he spun his wheelchair into position. By the time he reached the eight ball, though, he looked up at her and winked.

Gretchen had just returned with the beer. She pushed her hair behind her shoulder with the back of her fingers and handed Tamara a drink. **i don't believe it.**

can meat puppets *do* that?

shoot pool?

***win* at pool.** Gretchen leaned her shoulder on Tamara's so her bones bruised her sister's cage's flesh. Tamara sighed, comforted.

apparently, she answered, **some can.**

The male, leaning forward in his wheelchair to peer the length of the cue stick, did not glance at them. His eyes narrowed behind the glasses and the stick flicked through his fingers like a tongue. It struck the scuffed white ball, and the white ball spun forward, rebounding from the wall and striking the black at an angle. *Click. Hiss. Clunk.*

Eight ball in the corner pocket.

Pinky laid his stick across the table, spun the wheels of his chair back six inches, and turned to Tamara, holding up his hand. "Shark," she said, and put the beer into it instead of accepting the greasy clasp.

Pinky smiled at her and swallowed deeply as Gretchen passed her a second bottle. She was thirsty. She was always thirsty. "Go again?"

Beer was bitter in her mouth, cold and foaming where it crossed her tongue. She swallowed and rubbed her cage's tongue against its palate for the lingering texture, then gulped once more. The cold hurt the teeth of her cage. "Gretchen," she said, stepping backwards, "you play."

Gretchen beat him, but just only, and only because she broke. He laughed like a drain as she sunk the smooth, black eight ball, and raised his cue stick in his hands, holding it overhead as if it were a bar he meant to chin himself upon. He had blunt nails, thick enough that Tamara could see the file marks across them, and the tendons of his forearms ridged when he lifted them. "So," he said, "how would you feel about playing for forfeits?"

Gretchen smiled, and Tamara could see the difference. "What do you have in mind?"

The human lowered his cue stick and shrugged. "If I win, you come back to my place and let me feed you dinner." Tamara started, and he held up his hand. "Never fear; I don't have improper designs. And there are two of you, and only one of me, after all."

Tamara looked at Gretchen. Gretchen looked at Tamara, her luminous eyes huge, the pupils contracted to pinpricks. "Not to mention the wheelchair," Tamara said.

"Not to mention the wheelchair," he agreed. "And if you win, you can make *me* dinner." He let his cue stick fall forward so that it rested on the edge of the table.

Tamara smiled at him.

Tamara lingered in the bathroom, scraping her fingertips across pungent white soap to fill the gaps so her nails would stay clean. Through the wallboard, she could hear the clink of dishes and the rumble of the human's voice, the occasional answering chirp of Gretchen's. She turned the water on with the heel of her hands and cupped it to her mouth in brimming palm-fuls. It tasted faintly of Dial and made her blunt human teeth ache, her throat stretch and hurt when she gulped.

The smell of the alcohol the human was pouring reached her from the kitchen. She swallowed more tap water, filling the hollow spaces inside her, squinching her eyes against the following, welcome pain.

She straightened and turned off the tap, then checked her nails to see if the white crescents of soap had gotten loose. They gave her hands the appearance of a careful manicure. She stuffed them into her pockets as she walked down the hall.

As Tamara came down the hall, she saw Gretchen bent over the breakfast bar in the kitchen, a strip of pale skin revealed between her shirt and the band of her jeans. The male stumped about the kitchen on elbow crutches, which he had produced when Gretchen and Tamara helped him into his car. The wheelchair was because he couldn't shoot pool with something in his hands, he said.

Tamara had been all for eating him in the parking lot, but Gretchen had thought it better to wait. For privacy, and leisure, in which to enjoy their first good meal in days.

Tamara cleared her throat. And Gretchen jumped a little—guiltily? Tamara flinched in silent sympathy. *We cannot live like this. We just cannot.*

It was an effort to think *we*, and that almost moved her to tears. It was an effort, too, to remember divinity. To remember certainty. To remember what it had been like to be clean.

hungry, she said, and felt Gretchen stretch inside her skin. Gretchen grinned and ran her tongue over her teeth, and together they moved forward. Soon there would be blood and sinew, bone and flesh—and if not an end to thirst and hunger, sweet surcease, for as long as the dining lasted.

The air was cool and full of rich smells. Tamara's feet were springy on the floor. One more step forward. One more.

Over the spit of bacon, without turning, the male said, "I'd reconsider that if I were you."

Gretchen checked, and Tamara hesitated a half-step later. She hissed between her teeth as the male lifted bacon from the grease with tongs, set it on a paper napkin, and turned off the heat under the pan. Only then did he turn, leaning heavily on his elbow crutches.

tamara? Gretchen said, and Tamara's breath almost sliced her; the name struck her like a cue ball. Sisters did not need names. Not between sisters. Names were a human-thing, part of the lie.

She bit blood from her cheek as Gretchen said, again, **tamara?!**

The human male said, "He won't take you back, you know. You can starve yourself to the bone, starve yourself until you're blades, starve yourselves until your human hearts stop—and he will never forgive you. Time does not offer second chances. History does not give do-overs. It doesn't matter how hard you try to be entropy's angels again. The only kind of angel you can ever be from now on is fallen."

That whine. That was *her*. Or was it Gretchen?

The male—not a human male, no, she'd been fooled by his disguise, but she knew from his words that he must be an angel too, of some one of the dark Gods or another—continued. "Or you can learn to live in the world."

She should have stepped forward, rent him with her nails, shredded with her teeth. But she could taste it already, the grease of his flesh, the fat and the soil. She drove her nails into her own palms again. Gretchen crouched beside her. "You're not the Master's. You are not a Hound."

"No," the male said, leaning on his crutches so they squeaked on the linoleum. "I was born to the Father of Frogs. But I belong to myself now. Like you."

"You failed. You *fell*."

"I climbed, my angels."

And that explained why he smelled of sea air and not sour maggoty meat. Unlike Tamara, who could feel her own flesh rotting on the bones when she breathed too deep.

Filthy. Greasy. Everything was dirt. Tamara sobbed and licked blood from her nails, tasting the soap, stronger than ever. Some of it was her own blood. She wished that some of it was the watery blood of this smiling monster.

"I *won't* be dirty. I won't be hungry," Gretchen said, her hands bridged on the tile, one knee dropped. Her voice rose. "I won't be dirty forever. I *won't*."

The male's face was soft. Compassionate. Sickening. He tilted his head. "You'll be dirty," he said, pitiless as the Master, "or you'll be dead. Being hungry is being human. Can they bear more than you?"

Gretchen recoiled. Tamara thrust her thumb into her mouth, sucked the clean moon crescent of soap onto her tongue. She swallowed, hard, and again, and again, sucking each finger clean, feeling the soap reach her stomach, acid and alcohol hissing around it.

The male would *not* stop talking. She didn't think he'd stop if she jammed her fingers in her ears. "And that's the human condition. None of us can get clean. The world is sticky.

"And we don't have to like it.

"But you can't be an angel anymore. So you're going to have to learn to talk to each other."

you can't know that

Tamara didn't know if she'd said it, or Gretchen. Gretchen, from the lift of her shoulders, the upward glance, did not know either. The sound was dim, broken.

"I know," Pinky said, and held out one ugly hand, with its filed thick nails and its bulging knuckles. The webs that stretched between the fingers were vestigial, greenish, vascular along the underside of the membrane. He spread them wide. "I used to be a terrible angel too."

The soap, the words, the dirt, the blood. Something was coming back up. Something. Tamara went to her knees beside Gretchen, smacked down on the slate floor (so smooth, so hard, so planar). She retched. A thin stream of frothy bile trickled between her gritted teeth. She heard Gretchen whine.

And then someone was there, holding her, stroking her hair, pushing the flat feathered strands out of her eyes, his sleek aluminum props splayed out on either side. "Shh," said the monster, the fallen angel, the inhuman man. "Shhh," he said, and held her head as she bent down again and vomited soap and liquor on what had been a scrubbed floor, her belly clenched around cramping agony. "We don't eat soap," he said, and petted her until she stopped choking. "We don't eat soap. Silly angel."

She lifted her head, when she could, when the yellow slaver no longer dripped down her jowls. Pinky Gilman leaned over her, his wattled throat soft, tender, so close to her aching jaws. She lifted her head and saw her sister staring back at her.

A held breath. A quick shake of the head. Sharp silence, so hard that it might have ricocheted.

And Tamara, looking at Gretchen, heard the answer not because she *knew* it, but because she would once have known.

The Uninvited

CHRISTOPHER FOWLER

Christopher Fowler is the multi-award-winning author of twenty-six novels and collections of short stories. He is currently writing the Bryant & May mysteries. His latest novel is White Corridor *and his new story collection is entitled* Old Devil Moon.

His short story "The Master Builder" was made into a CBS movie starring Tippi Hedren and Marg Helgenberger, and his Left Hand Drive *won the London Short Film Festival's award for Best British Short Film.*

Fowler has also written the critically acclaimed graphic novel Menz Insana *and currently writes for the national press and the BBC. He lives in King's Cross, London.*

T he elaborate silvered gates stood wide apart, ready to accept guests. You couldn't arrive on foot, of course; there was nowhere to walk, except in the drive or through the sprinkler-wet grass, and it would have looked foolish climbing toward the house in the headlights of arriving cars.

Inside, the first thing I saw was an avenue of rustling palms, their slender trunks wound with twinkling blue and white lights, like giant candy sticks. Two robotically handsome valets in gold and crimson jackets were parking the cars, mostly sparkling black Mercedes, Daimlers, Volvos. The staircase was flanked by six teenaged waitresses in tiny red Santa outfits tentatively dispensing delicate flutes of champagne. A floodlit house, oblong, low and very white, was arranged on two levels between banked bottle green lawns. I could hear muted laughter, murmuring, a delicate presence of guests. I saw silhouettes passing before the rippled phosphorescence of a pool with translucent globes pacing its perimeter. There was no sign of our host, but on the patio a butler, chef, bartenders, and waiters were arranged behind banks of lurid, fleshy lobster tails and carrot batons.

There was a muffled beat in the air, the music designed to create ambience without being recognizable; Beatles' songs rescored for a jazz trio. It was the end of the sixties, the age of Aquarius. Smokey Robinson and Dionne Warwick were on the charts, but there were no black people there that night except me.

In Los Angeles, parties aren't about letting your hair down and having fun. They're for networking, appraising, bargaining, being seen, and ticked from a list. There were two kinds of guests roaming the house that night, ones who would have been noticed by their absence, and others who had been invited merely to fill up dead space. It goes without saying that I was in the latter group. Only Sidney Poitier would have made it into the former.

It was the home of Cary Dell, a slow-witted middleweight studio executive at MGM, and I remember seeing plenty of almost-familiar faces; Jacqueline Bisset, Victoria Vetri, Ralph Meeker, a couple of casting directors, some black-suited agents lurking together in a corner, fish-eyeing everyone else.

The important people were seated in a semicircular sunken lounge, lost among oversized purple cushions. The area was so exclusive that it might as well have had velvet ropes around it. Everyone else worked hard at keeping the conversation balloon-light and airborne, but couldn't resist glancing over to the pit to see what was going on at the real center of the party.

There was another kind of guest there that night. Dell had invited some beautiful young girls. No one unsavory—they weren't hookers—just absurdly perfect, with slender waists and basalt eyes. They stood together tapping frosted pink nails on the sides of their martini glasses, flicking their hair, looking about, waiting for someone to talk to them.

Parties like this took place all over the Hollywood hills; the old school still arrived in tuxedos and floor-length gowns, but studios had lately rediscovered the youth movie, and were shamelessly courting the same antiestablishment students they had ridiculed five years earlier. I had made a couple of very bad exploitation flicks, usually cast as the kind of comic sidekick whose only purpose was his amusing blackness. Back in those days I believed in visibility at any cost, and always took the work.

I had a feeling I'd been added to the guest list by Dell's secretary in order to make up numbers and provide him with a sheen of coolness, because I wore fringed brown leather trousers and had my hair in an Afro, and hadn't entirely lost my Harlem jive. He sure hadn't invited me for my conversation; we'd barely spoken more than two words to each other. If we had, Dell would have realized I came from a middle-class family.

I remember it was a cool night toward the end of November. The wind had dropped, and there were scents of patchouli and hashish in the air. The party was loosening up a little, the music rising in volume and tempo. Some of the beautiful girls were desultorily dancing together on a circular white rug in the lounge. I had been to a few of these parties and they always followed the same form, peaking at ten-thirty, with the guests calling for their cars soon after. People drank and drove more in those days, of course, but nobody of any importance stayed late because the studios began work at 4:00 A.M.

I was starting to think about leaving before undergoing the embarrassment of waiting for my battered Mustang to be brought around front, when there was a commotion of raised voices out on the patio, and I saw someone go into the pool fully dressed, a gaunt middle-aged man in a black suit. It was difficult to find out what had happened, because everyone was crowding around the water's edge. All I know is, when they pulled him out of the chlorine a minute later, he was dead. I read in the *LA Times* next day that he'd twisted his neck hitting the concrete lip as he went in, and had died within seconds. He was granted a brief obituary in *Variety* because he'd featured in a lame Disney film called *Monkeys, Go Home*. I remember thinking that the press reports were being uncharacteristically cautious about the death. I guess nobody wanted to risk implying that Dell had been keeping a disorderly house, and there was no suggestion of it being anything other than an unfortunate accident. Dell was a big player in a union town.

As I drove back to the valley that night, passing above the crystalline grid of the city, I passed one of the beautiful girls walking alone along the side of the road with her shoes in her hand, thumbing a ride, and knew she'd come here from the Midwest, leaving all her friends and family behind just so she could be hired as eye-candy to stand around at parties. I remember thinking how nobody would miss her if she disappeared. I felt sad about it, but I didn't stop for her. Black men didn't stop to pick up white girls back then; you didn't want a situation to develop.

The work dried up for a couple of months, but on a storm-heavy night in February I was invited to another studio party, this time a more low-key affair in Silverlake, where single palms crested the orange sky on the brows of hills, and Hispanic families sat in their doorways watching their kids play ball. You can tell poorer neighborhoods by the amount of cabling they carry above their houses, and this area had plenty. I pulled over by an empty lot and was still map-reading under the street lamp when I heard the dull thump of music start up behind me, and realized the party was being held in a converted brownstone loft—they were pretty much a novelty back then—so I parked and made my way to the top floor.

The building's exterior may have been shabby, but the inside was Cartier class. The whole top floor had been stripped back to brickwork and turned into one big, open space, because the owner was a photographer who used it as his studio. He handled on-set shoots for Paramount, and had coincidentally taken my headshots a couple of years earlier. It was good to think he hadn't forgotten me, and this event was a lot friendlier than the last. I recognized a couple of girls I'd auditioned with the month before, and we got to talking, then sharing a joint. The music was Hendrix—*Electric Ladyland*, I think. Pulmonary gel-colors spun out across the walls, and the conversation was louder, edgier, but it was still a pretty high-end layout.

It was the photographer's thirtieth birthday and he'd invited some pretty big names, but it was getting harder to tell the old money from the new, because everyone was dressed down in beads and kaftans. The new producers and actors were sprawled across canary-yellow beanbags in a narcoleptic fug, while the industry seniors stuck to martinis at the bar. I was having a pretty good time with my lady friends when I saw them again.

Perhaps because nobody had noticed me at Dell's house, I noticed everything, and now I recognized the new arrivals as they came in. There were four of them, two girls and two men, all in late teens to mid-twenties, and I distinctly recalled them from Dell's Christmas party because they'd stood together in a tight group, as though they didn't know anyone else. They were laughing together and watching everyone, as though they were in on a private joke no one else could share.

I admit I was a little stoned and feeling kind of tripped out, but there was something about them I found unsettling. I got the feeling they hadn't been invited, and were there for some other purpose. They were as observant as agents. They stayed in the corner, watching and whispering, and I wanted to go up to them, to ask what they were doing, but the girls were distracting me and—you know how that goes.

I left a few minutes after midnight, just as things were starting to heat up. I went with the girls back to their hotel. They needed a ride, and I needed the company. When I woke up the next morning, they had already vacated the room. There was only a lipstick-scrawled message from them on the bathroom mirror—plenty of kisses but no contact numbers. I picked up the industry dailies in the IHOP on Santa Monica, and there on page five found a report of the party I'd attended the night before. Some high-society singer I'd vaguely recalled seeing drunkenly arguing with his girlfriend had fallen down the stairs as he left the party, gone all the way from the apartment door to the landing below. He was expected to recover but might have sustained brain damage. Fans were waiting outside his hospital room with flowers.

Two parties, two accidents—it happens. There were studio parties all over town every night of the week, but it felt weird that I'd been at both of them. You had to be invited, of course, but there wasn't the strict door policy that there is now. No security guards with headsets, sometimes not even a checklist. People came and went, and it was hard to tell if anyone was gate crashing; the hosts generally assumed you wouldn't dare. They were insulated from the world. I remember attending a shindig in Brentwood where the toilet overflowed through the dining room, and everyone acted like there was nothing wrong because they assumed the maids would clear it up. Hollywood's like that.

Maybe you can see a pattern emerging in this story, but at the time I failed to spot it. I was too preoccupied; with auditions, with my career, with having a good time. The town felt different then, footloose and slightly lost, caught between classic old-time moviemaking and the rising counterculture. They needed to cater to the new generation of rootless teens who were growing impatient with the world they'd been handed. The producers wanted to make renegade art statements but didn't know how, and they couldn't entirely surrender the movies of the past. People forget that *Hello Dolly!* came out the same year as *Easy Rider*.

Strange times. In Vietnam, Lt. William Calley's platoon of U.S. soldiers slaughtered five hundred unarmed Vietnamese, mainly women and children, at My Lai. Many of us had buddies over there, and heard stories of old women thrown down wells with grenades tossed in after them. Those who were left behind felt powerless, but there was an anger growing that seeped between the cracks in our daily lives, upsetting the rhythm of the city, the state, and eventually the whole nation. I'd never seen demonstrations on the streets of LA before now, and I'd heard the same thing was happening in Washington, Chicago, even in Denver.

But nothing affected the Hollywood elite; they hung on, flirting with subversion when really, what they wanted to make was musicals. They still threw parties, though, and the next one was a killer.

This was the real deal, a ritzy Beverly Hills bash with a sizeable chunk of the A-list present, thrown in order to promote yet another *Planet of the Apes* movie. The sequels were losing audiences, so one of the executive producers pulled out the stops and opened up his mansion—I say his, but I think it had been built for Louise Brooks—to Hollywood royalty. This time there were security guards manning the door, checking names against clipboards, questioning everyone except the people who expected to be recognized. Certainly I remember seeing Chuck Heston there, although he didn't look very happy about it, didn't drink, and didn't stay long. The beautiful girls had turned out in force, clad in brilliantly jeweled mini-dresses and skimpy tops, slyly scoping the room for producers, directors, anyone who could move them up a career notch. A bunch of heavyweight studio boys were playing pool in the smoke-blue den while their women sat sipping daiquiris and dishing dirt. The talent agents never brought their wives along for fear of becoming exposed. I'd been invited by a hot little lady called Cheyenne who had landed a part in the movie purely because she could ride a horse, although I figured she'd probably ridden the producer.

So there we were, stranded in this icing-pink stucco villa with matching crescent staircases, dingy brown wall tapestries, and wrought-iron chandeliers. I took Cheyenne's arm and we headed for the garden, where we chugged sea breezes on a lawn like a carpet of emerald needles. Nearby, a fake-British band played soft rock in a striped marquee filled with bronze statues and Santa Fe rugs. I was looking for a place to put down my drink when I saw the same uninvited group coming down from the house, and immediately a warning bell started to ring in my head.

It was a warm night in March, and most people were in the torch-lit garden. The Uninvited—that's how I had come to think of them—helped themselves to cocktails and headed to the crowded lawn, and we followed.

"See those people over there?" I said to Cheyenne. "You ever see them before?"

She had to find her glasses and sneak them on, then shook her glossy black hair at me. "The square-jawed guy on the left looks like an actor. I think I've seen him in something. The girls don't seem like they belong here."

"What it is, I'm beginning to think there's some really harmful karma around them." I told her about the two earlier parties.

"That's nuts." She laughed. "You think they could just go around picking fights and nobody would notice?"

"People here don't notice much, they're too busy promoting themselves. Besides, I don't think it's about picking fights, more like bringing down a bad atmosphere. I don't know. Let's get a little closer."

We sidled alongside one of the men, who was whispering something to the shorter, younger of the two girls. He was handsome in a dissipated way, she had small feral features, and I tried figuring them first as a couple, then part of a group, but couldn't get a handle on it. The actor guy was dressed in an expensive blue Rodeo Drive suit, the other was an urban cowboy. The short girl was wearing the kind of cheap cotton sunflower shift they marked down at FedCo, but her taller girlfriend had gold medallions around her throat that must have cost plenty.

Now that I noticed, they were all wearing chains or medallions, The cowboy guy had a ponytail folded neatly beneath his shirt collar, like he was hiding it. Something about them had really begun to bother me, and I couldn't place the problem until I noticed their eyes. It was the one thing they all had in common, a shared stillness. Their unreflecting pupils watched without moving, and stayed cold as space even when they laughed. Everyone else was milling slowly around, working the party, except these four, who were watching and waiting for something to happen.

"You're telling me you really don't see anything strange about them?" I asked.

"Why, what do you think you see?"

"I don't know. I think maybe they come to these parties late, uninvited. I think they hate the people here."

"Well, I'm not that crazy about our hosts, either," she said. "We're here because we have to be."

"But they're not. They just stand around, and cause bad things to happen before moving on," I told Cheyenne. "I don't know how or why, they just do."

"Do you know how stoned that sounds?" she hissed back at me. "If they weren't invited, how did they get through security?" She reached on tiptoe and looked into my eyes. "Just as I thought, black baseballs. Smoking dope is making you paranoid. Couldn't you just try to enjoy yourself?"

So that's what I did, but I couldn't stop thinking about the guest dying in the pool, and the guy who had fallen down the stairs. We stayed around for a couple more hours, and were thinking about going, when we found ourselves back with the Uninvited. A crowd had gathered on the deck and were dancing wildly, but there they were, the four of them, dressed so differently I couldn't imagine they were friends, still sizing things up, still whispering to each other.

"Just indulge me this one time, okay?" I told Cheyenne. "Check them out, see if you can see anything weird about them."

She sighed and turned me around so that she could peer over my shoulder. "Well, the square-jawed guy is wearing something around his neck. Actually, they all are. I've seen his medallion before, kind of a double-headed axe? It means *God Have Mercy*. There are silver beads on either side of it, take a look. Can you see how many there are?"

I checked him out. The dude was so deep in conversation with the short girl that he didn't notice me. "There are six on each side. No, wait—seven and six. Does that mean something?"

"Sure, coupled with the double axe, it represents rebellion via the thirteen steps of depravity, ultimately leading to the new world order, the *Novus Ordor Seclorum*. It's a satanic symbol. My brother told me all about this stuff. He read a lot about witchcraft for a while, thought he could influence the outcome of events, but then my mother made him get a job." She pointed discreetly. "The girl he's talking to is wearing an *ankh*, the silver cross with the loop on top? It's the Egyptian symbol for sexual union. They're pretty common, you get them in most head shops. Oh, wait a minute." She craned over my shoulder, trying to see. "The other couple? She's wearing a gold squiggle, like a sideways eight with three lines above it. That's something to do with alchemy, the sign for black mercury maybe. But the guy, the cowboy, he's wearing the most potent icon. Check it out."

I looked, and saw a small golden five lying on his bare tanned chest. Except it wasn't a five; there was a crossed line above it. "What is that?"

"The *Cross of Confusion*, the symbol of Saturn. Also known as the *Greater Malefic, the Bringer of Sorrows*. Saturn takes twenty-nine years to orbit the sun, and as a human life can be measured as just two or three orbits, it's mostly associated with the grim reaper's collection of the human soul, the acknowledgment that we have a fixed time before we die, the orbit of life. However, we can alter that orbit, cut a life short in other words. It's a satanic death symbol, very powerful."

I got a weird feeling then, a prickle that started on the back of my neck and crept down my arms. I was still staring at the cowboy when he looked up and locked eyes with me, and I saw the roaring, infinite emptiness inside him. I never thought I was susceptible to this kind of stuff, but suddenly, in that one look, I was converted.

We were still locked into each other when Cheyenne nudged me hard. "Quit staring at him, do you want to cause trouble?"

"No," I told her, "but there's something going down here, can't you feel it? Something really scary."

"Maybe they just don't like black dudes, Julius. Or maybe they're aliens. I really think we should go."

Just then, the Uninvited turned as one and walked slowly to the other side of the dancing crowd until I could no longer see them properly. A few moments later I heard the fight start, two raised male voices. I'd been half expecting it to happen, but when it did the shock still caught me.

He was in his late fifties, balding but shaggy-haired, dressed in a yellow KEEP ON TRUCKIN' T-shirt designed for someone a third his age. I saw him throw a drink and swing a fat arm, fist clenched, missing by a mile. Maybe he was pushed, maybe not, but I saw him lose his balance and go over onto the table as if the whole thing was being filmed in slow motion. The kidney-shaped sheet of glass that exploded and split into three sections beneath him sliced through his T-shirt as neatly as a scalpel, and everyone jumped back. God forbid the guests might ruin their shoes on shards of glass.

He was lying as helpless as a baby, unable to rise. A couple of girls squealed in revulsion. When he tried to lift himself onto his elbows, a wide, dark line blossomed through the cut T-shirt. He flopped and squirmed, calling for help as petals of blood spread across his shirt. The music died and I heard his boot heels hammering on the floor, then the retreating crowd obscured my view. Nobody had rushed to his aid; they looked like they were waiting for the Mexican maids to appear and draw a discreet cloth over the scene so that they could return to partying.

Why didn't I help? I have no answer to that question. Maybe I was more like the others back then, afraid of being the first to break out of the line. I feel differently now.

Cheyenne was pulling at my sleeve, trying to get me to leave, but I was looking for the Uninvited. If they were still there, I couldn't see them. They'd brought misfortune to the gathering once more and disappeared into the despairing confusion of the Los Angeles night.

As I had twice before, I found myself searching the papers next morning for mention of the drama, but any potential scandal had been hastily hushed up. I lost touch with Cheyenne for a while, even began to think I'd imagined the whole thing, because the next month my career took off and

I stopped smoking dope. I'd landed the lead role in a new movie about a street-smart black P.I. called Dynamite Jones, and I needed to keep my head straight, because the night schedule was punishing and I couldn't afford to screw up.

We wrapped the picture in record time, without any serious hitches, although my white love interest was replaced with a black girl two days in, and our big love scene was cut to make sure we didn't upset the heartland audiences. Perry Sapirstein held the wrap party at his house on Mulholland because they were striking the set and we couldn't keep the studio space. I figured it was a good time to hook up with Cheyenne again—she'd been in Chicago appearing in an antiwar show that had tanked, and wanted to get a little more serious with me while she was waiting for another break out West.

I thought I'd know everyone there, but there were still some unfamiliar faces, and of course, the Beautiful Girls were out in full force, hoping to get picked for something, anything before their innocence faded and their faces hardened. The Hollywood parties were losing their appeal as I got used to them. I could see the establishment would never be unseated from their grand haciendas. They flirted with rebellion but would revert to type at the first opportunity, and everyone knew it.

I'd forgotten all about the Uninvited. People were caught up in the events unfolding in Vietnam, and fresh stories of atrocities on both sides were being substantiated by shocking press footage that brought the war to everyone's doorstep. I didn't meet anyone, ever, who thought we should be there, but I was in liberal California, and it would take some time yet for the mood to sink in across the nation. The sense of confusion was palpable; hippies were hated and feared wherever they went, and the young were viewed with such suspicion beyond the Democrat enclaves that it felt dangerous to step over state lines. Folks are frightened of difference and change, always were, always will be, but back then there were no guidelines, no safety barriers. There was no one to tell us what was right, beyond what we felt in our hearts.

We couldn't see how far we were blundering into darkness.

Even in the strangest times, somebody will always continue to throw a party and act like there's nothing wrong. So it was on Mulholland, where the gold tequila fountains filled pyramids of sparkling salt-rimmed glasses, and invisible waiters slipped between the guests with shrimps arranged on pearlized clamshells.

Everything was strange that last night I saw them. I remember being freaked by shrieks of hysteria that turned into bubbles of laughter, coming from the darkened upstairs floor of the house. I remember the hate-filled glare of a saturnine man leaning in the corridor by the bathroom. I remember going to the kitchen to rummage for some ice and seeing something written in maple syrup on the bone-white door of the fridge, the letters running like thick dark blood. I peered closer, trying to read what it said, expecting something shocking and sinister, only to feel a sense of anticlimax when I deciphered the dripping, sticky word:

HEALTH

So much for Lucifer appearing uninvited at Hollywood parties.

But the second I dismissed the idea as dumb, a scampering, shadowy imp of fear started scratching about inside my mind again. The more I thought about it, the more the room, the house and everyone in it felt unsafe, and the sense kept expanding, engulfing me. Suddenly I caught sight of myself reflected in the floor-to-ceiling glass that separated the kitchen from the unlit rear garden, and saw how alone I was in that bright bare room. There was no one to care if I lived or died in this damned city. Without me even realizing it, everything in my world had begun to slip and slide into a howling, emptying abyss. There were no friends, no loyalties, no good intentions, only the prey and the preyed upon.

No haven, no shelter, just endless night, unforgiving and infinite.

If this was the effect of giving up marijuana, I thought, I really needed to start smoking again.

But the line of safety was thinner then. We felt much closer to destruction. These days we live with the danger while cheerfully ignoring the data.

I once attended a class on the structure of myths at UCLA where we discussed the theme of the uninvited guest, the phantom at the feast, the unclean in the temple, the witch at the christening, the vampire at the threshold, the doomsayer at the wedding, and all these myths shared one element in common; someone had to invite them in to begin with. I wondered who had provided an unwitting invitation here in California.

I remember that night there was a very pretty blond woman in the lounge—although I only saw her from the back—whom everyone wanted to talk to. One of her friends was drunkenly doing a trick with a lethal-looking table knife, and I thought *what if he slips?* And just as I was thinking that, I became aware of them, standing right alongside me. I turned and found myself beside the square-jawed one who looked like an actor. His gray deep-set eyes stared out at me very steadily, holding the moment. The light was low in the main hall, which was lit only by amber flames from an enormous carved fireplace. I saw the Satan sign glittering at his neck, and he smiled knowingly as I flinched.

"Who the hell are you?" I half-whispered, finally regaining my composure.

"Bobby." He held out his hand. "You're Julius."

"How do you know who I am?"

"I have friends in the business. We know a lot of people."

I didn't like the way he said that. "I've seen you before," I told him. "Seen your friends, too."

"Yeah, they're all here. We hang out together." He pointed. "That's Abby, Susan, Steve."

They all looked over at me as if they'd picked up on their names being spoken. The effect of them moving with one shared mind was unnerving. I meant to say, "Who do you know here?" but instead I asked, "What are you here for?"

Bobby was silent for a moment, then smiled more broadly. "I think you know the answer to that. We're here to taste death."

"What do you mean?"

He looked away at the fire. "You have to know what dying is before you can know life, Julius."

"I don't understand you."

"I mean." Bobby leaned in close and still, his eyes filling with morbid compassion as they stared deep into mine, "we're leading the rise to power. We've already started the killing, and this city will become an inferno of revenge. The streets will run with blood. There will be a new holocaust, revolution in the streets, and the world will belong to the Fifth Angel."

"Man, you're crazy." I shook my head, suddenly tired of this white supremacy crap. I'd just spent two months mofo-ing around in some Stepin Fetchit role given to me by rich white boys, and I guess I'd just had enough. "Bullshit," I told him, "if the best thing you can do to start a revolution is shove a few drunks around at parties, you're in trouble. I saw you at Dell's place. I know you pushed that guy into the pool and broke his neck. I saw you in Silverlake, and at the house on Canon Drive where that guy was cut on the table. I know you don't belong here, except to bring down chaos."

"You're right, we don't belong here any more than you do," he said, distracted now by something or someone moving past my left shoulder. "There's no difference between us, brother. The rest of them are just little pigs." He exchanged glances with the others, and the two girls turned to go, slipping out through the crowd. He pushed back to take his leave with them.

"Wait," I called after him, anxious to keep him there. "How did you get in through security?"

Bobby looked over his shoulder, quiet and serious. "We have friends in all the places we're not invited."

"Nothing's going to happen tonight, right? You've got to promise me that."

"Nothing will happen tonight, Julius. We're leaving."

"I don't get it." I was calling so loud that people were turning to stare at me. "Why not tonight? You made this stuff happen before, why not now, right in front of me? Let me see, Bobby, I want to understand. You think you can summon up the devil?"

His eyes were still focused over my left shoulder. "The devil is already here, my friend."

I twisted around to see who he was looking at, but when I looked back he had gone. They had all gone. And the tumble of the party rushed into my ears once more. I heard the blond girl laughing as the man fumbled his knife trick, and the point of the blade fell harmlessly to the floor, where it stuck in the wood.

When the girl turned around, I saw that she was heavily pregnant, and heard someone say, "Come on Sharon, I'm going to drive you home, it's late. What if Roman calls tonight?"

She lived on 10050 Cielo Drive, I heard her say. And she had to get back, because the next night she was expecting her friends Abby and Jay, and they'd probably want to stay late drinking wine. She wasn't drinking because of the baby. She didn't want anything to happen to the baby.

The next day was August ninth, 1969.

It was the day our bright world began its long eclipse.

They caught up with Charlie and his gang at the Spahn ranch, out near Chatsworth, but by then it was too late to stop the closing light. There were others, rootless and elusive, who would never be caught.

I remembered those parties in the Hollywood hills, and realized I had always known about the rise of the Uninvited. Much later, I read about Manson's children writing *Helter Skelter* on their victims' refrigerator door, only they had misspelled the first word, writing it as *Healther*.

I saw how close I had come to touching evil.

The world is different now. It's sectioned off by high walls, no-go zones, clearance status, security fences, X-ray machines. The gates remain shut to outsiders unless you have a pass to enter. The important parties and the good living can only continue behind sealed doors. At least, that's what those who throw them desperately need to believe. That's what *I* need to believe.

I married Cheyenne. We have two daughters and a son. Against all reason, we stayed on in California.

And we no longer know how to protect ourselves from those who are already inside the gates. I guess we lost that right when we first built walls around our enclaves and printed out our invitations.

13 O'Clock

MIKE O'DRISCOLL

Mike O'Driscoll lives on Gower Peninsula, in South Wales. His stories have been published in genre magazines including The 3rd Alternative, Crimewave, *and* Interzone; *online at* Gothic.net, infinity plus, *and* Eclectica; *and in a number of anthologies including* The Year's Best Fantasy and Horror, Best New Horror, The Dark, Gathering the Bones, Lethal Kisses, Off Limits, Poe's Progeny, Darklands, *and* Neonlit Volume 1.

O'Driscoll's first collection of stories, Unbecoming, *was published in 2006. He writes a regular column on horror, fantasy, and science fiction,* Night's Plutonian Shore, *for* Interzone. *His story, "Sounds Like," has been turned into a one-hour TV movie directed by Brad Anderson, as part of the* Masters of Horror *series.*

The days were beginning to stretch out. Another couple of months and it would be surf and barbecue, cold beer out on the deck listening to Bonnie "Prince" Billy. Play some silly tunes on the guitar for Jack, teach him his first chords. Make some other kind of music for Polly. The sweet kind for which the diminishing nights left barely enough time. The cold still hung in the air at this hour though. Caleb Williams could feel it on his face as he followed Cyril across the rising field. He bent down, scooped up the mostly black mongrel terrier and boosted him up the stone ditch. He climbed up and over while the dog, resenting the indignity of having to be lifted, scrambled down by itself.

They crossed the dirt track to the garden, where Caleb paused to lean against the unpainted block wall. The sun was a ball sinking below Cefn Bryn, leaving the mid-April sky streaked with red. Gazing up at the house, he felt a sudden, unaccountable yearning. The otherness of dusk made the cottage seem insubstantial. Shrugging off this unexpected sense of isolation, he opened the back gate and let Cyril bolt through. They got the dog two years ago for Jack's birthday, but whether Jack had tired of it, or the dog had tired of the boy, it had ended up attaching itself to Caleb. Only now was he getting used to the idea of himself as a dog person.

In the living room, Polly was curled up on the sofa, dark red hair breaking in waves over her shoulders, ebbing across her blouse. She was channel hopping as he came in, and had opened two small bottles—stubbies, she called them—of San Miguel. "Saw you coming from Jack's room," she said, her gray eyes lucent with mischief. "You looked like you need one."

Caleb took the beer and sat next to her. "Is it me," he said, "or is the climb up from the bay getting steeper?"

His wife swung her feet up into his lap. "It's decrepitude," she said.

"Good. For a moment there I thought I was getting old." He tapped his bottle against hers and took a sip.

She smiled for a moment, then her expression changed. "You didn't hear Jack last night?"

"No. What?"

"I meant to tell you this morning. He had a bad dream." She frowned. "More than that, I guess. A nightmare."

"There's a difference?"

"Of course there is, fool." She jabbed a foot playfully into his thigh. "This was a nightmare."

"How could you tell?"

"I'm serious, Cale. He was petrified. He screamed when I woke him."

"Was he okay?"

"After a while, yes."

"What did he dream?"

"He was alone in the house at night. That's scary enough for most eight-year-olds."

"Poor Jack. How is he tonight?"

"He's fine. Has been all day. I was half-expecting him to say something but he never mentioned it. I guess he's already forgotten."

"Good," Caleb said, feeling a vague sense of guilt. Should have been there for him, he thought.

Polly sighed and rubbed her foot across his belly. "So, how was your day?"

Caleb said nothing. He was thinking about Jack's nightmare, trying to imagine how he must have felt. A yellow woman moved across the TV screen. He wondered where nightmares came from. What caused them?

Polly wiggled her toes in his face. "What's the matter? Got the hots for Marge Simpson?"

He laughed and grabbed her foot. "It's the big hair that does it for me."

She yanked her foot free. "There you go, making me jealous," she said, sliding along the sofa.

He drained his bottle and pulled her close. "I always thought blue would work for you," he said, before kissing her. He didn't think about Jack's dream again until after they had made love, and then only for a short while, until sleep took him.

Caleb taught basic literacy skills to young adult offenders, most of whom were serving community sentences for alcohol and drug-related crimes. Twice a week he held a class in Swansea Jail for those whose crimes were more serious. In all the time he had worked as an English teacher in a city comprehensive, he had seen countless faces just like theirs. The faces of disaffected boys who had never willingly picked up a book, or lost themselves in words. After ten years he had walked away. Now, watching these young men begin to find pleasure in reading, he felt he was finally doing something that mattered.

All the more maddening then, not being able to comprehend his son's terror. As he moved from one student to the next, his thoughts kept drifting back to Jack. He'd had another nightmare last night, worse than before. Hearing him, Polly had woken Caleb. When he'd gone to his son's room, the look of terror on Jack's face had shocked him. After he'd calmed the boy and returned to his own bed, he'd lain awake for hours, trying to comprehend the extent of Jack's fear. His inability to understand the dream left him feeling helpless, and this in turn had added to his confusion and guilt.

At lunchtime, he called Polly on her mobile. "Hi Cale," she said. "What's up?"

"You busy?"

"On my way to town. Got work to drop off at McKays." She worked part-time, auditing small business accounts. "Can I get back to you?"

"It's okay," Caleb sighed. "I was just wondering about Jack. How he was this morning."

"Okay, I guess." Caleb heard the doubt in her voice. "He dreamed about a stranger. He, uh—"

"He what?"

"He said a stranger was coming to our house."

Caleb tried to imagine his son's nightmare.

"We spoke at breakfast and he was all right. I think he forgot most of it. Not like he was last night. He's tough, you know, resilient."

"You're right," Caleb said. "I'll stay with him tonight, till he's asleep."

"He'll like that, Cale. Really." She broke the connection.

I hope so, Caleb thought, as he flipped the phone shut. Despite Polly's reassurances, he felt there was more he should be doing. Like being able to explain the dream to Jack, stealing its power through interpretation. Take away that ability to rationalize and he was no better than the most illiterate, most brutalized of his students.

In the evening Caleb put his son to bed and read him a chapter from *The Wind in the Willows*. Jack liked it when he put on different voices for the characters. High-pitched and squeaky for Rat, ponderous and slow for Mole. Toad was his favorite. He always laughed at Caleb's braying, exaggeratedly posh voice, but tonight there was no Mr. Toad, just the softer, more subdued notes of Rat and Mole as they searched the river for young Portly, the missing otter. He found himself strangely moved by the animals' mystical quest, experiencing an emotion akin to the yearning regret that was all the memory Rat and Mole were left with of their encounter with Pan. He closed the book and forced a smile, trying to hide his mood, but his melancholy was mirrored in Jack's eyes.

"What's wrong, Dad?" Jack asked.

"I was thinking about the story."

Jack nodded. "Me too. About the friend and helper." He frowned. "Why did they forget him?"

Caleb hadn't read the book since he was a child himself, and he'd forgotten how mysterious, how at odds with the rest of the tale, the "Piper at the Gates of Dawn" chapter had been. "So they wouldn't feel sad," he said, after a while.

"But he helped them find Portly."

Caleb nodded. "Yes, but there are things . . ."

"Why?"

Caleb wondered what it had felt like when he had first become aware of his own mortality. Choosing his words carefully, he said, "Sometimes people know things they're better off not knowing."

"Things in dreams?"

"Yes." Something resonated in Caleb's memory. He couldn't quite grasp it, though he suspected his feelings were an echo of Jack's empathy for Rat and Mole. "You remember anything about your dream last night?"

Jack shook his head.

"If you're scared, Jack, if something's troubling you, I want you to tell me."

"Are you okay, Dad?"

Caleb wondered why Jack would ask that question. It disturbed him, but he managed a smile and said, " 'Course I am."

"Right," Jack said, but the look of concern remained on his face. "I'll say a prayer."

"Why?"

"You're 'sposed to," Jack said. "Mrs. Lewis said you have to pray to Jesus to look after your family."

Mrs. Lewis was Jack's teacher. Caleb had nothing against religion, but he was troubled by the notion of Jack taking it too seriously. "You don't need to pray for me, son. I'm fine, really. Sleep now, okay?"

" 'Kay," Jack said, closing his eyes.

Caleb woke from a fretful sleep, scraps of memory gusting through his troubled mind. Though a film of sweat coated his body, he felt cold and vulnerable. A shaft of moonlight fell through the gap in the curtains, cloaking familiar objects in odd, distorting shadows that, in his drowsy state, unsettled him. He struggled to claw back the fragments of a dissipating dream and the sounds that had slipped its borders. A minute passed before he understood that he had followed them out of sleep, that he was hearing the same muffled cries from somewhere in the house. He sprang out of bed and crossed the landing to Jack's room. His son was whimpering softly, making sounds unrecognizable as words. As Caleb approached the bed, Jack's body spasmed and an awful scream tore from his throat. Caleb hesitated, unnerved by the intensity of his son's fear. He wrapped his arms around the boy and felt the iron rigidity in the small, thin body. Downstairs, Cyril began to bark.

"It's okay, Jack," he whispered. "I'm here." Jack's eyes opened, and in his disoriented state he struggled in his father's arms. Caleb made soothing noises and stroked his face. Jack tried to say something, but the tremors that seized his body made him incoherent. "Ssshhh," Caleb said. "It's over."

"Duh-duh, Dad," Jack cried.

"I'm right here," Caleb told him.

Jack struggled for breath. "He-he was here. He knew you wuh-were gone."

Caleb shuddered involuntarily at the words, and felt the lack of conviction in his voice when he said, "Nobody's here Jack. Just you and me."

Jack shook his head and looked beyond his father. "He came in the house. He was on the stairs."

Caleb held the boy in front of him and looked into his eyes. "There's nobody here. It was a nightmare. You're awake now." Cyril barked again, as if in contradiction.

"His face—it's gone," Jack said, still disoriented.

It was the same nightmare, Caleb realized with disquiet. Polly had said Jack had dreamed of an unwelcome stranger in their house. How common was it for kids to have recurring dreams? He wondered if it signaled some deeper malaise. "I'll go and check downstairs," he told his son, in an effort to reassure Jack.

"Please Dad," Jack was saying, his voice fragile and scared. "Promise you won't go."

A tingling frost spread over Caleb's skin, numbing his brain. His thoughts stumbled drunkenly, dangerously close to panic. He wondered if what he was feeling was, in part at least, a residue of his son's fear. He needed to be strong. "All right, Jack. You come sleep with us tonight, okay?"

Jack nodded, his gaze still flitting nervously about the room. Caleb picked him up and carried him back across the landing. He laid him down in the middle of the bed, next to Polly. She stirred and mumbled something in her sleep. He put a finger to his lips, signaling Jack to keep quiet. Then he left the room and went downstairs to the kitchen. Cyril was standing at the back door, sniffing. Caleb crouched beside the dog and petted him for a few moments. "What's wrong boy? You having bad dreams too?" The dog licked

Caleb's hand. He pointed to Cyril's basket, stood up and glanced through the kitchen window above the sink. Moonlight silvered the garden. Nothing was out of place. When he went back upstairs and climbed into bed, Jack turned and clung to him for a while, until fatigue loosened his hold and sleep reclaimed him.

The radio clock's LED screen pulsed redly in the darkness, as if attuned to the rhythm of Caleb's agitated mind. Vaguely disturbing thoughts had taken root there, but an unaccountable sense of guilt made him reluctant to examine them. They seemed born out of nothing. The darkness robbed him of reason, made his fears seem more real than they had any right to be. What could he do for Jack? Explain that his nightmares were the product of his own unconscious fears? As if reason could ever outweigh terror in the mind of a child. As if it could account for what seemed to him a strange congruence between Jack's bad dreams and his own fragile memories. He felt powerless and bewildered. Though he believed he would do anything for his son, he was plagued by a small but undeniable doubt. He couldn't escape the feeling that he was in some way responsible for Jack's terror, that it was connected to some weakness in himself.

Caleb strummed his guitar listlessly, his chord changes awkward and slow, like they had been when he'd first started playing. Maybe, once you got past forty, it was too late to take it up. The fingers were too stiff and the willingness to make a fool of oneself was not so strong as it had been. Yet, he didn't feel that way about himself. When Polly had bought the guitar for his birthday and told him it was time to stop talking and learn to play, it hadn't seemed such a crazy idea. And still now, after a year, the desire to play competently some blues and country tunes was as strong as ever. It was something else distracting him.

He leaned the guitar against the table, got up, and walked to the sink. Polly glanced up from the book she was reading. "Not there today, huh?"

Caleb shrugged and watched his son through the kitchen window. Jack was playing in the garden by the recently dug pond that still awaited its first koi carp. He was maneuvering his Action Men through the shallow water as if it were a swamp.

"You okay?"

Caleb looked at her. She'd put her book down on the table and was staring intently at him. He didn't want to talk. He knew already what she'd say. "I'm fine," he said, turning back to the window.

"It's Jack, isn't it?"

The boy was manipulating two of his soldiers into a fight. He paused suddenly, and cocked his head to one side, as if listening. Slowly, he swept his gaze across the garden. He seemed nervous, wary of something. After a moment or two, he continued with his game, but more guarded, as if aware that he was being observed. Caleb felt uneasy. He leaned closer to the window and let his gaze wander around the garden and down to the rear wall that backed onto the lane. Nothing appeared out of the ordinary.

"He's okay, Cale," Polly was saying. "He'd be even better if you'd stop fretting."

"I was trying to help him," Caleb said, still watching Jack.

"By interrogating him?"

"Talking about it will help him." Jack was shielding his eyes from the watery sun as he gazed south toward the bay. "Expose the irrational to the cold light of day and it loses its power. Making Jack talk about the dream will weaken its hold over him."

"Oh sure. After all, he's eight years old."

She didn't seem to get it. "What do you suggest we do?"

"Ignore them. They'll pass of their own accord if you stop bringing them up. Jesus, Cale, all kids have bad dreams sometime or other."

"I never did. Not like his."

"We all have nightmares. Why should you be different?"

He looked at her and heard himself say, "I just never did."

"Or you forced yourself to forget."

Maybe she was right. He turned back to the garden. Jack had laid one Action Man face down in the water. He was draping strings of pond weed over the doll. He paused and glanced up toward the house, before turning his attention once again to his game.

Polly came up behind Caleb and slipped her arms around his waist. "You just need to give him a little time," she said, pressing her lips against the back of his neck.

How much time, Caleb wondered, feeling an ache of tenderness as he watched Jack rise up onto his knees. The same nightmare four times in one week. How much time before reason was exposed as a hollow lie? He would not let it happen.

As if feeling his isolation, Polly pulled away. He was about to reach for her when he saw what Jack was doing. The boy was kneeling over the pond where the Action Man floated, covered with strands of weed. His hands were clasped together, his head was tilted skywards, and his lips were moving. Caleb's flesh tingled with disquiet. What kind of game was it that necessitated prayer?

Jack and Gary raced into the dunes ahead of Caleb and Cyril. A stiff breeze blew in from the east, across Oxwich Bay, unleashing small, foam-flecked waves to snap at the shore. Caleb followed the terrier up the steep, sliding bank of a dune. The boys were waiting for him atop the grassy ridge. Jack looked skinny and frail next to his friend, who, though only a month older, was a good six inches taller and a few pounds heavier. Sometimes Caleb feared for his son when he watched the rough and tumble of their play, but he was glad too that Jack had such a friend. Gary seemed to him in-domitable, and he hoped that some of that strength would rub off on Jack. No nightmare last night. Third dreamless night in a row. Perhaps Polly had been right after all.

"We're gonna hide now," Jack said. "You gotta count a hundred."

Caleb nodded. He called Cyril to him and held on to the dog while the two boys took off. He began counting out loud as he watched them scramble farther up through the tough marram grass. Cyril whined and struggled to chase after them, but Caleb held him until he had reached fifty. Then, still holding the dog by his collar, he crawled up the slope and peered over the crest of the dune. Jack and Gary were sixty or seventy yards ahead, running through the small dip toward another rise. He waited until they had disap-peared around the side of the hill, then called out that he was coming. Let-ting Cyril race ahead of him, he followed their path, before cutting across and up the dune at a steeper angle. Crouching as he came over the crest of the hill, he scanned the dune slack below, searching the bracken and coarse grasses for anything other than wind-induced movement. He spied a patch of yellow moving beyond the pink and white trumpets of a bindweed-choked tree, and quickly chose a route that would allow him to get ahead of the two boys.

Soon after, he popped up from behind a thick mound of marram grass and made booming noises as he shot them with his forefingers. After yelping in surprise, the boys collapsed spectacularly into the scrub.

By the time they had picked themselves up and started counting, Caleb was already heading deeper into the dunes. He ran for about a hundred yards, found cover in a clump of bracken, and lay on his back to watch the cirrus clouds race across the sky. He could hear the sea rolling in over the long flat stretch of the bay, the screech of gulls and the wind whistling through the dune grass. He closed his eyes for a moment and heard voices carrying on the breeze. He was surprised at how much distance and the wind distorted the sounds, made them indecipherable, barely recognizable as hu-man. The vastness of the sky overhead instilled in him a sense of isolation, which added to the strangeness of the voices. Despite the coolness of the breeze, he felt trickles of sweat on his back as the words shaped themselves in his head. Something about time. He listened more intently, made out Jack's voice, frightened, asking what happens at thirteen o'clock. A sudden rush of panic swept through Caleb. He sprang up from the bracken and spun round, searching the immediate vicinity for his son. There was no sign of either boy. He was about to call out when he heard Jack shouting from the top of a dune some sixty yards away. The boy waved to him, then followed Gary and the dog down the slope.

"You're 'sposed to hide, Dad," Jack said, as they arrived, breathless, beside him. "That was too easy."

"We would have found you anyway," Gary said. "Cyril had your scent."

There was nothing in either boy's faces to confirm what Caleb had heard. He had imagined it, he told himself. The wind and his own anxiety about Jack. Understandable, if foolish. He thought the boy looked a little pale, but he seemed untroubled. "Okay," he said. "I think it's time to go."

"Not yet," Jack said. "We only had one go of hiding."

Gary nodded, and without waiting for Caleb to agree, he tore off up the nearest slope. Caleb felt a surge of anger but he suppressed it. He gestured to Jack. "Get going," he said. "Make it good."

Jack sped off after his friend. Cyril stayed with Caleb of his own accord. It was getting on for seven and a chill lingered in the late April air. As he watched them disappear over the top of a high dune, he regretted letting them go again and considered calling them back. But they were gone now, and despite his sense of unease, he didn't want to spoil their fun. He counted slowly to fifty, then set out on their trail. He climbed the dune and scanned the nearby hollows for any trace of them. "Where they go boy?" he said, more to himself than the dog, who had stopped to investigate a few pellets of rabbit shit. Caleb shrugged, scrambled down the dune toward a trail that skirted the copse separating the dunes from the marshlands beyond. He followed this path to the end of the trees, then climbed up the nearest slope to get a better view. From the top, he saw the gray ocean and a thin line of sand, separated from him by the expanse of green, cascading dunes. A sudden, intense fear bloomed inside him as his eyes searched the windswept slacks. "Jack," he cried out. "Time to go, son."

No voice came back to him, just the moan of the insistent breeze through the coarse grass and brittle sea holly. He moved in a shorewards direction, clambering down one dune and up the next, calling Jack's name. He felt a tight knot in his stomach as he forced himself up the yielding slope. It sapped his strength and robbed him of breath. He reached the top, lightheaded and panting. Cyril scampered up the path behind him, tongue lolling out of his mouth. He stopped abruptly and turned, just as a figure burst out from the scrub.

It was Gary. Caleb's relief dissipated when he saw the boy was alone. "Dammit, Gary," he snapped. "Where the hell is Jack?"

Gary's grin slipped. "I—I'm sorry Caleb. We didn't mean to—"

Caleb saw that he had frightened the boy unnecessarily. "It's all right. Just tell me where he's hiding."

"I didn't see," Gary said.

Caleb's fear intensified. "Which way did he go?" he said, trying to keep his voice calm.

Gary looked around, then pointed back toward the marsh. Caleb took his hand, and together they headed down the slope. The sweat chilled his body as he raced over damp scabious, calling out. The minutes ticked by and dusk began to roll in from the bay. Odd terrors clawed at the frayed edges of his mind, and his limbs shook with fatigue as he searched through the trees. What had he been thinking, especially after what Jack had been through? Please, please, let him be okay.

A whispered sound caught his attention. He turned and saw the dog running along another path back into the dunes. "There," he shouted at Gary, a sharp pain piercing his side. He staggered after the boy and dog. Beyond them, he caught a glimpse of yellow through the scrub, lost it, then saw it again, unmoving on the ground behind a stunted tree. His heart was pumping furiously and the cry of despair was on his lips as he came round the tree and nearly crashed into Gary, who stood over the motionless form.

Jack was grinning up at them. "What took you so long?" he said.

For a second, Caleb teetered on the edge of rage, then he fell to his knees and hugged Jack tightly to his chest.

Caleb turned into the school carpark. Beside him, Jack stared blankly ahead. He'd not spoken in the six-minute drive from the doctor's surgery to the school. After a dreamless week, the nightmare had returned to ravage the boy. Caleb had heard him cry out sometime after midnight. He'd run to Jack's room and had found him sitting upright, his gaze fixed on nothingness. Traces of whatever haunted his dreams lingered in his eyes even after Caleb had woken him, but he had been unable to ascribe it a material substance or meaning. And all the doctor had had to say was that there was nothing physically wrong with Jack. Jesus Christ—what did he expect? Broken bones? A gaping wound? Caleb had wanted answers, not fucking platitudes. Tell him why Jack was having these nightmares, what was scaring him. Instead, he'd had to listen to bullshit reassurances about Jack's overactive imagination and how they should maybe monitor his TV viewing and ease up on the bedtime stories. Polly would be relieved, even if she had more or less predicted what the doctor would say. Maybe he was overreacting.

Caleb turned off the ignition, his body tense with anger and concern. He glanced at his son in the passenger seat. Jack looked too fragile, he thought, too lost inside his own head. He wanted desperately to hug the boy, to let him know that he would do anything for him, but he was afraid that Jack would somehow see the truth.

"You sure you want to go to school?" he said. "I can take you home if you want."

"I'm okay," Jack said.

Caleb felt sick with anguish. He didn't want to quiz his son but felt he had no choice. "Jack, the other day, when you asked Gary about thirteen o'clock, what did you mean?"

"About what?"

Caleb forced a smile. "When we were down at Oxwich. You asked him what happens at thirteen o'clock."

Jack seemed confused. "I don't know what you mean, Dad."

Caleb wondered if his son was being evasive. "Maybe, like Rat and Mole, you feel that it's better to forget some things?"

Jack shook his head, making his uncertainty evident. "I never heard of it."

Caleb believed the boy. He leaned over and hugged him, trying to squeeze strength into his son. "I love you, Jack. You know that?"

"Yes."

"I won't let anything hurt you."

"Dad," Jack said, his voice muffled against Caleb's chest. "I don't want you to go."

Caleb stifled a sob and patted him on the back. "I got work, Jack."

The boy pulled away from him. "I didn't mean—" He stopped then, kissed his father, and got out of the car. Caleb waved after him as he ran across the schoolyard, but Jack didn't look back.

Alone, his eyes watered, and he felt overwhelmed. His love was compromised by a sense of powerlessness, of having failed his son. He felt guilty too, at being afraid, not for Jack but for himself. He was ashamed of his weakness and angry at what he saw as the failure of his reason. He caught sight of something in the rearview mirror, a child's bewildered face staring at him from the back seat. Jack's, he thought at first, but after a moment he realized it was his own, as it had been thirty years ago. The cheeks were pale, the lips thin and trembling, the eyes haunted. Caleb felt the glacial creep of fear across his skin. Wanting to connect with the abandoned child, he reached up, touched the mirror, and saw the child's features blur and reassemble themselves into his own harrowed face.

Discordant sounds frayed Caleb's nerves and a harsh chorus of jeers echoed from the far end of the bar. He realized Polly wasn't really listening to what he was saying. Her attention was elsewhere; on the football match playing on the big screen television, or maybe on the people gathered in front of it. As if sensing his scrutiny, she returned her gaze to him and said, "I'm sorry, Cale. It's just that I thought we could, you know, talk about something else."

"Something else?"

She sighed. "We don't often get the chance to go out for a night. We've both been under a lot of strain lately, I thought it would do us good to be alone together."

Caleb frowned, frustrated at what he perceived as a lack of concern. "You don't think we owe it to Jack to—"

"Please don't play the guilt thing on me," she snapped. "Of course I'm concerned, but Jesus Christ, Cale, we just have to be patient."

"I think we should take him to see a specialist."

"If they continue, yes, maybe we should take him back to Dr. Morgan and get him to refer Jack to someone. But just for tonight, can't we talk about something else?"

It was a reasonable request, he knew. Jack's problem had taken its toll on them both. And yet, he was wary of looking away. "All right," he said. "Let me just say something, then we'll talk about whatever you want."

Polly's lips tightened and she leaned back in her seat, away from him.

"The common thing is a stranger," Caleb said. "Think about what that means. For a kid it signifies danger, right? What are kids told all the time? Be wary of strangers, and this is drummed into their unconscious." He spoke quickly, trying to flesh out his still sketchy interpretation, how Jack's fear of strangers was manifesting itself in his dreams as someone coming to kidnap him. Stories in the papers and on the TV about kids being abducted and murdered. That young girl found strangled in the woods outside Cardiff a couple of months ago, and more recently, the teenage boy whose naked body was found beaten to death on the sands along Swansea foreshore. Kids weren't impervious to things like that, he said. They made connections, even if they weren't conscious of doing so. In bad dreams, the most irrational things became real.

Polly finished her bottle of Corona. She tried to sound reasonable but Caleb could hear the frustration in her voice. "It's not that what you're saying isn't plausible, Cale. Maybe it is, I don't know. I'll read up on it. But I think you're becoming obsessed with this. What chance has Jack got of forgetting the bloody dreams if you keep on about them?"

"Ignoring it isn't going to make it stop."

"It sounds to me like you don't want them to."

"Shit, Polly, what the hell is that supposed to mean?"

She got up from her seat. "I want to go," she said. "I can't talk about this anymore."

Caleb grabbed her arm and said, "This is Jack we're talking about."

She pulled her arm free. "No it isn't. It's you." She hurried from the bar.

He sat there for a few moments, immobilized by panic and fear. How could she not sense the threat to their son? Slowly, his panic subsided and he followed her out onto the street. He saw her crossing the main road to the carpark. A mild rain was falling and the lights of Mumbles flickered on the dark bay like fragile memories. Caleb felt alone as he walked after her, distanced from everything he held dear. How does a man get back what he's lost, he wondered, puzzled at the question. He wasn't even sure what he had lost. Some memory, or maybe some part of his self-belief.

Anna, the baby-sitter, was watching *The O.C.* when they got home. Jack was fine, she said. Not a peep since she'd put him to bed at nine. Polly asked Caleb to check on him while she ran Anna home.

Alone, Caleb headed upstairs. A wave of relief swept through him when he saw Jack was sleeping soundly. The muscles in his legs quivered, and fearing he would collapse, he went and sat on the edge of his son's bed. Wan light edged into the room through the open door, falling on Jack's slippers and a couple of PlayStation games at the foot of the bed. A Manchester United poster was on the wall over Jack's head, and other posters around the room depicted Bart Simpson and scenes from the *Harry Potter* movies. Caleb felt a surge of tenderness. The sight of *The Wind in the Willows* on the night table filled him with sadness and a deep sense of regret.

I'm sorry, Jack, he thought, as he stood up to leave. The boy stirred and rolled onto his back. Caleb's breath caught when he saw Jack's eyelids were flickering crazily. His lips moved as if he were trying to speak, but no words came out, only the muted sibilance of dreams. "Jack," Caleb said, but the sound was less than a whisper. He turned, saw the small armchair beneath the dormer window. He pulled it a little closer to the bed and sat in it. Jack continued to make soft, indecipherable noises on the bed, one hand above the sheet, the fist clenching and unclenching.

Caleb wondered what his son was seeing. He tried to will himself inside Jack's head, to witness the slow unfurling terror. "Stay with it, Jack," he said to himself. "Be strong."

Jack began to toss and turn on the bed, his legs kicking sporadically beneath the sheets. His voice grew louder, but Caleb was still unable to recognize the sounds as words. His movements became more agitated, more violent. Caleb leaned forward in the chair, peering intently at his son. He anticipated some kind of revelation, as long as he didn't weaken and let his attention falter. That was the mistake he had been making, he realized, as Jack started to scream. Waking the boy too soon. Have to let him go further into it, see what he needed to see. Maybe then it would end. Recalling it in the daylight hours, his reason would overcome the nebulous fear. Jack was writhing now, his lips pulled back in a rictus grin as scream after scream tore from his throat. As awful as it was, Caleb felt he had to let it go on, for Jack's sake, he told himself, his vision blurring through tears.

The only problem was Polly, standing in the doorway, screaming at him to make it stop. He tried to explain what was happening, but it was no good. She ran to the bed, gathered Jack up into her arms, and carried him from the room. Caleb sat there, appalled at what he had done. At what he had failed to do. The terror wasn't Jack's alone, he felt. It was his nightmare too.

Throughout the day Caleb struggled with his fears, barely able to keep his mind focused on his students. Their demands oppressed him, their need for reassurance wore him down. He grew more irritable and short-tempered, so that for the final session of the day, forewarned by the morning's students, fewer than half the afternoon group turned up. Afterwards, he sat alone for an hour in his office, trying to make sense of what was happening to him. The persistence of Jack's nightmare scared him and his need to make sense of it had become an obsession. He had come to feel connected to it in some way, to believe that the key to deciphering it lay somewhere in his own past. All day he'd dredged his subterranean memories but had come up empty. As he left the building after six, he wondered if in fact he was afraid to probe too deeply. Maybe there was something there he wasn't ready to deal with, some secret he didn't want to discover about himself. He stopped in the Joiner's Arms on the way home, but found neither relief nor pleasure in the two pints of Three Cliffs Gold he drank, nor in the company of the few regulars who acknowledged his presence but who, faced with his patent desire for isolation, left him to his fretful ponderings.

Jack was watching TV in the living room when Caleb got home. He glanced in at his son then walked by the door and on through to the kitchen. Polly was reading a book at the kitchen table, sipping a glass of red wine. She looked up as he came in and managed an uneven smile. "You okay?" she said.

Caleb shrugged, took a glass from the wall unit, and poured himself some wine. "How is he?"

"Okay, I think. Keeps asking about you."

"What's that?" he asked, meaning the book.

She showed him the cover. It was called *Children's Minds*. "Picked it up in town today. Thought it might help us figure out what's going on with Jack."

"And does it?"

"It helps me."

"I'm going to sit with him tonight," Caleb said. "Watch him. I'll try to wake him before it takes hold."

Polly frowned. "You really think that will help him?"

"As much as that book."

She got up from the table and took his hand. "Caleb, can you be honest with me?"

"I thought I was."

"About Jack, I mean. About why he's so afraid for you."

"Jack's not afraid of me," Caleb said, agitated.

"That's not what I said," Polly said, confused. "Jack's afraid for you—not of you. Why? Have you told him something? Something you're not telling me?"

Her questions shook him, filled him with doubt. "Don't—don't be stupid."

"I'm not," Polly said, her voice rising. "I'm scared for our son and I'm worried about you. You're not yourself, Cale. Something's eating you up."

"Please, Polly," Caleb said, trying to hold himself together. "Don't presume you know what's going on in my head. Can you do that? Is it asking too much?" He didn't wait for an answer but hurried upstairs where he stripped off his clothes and took a long, almost scalding shower, as if to burn away the stain of some long forgotten sin.

Later, Caleb apologized to Polly and told her he'd look at the book she'd bought. Maybe it would help him understand what Jack was going through. After dinner, he went to his son's room. Jack was already tucked up in bed, and despite the broad smile that crossed his face, Caleb could see none of his usual vitality and zest for life.

"Mum said you're going to stay."

He stood by the edge of the bed, feeling a sudden, intense pang of guilt. "That's right," he said. "Keep the bad dreams away."

"Are you going to read to me?"

Caleb saw *Wind in the Willows* on the night table. He shook his head. "Not tonight."

"D'you read it when you were a boy?"

"Yes, though I'd forgot most of it until I started reading it to you."

"D'you forget your dreams too, Dad?"

Caleb stared at his son, not sure how to respond. He wanted to say the right thing, but he no longer knew what that was. "Most of them."

"Did you dream about—"

"Ssshhh, Jack. Go to sleep."

Jack was silent a moment, his face troubled. Then, as if having plucked up the courage, he said, "Will I die if I dream at thirteen o'clock?"

Caleb leaned over the bed and took hold of Jack's hand. "No," he said, squeezing. "There's no such time as thirteen o'clock."

Jack nodded but seemed unconvinced. He reached up and kissed his father's cheek. "I'm okay, Dad, really," he said, but Caleb saw a wariness in his eyes.

"I hope so, son," he said, letting Jack's hand fall. He moved to the window and sat in the armchair, watching as Jack turned on his side to face him. He'd brought Polly's book upstairs, but after flicking through the first few pages, he let it fall to the floor and focused his attention on his son.

He woke that night with the sound of screams still echoing in his head. Violent tremors shook his body as he crouched in the shadows, clenching his teeth to still their relentless chatter. A sickly, cloying dread hung in the air, and his flesh recoiled from its touch. Through the fog of dreams that swirled all round his semiconscious mind, he recognized Polly's voice, splintered to a thin, fragile whisper. "Caleb," she was saying, "what happened to you? Where have you been?"

The stench of foam was in his nostrils, the taste of salt on his lips. "Poh-Polly?" he groaned.

"Jesus, Cale." Her arms were around him and he felt the heat from her body seep into his cold, damp flesh. "It's okay, you had a nightmare."

He saw the darkness outside the kitchen window. He was crouched on the opposite side of the room, the slate tiles wet beneath him, and the distant pounding of surf reverberating in his head. Cyril cowered behind Polly, as if wary of him. "How did I get here?" he asked.

Polly shook her head, her face drained of color in the pale light. "Something woke me and you weren't there. I was going to Jack's room when I heard you cry out down here."

"This can't happen, Polly," he said. "I—I can't let it happen to him."

"What can't happen, Cale?" Her gray eyes searched his face. He felt cut off from her, drifting beyond her zone of familiarity. "What are you talking about?" she said.

He wondered at her inability to comprehend the vague shapes and shadows that flowed around him. Nothing he saw reassured him, not even her face. Her lips were moving but the words were drowned by the sound of the blood rushing through his brain. Someone had been outside, watching the house. Was he still there, waiting? For Jack? "Listen to me," he said, trying to warn her, but there was something else too, something he needed to know. The shadows beyond Polly were melting into the floor.

"It's all right, Cale. It's over."

She didn't get it. The dream was there, but all scrambled in his mind. He'd seen this before. Years ago, he thought, when he was a child. The same nightmare Jack was having. A pitiful cry came from elsewhere else in the house.

"Oh please no," Polly whispered, rising to her feet.

Instinctively, he grabbed her hand and said, "What time is it?"

"It's Jack," she said, pulling away from him, heading toward the stairs.

He realized what it was she'd heard. Jack was screaming upstairs. He struggled to get up from the floor. Heart pounding ferociously, he forced himself to look at his watch. It was twelve forty-five. Bad memories stirred inside him.

Caleb looked out through the crack in the curtains, at the three-quarter moon hanging over Three Cliffs Bay and the mist rising silently up over the fields toward Penmaen. He leaned back in the armchair. Jack was sleeping. Polly had phoned the doctor again that morning, asked him to refer Jack to a child psychologist. Caleb knew it would do no good but he hadn't stopped her. He'd wanted to tell her that only he could help their son, but fear, and a sense of his own weakness, had prevented him from articulating this certainty. What mattered was the hour in which Jack's nightmare came. The same hour in which it had come to him when he was a boy. The thirteenth hour. How many times had it haunted his sleep thirty-odd years ago? That sense of uncertainty. A feeling of being apart from the world, an isolation that had filled him with absolute dread. Lying in bed at night clinging to consciousness, fighting to keep the terror of sleep at bay. At least until the hour was past and even then not letting himself fall all the way, anchoring one strand of thought to the shore of reason.

It had withered inside him, he supposed. Withered but not died. He'd buried it deep down in the darkest recesses of his brain where it had lain in wait all these years till it had sensed the nearness of an innocent mind. The idea of it appalled Caleb. Every fiber of his reason screamed against the possibility. Yet he could no longer deny that his own childhood nightmare had transmigrated into the fertile ground of Jack's unconscious.

All day Caleb had thought about the nightmare, trying to collate his own hesitant memories against Jack's fragmented rememberings of the dream. They had both sensed a presence outside, watching the house. Jack had heard the stranger calling out, but he said it sounded a long way away. Sometimes he was inside the house, in the hall or on the stairs. Jack had never seen the nightmare through to the end, and if Caleb had ever done so, he'd forgotten what he'd seen there.

In the dim light, Caleb glanced at his watch. Eleven-thirty. Knowing that Jack would soon begin to dream, he prepared to abandon himself to the lure of sleep. Even as it tugged at his mind, he felt the stirring of a residual fear, urging him to resist. His eyes flickered open for a moment but darkness breathed over them, drawing them down. The strands of reason stretched one by one and snapped as he hovered a while on the edge of consciousness, before drifting across the border into the deep of dreams.

Nothing moved in the room. The chill cloak of darkness made everything one and the same. Caleb held himself still, waiting. His hands hurt from gripping the arms of the chair and every nerve in his body strained for release. He listened, trying to shut out the pounding of his heart and the crackling white noise of nameless fears. Until, above the sound of his own terrible thoughts, he heard again a muffled footstep on the stairs. Silence again for a moment, followed by more footsteps, coming closer. He caught his breath as they stopped right outside the door. Where was Cyril, he wondered. Why wasn't he barking? His flesh crawled as he waited for the sound of the door handle turning. Instead, the footsteps began to recede. He exhaled slowly, peering into the darkness where he imagined the door should be. He turned on the lamp. Dim light pushed feebly at the shadows, barely strong enough to reveal the open door, the empty bed.

He choked back a cry and rushed out onto the landing. There was still time, he told himself. His breath misted in the chill, salty air. There were damp footprints on the stairs. Following them down, he felt the fear clawing at his back, wrapping him in its clammy embrace. The wet prints marched along the hall, through the kitchen, to the open back door. A shroud of mist hung over the garden. Caleb hesitated, his arms braced against the doorframe. His son was out there. "Jack," he whispered, despairingly. "Please Jack, come home."

Hearing the dog bark out there, he forced himself to move, out across the crisp grass, which crunched underfoot. He went through the gate at the bottom of the garden, then turned and saw the house rising up out of the moon-yellowed mist. He felt a terrible loneliness and could barely keep himself from rushing back toward it. But he caught the sound of a soft voice calling to him. He hauled himself up over the ditch and ran on through the fields that sloped down into tangled woodland. He could no longer hear Cyril as he beat his way through trees and undergrowth, slipping and sliding on the soft earth, until finally he stumbled out onto the muddy banks of Pennard Pwll. He followed the stream as it meandered out of the valley into the bay. Above the rustling of the water, he could hear his son calling to him.

Impatient, he stepped into the stream, wading across the gushing, knee-high water. He stumbled over a rock, fell and picked himself up again. "Jack," he cried, as he struggled up onto a sandbank. Some distance ahead and to his left he saw the three witch-hat peaks that gave the bay its name clawing the night sky through the mist. Having got his bearings, Caleb raced across the sand toward the sea, energized by the blood pumping through his veins. The jaundiced mist billowed around him as he splashed into the wavelets lapping the shore. He waded out deeper, ignoring the current that tugged insistently at his legs. He beat at the mist with his arms, trying to open up a space through which he might spy his son. The sea was perishing, forcing him to snatch shallow, ragged breaths. One moment it was swirling around his waist, the next it was surging up to his chest. The mist seemed to be thinning out and he caught glimpses of the moon up over Cefn Bryn. A wave swamped him, leaving him treading water. The current began to drag him away from the shore. "Jack, please," he called frantically, as he tried to keep his head above the surface. Another wave washed over him and when he came up he could see clearly out into the bay. The sea sank its bitter teeth into his flesh. He was swimming hard now, just to stay afloat. He was growing weaker but still he searched for his son, chopping through the moon-silvered water, all the time following the sound of a voice, his own voice, but distant and younger, calling to him from out of a long-forgotten nightmare. More water poured into his mouth as he went under again, still fighting. He rose in time to hear a distant church bell strike the hour. At one, there was still hope. At two, it began to fade. He heard the thirteenth strike as a muted sound beneath the surface, a strange echo of the pressure of the sea filling his lungs.

It seems like dawn, or maybe dusk. He has difficulty now, telling the time of day. It seems to be always twilight. But still he waits for them, anticipating the moment, imagining a different outcome this time. But when they appear in the garden, the desperate longing he feels is as overwhelming as it always was. Jack looks bigger, more filled out. He must be ten, at least. Color reddens Polly's cheeks again, and the small lines around her eyes signify acceptance more than sorrow. He wonders what that means. He places a hand on the garden wall and as he does so, the house recedes a little, as if wary of him. He calls out their names and for one second, Jack looks up and stares directly at him. "Jack," Caleb cries out again, waving to him. "I'm here." For another moment, Jack continues to look his way, shielding his eyes from the sun. But then he turns and as Caleb looks down in despair, he sees no shadow on the garden wall, only sunlight falling right through the place where he stands.

Lives

JOHN GRANT

John Grant (real name Paul Barnett) is the author of more than sixty books, of which about one-third are novels. His The Encyclopedia of Walt Disney's Animated Characters *is regarded as the standard work in its field. As coeditor, with John Clute, of* The Encyclopedia of Fantasy, *he received the Hugo Award, the World Fantasy Award, and several other international awards. He received his second Hugo in 2004 for* The Chesley Awards: A Retrospective *(with Elizabeth Humphrey and Pamela D. Scoville). As managing editor of the* Clute/Nicholls *Encyclopedia of Science Fiction, he shared a rare British Science Fiction Association Special Award.*

Recently published books, all written as John Grant, include the "book-length fiction" The Stardragons *(illustrated by Bob Eggleton), the novel* The Dragons of Manhattan, *the children's book* Life-Size Dragons, *and the nonfiction* Discarded Science. *His story collection,* Take No Prisoners, *was published in 2004. The editor of the recent anthology* New Writings in the Fantastic, *he is currently at work on an encyclopedia of film noir and a "story-cycle,"* Leaving Fortusa, *while awaiting the imminent publication of the nonfiction book,* Corrupted Science.

We are waiting for Christopher to get home. Sipping wine around the kitchen table, Alice and I are just at the stage of starting to get worried. He's all right, we say to each other occasionally, betraying our concern that there might be something wrong. He's all right: Dick Charters will have picked Chris and Harry up okay from after-school drama practice, it being neighbor Dick's turn this week to fetch the two nine-year-olds. Maybe the traffic's hellish. Maybe Dick's run out of gas—wouldn't be the first time he's done that—and even now they're waiting for the rescue vehicles. Something like that.

Still, it's after nine o'clock, and we'd expected Christopher home by seven. . . .

The phone rings and it's Marian Charters, Dick's wife, Harry's mom. Do we know where they are?

Alice, who was the one to pick up the phone, tells Marian to come over to our place—help us with the wine while we're waiting for the truants, why doesn't she?

Marian says yes, and she's with us within ten minutes. Before she gets here we've opened another bottle of wine and swiftly knocked back a glass apiece to pretend we haven't.

As usual I pretend not to notice that Marian's very pretty. Alice is watching me to make sure I'm not noticing.

Twenty minutes later, a ring at the doorbell.

That's them, announces Marian, a slight drawl in her voice. Anxiousness has shoehorned her swiftly into a state of minor inebriation.

But it's not them; it's a man and a woman in blue, with faces as long as empty roadways.

A drunk started driving his SUV on the wrong side of the freeway. Took out four cars, another SUV, and a plumber's van before swerving right off and hitting a tree. Seven dead including the drunk driver. Three of the dead—an adult and two children—in the burned-out wreck of a blue Neon registered to Richard G. Charters, Jr. The cops called first at Dick's and Marian's home, and were sent here by a neighbor. . . .

All three of us on the couch in tears, me in the middle with my arms around the shoulders of the two women, as the cops do their best not to transgress their professional code of noninvolvement.

The bell goes again, and the lady cop murmurs to us that she'll get it.

Moments later she's leading a small wan figure in by the hand.

Christopher.

Of course, Alice and I are all over him, and for some minutes we completely forget about Marian, still on the couch, still grieving for her husband and son. The lady cop—professional standards be damned—goes to sit beside her, comforting her in the clumsy way strangers have. Soon the lady cop is weeping too. The guy cop doesn't know what to do with his emotions, just stands there wishing they'd go away.

What happened? we ask Christopher once we have our throats under control. What in the hell happened? Why weren't you in the car with? . . .

A guilty look at the couch and Marian, but her face is buried in the blue of the lady cop's shirt so she can't hear anything we say.

Something about the Cowardly Lion not being needed in tonight's rehearsal so, rather than hang around a couple of hours waiting for his lift with Harry and Mr. Charters, Christopher decided—bizarrely, as nine-year-olds can behave—to walk home instead.

All fourteen miles home.

There's nothing serious in Alice's scolding of him for being such an idiot, he's been told not to be out after dark on his own, doesn't he realize his route must have taken him through some dangerous areas?

Not as dangerous as Dick Charters's car on the freeway, I don't say.

It's a long night. The cops are the first to escape from it, of course, closely followed by Christopher, filled with a brace of comfort sandwiches and some M&Ms ice cream and a mug of cocoa. We decant the rest of the wine into Marian—no question of her going home to an empty house—and then pitch into the liquor cabinet until there's little sense in her trying to get any further cousins and aunts on the phone. At last we're able to haul Marian up the stairs to the guest room, which Alice has carefully cleared of anything reminiscent of childhood. Marian is snoring like a flooded drain when we tiptoe away to our own room to see if we can find some sleep ourselves.

It's a week before we let Christopher back to school, and nearly a month after that before we go to see him be the Cowardly Lion on stage with Dorothy and the rest, including an underrehearsed Tin Man who isn't Harry Charters.

Waiting outside while the shrieking thespians are changing back into their ordinary clothes, we chat with Bill Slocombe, the drama coach, telling him what a fine performance it was, especially given the circumstances.

We just thank every god in the heavens, says Alice, that our Christopher wasn't needed for rehearsal that fateful night. .

Bill looks at us oddly, puzzled by her meaning.

Her voice falters. The night, she reminds him, when (and the need to euphemize takes her over) you lost your Tin Man.

He says nothing, and later I discover why.

2

The natural state of everything is unpredictability.

Once-widowed Marian and I are in bed on a Sunday morning. We share custody of Christopher with Bill Slocombe and my ex-wife Alice, Chris's mother, and this is one of our weekends off. When you've been married only six months, living together only a few months longer than that, there is nothing else to do on a Sunday morning when you have it to yourselves than stay a long while in bed. Curiously, Marian finds it more of a wrench to see Christopher go off to his other home than I do; he has become her substitute for her son Harry, I think, but I have never dared ask her.

It's predictable that when parents lose a child they may either be bound closer together or they may be driven apart. It is not predictable that the death of their own child's friend should drive them apart. Yet something flickered that night between Alice and Bill Slocombe after the Wizard was revealed for the sham he is. Such things happen fairly frequently to all of us, of course, and they make no real difference to the orderly progression of living; but this time it coincided with the start of a veering apart of the hitherto parallel lines which were Alice and myself, and that drift led us to the places where we now are, and both probably the happier for it.

Alice and I have become better friends than we have ever been, and if occasionally nostalgia leads us to stray beyond the borderlines of friendship, well, who's to know? Not Marian, probably. Not Bill, certainly.

But I'm not thinking about any of that right now because Marian's relaxing with her head on the crook of my shoulder and there's sweat on her forehead that I'm in the process of licking off in between drowsy phrases of a meandering conversation concerning the depleted contents of the fridge and whose turn it is to get brunch together. There is nowhere in the world I believe I'd rather be right now, nothing else in the world I'd rather talk about.

So, of course, the phone has to go.

Leave it, I say.

It might be Alice or Bill calling about Christopher, Marian says.

She gets up, wrapping a light robe around herself as if a curve of breast or buttock might be glimpsed through the telephone. I watch, looking forward to the unpeeling of the robe, then let my eyes close.

Distant sounds of Marian's voice, then it's rising and not so distant anymore.

And she screams.

I'm beside her by the phone, arm around her waist, chilly in all the wrong places.

She can't speak anymore. Her mouth is just a cavern, her face one of the crumpled pillows I've just left. She holds the phone toward me as it were a furiously fighting rat.

I take it.

Mrs. Harbren. Lives just down the street from Alice and Bill and, this weekend, Christopher. A fire.

We're in our clothes somehow, and filling the car with the smell of sex as we cross solid lines and run lights on the orange. Then we're being enfolded into the crowds around a place that stinks of wet ash and misery, and somehow we make ourselves known to a cop so that we pass on through to where the firemen are looking at the steaming remains of their industry. There's a bit of the kitchen wall still standing, with a window in it that's like a five-year-old's grin. A fridge. A cooker. The seventeen-inch monitor Christopher was so pleased with. The three charred bodies are long gone, we're told as we look unbelieving at the bones of three lives; to judge by where the bodies were found, says a fireman from whom I think I sometimes buy pickles when he's not being a fireman, all three of them slept through it all and never felt a thing. It was the suffocation to blame, not the flames. The flames reached them later. An electrical short in the basement or the garage. . . .

Back in the car, we follow the road the three of them took. I can hardly see to drive.

Of course, there's not much anyone can tell us when we get there, and far less are they yet going to let us see what's left of Alice and Christopher and Bill. At any other time we'd probably joke about being just redundant thumbs and cope with our feelings of uselessness that way, but as it is there's nothing we know how to do except cling to each other and wish the world were some other place than this.

And then there's a doctor in our faces, failing to make us understand what he's saying. He has a brown face from generic southern Asia, and soft brown eyes like a lover's.

So at last we follow him to where Christopher's just beginning to sit up in bed. Christopher has a burn on his bottom that's going to trouble him for a few days, Doctor Seepersahd tells us, but aside from that he seems to be fine even though the paramedics in the ambulance could find no pulse and thought he was dead, and even though his bedclothes were charred beyond all recognition like Alice and Bill were, and even though his bed dropped through his bedroom floor and then the roof collapsed on top of it. They'll keep him in overnight, says Doctor Seepersahd, to check for any lung damage there might be consequent upon smoke inhalation, but right at this moment he looks to be fine.

A lucky escape.

A miracle.

These things happen, Seepersahd assures us, with the kind of smile you reserve for times when all the other news is incomprehensibly dark but the single gleam of light is dazzlingly bright.

Marian has fewer inhibitions. She'll mourn later for her two friends. I try to imitate her, for her and Christopher's sake, though it'll be forever before the pain will subside in the place where Alice used to live.

Christopher is well enough to smile, and to cough out a few hoarse words.

For the moment, that's all that can be allowed to matter.

3

The first we hear about the summer-school disaster is on the news that night, when somebody we recognize comes up on screen while we're eating our salads and so we turn off the mute. It's Gene Sendak, who's one of the teachers at the school, and he's letting the paleness of his face do most of the talking for him as he blurts out his horror at how a whitewater expedition could go so disastrously wrong for all concerned. No names because all of the parents haven't been contacted yet, which means us.

I sort of know what's going to happen next, but when I say so it doesn't calm Marian down and I realize it doesn't really calm me down either. She hits the phone while I pour some scotch for the both of us, being extra careful so that the shaking of my hand doesn't make the bottle's neck crack the rims of the cute crystal glasses we got at a yard sale somewhere.

Minutes later we're in the car, with Marian driving because I had to finish both of the scotches so they wouldn't go to waste, plus a gulp or two more straight from the bottle when she wasn't looking. It's sixty-five miles to Harmony Canyon and she does it in something under an hour, by which time I desperately need to pee. I seize onto the urgent call from my bladder as something to think about because it stops me from having any brain space left over to think about what we're going to discover.

Yes, sure enough, Christopher had a bad dose of the runs this morning so he stayed behind while the others went out on the boat.

Only Gene Sendak didn't know that when he was talking to Marian on the phone an hour ago, and he looks as if he's not terribly happy about knowing it now.

I don't blame him.

I think Gene Sendak watched with both eyes as Christopher climbed into the boat, and saw Christopher there as the kids waved him good-bye on their way off to the biggest and, as it proved, final adventure of their lives.

At least, or so Gene Sendak must be reassuring himself, he has one less lawsuit to cover his ass against. It must be every educator's nightmare—having some fatal accident happen to a kid whose parent happens to be a lawyer.

Christopher himself is almost as pale as Gene Sendak, and all the way home in the car he doesn't have more than half a dozen words for us. Marian more than makes up for the paucity, holding the steering wheel so tight her knuckles show bone, chattering away about relief, about good fortune, and about guardian angels working overtime—most of the words complete shit, of course, but most of the meanings behind them having a core of truth.

Tonight as I tuck Christopher into his bed—something I haven't done for years, because he's thirteen coming on fourteen now and I should respect his privacy as a young adult and all, but which seems very necessary tonight—I ask him to tell me what really happened.

His eyes are confused as he looks at me. Just like I said, Dad, he says. I think it was the fried chicken we had last night that did it, but I was in the latrines before dawn and it was the middle of the morning before I dared get too far away from them.

And I believe him because I have no other choice.

From the corridor Marian overhears my questioning him and it opens up a fissure between us.

4

The air's like chilled white wine up here on the slopes as I wait for Honey and Chris (as he now prefers to be called, the name being, he claims, "more adult"). They were still finishing breakfast when I set off for the ski car, ostensibly to check out the condition of the snow at the top but in fact because I want some time on my own to think. Honey believes we should get married and, while I imagine it perfectly possible that I love her, I'm not so sure

I can face being married again. I loved Alice and I loved Marian, and I married them, and, although I still love both of them—hell, I still have *the hots* for both of them—well, look where it led us. I scattered Alice along the shorefront where she and I spent our honeymoon, and Marian is living with a stockbroker who hits her and/or Chris when the Nasdaq takes a plunge, which is why Chris is here with Honey and me in Switzerland, complicating logistics and emotions alike.

It crosses my mind that in a couple years' time I might have to worry about leaving him and Honey too much alone together. I've seen his glances at her, and how she sometimes gets semiconsciously puzzled about the way she can't figure out whether to react to him as a child or as an adult.

There's a little chalet up here where they'll sell you schnapps to bolster your breakfast, and I've already done a little bolstering. It's not helping me come to any conclusions about the desirability of the marital state, but it's making the internal argument seem remote from me.

It's too far away for me to see the ski car at the bottom of its course as more than a little brown dot among slightly larger brown dots that are the buildings of the resort, but I imagine I can watch Honey and Chris boarding, him still somewhat clumsy and overlimbed as boys his age are, her with a few blond strands sticking out like wayward optical fibres no matter how hard she's tried to get them all tucked neatly away under her woolly hat. Then the car begins its lurching course up toward me. Nearby I can hear the machinery grunting as it hauls its load summitwards.

As soon as the noise of the engine changes its pitch I realize I've known all along that it would. The other trippers around me start looking at each other with concern, mouthing imbecilities in several different languages, but I stay absolutely motionless, possessed by the inevitability of the tragedy that will soon start to unfold.

And sure enough it does.

Bad maintenance? Freakish circumstances?

A million lawsuits will determine something everyone else but me can accept as the truth.

Whatever the cause, there's a sound like a rifle being detonated close to both of my ears at once, and then all the rest of the anxious awaiters are throwing themselves to the ground as the cable whips over our heads.

Why should I bother ducking? I know I'll be—physically, at least—all right.

So I stand where I was, hands knotted around the rail of the railing in front of me, watching the ski car lurch to one side as if it were throwing out a hand to seek invisible support, then, seemingly in slow motion, topple forward as it begins its inexorable plummet to the rocky snowy slope a thousand feet below, black insects spilling from it as it falls.

Only a few seconds later do we hear the tiny screams, like poppings among the hiss of an old vinyl LP.

Some of us, me among them, ski down to where the wreckage lies.

The other "rescuers" have just bodies and debris to examine, searching hopelessly for fickle signs of life. I have a boy to fetch.

5

Like recidivist alcoholics who, having lost yet another battle with the bottle, decide they might as well opt in future to embrace it as a way of life rather than fight it any further, Marian and I are back together again. No talk of re-marriage: we've both been down that road too often before. Chris says he approves of the relationship, and I think I believe him, even though perhaps he says it a little too frequently and a little too spontaneously.

We're comfortably off, of course—more than comfortably. My law practice has flourished over the years, and has now reached the point where I need to do little work there myself, just show up as an appropriately gravitas-endowed figurehead at partners' meetings or to impress the more moneyed clients. One of the last occasions I actively participated in a suit myself was getting compensation out of Marian's stockbroker for all the abuse to which he'd subjected her, and I got plenty. Before that, I personally handled the class action for the ski-car tragedy.

Of course, I know the *status quo* can't last. Marian poo-poos my apprehensions, so I've largely given up talking about them to her, but I spend most of my life just waiting for the axe to fall. I assume that this time it'll be her that'll suffer from being around Chris, but it could as well be the girl he's been going with steady the past year or more, a pretty little thing called Andrea whom I judge to have quite considerably more brains than she deems it fashionable to reveal. He brings her home from college sometimes during the vacations, and Marian and I show how openminded and in-touch we are by letting them share the guest room.

So there's no surprise for me when I get the phone call during one of my increasingly rare afternoons in the office to inform me that the car I gave Chris for his eighteenth birthday, with Chris at the wheel, has been involved in an inferno on I-80 when a gas truck jackknifed and exploded and twenty-four other vehicles piled into the flames.

No: one surprise.

Marian was in the car as a passenger along with Andrea, so he managed to take both of them out at once.

As I put down the phone I notice that my hand no longer even shakes when I hear news like this.

I go home and wait for Chris to arrive. Somehow I cannot conjure up any interest in what his explanation might be.

6

As a young assistant professor seeking tenure, Chris takes like a duck to water to the traditional academic pastime of screwing the prettier and more impressionable students. I will never know if he is aware of the fact that he's been infected at some stage of his enthusiastic sexual career with the HIV virus. Eight of the girls contract full-scale AIDS, and before you know it there's a mini epidemic going on at the college. There are plenty of indications that Chris is the root source of it all, but he's lucky enough to have a lawyer as a father and I'm able to use a mixture of litigation threats and general obfuscation to make sure no retaliatory measures are ever taken—except, understandably, that his tenure is not granted.

Chris himself is, of course, completely unaffected by the disease, and the medics are astonished by how efficacious their treatments are in expelling the virus from his bloodstream.

7

Three days after the disaster of 9/11, Chris walks on his own two feet out of the wreckage of the Twin Towers. His latest girlfriend, Jennifer, is less lucky.

A pity. I liked her.

8

No one is ever able to ascertain the identity of the organization that planted a bomb aboard flight 063 from New York to Paris, leading to the deaths soon after takeoff of all 271 passengers and crew aboard the aircraft, but the government uses the event as an excuse to go off and blitz some obscure Middle Eastern nation that most of us couldn't before have found on the map. Thousands die on both sides, although the vast majority of the casualties are comfortably foreign, dusky-skinned, and thereby anonymous.

Chris and I watch the news bulletins about the war on television together. Although the airline records are insistent that he boarded the plane, and although some of his personal belongings have been found among the debris scattered across Long Island Sound, in point of fact Chris changed his mind at the last moment, for reasons unspecified, and never showed up for the flight. I know this to be so, for he was here at home on the fateful morning in question, even though I cannot recall him being so. If the feds knew he was still alive, they would undoubtedly have some probing questions to ask of him.

He is speaking now, I think to me, although he seems to be addressing the screen. I have too many thoughts of my own to be willing to let his intrude upon them. Even the scattered phrases that dart in slyly to pierce my mind's shell are distraction enough. "I do *feel* things, you know, Dad?" and "I can't help the way I'm made—you and Mom did that" and "Whatever my body needs to do to survive, it does" and "I wish we could speak to each other more, Dad" and "I wish I could think you were listening."

Gadfly thoughts. Reflexively I swat them away.

Time passes.

He falls silent.

The evening crawls onward.

I glance frequently sidelong at Chris's eyes, glittering with reflected light from the moving images on the television screen, and realize from the relaxed way he slumps on the couch that it has never crossed his mind to do some requisite counting.

9

But *I* have been counting his lives.

I am in the garage. Chris has gone to bed a half-hour ago or more, and I will give him another hour to make sure he is sound asleep. I have written a letter of explanation and left it sealed in an innocuous white envelope in the middle of the kitchen table, so that it cannot fail to be discovered in the morning. I have checked that the little diesel tank of the chain saw is full, and that the motor is completely functional. I have checked that the horrible little revolver I bought yesterday is loaded, and that the mechanism functions smoothly. In theory the revolver should be enough on its own, but people have been known to recover from supposedly lethal gunshot wounds, even from multiple bullets in the brain, and I anyway am not certain enough of my own competence in ensuring that the shots I fire will be fatal. The chain saw will, I hope, guarantee the efficacy of my efforts.

The revolver should be enough for myself, afterwards.

I have nothing to do for the next hour or so except remember Alice, and Honey, and Marian, and Andrea, and Jennifer.

And Harry.

Dick.

Bill.

People I have loved, or some of them people I have simply liked.

All of them are gone now. All of them have been *outlived*.

I bought a pack of cigarettes as well as a revolver yesterday. I haven't smoked since high school, having been permanently frightened away from the weed by all the reports on the health dangers. No need now for such fears. I tap one out and light it, then pour myself another single-malt scotch, reminding myself that I must take care to remain sober enough to perform this night's task successfully.

Before he went to bed, Chris stopped at the bottom of the stairs and for once looked me straight in the eye. "I'm not the only one who's survived, Dad," he said. "There are dozens of different ways people can learn to survive things. You're a survivor too, in your own way."

I didn't understand him.

His gaze dropped, and he turned away.

Now I sit on the workbench I've never thought to work on and enjoy a perfect calm as I watch the clouds of my gray cigarette smoke swirl, dissipate, and very swiftly die.

Ghorla

MARK SAMUELS

Mark Samuels is the author of two collections, The White Hands and Other Weird Tales *and* Black Altars. *His third collection of short stories is provisionally titled* Glyphotech and Other Macabre Processes, *and is scheduled to be published by Midnight House in 2008. He has been nominated twice for the British Fantasy Award.*

For more information, his Web site can be found at www.mark-samuels.net.

My contention is that high-level sentience collapses in on itself near death in a manner akin to the demise of a massive star and that dying thoughts approach infinite duration. Postmortem, these thoughts, if driven by a will of sufficient power, can tumble over a synaptic event horizon and subsequently appear in another body with an almost exact genetic identity. Such "heirs" are subject to the invasion of their minds by ideas and emotions that originate with the dead. The living are simply vehicles for a series of disturbing and broken alien responses that we take to be our own personalities. I now believe that the majority of thoughts we think actually come from the "ghost shells" of ancestors in varying states of psychical decay. They are the products of disintegrating remains, frightful masks that have not been shed. Afterlife geography is seen in the UHF frequencies between TV channels, consisting of immense steppes of static. It is a projection in time, comprised of antimatter and populated by the dead.

—Julius Ghorla, *Black Holes* (1983)

T he 9:35 A.M. bus approached Crawborough railway station. It was a wet, miserable morning in late October. The rain had not ceased for three days and the weather forecasts predicted another week more of it. All the holidaymakers were long gone from this stretch of the Yorkshire coast; no more backpackers, elderly couples, or dirty weekenders used the bus service to ferry them north. Most of the time, except during school-run hours, the bus was empty save for one or two lone shoppers ferrying their heavy bags back from the supermarket to home. Even they usually traveled only as far as four or five stops.

The driver of the bus, one Bill Jones, was confident he would not have to take on any passengers for this service from Crawborough to Banwick. The incessant rain seemed to have forced everyone off the streets. This pleased him quite a bit because it meant he could enjoy the luxury of smoking whilst he drove, instead of waiting until he reached the depot at Banwick, well over an hour away. There would be no one to comment, or worse—report—on his flouting the bus company's regulations.

But as he pulled into the turn near the railway station, he was disgruntled to see a lone figure waiting underneath the bus shelter ahead. The prospective passenger had a large suitcase with him, two plastic carrier-bags, and a wicker basket for carrying a small dog or large cat.

When he pulled up alongside the shelter and opened the doors, Jones saw that the man was glancing accusingly at a fob watch he'd produced from the left pocket of his shabby beige mackintosh.

The man immediately struck Jones as being a difficult passenger. He tut-tutted loudly as he put away his watch as if to insinuate that the bus was running late. Moreover, his appearance and demeanor gave the overall impression that he fancied himself an eccentric. This did not endear him to Jones, who regarded any person even remotely out of the ordinary as highly suspicious; perhaps even of having come up from London. The passenger wore a black porkpie hat and sported a polka-dotted bow tie. He looked to be in his middle fifties. His thin face was a network of worry lines, as if he had analyzed all the problems of the world and come to no solution for them. His complexion was sallow, like candlewax, particularly around his cheeks. He had a long, aquiline nose, beady little eyes, and a small chin as smooth as a billiard ball.

The passenger began to haul his luggage up into the bus and crammed it in the storage space just in front of the seats on the lefthand side of the aisle. Jones noticed that the two carrier bags were stuffed full of paperback books. They smelled musty with age. When the passenger turned back to collect the wicker basket, which had been left until last, Jones called out in a flash of spiteful inspiration:

"Hurry along there, you're holding up the bus."

The man glared back coolly and then, with an air of studied irony, began to look around him, making it perfectly aware that he knew he was the only passenger boarding at this stop.

"My good fellow," he replied in a wearied tone, "kindly refrain from being objectionable." His was the type of voice passed down by generations of BBC broadcasters until regional accents were finally ushered in.

After he'd paid his fare, the passenger, whose name was Arthur Staines, carried the wicker basket with him to a seat close to the back of the bus. He wanted to be as far away as possible from the oafish driver. From inside the basket there came a long meowing noise and Staines lifted the lid to allow his cat Edgar to examine their surroundings. The creature, a fat and bad-tempered beast with mangy black fur, poked its head out and looked around with evident distaste. The cat lay a paw against the edge of the basket and dug its claws into the side. Staines feared that it might, at any moment, waddle forward and attempt to attack the driver, so he persuaded Edgar to settle down again before it was too late.

Edgar was Staines's sole companion. The two had been together for over ten years. Once the cat had reached maturity it decided not only that it preferred never to be left alone but also that it was no longer prepared to walk anywhere at all. Occasionally it would drag itself from one side of a room to another in order to eat or defecate, but its great bulk now meant that even this concession was haphazard.

Outside the rain lashed across the landscape of rolling fields and hills. Staines gazed absently at the deluge, more interested in the streams of water coursing down the glass of the bus windows than in the vistas cloaked by the low gray clouds. The vehicle crept along narrow roads between towns and along the sides of valleys, throwing up gigantic splashes as it motored through puddles and pools that had formed on the route.

He took a map from the breast pocket of his shabby mackintosh, unfolded it, and spread it out across his knees. His destination was an old fishing village called Scarsdale Bay, not far south from Banwick. Staines had carefully circled the coastal town on the map.

For some time he had been engaged upon research concerned with an obscure author who had made the village his home during his latter years. This writer, Julius Ghorla (1930–1985), had scraped a living writing pulp novels. Staines planned to make Ghorla the exclusive subject of the next installment (the third) of his limited-circulation periodical *Proceedings of the Dead Authors' Society*.

Staines was one of those obsessive bibliophiles who are unable to take any interest in fiction unless its creator had long been in the tomb. Had Ghorla been alive and still writing it is certain that Staines would have thought his work insignificant. Moreover, Staines even ignored prestigious dead authors, reserving his praise for those sufficiently obscure to have escaped critical attention almost altogether. It was as if by championing those writers who had been unfairly overlooked, and who were safely dead, he might thereby obtain for himself some measure of the reputation they had been denied. Vanity had turned him into a ghoul of letters. Ghorla's books had appeared only during the boom in cheap glue-bound paperbacks, never seeing print in hardcover, and issued solely by Eclipse Publications Ltd, an imprint of a disreputable firm whose catalog otherwise consisted of risqué or "spicy" novels.

Staines calculated that it could not be more than a forty-five-minute journey from Crawborough to Scarsdale Bay, despite the tortuous route that this particular local bus service followed. He had traveled all over the country in search of recondite literary discoveries, indulging his own predilections, although he made his actual, meager living from what little freelance journalism he could sell to local newspapers and the likes of specialist glossy monthly magazines such as *Paranormal* and *UFO Times*.

Julius Ghorla had been a favorite writer of his ever since he'd stumbled across a tattered paperback copy of the author's best known (inasmuch as "best known" is applicable) and final work back in 1984. The book was Ghorla's episodic novel *Black Holes*, a series of short stories joined together to form a reasonably lengthy opus of some 50,000 words. These stories were concerned with the interior experiences of the dying brains of several characters. Ghorla had come up with the intriguing idea that consciousness slows down at the point of death to a degree whereby interior time bears no relation to the passage of time in external reality.

Edgar began to meow again. The cat was in a state of agitation and showed his displeasure by rocking back and forth inside his wicker basket. Staines was momentarily at a loss to account for the cause, until he caught a faint whiff of what appeared to be cigarette smoke. He looked up toward the front of the bus and saw a wispy curl of blue tobacco vapor float out of the driver's cabin.

Staines was not especially puritanical when it came to smoking, but the effect it had on Edgar was not to be ignored. He got up from his seat and wandered forward, hoping to catch the driver in the act. However, by the time he was staring through the glass partition at him, there was no trace of the offending cigarette. The driver's window was slightly open and it looked as if he had managed to flick the butt outside moments before Staines's investigation.

"Have you been smoking in here?" Staines said, whilst tapping on the partition.

"What?" he responded, as if he didn't understand the question. There were telltale traces of ash on the sleeve of his uniform.

"I shall report you," Staines continued, "you have greatly upset my cat with your thoughtlessness."

"If you don't get back in your seat and shut up," the driver replied, raising his voice, "I'll throw you and your bloody cat off the bus."

Staines took a quick look at the still-raging downpour outside. It really would not do to have to walk the seven or so miles remaining before they reached Scarsdale Bay, especially in this foul weather. He doubted that Edgar would survive such a trauma. Loud caterwauling emanated from within the wicker basket. Doubtless Edgar wondered where Staines had gone.

At the top of Scarsdale Bay, Staines stepped down from the bus and joined the luggage he'd deposited on the pavement. He heard the driver mutter something obscene as the doors closed.

The rain had eased and was now no more than persistent drizzle. Staines looked back and forth along the deserted lane until he spotted a sign indicating that Scarsdale Bay town center was to his right, down a turning. As yet he could not see his destination but supposed it could only be a few minutes walk downhill. He tied the carrier bags of books around the outside of his suitcase. It had a retractable handle and little wheels at the base so that he could haul it along after him relatively easily. In his other hand he carried the basket containing Edgar. Mercifully the cat seemed to have fallen asleep after the excitement of the bus journey.

Once he'd turned the corner he had his first sight of Scarsdale Bay. It was situated on the side of a steep cliff and he saw a jumbled panorama of red-tiled rooftops and chimney stacks. Cottages jostled one another over the warren of tiny and narrow stairways and lanes. It had doubtless been a haven for smugglers a few centuries ago. Staines made his way down the central street, Ormsley Parade, passing a series of overhanging upper stories, dilapidated arches, and little flights of steps for pedestrians that were designed to break up the extremely steep gradient. Really, thought Staines, this curious little place might have been designed by an admirer of the artist Piranesi. It was certainly a fitting town for Julius Ghorla to have chosen as a retreat in order to pen his outré series of tales.

A sea wall had been erected in the 1950s near the bottom of the village to prevent any more of the fishermen's cottages being washed away by waves during storms. Ormsley Parade wound all the way to the very bottom of the cliff. During high tide the waves lapped halfway up the cobbled and seaweed-coated steps leading to the beach. When the sea was rough Staines could easily imagine that it spilled over the steps and into the Parade in a foaming torrent.

The hotel in which Staines had booked a room loomed large to his left. It was the sole guest house in Scarsdale Bay. Although most of the cottages here were let out to tourists during the summer season, such an expense was beyond his limited means. This hotel, called Shadwell Vistas, was very cheap, especially at this time of year, and he anticipated that he was unlikely to be bothered by any other guests. He paused outside the building, looking up at the timbered mock-Tudor structure with its bull's-eye windows, and then made his way inside to the reception area via a set of paneled double doors.

He crossed a threadbare carpet. The room had a sofa, a few chairs, and some black and white photographs in frames by way of decoration. They depicted scenes of Scarsdale Bay taken during Victorian times. From another room close by he heard a discordant conversation punctuated by bursts of static that sounded as if it were coming from a television set. There was no one manning the reception desk and so Staines rang the bell to signal his presence. A miserable-looking man in his early sixties emerged from a back office. He'd doubtless been engrossed in watching the television that Staines had heard. He was bald with a thin Orwellian mustache, and wore an undone waistcoat with check trousers. Staines noticed that he wasn't wearing any shoes, or even socks.

"Can I help you, Sir?" The man said without enthusiasm.

"I made a reservation by telephone. The name's Arthur Staines."

The man appeared to consult a list that he kept beneath the desk.

"Single room, staying for a week? Nonsmoking?"

"Yes, that's it. Thirty-five pounds a night was the figure I was quoted."

"I have the booking here, Mr. Staines. Quite correct. By the way, I'm Charles Browning, the acting manager here during the off-season. Anything I can do for you please don't hesitate to ask."

Staines signed the register, was told breakfast was served between 7:00 A.M. and 9:00 A.M., and then was given a key with the number seven tagged onto it. Just as he began to climb the stairs with his luggage, the man came around the desk and caught him up. "Forgot to tell you, Mr. Staines," Browning said, "there's a letter here for you. It was delivered yesterday."

Staines looked bewildered. He wasn't expecting any letter. Perhaps it was from a correspondent, one of those who shared his enthusiasm for Julius Ghorla's work, with late information concerning the village. He stuffed the envelope into his pocket, nodded at Browning, and continued up the stairs. When he reached the landing on the first floor he noticed that all the doors had bolts on the outside in addition to the standard locks.

Edgar was peering out of the basket and refused to leave it; he seemed decidedly unhappy about his surroundings. The hotel room was shabby and tiny. The mattress on the bed had been thinned by the weight of hundreds of guests. Staines imagined that someone deranged had chosen the wallpaper; it was a confused jumble of red whorls and spirals on a garish yellow background. He was glad it was so old that the colors had faded. When new it would have driven anyone mad.

He'd unpacked his belongings and now turned his attention to the letter. His name and the address of the hotel had been typed on the envelope, so he had no clue as to the sender. Even the postmark was smudged, so its point of origin could not be determined.

He tore open the envelope and recognized the handwriting at once; a numbing sense of dread rose up from his guts as he read the abrupt missive:

Heard about your good fortune in discovering that Ghorla's hitherto unknown sister is living in Scarsdale Bay. Will join you as quickly as possible. Do nothing until my arrival.

Your friend
Eric

Staines crumpled the letter into a ball and threw it across the room. That blasted Eric Cooper! Always dogging his footsteps! Cooper, like Staines, was obsessed with Julius Ghorla and was conducting his own research into the writer's life and work. By the weekend he, too, would be in Scarsdale Bay, pestering Staines to share what information he had gathered and then taking credit himself for what discoveries were previously made. Well, thought Staines, this particular act of treachery would not succeed. He had the head start and resolved to press his advantage. By tomorrow he was determined to find and interview Ghorla's sister. Moreover, he would warn her in no uncertain terms to have nothing to do with Eric Cooper. By the time his adversary arrived he would be too late.

Edgar purred from his basket. It seemed that he'd finally become accustomed to his surroundings and it was time to feed him his evening meal; three tins of Swedish meatballs in tomato sauce. He opened the cans with the Swiss Army knife that he always carried with him. The cat shied away at first sight of the implement, and became calm only when it was returned to Staines's jacket pocket.

Breakfast at the hotel consisted of a plateful of fried sausages, bacon, mushrooms, eggs, and bread. Staines managed to eat around a quarter of it washed down with greasy tea, and fed the rest to Edgar who was lurking in his basket underneath the table.

The breakfast room was deserted except for Staines. He'd been right in assuming that there would be few, if any, other guests staying at the hotel. Mr. Browning appeared periodically to see whether Staines required anything further. Staines wondered whether the man did all the work in the hotel during the off-season. It seemed plausible.

When Browning returned to take away the crockery and cutlery, Staines asked him whether he knew anything of a "Miss Ghorla" and where she lived. The town was so small and had so few permanent residents that it seemed inconceivable he would not know of her.

"Oh yes." Browning responded to Staines's query with a wry smile, "I know about her. Everyone here does. She's quite a local celebrity."

He said nothing more on the subject, but wrote down her address and directions to the place on a table napkin. Her cottage was located about three-quarters of the way up the cliff in a cul-de-sac.

"One more thing," Staines said, "why the bolts on the outside of the guest-room doors?"

"Oh that," Browning replied, "just a mistake. We never use them. They should have been fitted on the inside. Cowboy locksmiths—you know how it is. We haven't got around to changing them yet."

Within twenty minutes of Staines finishing breakfast he was traversing the labyrinthine series of stairways, raised pavements, and house-to-house archways in search of the cottage. He finally found a cobbled little turning, terminating in a high brick wall, where her home was located.

Staines knocked on the door three times and waited. In one hand he had a carrier-bag of books by her late brother, to prove his credentials as a scholar of his work, and in the other he carried the ubiquitous basket containing his cat. He'd covered the top of the basket with a sheet of plastic so that Edgar didn't get wet. The rain, though less ferocious at times than yesterday, was nevertheless still persistent.

The door finally swung open and the sight of one of the strangest women he had ever seen confronted Staines. The thing that struck him first was the uncanny Ghorla family resemblance. He recalled a photograph he'd once seen of Franz Kafka with his younger sister Ottla; the two might have been identical twins. The case of Julius and Claudia Ghorla was much the same. Yet the appearance of the woman was remarkable in itself; and this was the judgment of a man who prided himself on being regarded by others as an eccentric in his own dress. Claudia Ghorla wore a blond wig with a long fringe, a carefully sculpted coiffure in the 1950s beehive style. She could not have been any younger than seventy years of age. Her face was pinched and withered, and she wore an obscene amount of foundation, rouge, and lipstick. Her blue eyes, almost hooded by false lashes, peered at Staines with contemptuous disinterest. The woman was emaciated. The off-black velvet dress she wore hung from her skeletal body as if displayed on a clothes hanger in the window display of a rundown charity shop.

She looked him up and down.

"I don't want to buy anything," she said in a throaty voice, "now go away you awful little man."

Staines was taken aback at the idea anyone might mistake him for a traveling salesman or hawker of any description.

"Madam," he said, raising the cultivation of his accent several degrees by way of emphasis, "you misunderstand my motives in coming here."

"Nor," she replied, adopting a tone of hauteur even more cutting than her last effort, "do I wish to be bothered by—ugh—journalists."

This second assault was harder to bear, since it possessed an element of truth. Nevertheless Staines tried to shrug it off. He had not come this far to fall at the last. Not with Eric Cooper coming up along the rails close behind him.

Edgar let out a loud meow from inside the basket. He had endured quite enough of being outside in the damp air, alerting Staines to the fact.

"What's that you've got in there?" she said, her expression changing from one of stony hostility to one of interest.

"It's my cat Edgar. I take him with me wherever I go. . . ."

"You drag a poor animal around in this foul weather? Bring him inside where it's dry you wretched man, before you kill the helpless creature!"

Staines had been trying unsuccessfully for over three hours to elicit information from Claudia Ghorla about her brother. The sticklike woman fussed around Edgar, making the cat the center of her attention and practically ignoring whatever questions Staines asked that related directly to the author's life and work. It was as if she'd forgotten all about the existence of her late brother.

Staines sat in an armchair in her small drawing room, sipping at a cup of lukewarm tea. On the carpet were piled the paperback editions of Julius Ghorla's fiction. They failed to arouse any curiosity in her. When advised that Staines was planning a special issue of his little periodical, *Proceedings of the Dead Authors' Society*, in her brother's honor, she'd taken the news with no more than a noncommittal shrug. She was fanatically neutral about it all. He mentioned how unscrupulous his rival, Eric Cooper, could be, but she took the news calmly. Even Staines's claim that Cooper would rifle through drawers and cupboards in search of papers the moment her back was turned was met with nothing more than raised eyebrows.

He'd managed, at least, to convince her that he was not a journalist in search of a story, simply an amateur scholar engaged on private research for a small group of devotees. If he had not achieved this immediate aim he had no doubt that Claudia Ghorla would have taken no notice of him at all, except perhaps to contact the nearest branch of the RSPCA and have him reported for possible cruelty to his cat.

It had finally stopped raining and Staines suggested by way of a diversion that they might take a short walk while the weather was good.

Although Staines was still anxious to turn the subject around to Claudia Ghorla's brother, she persisted, instead, in discussing whatever came into her mind.

They sat upon an old bench overlooking the bay. It commanded a magnificent view of the jumbled house and cottage rooftops, the tangled alleyways and bridges. The turbulent waves crashed up against the sea wall far below. It was high tide now and no trace of the weed-choked beach below could be seen. Behind the bench was the former cemetery, overrun by the expanse of woodland, its boundary walls mere ruins where exposed roots and twisted trunks had pushed their way through. The wind swept up from the bay and whistled past them.

"Quite a pleasant spot. The beauty of nature errm . . . and all that sort of thing," Staines remarked, looking behind and then in front of him, comparing the two aspects of the scene around them. He said it to be polite. Frankly he was very much of the view that the countryside was something green-colored that you traveled across in order to get from one city to another.

"The modern world . . ." Miss Ghorla responded ". . . I find its sentimentality for Nature pathetic. Mother Nature! As if it concerns itself with the welfare of human beings! Or, for that matter, with any other creatures. Nature is an idiot, a mindless force that fumbles across this black planet. And yet the stupid people worship it!"

"It's very inconvenient sometimes. Perhaps a little too wild. . . ." Staines mumbled.

"When Nature acts in a way that is inimical to mankind, then we hear cries that hurricanes, floods, and droughts are somehow unnatural! During one decade society claims we are on the brink of a new ice age, during the next that global warming will finish us all off! All this is the consequence of our worshiping Nature! We think of it as a mother, and cannot bear the idea that it has no regard whatsoever for us. We fret and wail looking for signs of her displeasure, convincing ourselves that we have wronged her, as if she ever cared—or even noticed—our existence in the first place."

"I wonder if your brother shared your . . ." Staines said, before he was cut off yet again.

"Plagues and cancer," she spat, "aren't these too a part of Nature? Yet we do not hesitate to try and eradicate them! Mother Nature is riddled with venereal disease!"

Edgar began to meow from inside the large wicker basket that Staines had put down carefully next to the bench. The cat had also reached through the grill at the front and was clawing at the air in order to catch Staines's attention. The feline appeared to have had enough of Miss Ghorla's theories on mankind's attitude to the natural world.

The whole thing was a dead loss, thought Staines. The woman was useless to him. Let Eric Cooper see what he could do with her. Staines had endured enough of the old crone's nonsense.

"I really must be getting back to my hotel," he said. "They serve dinner at six and I'm famished."

"For a journalist, you've been quite entertaining," she replied. "Here, take this. Look it over and I'll visit you this evening at your hotel around nine, once you've eaten. We can talk privately about my brother's theories then. Perhaps even try some of them out in practice."

The old lady took a loose-leaf notebook from her handbag and passed it to the astonished Staines. He rifled through it as she got up, spoke a few more words, and then turned away to vanish into the warren of streets below them.

"I've underlined some passages for your convenience that I think you'll find of particular interest."

The notes related to Julius Ghorla's episodic novel, *Black Holes*.

Long after Claudia Ghorla had departed, Staines could still be found sitting on the bench. He was poring over the notebook in a state of total fascination. It was only once it had got dark and become difficult to read that he noticed night had come. Edgar had fallen asleep; he'd given up trying to attract Staines's attention. Luckily the advent of a rising moon provided Staines with sufficient light to carry on reading the handwritten text without interruption. This might be his only chance to do so. The old lady was capricious and could well change her mind about providing him with further information later on.

Staines was surprised to find that Claudia Ghorla had added the following entries of her own toward the end of the notebook, having scored out her brother's own pages with a black marker pen.

12th July 1985

Well, it's done. Last night I followed the instructions left by my late brother and drilled a hole in the front of my skull. It was an incredibly messy business. I really had no idea that there would be so much blood. The thick strip of bandage that I had wrapped around my head (just above my eyebrows) was soon soaked lipstick red.

I had to cover the carpet in the bathroom with plastic sheeting. Mirrors were placed at precisely the correct angles around my head so that I could see the progress of the operation clearly. An injection of 2ccs of lidocaine in my forehead served as an anesthetic. I cut a V-shaped flap of skin, drew it back to expose the skull beneath, and proceeded to drill through bone and marrow. The noise and the vibration were terrible. The drilling went on for an hour. Often I had to stop in order to wash away the blood running down my face and into my eyes. I felt as if my head would split apart before I reached the surface of the brain and finally created the socket for my Third Eye.

I knew the consequences of the operation going wrong; possible brain damage causing paralysis, idiocy, or blindness. But I had sworn to carry out my brother's last wishes. Even though his attempt to do the same thing had ended in his destruction.

My thighs are dotted with cigarette burns. Often, when I am smoking, I turn up my skirt and press the burning tip of my cigarette onto the cold white flesh there. The pain temporarily distracts me from the mental anguish I feel at my own helplessness. I am setting down this cheap autobiographical episode to prove to myself that any good liar can write convincingly. Now to await the changes that Julius predicted.

14th July 1985
What I still saw was the same thin, not unattractive woman with silvery, shoulder-length hair: a female version of my dead brother. Her body is almost emaciated and possessed of an awkward gait. Her skin is pale and unblemished, and her cheekbones elegantly distinct. Perhaps the lips are a trifle too thin, but the perfect regularity of the tiny teeth that they reveal more than makes up for any slight imperfection. Curved eyebrows arch above dazzling, glacial blue eyes.

This morning that face is almost the same, except for the ugly, sutured wound in the middle of my forehead. I am somewhat afraid of what lies beneath that stitched flap of skin. And of what it will be able to see if I remove that freshly made eyelid.

20th July 1985
Summertime in England: warm rain and leaden skies. A seaside town in the middle of July. Mercifully it is off the tourist routes and has nothing that would attract a holidaymaker. The beach is all shingles and pebbles, not sand, and miles from the nearest railway station or main road. The people here are unspeakably ordinary, and they blur into the background of the gray cliffs and the North Sea. There are no churches, piers, ancient monuments, or amusement arcades.

In the afternoon I walked along the beach in the uncomfortable humidity. I wore my green silk headscarf to cover the V-shaped wound, and a half-length mackintosh. I expect that I should have also taken an umbrella. The skies, as usual, threatened rain. Despite the rubber grip of my plimsolls I once or twice slipped on the stones underfoot. They were still slippery, for the tide had only just turned, leaving foam and kelp in its wake. Mother often told me that my feet were too small in relation to my height, so it was scarcely surprising that I was destined to stumble through life (metaphorically as well as literally) rather than advance boldly.

I wanted to find a deserted spot someway outside the town where the sea spray crashed up across the rocks, where I could be alone. Then and only then would I unveil my new Third Eye, gaze out across the ocean and see as I had never seen before.

Doubtless I must have been an odd sight to any observer; a grinning middle-aged woman with thin limbs, scrambling wildly along the shoreline. The fact is that I did not care. I was in the grip of a wild exultation. Part of me was unsure whether I was simply overcome with a sense of relief at having survived operating on myself.

There was a natural ledge set in the cliff face ahead of me. It was easily reached by clambering over some boulders and proved to be the perfect vantage point. I settled down on the rough surface, using my raincoat as a cushion on which to sit. I fairly tore the headscarf off me and my fingers worked on the sutures. I cut them away with tiny scissors and eagerly unpicked the strands with my long painted fingernails. Then I pulled back the V-shaped flap of skin. As I did so I closed my old eyes in order to see the world purely through my new one.

The light was so intense, so white, and yet so cold, that I screamed with shock. It seemed that the surface of my brain was freezing over.

A moment before, the sea was a foaming expanse of gently rolling waves. The next it was a solid white mass of ice stretching to the horizon, like that of the Arctic wastes or the surface of some frozen moon at the edge of the solar system. I now opened my old eyes too but my overall sight remained unaffected as if, with the dominant contribution of my Third Eye to the other two, I saw a new dimension for the first time. Only when I covered my forehead with my palm did the sea again become liquid and its waves break upon the shore beneath me.

And the sky! Before it had been dull, cloaked with low gray clouds, oppressive, and trapping the sticky heat beneath its leaden folds. Now it was crystalline blue, clear and vivid, a sheen of gaseous frost beneath abysmal outer space. Starlight shone straight through the chill and thin atmosphere, even now in the daytime.

Far away, at the limit of my vision, there was a great wall of ice. It looked like a frozen continent visible at the horizon's edge. Was it just my imagination or did it advance closer, albeit almost imperceptibly, as I gazed across the expanse separating it from the shoreline? Its motion was like that of the minute hand of a clock; so gradual that it exists on the borderland of optical illusion and reality.

I pulled down the V-shaped flap of skin, closing my Third Eye, and covering the self-inflicted wound from view with my headscarf. The world was no longer encased in ice. It was once again a typical miserable English summer's day. But I could feel the presence of my Third Eye in the socket I had created. The orb turned and rolled wildly beneath the thin layer of flesh on my forehead that covered it.

It was suddenly vital that I return to my dwelling and gather together my thoughts. They were racing through my brain with such rapidity as to be maddening. Ideas jostled for precedence in my mind, but I could scarcely make sense of them. They were haphazard and dreamlike, beyond the scope of my ability to render into words. These concepts were more like patterns or designs than a linear sequence of fictional events. In one of these flashes of inspiration I had the notion I might delineate the horror of an ice crystal in the decay of its symmetry or participate in the madness of a reflection produced by a shattered mirror.

Snowflakes continuously dance around me, like the static between TV channels. This is the beginning of a new Ice Age.

The dying sun casts shadows across the frozen beach as it sets behind the seafront trees and buildings. The ice is streaked with darkness. I think of the reflection of my own face I'd once seen in a shop window: an empty shell of a face, like that of a mannequin left out in the rain, cheap mascara dribbling from its lifeless eyes.

My Third Eye is invariably uncovered. I wonder if my two original eyes might atrophy in response to the dominance of my third eye. Perhaps they will begin to wither away, dissolving in the sockets, like mollusks that have had salt sprinkled on them. Eyes are the windows of the soul, but the Third Eye is a doorway, through which my brother's thoughts come and go. It is his eye. It is green—mine are both blue. What other physical features possessed by Julius might transfer to me?

Staines looked up from the notes resting on his lap. He felt a sense of dull sickness in the pit of his stomach. The old woman must have gone mad immediately after the death of her brother. Their relationship seemed to have been abnormal, possibly even incestuous. He wondered if they'd made some bizarre suicide pact that Claudia had failed to honor.

The sea rolled back and forth in the near distance beyond the muddle of moon-drenched rooftops. Above the waves, across the night sky, thousands of stars stood out in the blackness. He wondered if he might see one of them suddenly blink out of existence as he watched, collapsing in itself like one of the dying minds Ghorla had described. He had no idea how long stars took to perish but suspected that their life span dwarfed that of a man's into insignificance. The thought of time reminded him that he'd no idea how late it was now and he took his fob watch out of his mackintosh pocket. It was eight-thirty precisely.

He'd missed dinner at the hotel and realized he'd have to make a meal of Swedish meatballs from a can. But if it was good enough for Edgar it was good enough for him too. He picked up the basket (containing the still-slumbering cat) plus his bag of paperbacks and hurriedly made his way to the hotel through the crazily angled passageways of Scarsdale Bay. He didn't wish to be late for his appointment with Claudia Ghorla at 9:00 P.M.

Only upon opening the basket when back in the hotel room did Staines discover that Edgar was dead. The cat was curled up; its body rigid and cold, its eyes open and staring sightlessly up at him. He couldn't bear to remove the dead animal and sat down on the edge of the bed, trying to decide just what to do next. Eventually, Staines resolved to go downstairs into the hotel's lounge bar and drink himself into a stupor. He could deal with the disposal of Edgar's body in the morning. He had quite forgotten about his appointment with Miss Ghorla.

Just then someone knocked at the door to Staines's room. He opened the door and standing on the threshold was Miss Ghorla. She was clad in a ratty blouse and skirt. Her face was solemn and, at this precise moment, she was the very last person Staines wanted to see. He was incapable of questioning her closely or paying much attention to her responses even should they reveal some insights into the life and work of her brother.

"Mr. Browning directed me to your room," she said. "I thought it best if we talked in private rather than downstairs where we might be overheard."

"I'm sorry, Miss Ghorla, but I've had a shock, it's my cat you see . . ." Waving aside his faltering objections the old lady wandered into the room and cast a glance over at the basket containing Edgar's corpse.

"I warned you to take better care of that poor creature," she said in a low menacing voice.

Staines felt a wave of annoyance rising up inside him at the sheer bloody cheek and lack of tact that the woman displayed. He was about to let loose with a stream of abuse when he noticed a trickle of blood making its way down the center of her forehead from her beehive wig.

"I think you must have hit your head. . . ." Staines said.

She ignored his remark and picked up the notebook jointly written by her and Julius that Staines had left on the bed.

"Well," she said, "now you know some of it. But not, as yet, of the process akin to hypnosis whereby a mind in a healthy body might also be induced to collapse in on itself . . . but I can show you. I've sometimes wondered whether transfer between radically dissimilar genetic material is possible."

Another trickle of blood ran down her forehead and around her nose, dribbling along her right, foundation-caked cheek. She raised an attenuated, veined hand and dipped her long fingers into the coiled mass of hair covering her forehead, unpicked some sutures, and parted her fringe.

Eric Cooper set down his carpetbag in front of the reception desk in the Shadwell Vistas Hotel. He rang the bell in order to attract someone's attention. Eventually the temporary manager saw fit to drag himself away from the static between channels that he'd been watching on television in the back room and attend to the visitor.

"Do you require a room, Sir?" Browning said. "We've plenty available."

Eric Cooper looked around disdainfully at the sorry-looking foyer and curled his lip at the thought. After he'd caught up with Staines he intended to have a wash and brush up at the luxury cottage (with full mod-cons) that was to be his base during his visit to Scarsdale Bay. It might suit Staines to stay here in this godforsaken flea pit, but not Cooper.

"No," he said, "I believe a friend—ah—colleague of mine is a guest here. His name's Arthur Staines. I want to surprise him. Can you show me up to his room?"

Browning smiled at the well-dressed visitor. Cooper was a tall man with round eyeglasses, immaculately dressed in a navy double-breasted pinstripe suit with a striped tie done up in a Windsor knot. The only blemish in his appearance was an ill-fitting wig that was a slightly different shade of gray-brown to the natural hair left on his head.

"Very popular tonight," said Browning, "is our Mr. Staines. He's with a lady friend at this moment, one of our local celebrities."

"What?" Cooper responded. He had a sinking feeling of dread at what might be coming next.

"Yes, Miss Ghorla. She went upstairs to see him about a half hour ago." Cooper passed a ten-pound note across the desk.

"Can you show me up straightaway? I'd like to see them both if it's possible. Presumably you have a passkey."

If I can gain the element of surprise, thought Cooper, all might not yet be lost. Were he to arrive unannounced he might interrupt some conversation of import relating to Julius Ghorla that he might otherwise not hear.

Browning covered the bank note with the palm of his hand, slid it toward himself and nodded.

"Right away, Sir. Please follow me. It's only on the first floor, not far." When the two arrived at the door to Staines's room, Browning knocked once perfunctorily and immediately unlocked it. He let Cooper enter by stepping aside and discreetly moving back just outside the doorway.

The shabby little room was in semidarkness. Moreover, it was like walking into a huge freezer. The temperature within was some twenty or so degrees below zero. Cooper saw a dingy bed that looked fit only for the rubbish dump and was appalled by the sight of the most garish wallpaper he'd seen since the mid-1970s. It could even have been an authentic relic from that era. Then his attention was drawn to an armchair in the corner of the room, back amongst the shadows. A peculiar gurgling noise came from its occupant. At first Cooper thought it was a life-size dummy dressed in charity clothes, something left over from a stage show.

But he realized it was actually a very old woman—or something much like one. For although it was clad in a blouse and skirt, the skirt was pulled back over its withered navel, its stockings and knickers were around its ankles, and it was stubbing out a cigarette on a burn-dotted left thigh. Just above the score of burns rested a flaccid penis. Its beehive wig was askew and in the center of its forehead was a bloody third eye that stared unblinkingly.

Just before Cooper backed away in shock, a hitherto unseen figure crept out from around the side of the bed. It was Arthur Staines and the demented man was crawling on all fours like an animal, his breath like steam in the frigid air. A grotesque mewing bubbled in his throat.

"Did the bad man hurt poor kitty? Now all's well, now all's made well again," said the croaking voice of the figure in the chair.

Cooper took a long backwards stride in the direction of the door behind him, but Mr. Browning had already taken the opportunity to quietly close it and draw shut the bolt on the outside.

"We don't like to see Miss Ghorla distressed, Sir," said Browning, through the paneling, "so if you'd be kind enough to accommodate her it would be easier all round. It's only what we've all had to get used to, here in Scarsdale Bay."

Face

JOYCE CAROL OATES

Joyce Carol Oates is one of the most prolific and respected writers in the United States today. Oates has written fiction in almost every genre and medium. Her keen interest in the Gothic and in psychological horror has spurred her to write dark suspense novels under the name Rosamond Smith, to have written enough stories in the genre to have published five collections of dark fiction, the most recent, The Female of the Species: Tales of Mystery and Suspense, *and to edit* American Gothic Tales. *Oates's short novel,* Zombie, *won the Bram Stoker Award, and she has been honored with a Life Achievement Award given by the Horror Writers Association.*

Her most recent novels are The Stolen Heart, Missing Mom, *and* Blood Mask. *Oates has been living in Princeton, New Jersey, since 1978, where she teaches creative writing. She and her husband, Raymond J. Smith, run the small press and literary magazine* Ontario Review.

S tay away from her, they said. Don't even look at her. Don't let her see *you*.

She was one hundred years old. Nobody could remember a time when she'd been younger. She had a thing growing out of her neck, swollen like a goiter and the bright color of a rooster's erect comb. Stay away from her and don't let her see *you*. But the children hid in the tall marsh grasses beside the lane to spy on her, excited and frightened, and they could hear the old woman speaking to herself in a language they couldn't comprehend; maybe it was no language at all only just rapid muttered sounds punctuated by laughter, quarreling; you could see the thing pushing out of her neck, tight smooth shiny hot-looking skin of a texture different from her own raddled skin, like a balloon blown tight to bursting. It was the beginning of a face, maybe. Didn't it have tiny indentations where the eyes would be, a hollow for the nose, a tiny pit of a mouth? First they'd seen it was the size of a peach, then the size of an apple, then the size of a melon forcing the old woman's head to one side like she was laying her head on her shoulder.

Her back was twisted, too. Her spine you could almost see through her dirt-stiffened clothes, like a bow. When she walked it was a crab-scuttling, you could hear her harsh quickened breathing.

Through the mud puddles in the lane the children rode their bicycles, through the ragged corn fields the children ran, and in the straggly lilac that grew wild amid the ruins of the old cider mill they hid to peer at the old woman as the old woman passed by, and sometimes they dared to approach the old woman's house that was a falling-down unpainted farmhouse at the end of the lane and they tried to look through the windows (but they could not, the blinds were always pulled down); and they stole tomatoes from the old woman's weed-choked garden, and ate them unwashed, seeds and juice running down their chins; and sometimes they threw the tomatoes at one another shrieking with laughter. For the hell of it the boys trampled down the old woman's pole beans, tore at the blue morning glories growing in the fence, and the pink sweetpeas; they threw dried clumps of mud at the squawking red chickens and the rat-tailed barn cats that hissed and bared their teeth. The old woman stumbled from the rear door of the house screaming at them, swearing at them, Get away! Get away! Damn devils get away! The old woman ran at them with a broom, a mop, an ax propped against the side of the house, threatened to call the sheriff, have them all put in jail, in hell, damn devils where they belonged was hell.

If the shotgun wasn't broke, the old woman said, she'd blow them to hell.

The old woman lived in that house by herself, there'd been an old man who had died before any of the children could remember, except maybe the oldest could remember: a siren in the night, the sheriff's car with its flashing red light like summer lightning wild and flashing through the darkened windows of the children's house, and afterward the deputies asking questions of their parents, people talking of it for a long time: *Why? Why'd he do it?* The children were not supposed to know, the old man had killed himself with his own shotgun, which was a twelve-gauge double-barrel like all the men had; he'd blown most of his head off with the buckshot blast but it had been an accident, the old woman claimed, he hadn't mean it, hadn't been drinking or anyway had not been drinking much, only just hard cider not whiskey; he'd been trying to clean the gun that wasn't firing right, needed oiling and polishing and there'd been a time, the old woman said, he'd just been back from the War and built this house and barns and he'd took such pride in his guns, the shotgun and a twenty-two Springfield rifle, but lately he'd been letting things go, had not been well, his broke hip, his broke ankle from the damn horse kicking him, and that sickness he had he'd thought was t.b. but only just bron-ki-tis kept him coughing and sick for a year, so he'd gotten tired and careless at the end, mean and foul-mouthed, yelling at the neighbors to get off his property when it wasn't his property where they were—like the Quick family's back pasture where the fences were falling down—the old man prowled the fields, his neighbors' back lanes, close up behind their barns, his beard not trimmed like it used to be but a rat's nest and stained around the mouth and his old coveralls stiff with dirt and carelessly buttoned or not buttoned at all; nobody wanted to accuse the old man of stealing from them, but sure he'd walk off with things where he found them if no one was around—hand saw, paint bucket, wheelbarrel left in the Pinchbecks' pear orchard. Years ago when the children's parents were just children themselves the old man had gotten into a feud with one of his neighbors and some time later the neighbor's barn burned down. But it was never proved against him.

One of their boys died of a burst appendix aged eleven, because the old man hadn't wanted to call for a doctor, hadn't wanted to pay. It was his pride, too, they didn't have a telephone and he'd have had to ask a neighbor to call for him and God damn he wouldn't lower himself to begging, nor would he let the old woman go begging either, the kid had a stomach ache that was all, some kind of flu you'd expect to pass away except it wasn't flu but appendicitis so Calvin died. The children's parents said afterward they'd have paid for the doctor for God's sake letting a child die like that, worse than murder. The other children in that house were two boys and a girl and they'd been older and they moved away and no one knew where they were or even if they were still alive, it wasn't a question you could ask of the old woman for no one spoke to the old woman, not for years.

She was in the habit of prowling the roads early in the morning, looking for things in the county dump, clothes mostly, though the clothes she wore were always the same—men's coveralls, men's work pants, bulky sweaters, in wet weather work boots and in the summer sneakers with rubber soles. She wore an old windbreaker that had belonged to her husband, she wore his old wool-knit cap. Hadn't given herself a bath in years, people said. Hadn't washed her hair that had to be running with lice, so matted, greasy, in gummy clumps. But sometimes at the county dump the old woman would find plastic flowers, or a cloth flower, or ribbons like from Christmas wrappings, and she'd wear these for a while with the coveralls until they fell off and you'd find them in the lane, in a mud puddle, or in the dirt.

One day when the girl was nine years old she was riding her bicycle in the lane when the old woman approached. The old woman was walking with a cane, wearing the filthy windbreaker though it wasn't a cold day, coveralls and rubber boots and a bright pink silky scarf around her head she must have found at the dump. When the old woman spoke to her, the girl was too po-lite and too frightened to bicycle away, and it was a surprise to the girl, the old woman didn't shout at her, or swear at her, but was asking her questions she couldn't comprehend, for instance was she Beth Dorr's little girl?—when Beth Dorr was the girl's grandmother, so the old woman was mixing her up with her own mother, and this made the girl laugh nervously wishing to think it was a joke. The old woman's eyes were yellow-white and watery as if with mucus, the girl could see tiny red threads, worm-like veins in the eyes, the face was so old and creased and withered it looked as if the bones were trying to poke through; she'd taken care to cover up the goiter-growth on her neck but as she talked to the girl, shaking her head, shaking the cane, from time to time laughing, as if with mounting anger, the bright pink scarf worked loose and the thing was exposed—shiny and red-skinned like tumor, or a bladder, something you weren't supposed to see or even know about, it was so nasty. And the girl remembered being told *Stay away from her. Don't even look at her. Don't let her look at you.* But the girl was afraid to run away. She would have to leave her bicycle in the lane, she was too clumsy to ride

while the old woman was watching her. The old woman was asking her questions and she was saying, I don't know, I don't know; her voice was a shy
stammer, she was itchy-hot inside her clothes, she was miserable and frightened of the thing growing out of the old woman's neck, not wanting to see
it but unable to look away. The thing was so much smoother than the old
woman's face, it had grown to the size of a small melon and so it was forcing
the old woman's head to one side, which was why she walked off-balance, in
that crab-scuttle way. It had not any marks for a face, that the girl could see.
The old woman saw where the girl was looking and made an angry hissing
sound Shhhh! like scolding a cat and bared her stained and cracked teeth in a
nasty smile, You're not a pretty girl, you will have a hard time, like me. The
eyelid over one of the red-veined eyes dropped and winked and the girl felt
faint, for all this while she'd been smelling the old woman's stink, that had
worked its way up her nostrils and into her brain.

The old woman died that winter, back in the falling-down farmhouse where
no one ever visited, and it was said that the county coroner found part of a
tortoise-shell comb grown into her scalp inside the matted gummy gray hair
and that her scalp was reddened and swollen with hundreds of insect bites
and that her shriveled and wasted body was covered in insect bites beneath a
patina of grime. It was said that the thing on the side of her neck had grown
so big it was like a second head, it had tiny eyes like a fish's eyes beginning to
poke through the skin, tiny holes for nostrils, a small moist mouth the size of
a cherry pit. The old woman had died in her filthy bed and had lain there for
more than two weeks by the time anyone found her, but the thing on her
neck was still alive, quivering, pulsing, warm, making a low squeaking noise
like it was begging to be cut loose from the corpse so that it could have its
own life. Whether they killed it then or it died at some later time was not
clear. The girl never told anyone about the day the old woman had stopped
her in the lane, but for a long time she dreamt of the old woman, her nostrils
pinched with the stink, compulsively she touched her hair dreading to feel
that it had become matted and gummy; she had only to shut her eyes to see
the face pushing out beside the old woman's face, the tiny unblinking eyes,
and now, nearly fifty years later and hundreds of miles from her childhood
home, she finds herself unconsciously stroking her neck, seeing in the glassy
surface of the computer screen at which she is working, when dusk enters the
room and she hasn't yet switched on a light, the face reflected there; it is not
a face she knows except it is her face, and her fingernails scratch at the itchy
skin, the flaming welt, this sinewy growth on her neck, at the very base of her
neck at her shoulder bone, hidden by her collar, throbbing with furious heat.

An Apiary of White Bees

LEE THOMAS

Lee Thomas is the author of dozens of stories and nonfiction articles. In addition to magazines and new media, his fiction has appeared in the anthologies A Walk on the Darkside *and* The Book of Final Flesh.

His first novel, Stained, *won the Bram Stoker Award. He is also the author of the critically acclaimed novella,* Parish Damned, *and the novels* Damage *and* The Dust of Wonderland. *His short fiction is collected in* In the Closet, Under the Bed, *forthcoming from Haworth Press in early 2008.*

Writing as Thomas Pendleton, he is the coauthor (with Stefan Petrucha) of Wicked Dead, *a series of edgy teen horror novels from HarperCollins. His novel* Mason, *also under the Pendleton name, is forthcoming from HarperCollins.*

Thomas currently lives in Austin, Texas, where he's working on a number of projects.

Oliver Bennett walked across the lobby of the Cortland Hotel, nodding to his employees and guests. The floor, a lake of travertine marble, swirling with veins of cream- and beige-colored stone, absorbed the dull light of a stormy afternoon. Behind the concierge desk and sitting area, French doors ran the length of the west wall; their white slats parceled the concrete promenade, the grounds, and the cloud-veiled mountain range beyond the glass into a precise grid.

Oliver didn't care much for the Cortland. It was a landmark, decorated with extravagance and taste, but without a single concession to warmth. His wife Amanda wanted it, so he bought it, and they lived here because she wanted that too, but it was hardly a home. A home should be filled with personal belongings and intimate, happy memories. And at least one person in that place should love you.

The Cortland was an adequate shelter, Oliver supposed, pausing at the French doors, clasping a chilled silver handle in his palm. He looked over his shoulder at the lobby, observed the patrons, dressed in elegant wools, silks, and fur, moving gracefully amid the stiff-backed employees in their crisp black uniforms. Above, a Lalique chandelier hung like an immense pellucid beehive.

Oliver never noticed the similarity of shape before. The swollen center. The tapered extremes. *It really is a beautiful fixture*, he thought.

Outside on the veranda, he zipped his jacket against the chill and looked north over the lawn toward the swimming pool, now covered in a sky blue tarp. The swimming season ended over a month ago, making the destruction around the pool less of an inconvenience, though no less of an eyesore.

The earth beyond the broken pool was wounded and raw. Ridges of dirt rose in a ring behind a run of yellow warning tape. A bulldozer squatted on the lawn. Oliver checked over his shoulder to make sure that Amanda wasn't watching him—a reflex only. His wife never watched him, never followed. He knew she couldn't be bothered to keep track of a man she felt, on kinder days, was simply an obstacle on the way to a bank account. That didn't stop her from complaining about his behavior, however. If she caught him lighting up, she would use it as an excuse to berate him for the rest of the day. But since she was nowhere to be seen, Oliver pulled a pack of cigarettes from his jacket and lit one. With his lungs warmed by the smoke, he crossed the lawn toward the hole in his property and the wonderful thing it held.

Two weeks ago, while digging a trench in an attempt to repair the pool's broken plumbing, a work crew was interrupted by the discovery of a brick barrier. As the excavation continued, the barrier revealed itself to be a wall—one of four creating a vault buried deep in the ground. Oliver was there that day, standing on the lip of the gouged earth when the door was revealed. His anticipation of its opening had been wonderful, the only good thing he'd felt in years.

Despite the protests of Joe Hopkins, the crew's foreman, Oliver insisted on being among the first group of men to examine the contents of the strange brick building. After all, it was unearthed on Oliver's property. It was his, and he had every right to be part of the discovery.

And what a find it was. Inside were crates of alcohol, stacked floor to ceiling. Narrow passages cut between them, so that Oliver, Hopkins, and two of his workmen could navigate the length and depth of the chamber.

They must have hidden it here during prohibition, Hopkins said.

And nobody remembered it was here?

Apparently not.

Amazing.

Oliver stepped forward, out of the memory, and drew deeply on his cigarette. He ducked under the cordon of warning tape and stepped over the thick cable feeding electricity to the lights Hopkins had strung in the vault. He looked into the hole. Scabs of dirt marred the brick wall and filled the creases in the door's planks.

Though he knew this was his property, and he had every right to be here, Oliver hesitated before stepping onto the steep grade that would take him down to the door. He wasn't doing anything wrong, but he felt wrong, and the sensation brought a distant memory, which made the afternoon chill several degrees colder.

I want to show you something.

Where are we going, Kyle?

Come on. It's okay. Your dad showed me this.

Oliver drew away from the hole, just one step, a minor concession to fear. Then he thought, *No, this is mine.* He dropped his cigarette on a mound of upturned sod and walked toward the door.

Square-faced lights glowed high on the walls, catching the grain of the crates in their cast. Walking through the narrow paths, Oliver imagined he looked much like a giant passing through a city of wooden skyscrapers. The air was thick with dust and the scent of rotted pine and oak. He paused and read the labels stenciled on the sides of the crates; some were still legible, others had faded to little more than stains. Of course, the names meant little to him. He had neither the mind nor the tongue of a connoisseur. Still, he wondered what these aged liquors might taste like after so long. Was time generous, giving the spirits some special properties, or had it sapped them of essence as it did so many other things?

He searched, looking for some indication on the wall of crates for the case that most deserved his attention. Among the labels he could read, he found some self-explanatory—*Gin*, *Scotch Whiskey*, *Bordeaux*, and *English Rum*—and others told him nothing—*Belle of Anderson*, *Crown Prince*, and *Old Cabin Still*.

The more he explored, the more intriguing he found the vault, and Oliver believed he was working out a pattern in the room's organization. The pedestrian liquors—the whiskeys, the gins and rums—were at the front, while the middle of the room was filled with more exotic beverages—brandies, liqueurs, and aperitifs. Further back, deeper in the maze of crates, the wines took hold. When he reached the back wall, he recognized the Dom Pérignon crest on two stacks, though the letters were ghosted to indecipherability. Finally, he came to two crates set aside in a corner, not touching any of the other containers. These made him all the more curious for their total lack of identification.

Every other box in the chamber carried some blemish of ink, but not these. To Oliver's mind, this was the trove he sought—its value corroborated by its anonymity. Using the knife on his key ring, he pried the lid. Aged wood and nails whined against his efforts. The edge he worked splintered. He dug in again and cracked the wood enough to glimpse the contents.

The bottles appeared yellow, but it was too gloomy to tell. They were uniquely shaped—six-sided and nestled together like glass honeycombs. Each bottle was capped in wax that ran in clumped rivulets down the neck. They would do fine, he decided, and set to completing the task of opening the crate's lid.

Once the boards were torn back, he gazed inside. The case was designed to hold eight of the hexagonal bottles—three to a side, nestling two in the middle. But the two central bottles were missing, and a profound disappointment settled on him. Though, certainly, the culprit had absconded with the bottles nearly three-quarters of a century ago, he couldn't help but feel somehow violated.

Oliver carried a bottle of the mysterious liquor to the front of the vault and sat on a crate. He scraped the wax away with his knife, then brushed cream-colored flakes from the thighs of his trousers. Beneath this, a simple cork sealed the bottle, and it pulled free easily. He sniffed, and a sweet yet bitter odor climbed into his nose. Oliver swirled the liquid around in the bottle, and yes, the glass was yellow. Then, he drank. The liqueur cooled his throat instead of burning like so many spirits burned; it numbed his tongue, his stomach, his muscles.

He prepared himself to feel sick, perhaps poisoned, but the drink enlivened his system. Taking another sip, he leaned back on the crate and observed the vault and found it much to his liking.

Unlike Amanda, Oliver didn't need everything in his world to be polished and precious. Whenever he could sneak away for a week or two on his own, earthier places beckoned him. Dockside bars where the men and women were calloused and broken; musk-reeking video arcades with black-walled mazes, leading from one erotic shadow to the next; sweating alleys, running like veins through terminal neighborhoods—these were his places. They tarnished the silver of him and the secret of their visiting made him feel alive.

Where are you taking me, Kyle?

It's a special place. A secret.

Lifting the bottle to his lips again, Oliver closed his eyes. The childhood recollection was back, and instead of fighting it, he entertained the memory, remembering a fine young man that he once admired, even worshiped.

Kyle was the son of the gardener who kept the grounds of the Bennett Estate. Two years Oliver's senior, Kyle was strong and tanned and confident, with a mop of blond hair and sinewy arms corded with veins. He was everything that Oliver was not, and as a boy, Oliver spent hours at windows or pretending to read by the pool to watch his hero work in the yard.

Succumbing to intoxication, Oliver remembered one day in particular. He was twelve years old and following his hero through the wooded area running at the back of his father's estate. Kyle's back muscles flexed as the boy pushed aside tree branches and leafy shrubs, leading Oliver away from the house. After hiking across the property, Kyle stopped at a large shed and opened the door.

Come on. It's okay. Your dad showed me this.

A ringing came up in Oliver's head. The sound grew shrill and then flattened out into a massaging resonance. With the monotonous hum buzzing behind his eyes, the memory skipped, turned sharp and painful.

Kyle was angry with him, shouting. Oliver ran away, confused and hurt and needing to be in his comfortable, familiar room. Desperate to be there. Panicked. He raced through the shrubs and low tree branches. Then he tripped on a root. Fell.

A thousand bees surrounded Oliver's head. The world shattered into a dozen dislocated images, stacked in a trembling array before his eyes, and the horrible words, words spat at him by the gardener's son, took on the drone of the swarming bees, grinding terrible accusations into his brain.

Oliver opened his eyes and waved a hand in the air to rid himself of the daydream bees. He couldn't remember why he was running, couldn't recall why Kyle was so angry with him when Oliver did nothing more or less than what his hero asked, but he remembered running. In his panic he'd tripped and fallen, crashing through a low-hanging beehive.

Over thirty years had been lived and worn since that afternoon, but now, in this place he felt where each of those vicious creatures had stung him. A spot just below his left ear sang a particular ache now.

Despite the chill in the shadowed chamber, Oliver was sweating, and his breath hitched rapidly. The memories he indulged fueled an irrational yet intense erotic response in him, an aching heat that demanded release. Oliver put the bottle down on the crate beside him. He went to the thick wooden door and pushed it closed, cutting off the gray afternoon light. With his back to the door, he unsnapped his pants and stepped out wide to keep them from dropping to the dirty concrete.

He felt like a boy again, locked in his bedroom, his bathroom, a small wooden shack. The stinging at his neck aroused like a kiss, and the hive in his mind dove, tracing along the back of his throat, abrading his esophagus and gathering in his belly before working further into his system and down. The palm on his cock felt rougher than his own, more experienced. The shaft filling his hand was unfamiliar; it was too thick, too ridged with veins.

He squeezed his eyes closed to more perfectly feel the sensations.

The hive in his groin crawled frantically, seeking some means of escape. He inhaled and the bouquet of the liquor, the honeyed bitter scent, filled his head and triggered a painful yet perfect climax.

The thrumming ache of the fleeing swarm tore through his shaft as the imagined bees escaped into the black room. His ragged breath coaxed them out; tears wet his eyes.

In his ear, a single insect buzzed. A moment later, sharp pain flared on his cheek. He made a sound—almost a chuckle, more nearly a pant. Oliver's eyes sprang open. Before them, tiny pale dots like those following a particularly bright camera flash, dotted the gloomy air. He touched the wound on his cheek, already feeling the welt of a sting rising there. Covering this blossoming bump was a bit of fluid, thick and sticky to the touch. He searched his clothing and the floor for the body of the attacking bee, but found nothing. When he returned his attention to the vault's gloom, the pale dots were gone.

He shook his head in wonderment. Then, Oliver pulled the handkerchief from his pocket.

Go wash your hands, boy.

In the suite he shared with his wife, Oliver stared at the red welt just below his right eye and wondered on the coincidence that he should have been thinking about bees moments before being stung. The notion amused him. Indeed, he felt so good that he didn't care about the sour looks Amanda cast at him, as she dressed for dinner.

"What did you do to your face?" she asked, suddenly beside him at the mirror. She held a diamond teardrop to her ear and jiggled it to catch the light.

"Bee sting."

"There are no bees this time of year," Amanda said, dismissing his claim outright. She shoved against him to get a better look at herself, and Oliver walked away.

"Let's just hope that thing heals before Friday," she said.

"Friday?" he asked.

"Idiot," Amanda whispered just loud enough for Oliver to hear. "We're celebrating our find. I'm expecting everyone to attend. It'll be the usual crowd, and some new faces. I've invited that Joe Hopkins because he found the place, and I want the auction director to attend."

"What auction?"

"Well, we're not keeping those crates for posterity, Oliver. The auction house is having them removed and appraised. We'll find out exactly what they're worth, and I don't want you out there drinking all of the good stuff before they come, so you'll have to find another place to sulk until they're done."

The gardener's son led him through the trees and the shrubs. Sweat painted Kyle's back in a glistening sheen that Oliver wanted to touch. A trickle of perspiration ran along the boy's spine as he pushed aside branches and stomped forward; it pooled at the elastic band of his shorts, absorbed, turning the fabric at his waist from powder blue to navy. Oliver followed obediently. Something was different about Kyle that day; he seemed on edge, as if having Oliver along was an annoyance, even though he had extended the invitation. At the tool shed, far to the back of the property, the gardener's son stopped and put his hands on his hips.

In here.

The shed smelled of old grass and gasoline, dirt and paint. The fan of a willow branch curtained a small window high on the east wall.

A hand touched Oliver's face, and his breath came in tight, painful gasps. The gardener's son unfastened Oliver's belt and unsnapped his trousers. A rough hand slid over his belly, under the waistband of his boxers. . . .

Breathing deeply against a wave of emotion, Oliver lifted the oddly shaped bottle, stared at the amber glass. Something about the drink. Some incredible element of the alcohol. It sharpened his fantasies, gave them a life, made them tangible and teasing.

All but lost in this consideration, Oliver was startled by the sound of someone calling his name. He corked the bottle, set it on the crate and stepped outside, where he met Abe, the groundsman.

"You needed me, sir?" Abe asked.

Oliver told him about the crates he wanted moved. As he spoke the instructions, Abe's wrinkled old face clouded with worry.

"Mrs. Bennet said . . ."

"She doesn't pay you," Oliver said. "There are two crates. I'll show you the ones I want. Take them up to the second floor. Room 206."

He would be moving into that room for a few days. Amanda wouldn't mind; she never did.

Likely, she was courting a new lover. Amanda's mood toward him always soured when someone else was fucking her. Probably because her parade of men served to remind her that she'd settled for too little in marriage. They both had, and though Oliver considered leaving many times, the idea of being so completely alone was disturbing. Amanda took care of things—finances, social engagements, what clothes he should buy and when he should wear them. Such distractions were a burden, and he was content to leave them in her hands. Of greater importance, a companion, even one so incongruous to his needs, defined his place in the world and gave him a sense of belonging.

Why he should, in that moment, realize that being needed was wholly different from being necessary, he couldn't say.

Oliver closed the door to Room 206 and walked along the crimson carpet to the staircase. He paused on the landing, peering over the lobby's expanse. The crystal chandelier caught his eye. More than ever it looked to him like a giant beehive, made of gleaming clear gems rather than the fragile gray parchment of traditional nests. What wonderful creatures might create such a place? he wondered. This fanciful thought took hold in his mind, and his imagination filled the lobby with a swarm. Like soaring shards of glass, the bees flitted and danced in the air, climbed over the crystals of the fixture, disappeared inside to be warmed by two dozen low-watt bulbs.

The fantasy was all very beautiful to Oliver, who reached out a hand to grasp the carved banister. The people below, oblivious to his imagined swarm, chatted and wandered, read tourism pamphlets, while the air around them lit with a thousand specks of twinkling light.

"Mr. Bennett?"

Oliver started, and his magnificent swarm vanished. He turned away from the lobby and found Joe Hopkins smiling at him.

The foreman was a fit man in his mid-thirties with a brush of black hair framing strong and handsome features. Today he was not in his customary jeans and chambray shirt, instead wearing khakis and a black knit shirt beneath his leather jacket. Oliver returned the man's smile and nodded his head.

"Mr. Hopkins," he said.

"Surveying the kingdom?"

"Just gathering a bit of wool," Oliver replied. "What can I do for you?"

"Well, I thought you might be interested in the history of that wine cellar we dug up in your backyard."

Truth be told, his interest in the chamber had declined considerably. Amanda saw to that by having the hotel's publicist push the story to every reporter in town, making a spectacle of the place. It wasn't his anymore, not in any sense that mattered. Now that the crates of liqueur he wanted were stacked in his room, the speakeasy cellar was merely a curiosity. Still, he didn't want to seem impolite, and he found Hopkins pleasant enough. He leaned back against the banister and said, "What did you find?"

"We were right about the whole prohibition thing. It was a hooch hut, sure enough," Hopkins said, grinning at his turn of a phrase. Oliver couldn't help but notice the thick muscles in the foreman's neck, pronounced and corded when he smiled. "Davis Cortland had the place built so his guests wouldn't have to go dry, had it buried deep."

"Are you saying they had to dig their way down every time they wanted a cocktail?"

"Didn't have to dig. There was a tunnel connecting that vault to the basement of the hotel. If we'd excavated the east side of the thing, we would've found it. Anyway, Cortland had the whole place sealed up before he went to sell the hotel. Bricked up the basement and the vault. Apparently, he didn't mention it to the buyer, and the place was forgotten."

"And how did you find out about this?"

"They keep the Cortland family genealogy at the library. It's all on their computer system, so I just plugged in a couple of key words and Davis

Cortland's journal popped up." Hopkins paused and ran a hand through his hair. "Near the end there, old man Cortland was in pretty bad shape."

"How so?" Oliver asked.

"Well, both his sons died within about a month of one another. Both accidents. Cortland snapped. He found God in his own way, and he became convinced that his cellar, that's what he called the place, was cursed. Actually, he called it damned, but I guess it's about the same thing. Just craziness. He said that the boys were corrupted, led into sin by a low woman. That's what he called her anyway."

"Interesting," Oliver said. But he already projected the fallout of this discovery, and disappointment pushed in. Surely local journalists would dig up the same information, maybe more. As such, it was just something else to lament, another precious cache forcibly shared with the world and therefore meaningless.

Though he didn't exactly wish to remove himself from Hopkins's presence, he grew agitated with the conversation. But the foreman kept talking, telling Oliver about the Cortland family, and the patriarch's burgeoning madness—selling the hotel and starting a fundamentalist church in the family home, denouncing the decadent and opulent lifestyle his hotel once represented. Only when the conversation returned to the matter of Cortland's sons, Reginald and Michael, did Oliver's interest pique.

"I guess I can see how the old guy saw divine punishment in it. I mean, it's a pretty bizarre coincidence . . . for it to happen twice, in two different parts of the hotel."

"Both boys died the same way?" Oliver asked.

Hopkins nodded his head. "They were stung to death."

A tingle of excitement flared in Oliver's midsection. "They must have been delicate boys to die that way," he said. "Were they allergic?"

"Couldn't say. Cortland gave the impression that both were stung numerous times. They probably upset a couple of hives."

"Remarkable," Oliver said.

"It's all really fascinating," Hopkins continued. "When Mrs. Bennett asked me to check into the property history I was dreading it. I'm not much of a bookworm, but I got so damned curious, I kept digging."

Of course Amanda was behind this. "I see."

"Uh oh," Hopkins replied quickly. "The look on your face is telling me I should have kept my mouth shut."

"Not at all," Oliver said. He reached out and patted the foreman's shoulder. "Just a difference of opinion between my wife and me. I find her outlook unfortunate and a little sad. Amanda doesn't see a thing's value until she's envied for having it."

"And you like to keep things quieter?"

"Simply put . . . I like my secrets."

The day of his wife's party, Oliver sat at the window in his room and watched movers, under the vigilant eye of a slender man in tweed, remove the crates from the brick vault. The man in tweed, Amanda's assessor, made notes on a clipboard, and pointed and shouted. He read the labels on the crates, made more notes, pointed again.

Oliver closed the curtains, then drew the heavy shades as well. He went to the cases in the corner and pulled a bottle free. It was half empty. The last in the crate. He still had the second crate, though. Eight more bottles. They could last him another week, maybe two if he was conservative. Nonetheless, a flash of desperation, as if his supply had already run dry, tightened his chest. He fought to shake off this panic and studied the yellowish contents inside the glass.

Soon the ballroom below would fill with a miserable throng of the city's privileged. Oliver would have to smile and make small talk, pretend to care about exotic vacations and the tax benefits of buying bigger, more opulent homes.

Remembering what Joe told him about the Cortland family, he imagined little had changed over the years. They, too, probably held these kinds of affairs and likely spoke the same conversations. Oh, inflation changed the numbers being bandied about and trends changed the fashions, but Oliver couldn't imagine those long-ago conversations being any more interesting.

He opened the bottle and took a deep drink from the sweet fluid, immediately feeling its effects on his tongue. Oliver put the bottle on the nightstand and removed his clothes before stretching out on the bed.

He hoped to enjoy a brief period of bliss before putting on the host's mantle and indulging Amanda's need to be celebrated. He traveled through his memories, looking for a salacious moment on which to focus his attention, but his mind refused him. It kept coming back to the name Cortland. Oliver took another drink and stared at the ceiling, which was already shifting ever so slightly with his burgeoning intoxication.

Cortland had two sons. Both died from bee stings. The loss drove him mad. Joe had told him these things, but Oliver didn't want to remember them. He wanted to feel something good before being submerged in Amanda's fête.

But already he felt himself slipping away. He reached out and nearly knocked the bottle over. Once he had it firmly in hand, he brought it to his lips and sipped.

The room around him shifted, dissolved. Oliver replaced the bottle, struggled against the fantasy blossoming in his head, but failed. Instead of flesh and sweat and passion, he imagined . . .

A small dirty room, the walls and ceiling stained by cigarette smoke and dust. Water marks from faulty pipes spread over the plaster like monstrous amoebas. A bed was pushed against the far wall; it was the only surface in the room to be properly finished, with a delicate, floral-print paper. And on the bed, two boys in their late teens, tanned and lightly muscled, lay naked. One smoked a cigarette. The other looked toward the door. There, just crossing the threshold, a petite woman, naked and lovely, with short-cropped hair—a flapper's bob—cast a glance over her smooth white shoulder. Around her, a swarm of pearl-colored bees swarmed, filling the room with their buzz.

Oliver pictured all of this easily, the details painted in washed-out colors. He was disappointed to have entered the scene in the post-coital moments, having the heat of sex denied him, but something about this room, this place, felt so comforting he managed his displeasure and allowed himself to sink deeper into the fantasy.

Her name was Evelyn, he knew. Her small body moved gracefully amid her swarm, which cast a scrim of vague shadows, making the skin on her back and the supple curve of her buttocks appear to writhe and slide. Oliver followed her over the threshold and into another gloomy room, dominated by a single fixture.

It hung from the ceiling like a plump child, wrapped in a dirty shroud. The hive was enormous and the color of pastry dough. Opalescent bees by the hundreds crawled over its surface. Others flitted around the orifice at its base. On the floor beneath the nest, one of the oddly shaped bottles rested. A large metal funnel jutted from its neck. Honey dripped from the hole above, hit the funnel with a dull plunk, and slid down.

Evelyn slowly lifted her arms, disturbing the bees around her. With a gentle wave, she sent them to join their kin at the hive. In these few moments, Oliver felt the woman's control, her absolute command of the insects. He also felt her joy at adding numbers to their ranks. She walked to the hive, touched its surface with her fingertips, then bent low to retrieve the bottle. Evelyn pulled the funnel from its mouth, set it gently on the ground, before taking the bottle away. At an unmarked crate, previously unnoticed by Oliver (how could he notice anything but the wonderful hive?) she again bent down, lifted a cork, and popped it into the neck, driving it deep with a blow from her palm. She placed the bottle, which would later receive its cap of wax, in the crate and lifted an empty one from the floor beside it. This she placed beneath the dripping cavity and plugged it with the funnel.

Evelyn turned, a gentle smile pushing up the corners of her mouth. She ran her hands over her breasts and down her torso before lifting them to her hair, which she patted down.

Back in the room, the young man had finished his cigarette. He lay on his side, spooned by his companion, eyes filled with pleasure and dream. The second man's arm draped over the first, his palm gently caressing the belly of his brother.

For just as he knew the woman's identity, Oliver understood these two attractive boys were named Cortland. Reginald Cortland, the younger brother, looked content in the arms of his older sibling, Michael. Together, they tried to coax Evelyn back into the bed, but she was happy to stand apart, gazing at them.

A moment later, the dream changed. It happened so quickly, Oliver felt like he was dropping from a window.

Two broad men with flat features and stubble on their chins stomped into the room. They held short metal pipes in their gloved hands. The thugs observed the boys with disgust while the naked brothers yelped, then rolled away. They leapt from the bed, seeking their clothing. Another man entered the room. He was tall and straight-backed, wearing a fine woolen overcoat. His mustache was waxed neatly above his lips. He, too, looked with disgust at the young men scrabbling to dress, but fury was also in his features.

Evelyn protested, demanding the men leave her home, refusing to cover herself, even when one of the thugs slapped her harshly with the back of his hand and called her "whore."

Was Oliver the only one aware of the buzzing, growing louder in the next room? How could these thick men not hear it? It was nearly as loud as an approaching motorcycle.

The dignified man (Davis Cortland, he knew) ushered his sons out of the room and through the house. Behind him, his men cried out.

Cortland looked back and saw the air filled with what appeared to be snow, but his men cowered under it, slapped at it with fat palms. They screamed when any of the flakes touched them. And Evelyn, the beautiful Evelyn, stood at the center of this storm, looking serene as the men dropped at her feet.

The scene tripped again. The sensation of falling was worse this time, and Oliver nearly fell out of his dream.

He sat in the back of a great sedan, looking through the window at a house being consumed by flame. Oliver felt despair and horror, knowing Evelyn was still inside, trapped with her swarm between walls of fire. Davis Cortland stood outside the car, hands crossed over his crotch, watching the house burn.

Oliver shook himself from the fantasy.

194 ~ Lee Thomas

Emotions—hate, fear, anger, sadness in mourning the magnificent Evelyn's death—covered him like a thick syrup (*like honey*). He looked at the bottle on the bed table next to him, thought about the sweet liqueur held within and its origin.

He scratched his fingernails over his scalp, digging in deep until his neck tingled. He wanted the Cortland family out of his head, but they weren't quite ready to leave.

Though he did not return to the all-consuming fugue, Oliver caught glimpses, like memory, of the boys and their father: Reginald Cortland sitting in a corner on the floor of a hotel room, very much like the one Oliver currently occupied; he drank from one of the hexagonal bottles, his face streaming with tears, his hand masturbating furiously; the senior Cortland entered the room some time later to find his son dead on the carpet, the boy's body riddled with red welts, the bottle lying next to him; Michael Cortland, the older boy, sneaked through the hidden cellar, opening one of the crates Evelyn offered him and his brother as gifts; he sat in the tunnel that connected the hooch hut to the hotel, also crying, surrounded by the pale bees; he, too, was discovered with his skin destroyed and cold to the touch.

They couldn't control them, Oliver thought. Without Evelyn's command, the insects proved vicious and lethal.

He looked to the shadowy corner of his room. The bare wooden crates, holding the hexagonal bottles, sat there. Above them, movement like sliding wax caught his eye. He traced his gaze up the wall, saw similar movement against the ceiling. With a shaking hand, he reached for the bottle. Paused.

As for the father, Cortland believed his boys were corrupted by the beautiful Evelyn (though Oliver considered the act a generous seduction); the patriarch saw his sons' corpses, saw the bottles of sweet liqueur accompanying them, and with the shattered mind of one truly despondent, he cast his judgment against all vice and had the chamber of spirits sealed. He would no longer break the laws of man, nor sin against the laws of his God. He turned his back on capital and embraced an extreme and unforgiving faith.

Davis Cortland didn't understand. He was a conservative man with a shallow mind and no capacity for wonder. Oliver knew the type well.

Downstairs, Amanda was busy with caterers and florists. He needed to shower and dress and play the fine host. They were throwing a party to celebrate the opening of Cortland's vault.

He lifted the bottle from the nightstand, held it to his lips and again peered into the corner, at the motion along the walls' surface. *Cortland just couldn't understand*. Oliver corked the bottle and returned it to the crate.

———

The swing band played a midtempo tune. Ball gowns twirled and men in tuxedos smiled. Oliver stood away from the crowd, in a corner by the bar where he watched Amanda flirting with Joe Hopkins. With her arm on his shoulder, his wife laughed too loudly at something the foreman said and tossed her head to the side. She saw Oliver and her joyful expression switched off until she was again looking at Hopkins.

Oliver sipped from his martini, but the drink burned his tongue, tasted foul and poisoned. Throughout the evening, he had sampled the canapés and skewered delicacies circulated by the waiters, but they scalded and scraped his mouth, abrading his palate like bits of hot coal. He put the martini glass on the bar, wishing he had smuggled one of his bottles down to the ballroom. Nothing else would taste right to him tonight.

Amanda ran her palm down Hopkins's cheek. The man threw a nervous glance at Oliver, and Amanda laughed again. She slid her arm through Hopkins's and led him deeper into the party, out of Oliver's view. The music clanged in his ears, and the bustle of people now felt threatening, as if they were just amusing themselves until it was time to turn on him and attack. To add to his unease, his eyes were playing tricks on him, or they were failing completely. The room began melting into a single oozing image. Details blurred then bleached out. The ornate moldings dripped, and the far wall shrank as if collapsing. Around him, the smiling faces were little more than threatening smudges.

He had to escape. With the shrill banging of the music in his head, he fled back to his room.

Once the door was locked, he ran to the crates stacked in the corner. Desperate to have the music out of his head and the sick-making panic made numb, he pulled the bottle free and removed the cork. What remained wasn't enough to calm him. The final drops of fluid trickled over his tongue, a mere tease. Oliver corked the bottle and replaced it in the top crate. He set the wooden case on the floor and frantically opened the second. Once the covering boards were removed he snatched a fresh bottle and chewed away the wax seal. He yanked the cork from the neck. Then, he poured the liquid into his mouth until the disturbance in his system calmed.

He reached a hand out to steady himself and felt the wall shift and tickle under his palm. Oliver snatched his hand away.

"Sorry," he whispered, turning away.

Soothed but still uncomfortable, he removed his jacket and ruffled shirt. He slid out of his trousers and socks and stood in his underwear, already feeling the need for another sip.

He ran a hand over his belly and rubbed small circles, coaxing the swarm in his head to again fill his sex. Thoughts of Amanda and Joe Hopkins engulfed him.

They were together, he thought. Somewhere in that damned hotel, his wife lay beneath Hopkins. Her lips were on his chest, tasting his sweat and pushing into the muscle and hair. She'd encourage him with sounds Oliver hadn't heard in over a decade, voicing passion she had never shown her husband, and the workman, driving deep into Oliver's wife, filling her in a way Oliver never could, strained and flexed, showing her what a real man could offer.

Oliver poured a substantial slug of the liquid over these thoughts. It filled his head with a humming pulse, and his skin lit with friction.

The image of his wife laid back and wide open to the workman crystallized and a mouth fell on his. Hopkins's mouth. The weight of the workman's chest pressed down on him but he also felt the rise of Amanda's breasts under him. The duality of the sensations intensified until he felt hot sweat dripping from him and over him.

His fantasy, sparked by supposition and fueled by the numbing liqueur, did not position him between the two lovers; it fed him the sensations of both.

His cock grew warm, encased in wet skin as he thrust into Amanda's writhing body, and he felt the penetration between his legs, a thick shaft driving deep into his body, entering him through a channel he didn't possess. The smell of perfume filled his nose and was then replaced with a pedestrian aftershave. Hands stroked his ass and his chest and his back and his hips, and through it all, his sex burned with the gathering bees.

A solid rapping on his door snapped him from his fantasy, canceling the pleasure that tickled and stung the base of his cock, made it retreat. Instead of erupting from him, the buzzing ejaculate fled into his body. The bees were furious. Their furred bodies, their filament-thin legs, their beating wings prickled his gut, his stomach, and his sex. They clung to the membranes and jostled for space. The discomfort and frantic movement aroused him anew, and Oliver reached for the bottle on the nightstand.

The insistent knocking paused his hand. Oliver tried ignoring the summons, but it seemed the visitor would not be ignored. Oliver rolled off of the bed. He pulled his robe from the back of a chair and crossed the room.

Hopkins stood in the doorway. He greeted Oliver with a hello, rich in tone and salted with unease.

With the hive burrowing into his belly and the liqueur having numbed his mouth, Oliver said nothing, simply stepped back to allow Hopkins entrance.

Apparently uncomfortable and eager to hide it, Hopkins made a show of crossing his arms. Oliver noted the bulk of the workman's thickly veined forearms, and the hive ignited with frantic buzzing. Then, Hopkins unfolded the arms and shoved his hands deep into the pockets of his trousers.

"Mr. Bennett," he said. "I know what you must be thinking, but I want you to know I'm not the sort to get mixed up with a married woman."

Oliver stared at the handsome man and thought about the gardener's son. They were similar, he thought. Both shared a strength, a power that emanated from their skin in hot waves. The association further stirred the hive, sent it flying low in his belly and high into his throat.

"I just want you to know that," Hopkins said. "The last thing I need in my life is a jealous husband." The workman laughed haltingly, forcing the sound through his lips in an awkward attempt to lighten the mood.

Oliver stepped forward. "I've never been jealous of her," he said. The foreman seemed perplexed, but this simple man would never understand the importance of such a statement.

When Oliver imagined his wife and her lovers, he took her place in the fantasies, feeling the strength and the rough hands on his body. Her men became his hero, every one of them was the gardener's son—his Kyle reimagined. He wrapped an arm around Hopkins's shoulder, locking the man's neck in the crook of his elbow. "Never of her."

He leaned forward and put his lips on Hopkins's. The hive swarming at the back of his throat and deep within his belly grew to frenzy. Hopkins's lips were warm but rigid. Strong hands pushed, and then they shoved. Oliver stumbled back, nearly fell, and then regained his balance.

"What's wrong with you fucking people?" Hopkins yelled. He stepped forward and landed a fist on Oliver's jaw. The pain and concussion of the blow startled him but it was also exciting.

You liked that? You fucking freak? You rich boy piece of shit?

Kyle had struck him all of those years ago. Shouting obscenities and condemnations, the older boy punched and kicked and spat.

After their beautiful time together, while the resonating pleasure of their encounter still sang in his body, Oliver could make no sense of the abuse. Confused, Oliver fled the shack. He raced through the trees and the shrubs and into the waiting hive of bees.

Oliver tested his jaw, ran a hand over its pained arch. And the first of the white bees flew free of his mouth. It tested the air, bobbing and dipping with wings all but invisible from the speed of their beating. Another followed. Hopkins shouted a curse and turned to run, but he was too close to the door and clipped his brow on the jamb. The blow sent him back a step.

Oliver's mouth ached from Hopkins's fist and from the abrading wings and bodies of the emerging swarm. Dozens of the white bees flew from his mouth to fill the gloom. Across the room, Hopkins cradled his forehead, gazing in fearful wonder at the buzzing squadron. One of the white creatures landed on his cheek.

It stung.

The workman's eyes grew wide; he choked out a plea, and then slapped at the insect, crushing it to a smear of liquid on his already swelling cheek. Oliver watched calmly, his system and mind soothed by the rhythmic beating of thousands of wings. Hopkins backed to the wall, hands up, covering his face, as a vague mumble of panic tripped over his lips.

Oliver lifted his arms and threw a look over his shoulder to the corner by the crates, suddenly alive with activity. A thunderous buzzing filled the room, and Oliver beckoned his swarm.

Oliver walked back to the bed, but in his mind he was running through brush and speckled sunlight.

His face burned with bee sting and throbbed with the beating he'd taken from his former hero. Nearly blind, he stumbled across his backyard to the kitchen door and tripped over the threshold. He cried, then screamed.

A fresh pain shot along his palm, and Oliver looked down to find a stray bee squirming in a gout of pearl-colored fluid. The trapped insect jabbed its barb into the meat at the base of his thumb, protesting its capture.

His father appeared, hovering over him, shouting about Oliver's stupidity. Oliver held his hand out to show his father the monster that still clung to him, and his father fell silent. . . .

Your dad showed me this you fucking freak. And you like it? You rich boy piece of shit. I oughtta kill you and your faggot father.

The old man looked out the kitchen window, over the backyard, and perhaps all the way to the back of the property where the tool shed stood. Seeming dazed, red with flush, he told Oliver to wash his hands.

Wash your hands, Boy.

Ignoring his son's tears and pleas, Oliver's father walked out the back door. A housekeeper appeared moments later, drawn by Oliver's cries. She wasted no time in helping him to his feet and to her car. She drove Oliver to the hospital where he spent the night in pain, hallucinating about his father and Kyle and bees.

By the time he was released the following morning, the gardener had packed his family up and left the estate. Oliver never saw Kyle again.

In the dark room, Oliver reclined on the bed. Naked, aching and swollen, he let the roar of wings clear the thoughts from his head. Painful lumps covered his chest and his belly; his cock was raw and misshapen by a dozen stings. A tear of semen dripped from the welted head and upon touching his stomach came to life with fierce movement, wings flapping and tickling his skin before pulling away to join the droning swarm above him. The small white bees speckled the air, crawled over the walls, and dove from ceiling to floor. Their scent—bitter honey—filled his nose. On the nightstand next to him, the amber bottle stood empty.

He rolled his head, his swollen ear stinging when it touched the soft cotton pillowcase. Above the cases of liquor in the corner of the room, the ceiling already puckered with the foundation of a glorious shelter. The combed base of the hive was as big around as a serving platter and as white as snow. Drones scurried over the delicate construction, furiously adding material to the nest.

Somewhere below, the party continued. Amanda would be flirting with some new man, seducing him with Oliver's wealth, while degrading her husband with words of dissatisfaction. Here, though, none of that mattered, because, finally, he possessed something of his own, something his father's trespass could not taint, something Amanda could not imagine or covet or take. It was wholly his. The Cortland boys proved too weak for this responsibility. But not Oliver.

Like the lovely Evelyn, he would harbor and tend to his hive. He would be their master, their mother and their shelter.

His swarm would grow in number and strength, and by winter, the walls of the room would run with pearls of honey to be collected and stored. The two cases of bottles would never be enough to hold all of the magnificent liqueur.

"Oh please," he whispered to the room.

Six of his drones dropped from the platinum cloud to circle above him. Each beating of their wings brought the promise of pleasure and creation. "Please," he said again, and the white drones descended to penetrate his skin with their barbs. Agony erupted and was quickly numbed. Euphoria followed like an echo of the pain.

Beneath his hand, his anxious shaft, thick with knots, was already close to release. A sharp pain flared behind his ear. Oliver cried out, and the swarm's number increased.

The Keeper

P. D. CACEK

P. D. Cacek received a B.A. Degree in Creative Writing from the University of Long Beach in 1975 and has been working in her chosen field ever since.

She has won the Bram Stoker Award and the World Fantasy Award for her short fiction and is the author of six novels, three collections, and more than a hundred short stories; her most recent short stories were published in the anthologies Lords of the Razor *and* Night Visions 12.

Cacek is currently working on a nonfiction project involving haunted bed and breakfasts, as well as collaborating on a screenplay about Lizzie Borden based on new evidence. A hint: She did it—but not with an ax.

S he arrived just as the sun was setting.

Summer was over and the last of the autumn leaves—the ones that had for weeks filled my bedroom window with fire and gold—were gone. Only the gray branches and twigs remained, and it was through them that I first saw her.

"A cousin," Zaideh told the family last year at Hanukkah as he held the telegram that had come that morning and which had become the immediate focus of all our attention. All day we had waited and all evening, too; so that by the time he finally sat down in the big chair in the front room, our curiosity had built up inside us like steam in a kettle.

"Just one?" one of my aunts had asked.

And Zaideh had nodded. "Yoh, just one."

I can tell you that I wasn't the only one disappointed. All of us, the children, looked at each other and shrugged. We had cousins, more than we knew what to do with sometimes, so why did this one send a telegram? It seemed such a waste after so full a day of imagining. But our parents were moved by the news—some to tears, some to anger, some to a silence that went beyond all feeling—and it frightened us, making us draw close to each other. The petty squabbles and thoughtless words that were our usual playthings were set aside as we wondered and worried about this newly found cousin.

For almost a year we worried.

For almost a year we made up stories.

And, once again, we were disappointed.

From the few snatches of conversation I'd heard between Zaideh and my parents—conversations that always ended when they noticed me—I'd expected her to be bigger, almost full-grown . . . but she was younger than I was. Only nine, Mameh had told me that morning.

"And she's had . . . a hard time, so you'll have to be good to her. Like a little sister, yes?"

I'd never wanted a little sister, but because there'd been tears in my mother's eyes I lied. Yes, I said, of course I'd be good to her.

I barely let myself breathe until I saw her from my bedroom window . . . the little girl bundled into a coat that was too big for her. Just a little girl with pale skin and large dark eyes that looked up and caught me staring through the branches.

Just a little girl who didn't smile when I waved.

It was dark by the time the front door opened, closed, and the low, constant murmur of voices that had filled the house since midday stopped. Silence wasn't ordinary in our house . . . there was always noise of some kind or another—pots clanging, the rustling of my father's newspapers, the grinding hiss and occasional music from the old Philco radio that my grandfather insisted sounded as good as the day he bought it—and its absence made me press my arms against my belly.

She had stopped all that. My new, unknown cousin had killed the sounds that made our house alive.

I hugged myself tighter and watched the first stars appear, hoping my grandfather would forget I was there.

He didn't, of course.

"Sarah. Come."

His voice echoed in the strange quiet.

My aunts and uncles had wanted to bring their children, but Zaideh had told them no. *She*, the unknown one, would have more than enough time to meet and be met later on . . . tonight it was important that she be made to feel comfortable. Be made to feel at home.

I was the only *child* allowed to meet her this night.

"Sarah? *Eilt zich*!"

But I didn't hurry. All I could manage was a stiff, slow walk that carried me from my room to the hallway, and finally to top of the stairs. My Mumeh Rebecca was standing at the bottom of the staircase, crying softly into a handkerchief, breaking the terrible, unnatural silence that had filled the room. My heart was pounding by the time I reached her, and her fingers, usually gentle, dug into my shoulder as she pulled me into the front room.

"Terrible, terrible! *Gevaldikeh zach*! How could they do such a thing? *Viazoy? Viazoy* to such a little thing. To *kinder*? Children. She's the only one left. *Ver volt dos geglaibt*? Who would believe such a thing?"

Mumeh Rebecca kept muttering in Yiddish and English as she steered me through the sea of serge trouser legs and black crepe skirts. They had come dressed as if to sit *shivah*, and the pounding of my heart grew faster.

Zaideh stood by the mantel of the blocked fireplace, his head nodding as if in prayer, and waved me forward with his fingers.

"Sarah, here . . . *kum aher*." Then he turned his head and smiled down at the little girl who sat perched on the very edge of the old, overstuffed chair he never let anyone sit in.

Eyes down, hands folded in her lap, she looked smaller without the coat, my new cousin; small and frail and thinner than any nine-year-old should be. There were lines on her face, like Zaideh's. His, I knew, were from the smiles that always found a way to his lips, but I didn't think her lines were from the same thing.

She was pale as snow and the shadows beneath her eyes were the color of summer plums, the same color as the jumper she wore. Someone, maybe Mumeh Rebecca, had tied back her mud-brown hair with a red ribbon; but it looked too new and bright, out of place . . . like a rose left on a grave.

I jumped when Zaideh cleared his throat; but she just sat there, motionless, like stone.

"Sarah, this is your cousin, Janna."

Janna, her name is Janna.

"Hello, Janna."

If she heard me or not, I didn't know. She just sat there, staring at her hands while the lines around her mouth deepened. I looked up at my grandfather and he shrugged, then kneeled next to the chair and whispered, very softly, to my new cousin. For a moment she stayed frozen, then, very slowly, she nodded and raised her face toward me.

Her eyes were the color of amber and so empty they looked like a doll's. Her lips moved, trembled, then tightened against the pull of the lines on her cheeks. Zaideh sighed and placed his one hand over both of hers.

"Janna doesn't speak English, Sarah," he said. "She doesn't really speak much at all, so you will have to be patient, yoh? Help her?"

"Yes, Zaideh."

"Good. *Es iz gants gut.* It will be all right . . . you'll see. Yoh?"

I wasn't sure if he was talking to me or her, but I nodded and that seemed enough. He smiled at me but squeezed *her* hands. "*Gut.* Now, we eat . . . come."

Zaideh's smile stayed on his lips as he stood and waved toward the kitchen. Food was the binding cloth of my family. There was never any sorrow or joy so great that it couldn't be laid upon my grandmother's large wooden table amid the platters and dishes and jars and picked at. My grandmother had been dead for almost as long as I'd been alive, but the tradition remained.

So the family sat down and picked and talked until there was nothing left; but neither my new cousin nor I ate very much. She because all of it was too new, me . . . because she was there. She held the spoon my mother had pressed into her hand, only moving it to the food-laden plate in front of her and then to her mouth when someone, usually Zaideh, told her to eat. When no one said anything she lowered the spoon and stared . . . her amber doll's eyes reflecting the candles my mother had thought would add a festive touch, her gaze stopping somewhere in the middle of the table.

But every now and then those eyes would widen and her fingers would tighten against the spoon handle and the lines on her cheeks would deepen.

We were sent to bed early, she and I, but I went without one word of resistance. My stomach hurt and I didn't want to stay up and watch the family pretend it was a night like any other: my mother and aunts in the kitchen gossiping, my uncles and father on the porch smoking their pipes and arguing about the latest baseball scores, Zaideh—without me—listening to either the *Lux Radio Theatre* or *Fibber McGee and Molly* or *The Fitch Bandwagon* or *The Lone Ranger.*

Mameh came in to help my new cousin change into one of my old nightgowns, then sat down on the bed that had, until that night, only been mine, and sang a lullaby I had almost forgotten. It was for *her*, of course, *my new cousin*. I was almost twelve, too old for such things, but I listened and fell asleep with the sound of it in my ears.

And woke to screams.

At first I thought it was *her*, but when I sit up I see it's the children who are screaming. Boys and girls, naked . . . their skin and lips blue . . . eyes wide with fear as they run across the frozen ground . . . screaming even as the dogs get closer and closer. They're still screaming when the dogs reach them. Then it's their mothers who scream while soldiers in dark uniforms laugh—*they're always laughing*—and bet on which dog will finish its meal first. I try to bury my face beneath the blankets, but strong hands pull my arms away and shake me like a rag doll.

"No, no. You must watch, little one. How will you learn if you don't watch. It's just like when you were in school. See? Open your eyes . . . this is a lesson you need to learn."

The hands tighten on my shoulders and turn me toward the barbed-wire fence where the body of a woman hangs head-down like a chicken in a butcher's window . . . her throat cut . . . gutted . . . the blood frozen on the ground beneath her

"And this is another lesson. Do you want to see another?"

I don't know what to do. I don't know if I should answer or keep quiet. Sometimes they want you to answer . . . sometimes being quiet kills faster than the dogs or the knives. I don't know what they want this time.

"Did you hear me, little one? I asked you a question."

"N-n-n-"

"N-n-no? *You didn't hear? Or you already know all your lessons? No . . . I don't think so. I think you've forgotten everything we've tried to teach you. Yah?*"

The hands tighten on my shoulders and drag me toward one of the buildings . . . and I turn . . . somehow I manage to turn and look into the bright blue eyes that stared out at me from a grinning white skull.

"*Time for another lesson, little one.*"

"MAMEH!"

The headboard banged against the wall when I sat up . . . woke up. Sobbing, gasping for breath, I clutched the blankets in my hands and heard my father's yawning mutters and the soft whisper of my mother's slippers on the hall carpet and, from the small room downstairs, my grandfather's constant snores. I was awake, this time I was awake . . . but it didn't help.

"MAMEH!"

"Yoh . . . yoh, I'm here, I'm here, *maideleh* . . . shush, it's all right. Sha, sha, sha, sha . . ."

The next moment I was in her arms, biting the inside of my cheek to keep from crying. I was almost twelve and it was only a nightmare . . . and almost-twelve-year-olds don't cry over nightmares.

But I still burrowed into my mother's warmth until she pushed me away.

"Where's Janna?"

I looked and her side of the bed, *my* bed, was empty.

My mother's hands dug into my shoulders the same way the skull-faced soldier in my nightmare had.

"Where is she, Sarah, where is Janna? Simon! Simon, *kum*!"

The hall light came on and my father stumbled into the room—mumbling, rubbing his eyes, his robe untied. When he finally looked at us, he yawned.

"What?"

My mother let me go and stood up and her hands moved like birds in the yellow light from the hall.

"Janna's not here! Look! She's not in bed!" My mother's hands stopped moving and closed into fists. "Simon . . . where could she be?"

My father shook his head. He looked very big with the light behind him. I couldn't see his face.

"She's not here? How could she not be here? Sarah—" He turned toward me but I still couldn't see his face. "—where's your cousin?"

I didn't have time to answer, to tell him I didn't know. Zaideh came into the room, the crocheted blanket my grandmother had made before she died wrapped around his shoulders, his legs bare beneath the flannel nightshirt.

"*Vos tut zich?*"

My mother told him, and the tears that filled her voice made my eyes burn.

"Gone?" Zaideh asked. "Gone where? Where could she go?"

"I don't know! *Ich vais nit!*"

"Sha, Rachel, quiet." My grandfather's voice was soft as he touched my mother's cheek. "What are you talking? She's not gone. Look . . . she's there."

I looked where he had nodded and saw her . . . my cousin. She was standing next to the window, wrapped in the curtain, the dull yellow light from the hallway reflecting off her eyes. I watched my mother's shadow race across the room.

"Poor baby." My mother's voice was soft, almost a whisper as she picked my cousin up and carried her back to the bed. "Poor little thing. Did Sarah scare you?"

"*Me?* I didn't do anything."

My mother shook her head and made a face—at me—while she tucked my cousin back under the blankets.

"Of course you did," she said, "you frightened her."

"I had . . . a bad dream."

"You're too old to have bad dreams. Now, both of you . . . go to sleep. *A gute nacht.*" Then my mother pointed at me. "Sleep. Now."

As I closed my eyes, I heard my father whisper. "Funny. I thought it would be the other one who would have bad dreams."

Zaideh said something back, but it was lost in the sound of the door closing. When my room was dark again, I opened my eyes and listened to the sound of their steps getting softer and softer. She must have been listening, too, my new cousin . . . because the moment the house was quiet, she got out of bed and walked back to the window. Cocooned in the curtain she just stood there, looking out at the night between the bare branches of the maple tree.

I watched her for a few minutes, then turned onto my side—away from her. She was crazy, maybe *that's* what happened to her. She went crazy and her parents sent her here because they didn't want her anymore. No wonder I had a nightmare, sharing my bed with a crazy person. In the morning I'd tell my mother.

I fell asleep thinking about this and didn't dream for the rest of the night.

I didn't have time to tell my mother anything in the morning.

"I called you almost an hour ago, what took you so long?" She barely looked up from the pot of oatmeal she was stirring. "What are you standing there for? Hurry and eat or you'll be late for school."

My new cousin was already at the table, spooning oatmeal into her mouth as if she were a clockwork toy: Spoon into bowl, mouth opened, spoon into mouth, mouth closed, spoon back into bowl . . . over and over again even though it seemed her bowl never emptied. Zaideh looked at me from over the top of his newspaper then rapped his knuckles against the tabletop.

"Are you here to watch? Sit down and eat before it gets cold."

I sat. "Why does she eat like that?"

"Like what?" my grandfather asked. "She eats . . . so should you. Go on. Eat."

"But . . ."

"Enough with the talk. Fill your mouth instead of emptying it. Food is to be eaten; how it is, doesn't matter. You are lucky to have it, so eat." He glared at me for a moment, so I'd understand that what he said was important, then winked. "Is good, yoh?"

He waited until I nodded before turning his attention to her. My new cousin. "Gut, yoh? Gut . . . oatmeal, yoh. *Farshtaist?* Understand . . . oat . . . merely. You say . . . oat-meel."

She looked up, those wide amber eyes staring at his face.

"*Zie farshtait ir?* Say it." He tapped her bowl and said the word again, very slowly. "Oat . . . meel."

She looked down at the bowl. "*Kasha?*"

Zaideh laughed.

"No, *nain . . . nain kasha* . . . oat-meel."

"Ohmeel?"

You would have thought an angel had suddenly appeared in the kitchen.

"Yoh! *Yoh, iz gut, pisherkeh! Rachel*! You hear? Janna said oatmeal! She talked."

My mother dropped the wooden stirring spoon and oatmeal splattered against the green-and-white linoleum.

"She talked. A miracle . . . they said she might never . . . She talked. A real word."

"Of course a real word. What would she say—a made-up word? Rachel, shush. Janna . . . Janna, say again—oatmeal."

"Ohmeel."

Zaideh swept the air with his hands. "See . . . you hear? Janna, look. Look." He picked up the teaspoon he'd used to stir honey into his tea. "*Leffel, yoh . . . leffel?* Spoon."

"Spunah."

"Spoon! See . . . a genius we have."

My mother yelled for my father to come see, to come hear, while Zaideh pointed to other things on the table, then in the kitchen, then to me.

"Janna, say Sarah."

Our eyes met and I saw her lips move, but before she could say it, before she could say anything my mother dragged my father into the kitchen and then there wasn't any more room for my name.

And so our family grew by one.

For almost three months, it was like having a new baby in the house. Day and night, my aunts and neighbor women would find excuses to visit and always with something for *"the little one"* — a hand-knitted scarf, a box of hand-me-down clothes that were too good to throw away, a toy, a book, or maybe just a plate of cookies to *"fatten her up."*

For almost three months my new cousin was the center of the world, then the newness wore off. The neighbor women returned to their own families, and my mother and aunts went back to the day-to-day routine of cooking and cleaning and making sure each new piece of gossip was passed along. Zaideh and my father stopped puffing out their chests as if they'd done something important and started falling asleep again in front of the radio each night after supper.

Everything was back to normal.

For everyone but me.

Because I was the youngest and had "nothing else important to do," it became my responsibility to take care of my new cousin. I was to see that she ate and dressed warmly and practiced her English every day and wasn't ever left alone. Any toy or doll or book I had was to be shared with her. Any place I wanted to go, she was to come with me. My friends were to become her friends . . . my life devoted to hers.

Every moment I was in the house, I was to be by her side . . . talking to her, playing with her, reading to her, and helping her to forget.

But they never told me *what* I was supposed to help her forget.

"*Sarah* . . . *Janna*—we're going! Come give kisses."

It was Tuesday, canasta night.

My parents spent each Tuesday night playing canasta. Sometimes with the neighbors, mostly with my aunts and uncles; tonight with Mumeh Rose and Feter Aaron who lived in a wonderful apartment above the bakery.

I always went with them when it was at Mumeh Rose and Feter Aaron's, but not to play or even to watch the card game. I would go so I could sit in the kitchen that always smelled of vanilla and baked apples, eating cookies and listening to Bob Hope on the *Pepsodent Show*.

But not this time.

Father was already standing on the porch, shoulders bunched under his coat, his hat pulled down over his ears, the car keys jingling in his hand. My mother was busy with her hat in front of the mirror, her coat still hanging on the hook next to the door.

"Sarah, I need you to watch Janna tonight."

"But I—"

"We'll be home early."

"But, Zaideh—"

I stopped when Mother turned to look at me. "I need you to stay with Janna. Zaideh has gone to visit Mr. Katz over in the hospital. Poor man broke his hip. You're old enough to stay alone and watch Janna."

This month I was old enough, last month I wasn't? But I didn't ask out loud.

"There," she said to the mirror when her hat was finally perfect, "come help your mama with her coat and give kisses good-bye. Janna . . . *kumt aher*, come here."

I jumped as she brushed past my shoulder. She was so small and quiet, like the ghost of a mouse, easy to forget.

"You be a good girl, yes?" My mother held my cousin's face between her hands. "Yes . . . good girl, yes?"

My cousin nodded. "Yoh. Yez, goot girl."

She spoke English now. A little—not much and not well—but each word was like a pearl to my parents and grandfather. My mother smiled.

"Yes! Good girl!" She stopped smiling when she stood up and looked at me. "You be good, too, Sarah. And don't stay up late. Nine o'clock and be sure you lock the door. We'll be home early."

My father closed his hand around the car keys when my mother stepped onto the porch, pulling the door shut behind her.

"All right, all right, Mr. Impatient, I'm here now. Sarah—lock the door!"

Their footsteps didn't leave the porch until I'd twisted the lock shut. This was the first time I'd been allowed to stay home alone, more or less. Part of me felt very proud—my parents didn't think of me as a child anymore—but the other part wished they still did.

My cousin was sitting on the bottom step of the stairs when I turned around. Looking at me. Waiting.

"Are you . . . hungry? You know . . . food. You want something to eat?" I pointed to my mouth, then my belly.

She watched my hands and shook her head. "No."

It was going to be a long night.

"Do you want me to read you a story? *Buch*, you know, book?" Zaideh was always correcting my Yiddish, so I pressed my hands together then opened them at the thumbs. "Book?"

She shook her head.

"Radio?"

She just looked at me.

This time I shook my head and walked into the front room. It took a few minutes for the old Philco to warm up, but by that time she must have figured out what I'd asked and followed me. *I* sat in Zaideh's chair and she sat on the couch, tucked into one corner with her legs up tight against her belly, as the *Pepsodent Show's* theme music filled the air.

"Bob Hope," I told her.

She nodded. "Hope."

She fell asleep before the first commercial and stayed asleep when I got up to make tea after Bob Hope said good night. Zaideh always made honey tea after the program, and then we'd sit in the kitchen and tell each other the same jokes we'd just heard. I knew it wouldn't be the same, but I made the tea anyway and was spooning honey into two cups when I heard voices in the front room.

The kitchen clock showed only a few minutes after nine. My parents had come home earlier than usual, keeping their voices low so I wouldn't hear them. I let the jar of honey thump against the countertop to let them know that I had. *They hadn't trusted me to watch my cousin after all.*

"Do you want tea?" I called out to them. "I'm just making—"

But suddenly their voices got louder and I heard my mother scream.

I thought it was my mother until I ran to the front room.

The cups slip from my hands and bleed honey onto the floor as I stand and watch two skull-faced soldiers drag a woman with amber eyes across the room. The woman's face is thin and her head is shaved, but I know her eyes . . . I know her. I have never seen her before but I know her. The woman looks at me and her hand reaches out even as one of the soldiers strikes her across the mouth. Blood spurts, gleaming in light from Zaideh's reading lamp, and when she opens her mouth blood pours out with the words she screams: *"Janna! Janna! Es fardrist mir! Janna . . . gedainkst. Gedainkst!"*

And I understand them.

Janna. Janna, I'm sorry. Janna . . . remember. Remember.

I make a sound, just a little sound when the front door opens, but it's enough to wake her; and the moment my cousin's eyes opened, the soldiers and the screaming woman melted into the air like mist. Zaideh came in, his face red from the cold.

"*Vos tut zich?* I scared you?" Then he nodded when he saw the broken cups and oozing honey. "I scared you. Come . . . let's clean this up before your mama comes home. Go get a rag and water."

Zaideh went to hang up his coat as my cousin got off the couch and slowly walked toward me. The broken china made soft sounds when she gathered the pieces in her hand.

"*Es fardrist mir,*" she whispered—*I'm sorry*—as she held them out to me. "I can't . . ."

I ran from the room before she could finish. I didn't want to know.

I never wanted to know.

But I didn't have a choice.

She got sick the first week of winter.

"*Just a little cold,*" they said, "*nothing to worry about.*" But despite all the homemade tonics and teas my mother and aunts forced down her throat, my cousin's cough deepened into a wet, gurgling bark that grew worse and worse until it finally brought up blood.

I got back from school one afternoon just as the doctor was leaving. He smiled at me and patted my head, asked about my health and nodded without listening.

My mother was in the front room, standing next to the cot Zaideh had slept on during my grandmother's final illness. It was tucked into the corner nearest the fireplace, sheets and blankets at one end of the horsehair mattress, a blue-and-white striped pillow at the other. As I watched, my mother bent down and touched one of the blankets.

"I should get new ones. These wouldn't keep a dog warm."

"Mameh?"

There were tears on her cheeks and in her eyes when she turned around . . . and I ran to her, frightened, my own eyes filling as I felt her arms close around me.

"Mameh, what is it? What's wrong? What happened?"

For a moment she couldn't answer, and then we sat on the edge of the cot and she told me. I was old enough to know, she said. Janna was very sick and would have to sleep down here until she got better.

"She'll be fine . . . all she needs is a little rest. You'll see. Once she gets a little rest she'll be—" The lie choked her.

"Mameh?"

My mother was quiet for a few minutes, then took a deep breath. "She's not going to get better, Sarah. After what she's been through, to live through all that . . . she's not going to get better."

"What happened to her, mameh?

My mother pulled me closer to her.

"I don't know."

We held each other until my father came home from work and carried Janna down to the cot.

Later that night, when everyone was asleep, I found out what happened to her.

At first I think it's just a doll—one of her new dolls—that lays burning in the fireplace, but as I get closer I can see the blackened flesh curl away from the bones of a tiny hand and watch a perfect little face consumed. The child in the fire is no more than a baby.

And it's not alone.

There are hundreds of them . . . babies, children, men and women, naked, stacked up like branches . . . like pieces of kindling waiting to tossed into the flames.

Asleep on the cot, Janna whimpers and the sound of the fire gets louder, the smell of burning flesh stronger.

And I know what's happening . . . I finally know.

She's not just dreaming them, the bodies in the fire and the smell and the sounds, she's doing what the amber-eyed woman told her to do . . . she's *remembering* them.

I can hear the crackle of the nightmare fire as I crawl into the cot next to her. Her body is hot, the flannel nightgown I outgrew three years ago soaked through with sweat. She groans when I wrap my arms around her, but doesn't wake up, so the nightmare goes on and on.

I whisper to her, soft and low, like the lullaby my mother sang to her that first night.

"Janna, *veizen*. Show me."

Her body tenses against mine and the light from the nightmare fire changes into a bright white glare while she stands in the frigid air, shivering, holding tight to a hand almost blue with the cold. *Mama's hand*. She looks up and Mama smiles, but her amber eyes are pale in the camp's searchlights and she says something . . . but the light changes again and mama's gone and in her place is a tunnel leading down to a brightly lit bathhouse. There are two soldiers standing near the door. One handing out towels, the other soap. Both are smiling. Both have skulls instead of faces. Both of them wave and . . .

Another hand offers candy. Another hand tears off our clothes.

Another hand.
Another face.
Another body.
Another scream.

Janna stopped dreaming an hour before dawn, and I stayed with her until her body was cold. I remember she was smiling. I remember all of it . . . every horror, every pain, every memory that had festered under her skin.

She gave them to me to keep.

Now it's your turn.

With thanks to Naomi Birns

Bethany's Wood

PAUL FINCH

Paul Finch is a British ex-cop, now full-time writer, who works prima-
rily in television and film, but who is no stranger to short story markets.
His first collection, After Shocks, *published in 2001, won the British
Fantasy Award, while his short novel,* Cape Wrath, *made the final
ballot for the Stoker awards in 2002. His short stories have been pub-
lished in the anthologies* Shadows Over Baker Street, A Walk on the
Darkside, Quietly Now, Daikaiju! *(Giant Monster Tales), and* The
Mammoth Book of Jacobean Whodunnits.

Finch regularly writes for The Bill, *the popular British television
crime series, while* Spirit Trap, *a teen horror movie, which he coscripted,
was released to cinemas in 2005. He has just completed his first full-
length novel,* The Twisting Flesh, *and is currently working on a
movie adaptation of* Cape Wrath.

*He lives in Lancashire, northern England, with his wife, Cathy,
and his children, Eleanor and Harry.*

The eerie figures seen walking in Bethany's Wood on Bloodybush Edge last Sunday may have a perfectly mundane explanation.

Bestselling novelist Ariadne Jones, who owns the wood, and over three hundred acres of the surrounding pastureland, has admitted that the objects were almost certainly "mobile works of art" that she herself has erected in the densely-grown area of pine forest.

The incident caused a minor sensation last weekend, when ramblers, who didn't realize they'd entered private land, spotted what they later called "horrible shapes" moving among the trees. One rambler was so disturbed that he is alleged to have run three miles to the nearest pub, where he stammered out his story to an astonished taproom.

In a statement issued through her agents, Beckwith-Blenkinsop, Miss Jones, the famously reclusive authoress, who actually lives on the estate but has never received guests there or been photographed, said:

"I certainly apologize for any alarm I might have caused. The creation of these moving sculptures has been a project of mine for some time. It's my intent to eventually put the display on show, but not at present as there is still a lot of work to be done. In respect of this, I request that members of the public who are interested be patient and do not come onto the estate uninvited. Bethany's Wood is a carefully nurtured ecological environment, and even the most cautious trespassers could cause accidental damage."

—North Cheviot Gazette, Aug 29th 2005

Terri sighed and put the printout down. It was now dog-eared and tacky from her pondering and fingering it all the way up from London. How Mark had found such an obscure item as an on-line issue of the North Cheviot Gazette—a free newspaper with a rural readership and subsequent minuscule circulation—she hadn't yet discovered, but it was typical of him that he had.

She looked at the paper again. She supposed she could understand why it had caught his attention, but really . . . was something as oblique as this genuinely worth a spur-of-the-moment three-hundred-mile drive? There was a *thump* from the direction of the pub; its rear door closing. Terri glanced out through the Range Rover's front window. Mark was making his way across the car park, pulling on his waxed jacket. It was a cool day for early September, and the sky overhead was slate-gray and promising rain, as it always seemed to be doing in this desolate region. Terri was a Home Counties girl by origin, but well-traveled. In Europe, she'd been as close to the Arctic Circle as St. Petersburg; in North America she'd visited Vancouver. But never, even in those far more northern outposts, did she think she'd seen skies as routinely threatening as the ones that lowered over the north of England.

"Any joy?" she asked, as he climbed into the car beside her.

"Yeah." He slid his key into the ignition. "We're about three miles away."

"Thank God."

Getting to the Northumberland National Park had been easy enough. All they'd really had to do was travel north from London in a straight line, and stop just short of the Scottish border. But once there it became more difficult. They had their AA map book, which was so detailed as to indicate the presence of the spectacularly named Bloodybush Edge (an immense downward-sloping swathe of rugged and featureless wild country), but even on the local map they'd bought, there'd been no trace of Bethany's Wood. As such, they'd had to wing it, stopping at farms and country pubs like this one, The High Riding, to ask directions. Now at last, they seemed to be getting somewhere.

"I hope it's worth all this, Mark," Terri said as he started the car. She didn't want to annoy him with superficial gripes, but if a point *needed* to be made, she never hesitated to make it.

They drove out onto the narrow lane. Sweeps of tussocky, boulder-strewn grassland rolled away to either side, portions of it divided up by dry stonewalling. From this angle it looked flat, but that was deceptive. It actually undulated. Becks snaked across it, often concealed in swampy, low-lying valleys. Here and there, on raised ground, lonesome stands of fir made sentinel shapes against the rain-swollen clouds.

"When we set out this morning I was ninety-five percent sure," he eventually replied. "Now I'm ninety-nine percent."

"Okay?"

"I've just spoken to the landlord in there. He reckons he's actually seen these sculptures. He reckons they're really, to use his own words . . . 'shitty.'"

"I see."

Her doubtful tone led him to explain further: "Well . . . that's exactly what Zoe was into. She used to produce these metalwork figures."

"That were shitty?"

"I know what he meant by that," Mark added. "The stupid cow always thought she was *avant-garde*. These objects she made, they were like life-size re-creations from Picasso. You know, humanoid but distorted, impressionistic. Not true to life."

"Shitty."

"*I* thought they were shitty, yeah!"

"Yes, but Mark, the difference is that you thought they were shitty because they'd been made by your mum's girlfriend, and you hated her guts. This landlord chap might think they're shitty because they're a load of amateurish crap. You sure you're not confusing the two?"

Mark appeared to ponder this as he drove. Terri watched him furtively. He was a handsome, well-built guy, and his unruly, oil-black locks and square, frequently unshaven jaw gave him a rugged, masculine appeal that was quite at odds with the fact he was a vicar's son. Of course, at the moment, he was pale, sallow-cheeked. The inner turmoil he currently had to deal with was proving hugely stressful.

"Mark," she said, more gently, "I'm only making sure that we aren't still putting two and two together and coming up with five."

"Look at the rest of the evidence," he replied. "The place is called Bethany's Wood. My older sister is named Bethany."

"That could be a coincidence."

"This Ariadne Jones who says she put the figures up, and who no one's ever seen . . . she's a best-selling author. My mum was a best-selling author."

"Your mum was a romantic novelist. Ariadne Jones is famous for non-fiction, and concentrates mainly on New Age philosophies."

Mark shook his head. "Mum was starting to get into that stuff, especially when bloody Zoe came along."

"Yes, but it wasn't her bread and butter. Your mum was surely smart enough to stick to writing what she knew about?"

"All right," he said, "all right . . . they use the same literary agents."

"Beckwith-Blenkinsop probably have hundreds of top writers on their books."

He glanced at her. "Why are you giving me such a hard time, Terri? You know this is important to me."

"I know it is. I just don't want you getting terribly disappointed."

"You mean I should accept that Mum's dead?"

"I wish you would."

"And I should ignore tantalizing clues that might suggest otherwise?"

Terri considered. "I'm not sure they do suggest that."

"But if it was your mother wouldn't you at least look into them?"

A moment passed, then she nodded. "Course I would. Which is why I've not tried to talk you out of coming. Which is why I'm here with you now, being supportive."

Mark drove on, visibly uptight. She understood why. He'd only uncovered this unlikely piece of evidence two days ago, and ever since then had been planning his journey north. By this morning he'd been like a cat on hot bricks. The trip itself, dragged out through five hours of infuriating Saturday traffic, had also taken its toll on him.

As they cruised through the bleak but verdant border country, Terri thought about the strange family she was shortly to marry into. The Hagens were most famous at present for Anthony Hagen, Mark and Bethany's father, an Anglican priest and outspoken traditionalist, who was soon to be inaugurated as Bishop of Woking. Diane Hagen, his late wife, had been renowned in her own right, but was better known now for the manner of her passing than for the numerous books she'd written: the car in which she and her young protégé, Zoe Wroxeter, had been traveling, was found in the River Avon, having apparently crashed through the barrier fence on the Clifton suspension bridge. No bodies were recovered, but it was generally held that neither woman could have survived such an accident. That was ten years ago, however, and now Mark himself was following his mother's footsteps by making his name as a novelist, though in his case it was crime thrillers. He'd already had three published, to considerable acclaim, which wasn't bad going for a twenty-three-year-old.

And then all this business had started. He'd suddenly developed the conviction that his mother was still alive and living incognito somewhere. Terri knew that Mark had a tendency to obsess about things, but she didn't think he was beyond the reach of common sense. She was certain that when, or if, he finally met this Ariadne Jones and saw for himself that she wasn't his mother, he'd drop the whole thing.

It would be easier if they'd gone through the correct channels, though Ariadne Jones had no form for granting interviews, and she definitely wouldn't if by some unlikely chance she *was* Mark's mother. That said, Terri still wasn't happy with Mark's determination to see the woman even if it meant "fucking forcing his way in." As she'd explained to him, forcing your way onto private land was not generally a good idea; most people deemed it illegal. Mark's response to that had been to remain ominously quiet.

He only drove past the entrance gate to the estate once, in order not to attract attention, but Mark was in no doubt that they'd come to the right place.

There was no notice on the gate, but it was tall and made from wrought iron, with spikes running along the top. There was a mailbox to one side of it, and an intercom system built into a brick post, while from the high branches of a nearby larch, a security camera kept silent surveillance. Such protection of privacy was never a trait of his mother's in her old life. Even at the height of her popularity, she'd lived openly at the vicarage and had been more than willing to sign books for anyone who turned up at the front door. But then, he supposed, if she'd drawn a line under that existence and started something new, it was possible that everything else had altered.

They continued along a country road that was little better than a cart track. High embankments rose to either side, covered in gorse and bracken, so the only view was directly ahead, though that was now obscured by heavy rain, which had been drumming on the car's windshield for the last ten minutes.

"Just out of interest," Terri asked, "where are we going now?"

"Making a recon," he replied.

He did his best to make it sound as though this was part of a plan, but the truth was that he was winging it again. He had no idea of the geographic layout of the Bethany's Wood estate. He hoped they were skirting around its edges, and would soon come upon an access point, but it was equally likely they were actually driving *away* from it. It could only be a matter of time before Terri began to get exasperated.

He glanced sidelong at her. His wife-to-be was exceptionally pretty: pert-nosed, brown-eyed, with glittering brunette tresses falling well past her shoulders. Even in baggy outdoors clothes—a shapeless sweater and surplus Army trousers with pockets down the sides—her trim figure was unmistakeable. Not surprising considering that she was a fashion model by trade. He'd been going out with her for three years, and in that brief time he'd seen her progress from a youthful, coltish wannabe to a princess of the London and Paris catwalks. She was only twenty, but this last six months alone, the job offers and the cash had come pouring in. Thankfully, other less savory aspects of the fashion-world lifestyle hadn't yet afflicted her. She didn't do drugs, for instance, her drinking activities were confined to the odd glass of wine, and she had no time for the sort of tantrums that certain older members of her profession excelled at.

She now put another pertinent point to him: "I never knew your mum, Mark. But from what I've heard of her, she was a good mother and a devoted wife."

"She was," he replied. "I used to *think* she was, at least."

"Come on. You were thirteen when she died. That's long enough to form a very accurate impression of what someone's like."

Mark said nothing. He knew what she was getting at.

"Why would she deceive you in such a heartless way? Why put you through the agony of thinking she'd died? And not just you, your whole family and all her friends, of which I understand she had a lot?"

"She had a lot 'til Zoe Wroxeter came on the scene."

"Let's not change the subject. Look, stop the car."

Mark slowed to a halt and applied the handbrake. "Think this through," Terri said. "Do you believe that your mother loved you?"

Mark remembered blissful childhood evenings spent in the rosy glow of the hearth, seated on his mother's knee as she read him fairy tales or nursery rhymes. For a moment it was difficult for him to keep the tears from his eyes. Rather curtly, he nodded.

"So I ask the question again," Terri said. "How can you square *that* with her staging her death and abandoning you all, and not only that, abandoning her responsibilities and all the other things that were going on in her life? It doesn't make sense."

"She was a dyke."

"Oh, Mark . . ."

"Look, just because Mum loved us all, that didn't mean she wasn't confused about her sexuality."

"I'm not saying she wasn't," Terri retorted, "but she was a mature woman when she finally realized the truth about herself. I find it highly doubtful she'd have been so blown away with lust for this Zoe Wroxeter, who from what you say was a plain, bland little creature . . ."

"That's putting it mildly."

"It's highly doubtful she'd have chucked her entire life away just because she was bicurious. Not if she loved you all, Mark."

"It's *because* she loved us all."

There was a moment of silence.

"What do you mean?" Terri finally asked.

Mark tried to explain: "When Mum married Dad, she didn't know she was going to become a successful author. She went into that marriage with a strong sense of duty. Even later on, when she was topping the best-sellers list, she was by his side at church fêtes, at bring-and-buy sales, visiting the orphans and the OAPs."

"Doesn't that underline what I've just been saying?"

"No, it doesn't. She knew that copping off with this little gay vixen would be unforgivable, would tarnish everything. Don't you get it? My dad would never have lived it down. It would have been bad enough if she was seeing another bloke, but another woman!" He let his words hang, then added: "In pretending that she'd died, she was actually protecting us."

"And you hate her for that?"

"Yes. Because she was protecting us from something she could still have turned her back on. Something that, if she'd been strong, she could have ignored."

Terri didn't reply, and Mark knew why. It was because this was the part of the conversation where he and she had been certain to disagree. Though she might be a hometown kind of girl rather than a ball-breaking party animal, Terri was still part of the metropolitan set, still a progressive thinker. Perhaps to Terri's mind, the fact that Mark's mum had finally found fulfillment was justification enough for her turning her back on her original family, especially as they'd by then reached an age when they could fend for themselves. Maybe he ought to feel that way, too, but he didn't. No matter how hard he tried, the very thought of what he suspected his mother had done aggrieved him, hurt him so deeply that the pain of it too easily transformed into anger. And then he stared past Terri, across the road, and spotted a gap in the embankment, and on the other side of that, a low net fence, and the anger flared again.

He snatched the keys from the ignition, pocketed them, and climbed from the car. He stood beside the vehicle. The rain had eased off, but the air was dank and chill. Wind hissed on the saturated hillsides.

"What are we doing now?" he heard Terri ask from inside.

"Let's walk from here," he said gruffly.

"What if someone comes along and needs to get past?"

"Who's likely to on a Saturday evening?" He glanced at his watch—it was now well after six. "Even farmhands don't work Saturday evenings, and I doubt anyone else ever comes along this road. Come on, it's stopped raining."

Terri climbed from the car as well, but reluctantly, as though expecting to get drenched. The moment she was out, Mark locked the vehicle, then sidled around it to the break in the embankment. The trackside grass was deep and lush, and filled with nettles, and it soaked his jeans as he waded into it.

"Do we even know that this is part of the estate?" Terri asked.

She looked concerned. One of the things she'd insisted on when they'd first set out from London, was Mark's guarantee that he wasn't coming here for revenge, that there wouldn't be trouble if he found that Ariadne Jones *was* his mother. He'd promised there wouldn't be, advised her that, despite being so cruelly betrayed, he wasn't a killer.

"It never actually entered my head that you might kill her," Terri had said worriedly. "I just don't think it would help anyone if you caused a scene."

"Well, there are scenes and scenes," he'd replied enigmatically.

"Mark!" she'd snapped. "We're not going if all you're planning to do is start a fight."

Eventually, he'd assured her that he wouldn't start a fight, that all he wanted was some answers. But even then he knew that she was uncertain of his intentions. And as he climbed the raised ground toward the low fence, he did it heavily, stomping with his thick-soled hiking boots, finding secret pleasure in the knowledge that he was reawakening Terri's earlier concerns.

The fence only came as high as his chest, and it was old and flimsy; so flimsy in fact that it could easily be pushed down to allow them to climb over it. Beyond it, meadowland, glistening with rain, sloped downwards for about fifty yards before terminating in a wall of conifers. Without any doubt, that was the outer bulwark of Bethany's Wood. The trees ran north-south for as far as Mark could see, and were closely ranked together. This had to be the place. From what he'd learned, Bethany's Wood had been carefully managed and was composed exclusively of evergreens. It was also relatively young, as none of this wood's trees appeared to have grown over fifteen feet. He stared, trying to penetrate the trackless gloom behind the narrow trunks, and wondered how far into it the house actually was. In normal circumstances, perhaps if he'd been less driven, he wouldn't have fancied venturing in there, especially when he considered the newspaper report about the "horrible figures" prowling about, the "mobile works of art"—whatever the hell that meant.

Terri clearly shared the feeling. She hugged herself against the chill and watched the wall of woodland uncomfortably.

"You don't have to go in if you don't want to," Mark said.

"I said I'd come with you, didn't I," she replied. "Though I'm not sure who's the bigger maniac, you or me." She glanced up at the clouds. "I'll get my waterproof, yeah?"

"Sure," he said, handing her the car key.

As she turned back to the vehicle, he vaulted over the fence and landed in the meadow. He strode forward a few yards, all the time staring at the wood. At middle school he'd once gone on a field trip to North Wales, and spent most of that day orienteering in one such purpose-grown pine forest. It had been far more difficult than he and his friends had expected: there'd been no paths in there, no streams, hardly any landmarks at all apart from the occasional firebreak; only file after regimented file of identical pines, their foliage so dense and prickly and meshed together that it was a struggle to make headway in any direction. On that occasion, of course, he'd had a map and compass, so any difficulties he'd encountered then would be magnified tenfold this time.

Mark thought about telling Terri again that there was no need for her to go farther. But he knew she wasn't accompanying him solely to provide support; she wanted to ensure that he didn't do anything stupid.

Then he saw movement.

At first it was only a flicker on the edge of his vision. He turned his head left, gazing hard, trying to focus on the black spaces amid the matted, emerald boughs. And yes, for a fleeting second, a human figure was visible, but moving away into the dimness, rapidly vanishing, the way a sinking body descends into the murk of the ocean.

Instinctively, without really thinking, Mark started forward across the grass.

It was the first real surprise Terri had had since the start of her relationship with Mark: she'd got back to the fence and found no sign of him.

She pulled down the hood of her waterproof and stared across the meadow. Surely he hadn't gone on ahead without her? She reached for the mobile phone in her pocket. That was what she'd do if they ever became separated in a shopping mall or something. But now she remembered that when she'd been getting her coat from the car, she'd seen his mobile in the glove box.

Irritated, she climbed over the fence, and started forward toward the wood. The ground was so soggy that it *squelched* with each step, and as Terri only had trainers on, her feet were soon wringing wet. At last she reached the trees, but still there was no sign of him. She paused, peering as far into the depths of the wood as she could. Thanks to the way it had been grown, there was little ground cover, only a smooth carpet of needles. The downside, however, was that there was no light either. True, there were narrow passages between the rows of firs, and these led away from her in straight lines, but many soon became lost in dense brush and opaque shadow. Slowly, the enormity of what she was going to have to do sank in. It went against all logic for her to wander into a silent stretch of unknown woodland, even if her boyfriend *was* somewhere close by.

She listened in the hope that she'd hear him, but the only sound was that constant *hiss* of wind on the distant hilltops. Even birdsong was notable by its absence. Terri stood there for several minutes, then finally zipped her cagoule up and strode forward. This was a private estate; who was likely to be here who would offer danger? A gamekeeper would merely show her to the exit. Poachers, certainly in England, were better known for cutting and running when confronted than for attacking. A few minutes later, though, such easy rationalization seemed misplaced. Once she was inside the wood, its shadows closed around her; she pressed on, but soon was having to turn sideways just to make progress. The air itself changed. Outside, it was fresh, invigorating. Here, it was strongly scented—with sap from the young trees, and mold from the layer of mulch under her feet. Strands of cobweb were soon crisscrossing her path, glistening with raindrops; clusters of unhealthy-looking toadstools sprouted among the more exposed roots. As the wind couldn't penetrate very far in, the silence became sepulchral. There was a still-ness too: it was heavy, ominous, as though it forbade you to disturb it; the stillness you got in church, she thought.

Then a figure crossed her path.

Terri stopped dead. Chills ran up her spine like electric currents.

A rather unpleasant figure.

To begin with, it hadn't been walking. Whoever had reported that they'd seen figures *walking* in this wood was way off the mark. This thing had been sliding, or perhaps "gliding" would be a better term. It had crossed the path ahead of her in a single smooth movement, without any of the jerking, per-ambulating motions one normally associates with a legged animal. Not that she was convinced this figure even *had* legs. She thought it was wearing a ragged, shiftlike garment, almost a toga, with one section thrown over the left shoulder, as a result of which only the upper torso had been visible. If you could call it a torso. Because it was ghoulishly skeletal: a narrow, upright cage constructed of tubular metal and painted deathly white. Terri wondered if it was painted *luminous* white, if it would glow in the dark as it patroled these deep and silent groves. Despite that almost too eerie thought, she blun-dered forward to the point where she'd seen the thing.

She spotted it again, watching it for several moments before coniferous curtains sprang back into place to block it from sight. Terri stayed where she was, thinking quickly. It definitely had a humanoid shape. Its left arm was hanging by its side, and had looked visibly prosthetic—molded from pale plastic, jointed at the elbow with a screw—the sort of thing you'd find in a hospital skip. The right arm, however, projected out in front, and was nar-rower, longer, and char black, almost like a bar of burnt or badly corroded iron. There was a glove on the end of it, a leather gauntlet. The iron bar had been inserted as far into this gauntlet as the index finger; the impression cre-ated was that the figure was pointing ahead as it moved.

Terri thrust her way through the brush. There was nothing to be fright-ened of here. The object was a work of art, a sculpture, nothing more. She fought her way into open space, and looked around her. What kind of head did it have? She thought it was smooth and oval, egglike, with a see-through bag pulled down over it, tied at the neck. At the front there was a photo-graph of some sort, or perhaps an illustration.

"Hello?" she said aloud, only belatedly realizing how absurd she was be-ing. Artworks didn't respond to human contact.

Then she glimpsed it again. Or, at least, its back—thirty yards distant, once again receding through the green arches of the wood. It had apparently turned right, and as Terri started to follow, it turned again. This time it veered to the left, quite sharply, catching her by surprise. Though it wasn't too far ahead, this new maneuver threw her completely off-track. She spun around, confused. Branches obstructed her; pine needles prickled her cheeks. She scrambled on, but her quarry was no longer in view. She halted to listen, but could hear nothing except her own hurried breathing. She wasn't even sure now which direction she was facing in. If she decided to go back to the car, she wouldn't be able to find it easily.

"Mark!" she called out.

All of a sudden, she got angry. She was drenched, and not just her legs and feet, but her body as well: the inside of her waterproof now ran with sweat.

"Mark, where the hell are you?" she shouted. "God damn it, this is ridiculous!"

She entered another straight-line avenue. Following one of these passages would eventually bring her back to the outside world, though at which part of the wood's circumference she couldn't imagine.

"This is ludicrous," she said, checking her watch: it was almost seven o'clock.

She glanced overhead. The clouds—the few she could see through the interlacing branches—had broken a little. In fact, they were streaked with blue, were mackerel-like; it was more like an August evening than a September one. The difference was that it was now getting distinctly colder, and dusk was shortly due to fall. There was nothing for it; she was going to have to follow this particular passage to its end. The question was whether to go forward or to go back. She looked over her shoulder.

And saw a figure that had clearly been encroaching on her for the last half-minute.

Terri couldn't suppress a yelp. Instinctively, she started to back away. The figure continued to advance toward her along the corridor of trees. It was coming quickly, relentlessly. At first it was twenty yards away, now fifteen, now twelve. She continued her backwards retreat, knowing only that it wasn't the same one she'd seen before.

This one appeared to have been assembled from bin liners stuffed with straw, and bound into a human form with ropes, belts, and harnesses, many of the latter studded with iron spikes. Over that it wore a top hat and a tailcoat, both of which had seen better days. From each of its sleeves protruded a three-pronged steel claw, all the prongs purposely curved and sharpened. Terri saw that this object, too, was gliding rather than walking. Its feet wore black, high-heeled shoes, but they were mounted on a metal plate that seemed to skate along the woodland floor. Even though she retreated steadily, the thing was near enough for her to identify the white-on-black image plastered to the front of its straw-stuffed dummy head.

It was a human face.

Quite unmistakably, it was *her* human face.

Terri's breath caught in her throat. She muttered some nonsense about being mistaken, about hallucinating, but though that face was cast in photographic negative, the closer it got, the clearer it became.

And if that wasn't appalling enough, what passed for the thing's hands now visibly rotated. Its arms flexed at the elbows, then bent upwards. The forearms rose and spread themselves out. It was a greeting, she realized with numbing horror. Her demonic twin wanted to embrace her.

With a shriek, Terri turned and fled.

She weaved blindly away through the trees, slashing herself across the face and body, but stumbling on headlong. Sheer terror gave her heels wings, but she felt certain that she was being pursued. Was that the rasping of breath in her throat, or the *thrash* of foliage as her sisterly stalker gained ground? She could outrun it, she told herself; she was fit. She could easily outrun it. And then she tripped.

She tumbled forward and felt her ankle twist. Something *snapped*.

Terri wanted to scream, the agony was so intense. But fear of what followed her prevented this. She scrambled along on all fours, panting like a dog, clawing her way through the needles. After a dozen yards she tried to stand again, but that was a mistake. White fire shot up her leg. Reeling sideways and then falling against a trunk, the wind was knocked out of her. She rolled on damp earth, gasping for breath, her eyes filled with hot tears, and as a result, she didn't at first notice the figure that appeared to one side of her and now stood there in contemplative silence. She only realized it was there at all when it reached down and gripped her by the shoulder.

Mark thought he'd worked out how the figures moved.

He'd now seen several of them in the wood, all following their own mysterious paths. Having shadowed one for several yards, he'd finally realized that it wasn't sliding along a runner as he'd first thought, but was actually part of a huge chain-and-pulley system. Once the figure passed out of sight, he kicked aside the debris of the woodland floor and discovered a narrow, shallow trench, lined with greased enamel and with soft rubber flaps fixed over the top, one to either side, to prevent materials falling in and clogging it up. A chain, thick with oil, was moving steadily along inside it. Evidently, the pegs on which the figures were mounted were located at regular intervals on this chain, which probably meandered back and forth all over the estate. Likely, it was operated by a central mechanism, an engine of some sort, probably fitted with a wheel, the teeth of which caught the chain's links as it revolved. If that was correct, so long as the power was switched on, these odd beings would trawl spookily around Bethany's Wood until the cows came home. Weirder still, Mark also suspected that some of them had additional but independent power-sources: they looked to have been constructed on steel skeletons, which apparently had moving parts. As he'd spied on them, he'd noticed occasional animatronic hand and arm movements, which invested the figures with an eerie lifelike quality.

His objective now, however, was not to discover what purpose this immense, mobile grid-pattern served—though he'd be fascinated to know—it was to find out if, as he suspected, its focal point was the house where Ariadne Jones lived. The spider frequently sat at the center of its web, he told himself. Following one of the figures and seeing where it took him thus seemed the best option. The one he locked onto was broad across the shoulders and wore a shabby coat with its sleeves removed. This revealed that it had coiled springs for arms and shovel-blades for hands, which bounced up and down continuously as it rolled forward. A garish, carroty-red wig hung down its back. This doubtless signified something, but Mark didn't waste time trying to work out what, because he'd no sooner started to track the figure than a house came into view ahead. One glance told him it was *the* house. But it wasn't what he'd expected.

It was not well kept. The building was clearly old and grand, but was a dim shade of what it must have been in former times. It was a well-proportioned two-story affair, built from mellow, pinkish brick, with tall Georgian windows all along the front and a castellated porch tower. Many sections of its roof were visibly rotted or covered in fungus, however, while lichen grew in green streaks down its walls. The window boxes were full of unsightly weeds, and some of the windows themselves were cracked and papered over on the inside.

Mark emerged from the trees onto a pebble drive. He stared at the house, perplexed. His mother had always been an accomplished homemaker. The vicarage where he'd spent his childhood had never been less than pristine, either inside or out. Even when she'd begun to write seriously, she'd always found time to expertly housekeep. The sculpture he'd followed, meanwhile, was now halfway across the drive. The runnel—for that was how Mark had come to think of the channel containing the chain—led diagonally toward the west wing of the building. The figure entered the wing through a narrow archway that seemed to have rectangular strips of opaque plastic hanging from it. Whether this was an entrance to the building proper or just a short-cut through one of its annexes to the other side, Mark wasn't sure.

He looked the house over, then the drive: to the right it became a small path that circled around the corner of the building, and to the left it curved out of sight, presumably back toward the front gate. There was no sign that anybody was here: no one was visible through the windows, and there were no vehicles in sight. He walked furtively across the drive, trying not to *crunch* the gravel too loudly, and approached the plastic-covered entrance, which he pushed through without hindrance. Beyond that, he found himself in an arched passage that had a dank, fetid aura. Mold grew thick and scabrous on its whitewashed walls, though the floor was concrete and looked like it had been swept recently. The runnel led directly up it for ten yards, then passed through what looked like a pair of pink curtains. Mark strolled down toward them, and when he got there, saw that they were made from vinyl and had a slick, slippery texture.

He paused, listening. There was a low reverberation; the sound a machine might make, and, for some reason, that set him on edge. For the first time, Mark had the feeling that if he went any farther now, if he pushed through these curtains uninvited, he would at last be committing a crime, would finally be violating the privacy of this house. He pondered. He wasn't a criminal by nature. It went against all the modes of common decency that his father had drilled into him over the years, but he'd come this far. He was inches from answering a question that had tortured him for a decade.

"Fuck it!" he said, and he went through the curtains fist-first.

The room on the other side might once have been a garage: the floor was still concrete and the walls whitewashed, while the ceiling consisted of old planks. But if housing vehicles *had* once been the room's purpose, things had changed. There was a curious scent in the air—it was pungent, sickly sweet— and a reddish, low-key light emanated from niches in the walls where candle flames burned. On the opposite side of the room, a grill glowed orange in an oil black, furnacelike structure. The illumination this gave was so poor, however, that Mark stood there for several seconds before his eyes attuned. When they did, he saw that the runnel veered slightly to the left, then proceeded across the room, bypassing an oblong flagstone that had been set into the floor close to the left-hand wall, and from the side of which a coaxial cable snaked away and vanished through a socket in the skirting board. This flagstone seemed to be the source of the low hum that Mark had heard outside, and he deduced that the wheel mechanism was probably located beneath it. Doubtless the wheel itself lay horizontal so that it could manipulate the chain without interfering with the figures as they glided by overhead. It was clever, he admitted to himself. This whole thing was clever, if a trifle pointless.

He started across the room. There were two open doorways, one to either side of the furnace. The runnel led out through the left one. Mark peeked after it, and saw a passage that ran fifteen yards to the other side of the building, then exited through an outer arch. The shovel-handed figure was now framed in the middle of this as it trundled off toward a second wall of fir trees. He watched it until it disappeared, then turned back to the vinyl curtains. He didn't suppose it would be long before another one came rolling in. He didn't know how many there were traveling on this circuit, but he'd already spotted several different ones. Then he noticed something else; another kind of sculpture, though this one was unlikely to move because of its ungainly shape and position. Whereas the others were upright and basically humanoid, this one was totally impressionistic. It might, in the wildest flight of someone's imagination, have represented a person, but if so, its legs were fat stumps, its belly huge, its shoulders ridiculously narrow and its head the size of an orange. The whole thing had then been smoothed off and rounded, and, at the lower portion of its middle, now possessed a curved, worm-like object, which initially Mark thought was a phallic symbol. He then realized it was supposed to be a serpent, winding its way up the statue's globular belly from a hidden area between its legs. The entire thing was about the size of a large child, and it sat on top of the furnace on a timber platform; Mark hadn't noticed it before because the glare from the furnace grate had shielded it. Even now it looked colorless, probably having been molded from basic clay, though he noticed that silver candleholders were placed reverentially to either side of it. It was evidently an idol of some sort.

As he considered this, he heard the sound of someone approaching. He scrambled into the passage that led back to the outside, and waited there. A second passed, then footsteps entered. Mark risked a glance. A woman came through the door on the other side. She was short and stocky with severely cut dark hair, and wore sandals, baggy trousers, and a paint-stained smock. She was carrying three bowls, which she now laid in front of the idol. He was just close enough to see that the first contained nuts, the second apples and pears, and the third what looked like a piece of overcooked steak. The woman whispered something barely audible, possibly an incantation of some sort. Then she crouched in front of the furnace grate, opened it, placed the blackened meat on an iron skillet, and pushed it into the flames. After this, she turned and left by the door she'd come in.

Mark emerged from his hiding place and gazed at the idol. He couldn't imagine what it represented, if it represented anything at all. But the loathing he suddenly felt for it was corrosive. Then he sensed a new presence in the room. He spun around, panicking—only to relax again.

Another automated figure had slipped in through the pink vinyl curtains and was now gliding forward. This one was scarecrowlike: a thin crucifix of steel rods, with what resembled a black cassock trailing from it. Its head was a punctured football, so scrunched and weathered that the photograph-face attached to it was unrecognizable. Mark felt a twinge of revulsion as it slowly crossed the room toward him, only at the last minute to swerve left and go out toward the exit door. He watched it recede down the passage and saw additional movements. The steel-rod arms started to swivel, then to abruptly hinge at mid-length, one upwards, one down. The steel shaft that served as its neck was also jointed, for the head cocked first to the right, then to the left, in jerky, doll-like motions.

It was this that finally decided Mark he'd had enough. In truth, he'd already had enough when he'd seen the woman go through her clichéd, pseudo-Pagan routine. He had no doubt that it was Zoe. He hadn't seen her face, and she'd clearly put weight on over the last decade, but her stance and gait were the same, and anyway, who else would indulge in such juvenile New Age fantasies?

He strutted across the room, stopping once to hawk up some phlegm and spit it at the idol. Then he went out through the door the woman had taken. It connected with a passage that seemed to run into the main body of the house. Very soon, Mark saw that the interior of the building was as poorly maintained as the exterior. The walls were bare plaster, and though many of them had been illustrated with interwoven patterns of flowers, trees, and other pastoral imagery, they were now flaking and cracked. The main hall was lofty and oak-paneled. It might once have been imposing, but the woodwork had lost its luster, the carpets were worn, and there was a smell of damp. Its few items of furniture were shoddy and ill-matched, and thrust carelessly to one side. Here and there, Mark could identify faded patches on the walls where pictures might once have hung. Then he heard movement close by. He spied a pair of open double doors, and looking through them saw a large parlor or lounge area—though it appeared to have been converted into a multipurpose living and working environment. In one part of it, a sofa and coffee table sat in front of a beaten-up television set, and beside that, a once grand hearth, now with a portable electric fire placed inside it. More centrally, there were two big desks, both arrayed with office equipment and computer gear, but also strewn with discarded paperwork, as was the extensive floor. One entire wall was filled with shelves clumsily fitted, with no apparent care for appearance, and crammed with dog-eared books. Books were also jammed three-deep along the windowsills, blocking out a significant amount of daylight. In every corner, it seemed, there were piles of boxes, or bundles of string-tied newspapers and periodicals. Though it should have been a huge, spacious chamber, it felt cramped and squalid. As before, a smell of damp pervaded.

The woman was in there, sorting through a heap of documents on the right-hand desk. She clearly *was* Zoe. He could see that now. There was no mistaking her small round face, which, though it had grown pale and pudgy over the years, was as bland and uninteresting as it had ever been.

"So now you're Mum's secretary as well," he said aloud.

The woman started violently, then stared up at him, shocked and at the same time frightened. "Who are you?" she shouted. "How'd you get in here?"

Mark entered the room. "Don't recognize the thirteen-year-old whose life you screwed up?"

Several heartbeats passed, during which time she seemed too dumbstruck to speak. She stared at him, stunned. Then, abruptly, her head dropped forward onto her pigeon-chest, and she shook it, and Mark saw to his astonishment that she seemed almost relieved.

"I'm . . . I'm sorry, Mark," she finally stammered. "I thought . . ."

"You thought I was a burglar? A rapist maybe?" He snorted scornfully. "Don't flatter yourself, Zoe. I wouldn't touch your cunt with a cattle prod."

At which she looked quickly up at him again. Her mouth fell open. Evidently, the innocent, gawky young teen who'd always been quiet and obedient around his parents, and so polite to guests, had come a long way in the last ten years.

"Get out of here," she said. "Get out or I'll call the police."

"Please do," Mark replied. "Faking death to collect on insurance is a criminal offense."

"It was nothing to do with collecting insurance!"

"You think the cops'll believe that? Mind you," he added, glancing distastefully around. "Maybe they will. This place is a fucking shit-hole."

He began to circle the room, picking things up, examining them, discarding them. Some items he only poked at gingerly, as though afraid they'd infect him with something.

"What were you expecting?" she asked nervously. "A palace?"

"Yes, I was. Always thought houses like this were full of antiques and artworks. *Real* artworks by the way. Not those lumps of crapola you've got walking round outside."

"They're crude effigies, that's all."

"That's the very most they are. Jesus, I can't believe she gave us up for *this*."

"She wanted a new path."

"Yeah, straight between your legs."

"Is that so wrong?"

"Well it isn't right," he said.

"Why, because it's against the Ten Commandments?" Now it was Zoe's turn to sound scornful. "Don't tell me you believe in the Ten Commandments, Mark. The Anglican Communion doesn't even believe in the Ten Commandments. The slightest pressure from modernists, and they're ready to change everything."

"It was wrong for someone like my mother to do it," he retorted. "She used to be devoted to the Church until she met you. You must have brainwashed her in some way."

"I never did any such thing!"

Zoe was following Mark around as he navigated the room, still picking things up and dropping them. She didn't seem keen to get close though. He knew he was scaring her—by his tone, by his deep, angry breathing, none of which was a put-on. As a youth, she'd never known him to be capable of violence. But of course people change.

"I suppose to you the Christian Church is just another tyrannical patriarchy," he said, "obsessed with keeping women subservient."

"And you don't think it is?"

He rounded on her so quickly that she backed up a few paces. "I don't give a shit whether it is or isn't!" he barked. "But I know it's been around two thousand years and you and your crystal-worshiping lunatic fringe aren't going to replace it anytime soon."

"Please leave, Mark. It's serving no purpose you being here now."

"You want the truth, Zoe—I've got a natural antipathy to people like you. All this counterculture self-righteousness, it's just a front, isn't it. Deep down, you're all out for what you can get, just like everyone else." The woman shook her head, but Mark ranted on: "I still have vivid memories of you wheedling your way into our lives, first appearing as a fan of my mum's, then as a friend, then as a companion, until finally you were going everywhere with us. Every event and function, *you* were there. The only thing that stops me kicking myself for not realizing what you were sooner is the fact that my dad, who's no dimwit, didn't realize either. Not until it was too late . . . you bitch."

"Please, Mark . . ."

"As I say, though, you're only one of a type . . . a deluded little nobody trying to invent her own reality because there isn't a place for her in the real reality."

"*This* is our reality now."

"This is nothing! It's a hiding place for aggrieved, self-pitying failures like you . . . with your crappy artworks and your paint-covered overalls and your stupid fucking men's haircuts. Jesus, no wonder you fucked up in real life."

"And did your mother fuck up?" she retorted. "Did *she* fail?"

Mark didn't answer that. Or rather couldn't. Because his mother clearly hadn't failed—either at tasks society had set for her, or tasks she'd set for herself. Scowling, he set off around the room again, picking things up, disgustedly tossing them aside.

"Anyway," the woman added, "I don't know why you're pretending to be such a misogynist. You're not. We know that, we've read your books."

That stopped him midtrack. He turned slowly round. "You've read my books?"

"Yes. And we like them. You're not an insensitive person, Mark. Why are you behaving as though you are?"

"My books are crime stories," he finally said. "They're full of grime and foulness."

"They center around a female cop, who's clever and sassy and streetwise."

"Who's also a male fantasy figure," he replied.

Zoe shook her head. "She's blazed her way through a male-dominated world."

"That's because she's blond and pretty and got big tits."

"She's made a success of her life."

"Because she can flirt as well as fight."

"She's still in control, she does what she wants . . ."

"Oh, for Christ's sake!" Mark bellowed. "She's fucking fiction! Just like all this. I mean, just what the hell is *that* supposed to be exactly?" He pointed through the window, to where another of the automated dummies was slowly processing across the drive toward the door in the west wing.

And then, for an amazing moment, possibly because he was staring so intently at it, he thought he recognized it.

It was ludicrous surely? The dummy, which again was skeletal-framed but in this case swathed with alternate strips of bandage and silver foil, and heavily padded out so as to look like a rugby player, resembled nothing that might exist outside the pretentious world of modern art. And yet, bizarrely—possibly because of its head, which was an upturned bucket with a big moustache and an obscenely grinning mouth drawn on it, and wore a trilby—it reminded him of his second-cousin Fred, who was prone to Jack-the-laddishness and ran two nightclubs in west London.

"No way," Mark said, shaking his head. "No way."

"It's a supplicant," Zoe replied, answering his previous question. "It's on its way into the temple."

"The temple?"

"You were in there earlier. That's the only way you can have got into the house."

"Oh yeah, the temple." He jeered at the very notion.

"Don't you realize that that's what this is all about?" she asked him.

"You've been through the wood. Surely you've seen what's happening there. It's the ritual dance. The journey of the circles, the eternal labyrinth."

"For Christ's sake . . ."

"The journey through life," she added, "the only true way to find the Goddess."

"It's a pile of fucking horseshit!"

"You think so? Well *you've* done pretty well out of it." She glared at him defiantly. "Your father has too. And your sister."

Mark looked at her again. For a second he thought he'd misheard. "What?"

"Hasn't your father recently been appointed Bishop of Woking?"

For a few seconds crazy ideas spun in Mark's head, but he quickly dismissed them. "Okay . . . so you and Mum read the papers. Big deal."

"It's *because* of your mum that he's been appointed," Zoe said. "It's because of *her* that you're a successful author at so young an age, that your sister's already a barrister."

Mark shook his head, unwilling to listen let alone believe.

"What do you think your mother's built all this for?" Zoe asked him. "She might not live with you anymore, but you're still her family. She loves you all deeply."

Still Mark shook his head. But the more he considered it, the more he began to wonder. "That supplicant," he said, his voice tremulous, "the one that's just passed. It looked like a cousin of mine."

Zoe nodded. "You're *all* here. All her kith and kin. You're as much a part of the ritual dance as she is, probably more so. And all the while the paths are trod, you advance, you prosper. . . ."

"*This is a crock!*"

"I don't explain it very well, I realize that. I'm merely an acolyte."

"*And what's Mum supposed to be, the high-fucking-priestess!*" he exploded.

"Of a sort," the woman said, remaining calm, clearly understanding that his new anger stemmed from a dawning realization that she might actually be telling the truth. "She's the one the goodness comes from. The goodness that you *know* is real, because you used to bask in it yourself."

Mark tried not to remember those luxurious evenings by the fireside, seated on his mother's lap. Tried not to recall her kind, encouraging voice as he read his early lessons to her, or her soft hands helping him put his pajamas on. But probably because of the stress of the day, and the shock that the person he'd loved and worshiped throughout his most tender years was still alive, tears started to blur his vision.

"W-where is she?" he stuttered.

"She's walking in the wood," Zoe said. "She always walks in the evening. At moonrise the Goddess is most vibrant. . . ."

"Cut that crap!"

"She'll be back soon. She can explain it, herself. She's far more articulate than I am."

"She's going to need to be," Mark snapped. "Ten minutes after I get home, you'll have the world's press at your door."

"That would be your choice, of course."

"You mean I'm allowed one? In this domain of women."

"I know all this has come as a big shock to you, Mark," Zoe said, touching his arm, only for him to flinch away. "That's why we hid from you all. Ariadne was desperate not to hurt . . ."

"Diane! Her name is Diane!"

"Diane then—or perhaps Diana. The Roman mother-goddess, kindness embodied, the mistress of healing . . ."

"Jesus, Zoe! Grow the fuck up!"

"Who shares many attributes with the Virgin Mary, if you'd rather hear it that way."

"I'm not fucking interested!"

Mark used the heel of his palm to wipe the tears from his eyes, determined to regain his composure and, at the same time, his manly pride. It probably wouldn't count for much in a place like this, but Hell, by the sounds of things it was all he had left that was truly his.

"If you want to wait here, she'll not be long," Zoe said, moving toward the double doors. "Can I get you a drink?"

"Yeah. Make it a stiff one."

"There's no alcohol in this house. Will tea do?"

"So long as it's none of that herbal shit."

She nodded, and left the room.

Mark felt cold and alone, and not a little embarrassed. He wondered what his mother would say when she finally arrived. He also began to wonder what she'd look like. She'd been beautiful as a young woman, tall and shapely, with long fair hair and dazzling violet eyes. He'd only come to realize it recently, but he'd unconsciously modeled Laura Prince, his sexy policewoman heroine, on early photographs of his mother. She'd been stunning, which only added all the more to her mystique, and, now that he admitted it, increased his desire to see her again. Rather selfishly, he realized, he found himself hoping that time hadn't taken its toll on her; that she wouldn't have put on weight or grown haggard.

Then he heard a noise from the hall—the *click* of a latch.

He went straight out there, expecting someone to be coming in through the front door. But beyond the stained-glass fresco in its central panel there was no one. It was the wind, he realized. The rain had started again; gusts of it blew against the walls and windows. Mark relaxed, but decided he would wait here. He would be the very first thing his mother saw when she came in. Though he now ached to see her again (there was no denying that!), there was still some part of him that wanted to punish her.

And that was when he noticed the door on the other side of the hallway.

It was a single door, once handsome, carved with foliage and woodland faces, but now chipped and dull, and in fact vandalized because someone had chalked something on it. Mark idled over there and tried to read the graffiti. It was faded, only semilegible, but it appeared to read: *Disintegration*.

Curious, he pushed the handle down. The door swung open. He was confronted by what might have once been a small reception room but which now seemed to be used as a trash heap. Not that it contained trash of the common garden variety.

Stacks of portraits were propped against the walls. They were largely done in oils and portrayed typically regal subjects: redcoats, cavaliers, ladies of court. Old masters to be sure, yet all were grubby and torn, while some had been deliberately slashed. There were piles of broken crockery as well, and heaps of tarnished silverware. In the very center though, and this was the really surprising thing, lay a vast clutter of ancient weapons, apparently dumped there and allowed to gather dust.

Mark strode forward.

It was a perplexing sight. More so when he considered that, if these items were the real thing, they'd surely be priceless. Even if they were replicas, they looked so old that they had to be valuable. Long swords were present, alongside shields, battle-axes, maces. From later centuries, there were halberds, breastplates, sabers, flintlock pistols. All were aged in the extreme, many broken and rusty-edged, and just lying here in a heap.

Slowly, he understood. These weapons had probably once adorned the interior of the house, perhaps around the time his mother had first bought it. They'd doubtless filled the halls and passageways, hung in places of honor. They'd have added a touch of grandeur, there was no doubt. But in the light of what he'd learned today, it didn't surprise him too much to find them discarded like this. Nevertheless, it saddened him.

It wasn't right for all men to be lumped together under the same bloodstained banner. True, these weapons represented a solution to life's problems that was characteristically male. More to the point, perhaps, many of these arms visibly dated from the Cromwellian age, when *religious* warfare finally came to England, so the Church of Christ was also being denied by this irreverent action . . . but that was where the real irony lay. Because the horrors these weapons once wreaked had never been the responsibility of Christ himself. Jesus told people to love their enemies and forgive them, not kill them. Likewise, not *all* men were persecutors of women: Mark's father, for example. Anthony Hagen, the newly anointed Bishop of Woking, had always been a thundering voice in the pulpit, and a stern figure even in his own home. And yes, he preached that the old ways were best, he denounced the ordination of female priests, he believed that men should work and women stay in the home and raise families. And okay, in the eyes of some, maybe that was a form of female servitude, but was it really *so* bad? Was it genuinely fair to bracket men like Mark's father with the rapists and the witch-hunters?

There was another rattle from the front door. Mark turned, but nobody came through it. He glanced back across the room and the weapons, and saw a tall cupboard. It looked as forgotten and beaten-up as everything else in there, and he wouldn't have given it a second thought had he not spotted a black, tarry substance that seemed to be leaking from the bottom of it. He thought again about the word scrawled on the door: *Disintegration*.

When something disintegrated, it was over, finished, there was no way back for it.

Before he knew what he was doing, he was walking across the room. He rounded the pile of weapons and approached the cupboard. The liquid formed a viscous puddle in which three cockroaches wriggled helplessly. Mark watched them for a moment, chilled. Then he reached out, lifted the catch and opened the cupboard door.

And the smell hit him before the vision did: of burn, of char, of rancid flesh, of melted human fat.

The man in there, whoever he was, was naked except for a belt, which had been looped around his neck and used to suspend him from a coat hook. His flesh was streaked a variety of colors, mainly greens, purples, and yellows, and was crisped all over as though he'd been fried in batter. His hair, both on his head and his body, only remained in singed patches, and his eye-sockets were empty cavities.

Mark gagged, found himself swaying. He was about to topple forward, but at the last second he jerked away, tottering backwards and falling into the heaped weapons, sending them clattering across the room.

"What the hell are you doing in here?" a voice screamed from the doorway.

Mark looked dazedly around, and saw Zoe. She held two steaming mugs, but her face was written with outrage. And then she spotted the opened cupboard, and the thing inside it, and her cheeks, which had briefly flushed pink, blanched white.

"Should I ask you the same question?" Mark wondered, rising unsteadily to his feet, and only now realizing how lucky he'd been to stumble on this find *before* he'd had a chance to sample the drink she'd prepared for him.

Almost unconsciously, he reached down for a weapon, his hand finding the hilt of a chain-mace. "Tell me," he said, indicating the corpse, "is this another of your superior female values?"

Zoe watched dumbly as he picked the weapon up. It might have been old, but it still looked serviceable. Its chain was a foot long, and on the end of that swung a ball of spiked iron that was at least the size of a man's clenched fist.

"This is not what you think." she said, backing into the hall.

"Not what I think?" he replied, following her. "Was it a piece of this poor bastard that I saw you feeding into that fucking obscenity's fire-filled belly early on? A chunk of his buttock maybe, his inner thigh?"

"He was already dead. . . ."

"You maniac sow! What the hell kind of Satanist bullshit is this?"

They were now in the hall, and Mark lunged toward her. He tried to grab her rather than hit her, but the ball-and-chain was still in his hand. The woman screamed and dropped her two mugs, smashing them. She just managed to evade his reach. "Mark, you don't understand! He tried to interfere with the supplicants."

"What, those fucking walking piles of junk outside! He dared put his hands on one, so you killed him for it?"

"It's not that," she insisted, still backing away. "We didn't kill him. It was an accident. I'm just making use of the aftermath. And it wasn't *us*. You mother doesn't know anything about it."

"She doesn't know what's going on in her own house?"

"She lives in her head now, Mark." The woman continued to retreat. "All she cares about is her writing. I take care of everything else."

"You lying dyke harridan!"

"Listen to me," the woman pleaded. "He was a tramp, a vagrant. I don't even know how he got into the grounds, but he tried to interfere with one of the supplicants. And the power of the Goddess ran through him."

"Liar!" Mark shouted. "You killed him, didn't you! You pagan bitches, you fucking burned him!"

"No!" Zoe cried. Tears of fright appeared on her cheeks. "It was the Goddess who burned him. But it was unintentional. He tried to pull a supplicant down, and the power erupted inside him."

Mark now had her cornered, but suddenly her words struck a cord with him. Power—she'd used the word *power*. An image filtered into his mind—the coaxial cable that he'd seen snaking out from the mechanism that drove the dummies and connecting with the mains.

"*Jesus Christ on a bike!* Are you telling me those things out there are electrified? That a live current runs through them?" He thought of the mobile figures, and the many parts of them that were exposed metal. "Good God, are you evil or just plain loopy!"

"This is a holy place," she protested, "no one's supposed to come here!"

"You stupid whore!" he roared, and he slapped her across the face hard, before dashing back down the passage toward the temple. Terri was still out there. . . .

He entered the sacred chamber just as another of the effigies passed through. He didn't even look at it, but went straight across to where the flagstone lay. It was heavy, solid; but it wouldn't stop him. He put everything he had into the first blow, swinging the chain-mace down in a massive arc. There was a deafening *crunch*, and cracks shot across the slab's surface. Mark struck it again, and again, his efforts aided by the brutal design of the weapon, which had once crushed in steel helmets and shattered the skulls of men and horses alike. Only seconds later, the flagstone was in fragments.

Zoe now stumbled into the room behind him. She begged him to stop what he was doing. He ignored her.

Below the flagstone, as he'd suspected, there was a horizontal wheel. It turned against the links of the chain, keeping the entire ghoulish pantomime in motion. But a nest of live wires fed down onto it, dancing back and forth across its glinting steel surface, blue sparks flashing. Dear God, it had been set up like this *deliberately*; the whole thing was a deathtrap. For a minute he was too shocked to think clearly. But at last, he glanced up and saw the cable, and the spot where it entered the wall. Not willing to risk touching the wheel, he opted to make *this* his point of attack. He swung the mace sideways, hitting the wall in the exact place where the cable connected. A thin coat of plaster shattered, and underneath that there was a normal power point, put in place professionally and with full insulation. Mark struck at this as well, over and over, smashing it apart. Then he grabbed the cable and yanked it. Its roots now severed, it came out easily.

Immediately, everything stopped: the wheel, the chain; out in the passage, the retreating effigy also came to a halt. The live wires that had electrified the wheel ceased to jump and spit.

A taut second passed. Then, from behind him, Mark heard Zoe breathing heavily. He turned. She shrank back, wet-eyed. "Happy now?" she said.

"You think that's bad," he replied, "wait 'til you see this."

And he turned to the idol on the furnace, and raised his mace. He'd show them the meaning of disintegration. At *this* threat, however, the woman came violently to life.

"*NO!*" she howled, throwing herself onto his back, wrapping her arms around him.

He staggered forward and fell sideways, but managed to turn his body so that Zoe took the brunt of the impact. She gasped as he landed on her, then rolled away from him, agonized, clutching her ribs. He followed her on his knees, discarding the chain-mace and clasping his hands on her throat. "You want I should do *you* instead!" he panted. "You want I should make a martyr of you!"

And he began to squeeze. He hadn't intended to go this far, but he was livid with rage. He saw her eyes dilate, her mouth gape to impossible width. How soft the muscle tissue beneath his hands; how easily he could ply it, meld it, throttle it. He didn't want to do this, he told himself; he *needed* to. It *had* to be done. And then he heard something: a voice.

Slowly, dizzily, he came back to his senses. His hands loosened from the woman's flesh. Wheezing, she sucked at the air.

Shaking, drunk with emotion, Mark stood up and tried to locate the direction of the voice. It was somewhere beyond the curtains: outside the house. He picked up the mace again, and thrust his way through the hanging vinyl, stumbling down the entrance tunnel. Someone was definitely talking out there. It sounded like Terri.

". . . maybe I could understand," he thought she was saying. ". . . this would be the best opportunity . . ."

Mark stopped for a second, as realization of who she must be speaking to dawned on him. Then he gave a shout and dashed the few remaining yards of passage, bursting out through the plastic strips onto the drive.

Again, the rain had eased off, and was now only coming in spatters. But the two women, who'd just emerged side-by-side from the trees, had clearly caught the worst of it. Their waterproofs ran and sparkled with droplets. One of them *was* Terri—and thank God for that, thank God on high. The other, however, was taller and more buxom, and having just pulled back her hood, had unraveled long tresses of hair that were still a shimmering gold. She looked up as Mark lurched across the driveway toward her, and even from this distance—maybe twenty yards—he could see that age had barely touched her. She was as young-old as ever, as beautiful, as wise. Yet his presence didn't seem to register with her.

"Mum?" he whispered. Then, louder: "Mum, it's me!"

He was so focused on the woman that at first he didn't notice the supplicant standing still on the drive. Only when he walked past it, virtually rubbed shoulders with it, did he realize what it was. He stopped and stared round at it in disbelief. It might have worn a top hat and tails, and been bound around the body with S&M-type strapping, but there was no mistaking the negative photographic image that had been used to create its face. Because it was Terri.

They'd known about Terri as well?

Had they been watching him as closely as *that*? Had they manipulated even this most personal aspect of his life? And, if so, how close had they needed to get, and yet all the time remain hidden, watching from the shadows, interfering? Interfering for the better, admittedly, but still interfering—in fact controlling. Mark found himself shaking his head. It wasn't right. None of it. He loved his mother, yes, and he would show her that now they were together again, but he was an adult, and he made his own rules and he chose his own woman, and none of this was fucking right. With a strangled cry, he drew the chain-mace back.

"No!" he heard someone scream from the house. Zoe again.

He swept the weapon down.

"No!" he heard from another direction. Terri? It didn't matter, the hags would pay.

Deafening impacts followed as Mark assailed the supplicant. He struck at it front and back, and up and down, with great, savage, two-handed strokes. With each blow, pieces flew off it, the metal inside it rang out appallingly. . . .

"No," Zoe wailed, grabbing his jacket, trying to drag him back.

He shrugged her off, though it scarcely mattered now. The effigy of his fiancée still stood upright, but at a gruesome angle. Its garb hung in shreds, its straw guts were disgorged all over the floor, and in many places its iron bones were visibly bent and broken. He only realized the full extent of his victory, however, when Terri—the real Terri—came toward him. For a second she seemed unsteady on her feet. Then blood began to trickle from the corners of her mouth, and he saw that her hands hung askew at the ends of her twisted arms. Before he could say anything, she sank to her knees, and with lids fluttering on eyes now brimming with crimson tears, she slumped down onto her side.

Mark felt his world start to spin. It wasn't clear to him what had happened.

Somewhere behind, he could hear Zoe sobbing: "I told you, Mark, it's the Goddess . . . it's the power of the Goddess."

Still it made no sense to him. His gaze flicked back and forth between the two mangled forms. Then his strength ebbed, and he dropped to all fours. He wanted to reach out and touch Terri, but he couldn't. He couldn't do anything, except look up helplessly at his mother, who had now finally approached.

She stared down at him, but again it was as if she didn't know him. He looked into her violet eyes, which peered right through him, as though through mist, and seeing the serene smile on her face, with a sudden clarity of understanding he remembered the many things he'd read suggesting those closest to the deities were the completely innocent, the completely calm, the completely happy. And it struck him as perhaps inevitable, and maybe fitting, that after so many centuries of torture and torment—and being denied—the Goddess was mad.

The Ease with Which
We Freed the Beast

LUCIUS SHEPARD

Lucius Shepard was born in Lynchburg, Virginia, grew up in Daytona Beach, Florida, and now lives in Vancouver, Washington. His short fiction has won the Nebula Award, the Hugo Award, the International Horror Writers Award, the National Magazine Award, the Locus Award, the Theodore Sturgeon Award, and the World Fantasy Award.

His latest books are a nonfiction book about Honduras, Christmas in Honduras, *a short novel,* Softspoken, *and a short fiction collection,* The Iron Shore. *Forthcoming are two novels, tentatively titled* The Piercefields *and* The End of Life as We Know It, *and two short novels,* Beautiful Blood *and* Unknown Admirer.

Me and Molly Bruin were lying on our stomachs atop a sea cliff overlooking Droughans Beach, fresh from a fuck, and lolling there, our skins stuck with bits from the weeds and tall grasses that cloaked our sin, with the wind in our faces and our lives yet to be lived. For want of anything to say, I scooted forward and hung my head down so I could see beneath the overhang. Just below the lip, a chunk of earth had been ripped from the cliff face, laying bare a tangle of roots, some thick as a child's arm, from which sprang the spindly shrub that poked up beside me, producing from its topmost twig a single pink bloom, the sum of all that tortuous subterranean effort. It annoyed me, that flower, the way it was dandled, bobbing in a stiff breeze like vegetable laughter, and I snapped it off, intending to crumple it in my fist.

"For me?" asked Molly with mock delight, knowing I hadn't meant to give her the flower. She plucked it from my hand and sat up, fixing it in her black hair. Her torso was decorated with green and blue ink. Traceries of vines and leaves interwoven with the random grace of natural growth coiled about her breasts, trellised across her belly. With the flower capping her curly head, she might have been a nymph born of some mystic union, and not the daughter of a drunk and the bloated misery that was his wife. Even the scatter of acne across her cheek seemed put there by design.

"We should go down," she said.

"Not yet."

A hill sloped upward from the edge of the cliff and, just below its summit, gone to nature amid a wrangle of bushes and stunted trees, there stood a ruined cottage with a caved-in roof and a gaping doorway, home to mice and spiders, shadows and snakes. By unfocusing my eyes, I could make it into a soldier's remains, a giant fallen during an assault, his body collapsed to rib bones, tenting up the brown-and-black camouflage of the boards. A cover of soft gray clouds was being drawn across the sky.

"We should see what the others are doing," Molly said. "It'll be dark soon."

"In a minute." I rolled back onto my stomach. "You took the sauce out of me with that one."

Pleased, she lay down in the grass, nudging against my shoulder and hip, and went to braiding grass blades together. She stretched a hand out beside mine, as if comparing the two in size and pallor, then rested her head on her arm and said, "Let's stay here tonight."

"Where?"

"I saw a couple places back in town."

"Too expensive."

"We don't have to find a place, we can stay awake all night." She rolled over and grabbed a baggie from a purse, showed it to me—it held a quantity of white powder and, in a little plastic bottle, a rainbow confection of pills. "We have this," she said, and shook the baggie, making it rustle.

"Yeah, whatever," I said. "I don't care."

She pitched her voice low in imitation of mine. "'Whatever. I don't care.'"

"I don't."

"It's all so depressing." She threw herself down in the grass and pressed her forearm to her brow, as if overborne by the world's brutishness. "Whatever. I don't care."

There were five of us that day and, it seemed, all our days. Molly, me, TK, James, and Doria. We traveled in a small disheveled pod, when we traveled at all, and we liked to ride the driverless white buses that trundled up and down the coast, controlled by electric cells along the road. Often we rode them to Droughans Beach. I had stolen a tool from a repairman's kit that enabled me to open a panel on the floor and control the stops and starts. If there were other passengers on board, they would ask to be let off, and so we stretched out across the seats, scrawling our names (though not our true ones) and affections on the windows and walls, shouting, and pissing in the aisles, knowing that by the time anyone responded to the signal sent by the wounded bus, we would be off into the next chapter of our vandal's tale. We were none of us eighteen (I had almost reached that defining age), living in a city squat with half-a-dozen of our peers, surviving by means of stealing, prostitution, and panhandling, and these little excursions were the height of our criminal joy. We could all tell each other the same true stories of abuse, deprivation, rape, but there was no point to it, so we told one another the same lies, an equally pointless and dissatisfying exercise, but more fun. We lived to lie, we were professional quality liars, and the finest lies we told were the ones we could not help believing ourselves.

Close to where Molly and me lay, a wooden stair led to the beach, descending in two tiers past boarded-up cottages, though not so ruinous as the one on the clifftop. Near dusk we climbed down the stair, a precarious route due to broken steps and a rickety railing, and out onto the sand. Droughans Beach was approximately a hundred and fifty yards wide at low tide and stretched unbroken for nine miles. The sand was so fine that when Molly slid her bare feet along it, she produced a distinct musical tone. Facing the stair, a fragment of a giant's fossilized jaw thrust up some thirty feet from the shallows, gone a dull grayish green with age; two worn teeth of the same color, a molar and a canine, showed clear of a light surf—it had been lying there for so many centuries, it had blended with the landscape and might have been mistaken for a natural formation. To its right stood a massive rock over two hundred feet high, shaped like the giant's ancient tool shed, its peaked roof topped by greenery that sprouted from a thick layer of birdlime left by the gulls and puffins that roosted there in the thousands. That evening, water foamed around its base and waves broke over its sides, sending sprays into the air; once the tide receded, however, you could stroll out almost to its seaward end and keep your shoes dry.

Molly ran off to find our friends among the thirty or forty people who were walking the beach, and I hunkered on the sand close to the tidal margin. There was scant wind where I sat, but it was blowing hard atop the rock—the gulls went off balance as they landed, beating their wings to stay level, getting one foot down and tottering before they settled on their perch. Their distant cries sounded like a baying of tiny, trebly hounds. The landward face of the rock looked to have been sheared away down to a skirt of rough stone that spread out from the base; inscribed thereon, covering a quarter of its surface, was a great design of whitish lines that, although it, too, might have been a product of wind and weathers, revealed the aspect of the embryonic creature that had been sealed within the rock centuries before. I thought about that half-liquefied monstrosity, left to mature in the solitary dark, and wondered what shape it had taken, and whether it had grown to the limits of its prison or been stunted and deformed by the blackness.

I sat there for what seemed an hour, my thoughts plunging to places as black as that prison and soaring into bright fantasies wherein Molly and me, TK, James, and Doria, all our friends in the city, lived in a circumstance with good health and good food and drugs enough never to know a vengeful feeling or bloody desire; and then I lay down in the sand, not because I was sleepy, but because I was oppressed—it was as though a hand, irresistible in its power, were pushing me onto my back, I was so overcome with hopelessness, with the understanding that our fates already had been decided. As surely as I saw that design of white lines left by the ancients to warn against what was sealed within, I also saw lesser lines that described Molly beaten by a trick, TK overdosed, James done in by an untreated disease, Doria with her throat cut. All still young, still wanting life. The only death I could not see was my own, but I felt it closing around me.

Eventually I did sleep and when I woke it was dark. Most of the strollers and shell collectors had left the beach, and Molly and the rest, made visible by moonlight, were gathered around a boulder that the tide, receding now, had left bare. I was angry at them for letting me sleep and I walked toward them, brushing sand from my clothes, thinking how to express my displeasure. They were talking to an old man in a plaid cap and shabby clothing. He was holding a battery lamp that, now and then, he switched on, underlighting the other's faces and his own as he shined it over the pool. I could tell they were screwing with him. TK, with his rabbity bones, a few hairs on his upper lip playing at being a mustache, still a boy; James, sullen and muscular, yet half-a-head shorter than I; and Doria, her hair part-blond, part-blue, with a bitter, sexy face: they, and Molly as well, each wore sober looks, as if intent on what he said, but I knew they were repressing their derision.

"When I was no older than you kids," he was saying, "I was on patrol down here."

"You were a cop, huh?" asked TK.

"Oh, no! I was part of an environmental patrol. The town hired seven of us kids to make sure no one disturbed the tide pools. We'd catch someone sitting on the rocks, like you were doing, and we'd tell them they were sitting on living creatures." He played his light over the boulder. "See there? Acorn barnacles and tube barnacles. Anemones. Tiny ones. If you look close you can see 'em poking out their tongues."

"For real?" said Doria. "Sitting on them might get a girl off, huh?"

James said, "Why seven?"

The old man acted confused; he glanced at James anxiously.

"Why'd they hire seven?" asked James with studied thickness. "'Cause it was like a magic number?"

"It was just for the summer," said the old man weakly.

"Did you guys call yourself something?" asked TK. "Like, did you have a name? The Seven . . . you know. Whatevers."

"Beachmasters!" suggested Molly, provoking laughter from James.

"Assbags!" Doria looked to the group for approval, but no one found her remark funny.

"We weren't . . ." The old man blinked, licked his lips. "We . . ."

"Suppose you saw someone doing this?" James went tromping, splashing through the tide pool. "What would you do? Blow your little whistle?"

"I'd probably fucking kill you," I said.

The old man shined his lamp full on me.

I threw up an arm to shield my eyes and said, "Turn that damn thing off!"

For the reaction it brought, my voice might have been a roar. The old man dropped the lamp into the tide pool and stumbled back against TK. I shouldered past Doria and said to him, "You know this is an evil place. Especially at night."

He stared fearfully at me, one red-veined eye rolling like a horse's, a horrible, unlucky thing, and I told him to look away from me. When he had done so, I put my mouth to his ear and said, "Suppose you're here when the beast breaks loose? It would tear you apart."

He started to turn his head and I said, "Don't look at me!"

I laid a hand on his back—he was trembling—and told him to go. His trembling increased and I repeated my instruction. "Go now," I said. "Or I won't be responsible."

He took an unsteady step. I spanked his bony rear, setting him into a hobbling run; the others hooted and laughed.

"Shut the hell up," I said.

They fell silent, except for James, who said, "Fuck you! Who made you God!"

"I thought we cleared that up last month," I said. "Those ribs heal all right? That tooth still giving you trouble?"

I won the staredown and, to cover his shame, he bent to pick up the old man's lamp.

"Leave it," I said. "It looks cool."

And it did, it made the pool appear sacred, green watery radiance streaming up.

"Why were you bashing that old fart," I asked.

"We weren't going to hurt him," TK said.

"You know how it goes. You start off fucking with somebody, just fooling around, and it gets out of control. Someone takes a bite and the feeding frenzy's on." I sat on the boulder, unmindful of dying anemones. "We've all got wicked tempers and it doesn't take much to make us snap. That's how we hurt ourselves. Right, James?"

"I guess," he mumbled.

"Consider it a lesson," I said. "Why waste your anger on someone whose pain can't profit you? You have to conserve anger, nourish it. Like the beast. Imagine when it gets out, how strong it'll be. All those years with no place to vent . . . except on itself. It'll be strong enough to break the world. You need to be that strong."

Doria laughed nervously.

"It's not funny," I said.

"Hey!" she said. "It's just you talk so much shit, man, I can't keep it straight."

"You have to think," I said. "You have to decide what you need to survive and use your anger to take it."

They listened, but I detected boredom in their faces. They were too inured to my words to hear them. Of them all, only Molly displayed the wit to survive, and even she looked bored. I continued to lecture, hoping that sheer repetition would put the brake to their course of self-destruction. I told them to muzzle their whims, to devote themselves to strategies that would sustain them. And yet the more sense I made, the more certainly I lost them. They had begun to view me as they would another species. Soon I would be as irrelevant as the old man.

After I stopped talking, Molly distributed the pills. She offered me none, knowing that I would abstain. Drugs brought me perilously close to the source of my rage. The others wandered off along the beach, but I remained seated on the boulder. The light from the pool made me feel like a wizard who had, by means of some occult process, opened a portal beneath his feet into a bright submarine continuum, and, having used up the pleasures of this world, was contemplating a dive into those uncharted waters. I pictured myself as a shadow raised against a greenish glow, a demonic figure in a Buddha's pose.

The battery lamp had fallen into a niche in the rocky bank and nearby rested an anemone that had the approximate size and oblong shape of a woman's coin purse. It was a fancy thing, pale jade in color, beaded around its outline with what looked to be dark green florets. I was tempted to reach down and grab it, but feared it would be unpleasant to the touch or sting me with its acids. Best to imagine it in hand, I thought. Smooth and firm, a living stone. On the bottom, a crab no bigger than the joint of my thumb was negotiating a rise between two collapsed strands of kelp. I stared into that shallow depth with such intensity, it seemed I became a citizen of that savage, tranquil place.

When I was fourteen I struck my father in the face, putting an end to a decade of torture both mental and physical. The blow raised a lump the size of a hen's egg above his right eye, swelling up instantly, but had a more lasting effect on me. Frightened by what I had done, certain that he would call the police, I ran to Spetlow Hill and climbed the church tower (it was then under construction), and there I spent the night huddled under a tarpaulin, gazing out through a skeleton of masonry and steel at the tumbled roofs of the town and the listless ocean beyond. God knew me now, I thought. I had violated one of His taboos, no matter it had been in self-defense. His fierce eye had marked me. Yet when I recalled my father on his knees, clutching his injury, I felt a vicious satisfaction and joy. It was the best feeling I'd ever had and I wanted it again. I wanted to piss God off, I wanted another bloody victory. If I returned to home, I believed he/He would kill me, and so, after stealing clothes and some money, I fled to the city in search of that feeling. I never found it, but I found lesser feelings that sufficed. Amazing, how impotence itself can be rendered impotent by the sound of someone groaning in an alley or the impact of a boot on bone.

For nearly four years, I brawled and bullied my way through life. Not that it was all a triumph. Many nights I made my bed in an abandoned factory or railroad yard, beaten and degraded, terrified by every indistinct sound, by the rats that nested there; but I became, at last, the king of my own rat's nest. And now I felt the world pulling me away from childhood, from my hard-won sinecure. Even as I had lectured my brother and sister rats, recognizing they would suffer without my guidance, I was envious of their state. Seeing them at play on the beach, zooming about, falling to their knees, puking up the poisons they had swallowed, then vanishing into the dark, I felt love for them; but love was an emotion they did not respect and so, to honor their feelings, I dismissed them from my thoughts.

The tide had gone out. I walked toward the rock, scrambled up the skirt of rough stone, and found a spot where I could sit. It smelled of ruin, like a drowned cathedral in which the vestments and candles and incense had rotted away. The waves broke against it less vigorously than before, but cold sprays still spattered me with shrapnel bursts and my face grew numb from this constant booming assault. And yet I felt secure, sheltered by its darkness, as I had felt when, after a beating, my father would lock me in a closet and forget me for the night or longer—I thought that the beast, even in its desperation, must feel similarly secure. I tried to isolate its scent from the greater smell of the rock, the stink of the silent birds in their black nests.

Molly flitted past on the sand, pursued by another, less defined figure, both going out of view behind the rock. The sight gentled my thoughts, giving rise to a memory. I had stolen a car from the parking lot at the mall, punched through the glass and hotwired it, and the five of us tore out onto the interstate. Molly had called shotgun and, as I drove, she leaned out the window, shrieking, her hair flying, flashing her tits at the people in slower cars. She must have resembled a ship's figurehead stuck on sideways and come to life, yet they looked at her with dull, unsurprised faces, as if every day of their lives they were blessed with such insane beauty, or else this was something their television sets had warned them against and thus they were prepared to put up a stolid front. I could have written songs about their stuporous response.

Darkness closed down, a light rain fell, and once we turned off the interstate onto Highway 26 things grew quiet inside the car. James, sounding paranoid, asked where we were going, and Doria fired up a pipe, and TK was getting all film-geeky about a movie we had seen, pointing out flaws in its logic, saying that the metal tripods had been buried in the rock for millennia, withstanding a million tons of pressure, okay? So how come Tom Cruise could blow one up with a grenade?

"Because he's Tom Cruise, man," said Doria, trying not to exhale. Talking caused her to hack up smoke. "Shit!" She handed the pipe up to me, nudging my shoulder, leaning so far forward that I could feel the bristle of her dreadlocks (she had since changed her hairstyle) on my neck.

Molly snatched the pipe from her and that was good with me. I was high on crime and violence. Whenever a car rushed toward us, its headlights dazzled the raindrops decorating the windshield and it would seem I was driving into rings of fairy light; then darkness would swallow the road, a curving two-lane slicing through a spruce forest, and I had to refocus in order to steer. I needed to come down a notch and I told Molly to look out for a place where I could buy beer, explaining that I was having some difficulty.

"You can't see?" She laughed merrily, delighted by the prospect of my blindness.

"Want me to drive?" James asked. "I can drive."

"Fuck no!" I punched the gas, accelerating to shut him up. James could be a real pisser. His parents were religious zealots and that was most of his problem.

Molly switched on the radio, found a station playing rock, and turned it high, putting an end to conversation. She rolled down her window and played with her tongue stud, popping it in and out between her lips like a little gemmy bubble.

Twenty miles down the road we came to a convenience store with carvings for sale off to one side, gigantic things made out of stumps and fallen logs, animated by magic. It had stopped raining. Puddles like shiny black eyes dappled the gravel lot. I went inside, bought beer, stored it the car, all except a forty, which I cracked, and went over to where my friends stood, checking out a huge fir stump that some redneck necromancer had carved into a troll that kept walking into its cave house, casting a sour look back over his shoulder before shutting the door, then backing out and repeating the process.

"Who do you think buys this crap?" I karate-kicked the troll in the side, not disrupting its course in the slightest, though its eyes flickered redly.

"Nobody," TK said.

"I don't know," Molly said. "I think it's cool."

"Molly thinks it's cool!" Doria minced about, affecting the guise of a connoisseur. "It's so . . . so relevant, so . . ."

"It's absolutely relevant," I said. "The things going on today, the ancient magical shit that's reappearing . . . like these sculptures, the beast. And the new stuff. The white buses, the people with machines inside them. The fucking mind control exerted by Chairman Channel Twenty-five. It's all starting to come at once. Witches, mad science, stupid magic. All the things that were going to happen, that might have happened, are being crammed into our days. A sort of preapocalyptic meltdown. And it's going to get weirder before it's through."

They gaped at me, waiting for a punch line.

"It's still crap, though," I said. "We don't have to deal with it any different from anything else."

I set down my forty, unsheathed the hunting knife I kept strapped to my calf, and began hacking at the troll, slicing thick shavings from its bulging forehead, stabbing it until its eyes ceased to glow. The clerk yelled at us from the doorway. I started toward him, but James caught me from behind and wrestled me back.

"Jesus! You're a fucking wildman!" TK said as we piled into the car.

"Did you see the guy's face?" said Doria. "He was tripping!"

I was breathing fast, light-headed, but I got the engine going and jammed it; we sprayed gravel past the front of the store and fishtailed onto the highway.

"We should get off this road," James said.

I slowed, braked, and made a U-turn.

"What the fuck are you doing?" he asked.

"I left my forty back there," I told him.

Molly rested her head on my shoulder and sang a la-la-la song.

"Fucking wildman!" said TK happily.

"You can consider it a lesson," I said to James.

"What're you talking about?" he asked. "What kind of lesson?"

"A lesson in risk management," I said. "And in beer conservation."

A couple of hours after I had climbed onto the rock, I began to feel a vibration at my back—barely detectable, at first, and erratic, growing stronger and steadier. I thought it was the beating of my heart and ignored it; but then it stopped, starting up again a few minutes later, stronger this time, and occurring at such lengthy intervals I knew it could be no heart. I laid my head against the rock and listened. At length I managed to separate a faint thudding noise from the crunch of the waves.

The beast was trying to break free—that much was clear—and it was making headway, for I had never heard·that noise before. I wanted to be far from Droughans Beach should it succeed. But as I thought how to organize our flight, how to weld my drugged friends into an efficient force, I began to feel a kinship with the thing, a shared sense of purpose. We both hated the world and its people. Each morning they choked down another dose of everything's-fine or whatever bland preachment they had been induced to swallow, and went forth to mindfucking jobs where they would make a paper sandwich of some poor bastard's blood and bones; to fitness clubs where they believed they could perfect the unperfectable; to movies that persuaded them this death-in-life was preferable to an existence in which they dared to confront the truth of the human condition; and all the while a horrid tide was rising higher and higher, until one day, they would look out their windows to find streets choked with red water and corpses, and, mistaking the sight for normalcy, for another cold-meat Sunday with the living room dead, they would open their doors and drown.

Here, now, was the antidote to all that.

I had an epiphany—I pictured the beast sated with killing, the whole world in its belly, falling asleep on the sand, going into labor and dying midbirth, assaulted by giants come down from the hills where they had been hiding to rip the fetus out and lock it away in its prison rock, and I saw the process of civilization beginning again, the good and bad of it, leading ultimately to a moment such as this. I understood it was my duty to assist in the delivery of the new cycle on this primordial beach with magical light streaming up from the tide pool and no one to witness. I inched my way along the rock, stopping now and then to listen. The thudding grew louder and at last I found the crack the beast had made. It ran straight up the face—I could not see its end or judge how deep it went. I unsheathed my knife and reached with it into the crack, pried with the tip, with the edge, digging crumbles of stone from around a harder object. I was at it for the longest time. Someone called my name, but I continued to pry and dig.

"Hey! What you doing?" Molly flung her arms about my neck from behind; when I offered no response, she said, "TK wanted me to go down on him."

I felt a flicker of annoyance. "Did you?"

"No! I'm being more . . . like what you said."

"What did I say?"

I withdrew the knife, reached into the crack with my hand, and touched something colder than the surrounding stone. A metal projection, I thought. Part of a bulky mechanism.

"To respect myself," Molly said. "I was trying to be more self-respectful. TK really wanted it, so I came to find you. So he'd leave me alone." She turned my face toward hers and kissed me. "Let's go up on the cliff again."

In the moonlight, her pupils were enormous and her expression flowed from seductive to deranged to stunned, reflecting the action of the drugs she had ingested.

"Later." I reinserted the knife into the crack and pried at the metal, felt it shift the slightest bit.

"What are you doing?"

"Listen," I told her.

She cocked an ear and said, "Listen to what?"

"Try to tune out the sound of the waves. You can hear it."

She listened more attentively. "I think . . . maybe I hear something."

I encouraged her to put her ear to the crack.

Again she listened. "I think . . . Yeah. It's kind of a . . . a . . ."

"A thudding."

"Yeah! I hear it!" She looked at me in alarm. "What the fuck?"

"It's trying to get out," I said.

She was bewildered for a second or two, then her eyes widened. "The beast, you mean? That can't be. . . ."

A rending noise broke from the crack and I pulled her back, edged away along the face of the rock, for now that my part in things was done, I was afraid to see the issue of my labor. Despite all I felt about the world and its worth, I feared for my life and for Molly's. And TK's. He strolled into view, doubtless looking for Molly, and stood by the tide pool, staring down into the glowing water. He appeared to be picking his nose.

The thudding grew louder, more insistent, and, as if in sympathy with such relentlessness, a wave detonated against the seaward end of the rock, showering us with spray. Molly's shriek must have outvoiced the rush of water, for TK glanced toward us, and it was at that moment the beast broke free. I had expected a gush of blackness, the wall to shatter, slabs of stone to rain down, but all I saw was a dark shape eeling from the crack. It seemed a pipe had broken within the rock and was leaking oil. Yet as it continued to pour out, the beast gathered its substance into a more fearsome formlessness. It was fluid, it was living smoke, it was power adapted to the black medium in which it had been steeped. It boiled up into a cloud three times our height, and then condensed into a shape no bigger than a man's. It seemed to turn to Molly and me, though it did not truly turn—it rearranged its parts, moving its front to its back and hanging a face on its inky turbulence, a parody of rage with shadowy fangs and eyes emerging from a storm-cloud chaos . . . then it went flowing over the broken ground toward TK. I sprang after it, shouting a warning, but I was a foot short, a split-second late. By the time I dropped to my knees beside him, the beast had condensed a portion of its substance into an edge and sliced him across the throat. He lay with his head in the water, his blood roiling out in a cloud that crimsoned the light cast by the submerged lamp.

Grief, fear, and urgency were mixed in me. The beast had merged with the night. I could no longer see it, though I felt its presence along my spine. I shouted at Molly to stay where she was and jogged down the beach, peering left and right. The tide pool dwindled to an eerie chute of red light. The rock became a shadow and the giant's jawbone was lost to sight. After I had gone, I'd estimate, a quarter-mile, I regretted having left Molly alone, but I decided to keep searching a while longer, and shortly afterward I spotted two figures lying together in the sand. Not sleeping, though. One waved an arm, as if describing the wide arc of his existence. It had to be James. Though restrained in my presence, whenever he thought himself unobserved he was given to dramatic gesture.

I broke into a run and James came to his knees, wearing a look of terror. He must have misapprehended my intentions—I cried out, seeking to reassure him. Doria, too, got to her knees and screamed as the beast, materializing from the dark, flowed over them, a furious smoke that hid them from view. I flung myself atop it, stabbing and slashing with the knife, but it was impervious to my attack, and, when it had done with them, it flung me aside as if I were nothing and dissipated on the night wind, leaving behind a bloody human wreckage. I did not linger over their bodies—they each bore a dozen wounds, any one of which might have been fatal, cruel gouges made by teeth hardened from the beast's all but immaterial flesh, and I had no time to mourn. My mind was a flurry of red and black, a confusion of dim urges and fears, but I knew where the beast had gone. Molly. She would, I realized, have stayed by the rock for some minutes, but then, overcome by fright, she would have headed for the stairs leading up from the beach.

I ran, unmindful of my safety. She was all I had left, all that remained of my shabby kingdom, and I ran myself breathless in hopes of saving her. I felt the beast's sides heave, panting in its self-made shadow, and knew it to be near. She had started to climb the second tier of steps when I caught up to her. Seeing me, she sagged against the railing and said in a helpless voice, "Oh, no."

"It'll be all right if you don't run," I told her.

She said something I didn't catch and then, "God! This isn't happening."

I eased close, not wanting to alarm her with a sudden move, realizing

I must be a sight, covered in blood, and that she, like James and Doria, may have misinterpreted my appearance.

"It's not what you think," I said.

"I saw you," she said. "What you did to TK. . . ."

"You can hardly see at all, you took so much acid and speed," I said. "What you saw was me trying to protect TK. It was the beast killed him. But you're going to be all right. It's grateful to me for releasing it. At least it hasn't tried to kill me yet. As long as it knows you're with me, it won't hurt you."

A flicker of belief showed in her face, but only a flicker.

"Okay," she said.

"Please don't run! I understand you're scared, but you don't have to be scared of me."

"Okay."

I noticed a tension in her body and said, "Don't!"

She sprang up the steps.

This time I made no attempt to intervene.

I ran down the stair and out onto the beach, howling in grief and rage. I held my arms up to the jolly moon balanced on the peak of the prison rock, begging for blood to rain down and for everything to cease. I flung the knife into the ocean and fell on the sand and there I remained until the gulls made their first circling flights. When the sky had gone the deep holy blue of predawn, I went to the edge of the water and washed myself clean. I was almost empty, without purpose or direction. And then, glancing inland, I saw the beast gather itself into the form of a giant and go striding off over the hills, toward the mountains beyond. I was disappointed—I had hoped for the destruction of cities. The mountains were a place of rest, a country for old men. Yet I had no choice but to follow.

It's hard to be hopeful these days. I cling to life like an ant to a leaf blown along a storm drain, watching the world rip itself apart. I am old now, not so old as the decrepit old man we met on the beach that night, but old enough to value certain things I once perceived as foolish and unworthy. I don't go out much, don't have many friends. I live in a small mountain town with my family. My wife, a magical creature, though she would strenuously deny it . . . Each morning she walks out the door and vanishes. What she does with her days, I have no idea, but when she returns home of an evening, she brings with her otherworldly scents and I will discover scraps of paper in her purse on which are written the fragments of wicked spells. She hisses when I make love to her, she grunts in a language unknown to me and sometimes locks her teeth in the meat of my shoulder.

I edit the town's weekly paper, which I also founded. Each week I write a column citing some symptom of our cultural decay that is a predictor of doom and madness, columns that cause great amusement among my readership. They e-mail excerpts to friends in other towns and label me an eccentric, though lately, since I have won several regional prizes for journalism, they have been more respectful. Despite this, I know the prizes are awarded for my idiosyncratic style, that hardly anyone listens to me, that few believe in beasts, in apocalypse—they believe, instead, that they will pass through the black wall toward which we are all speeding, that it is permeable and may even form the gateway to a better life. Thus the paper no longer interests me, and for some time now I have devoted the bulk of my energies to my son, a sturdy eleven-year-old.

I don't entirely understand what the cycle of giants and children and beasts means in the scheme of things, but I suspect that my son will understand. Whereas my father's training was haphazard, born of his intemperate nature, mine is carefully thought-out, scrupulously planned. I beat my son, I lock him away, I control his reading, I keep him friendless, but all apportioned so that these torments have formed a bond between us. I have told him that it is done to strengthen him, and he has accepted the pain as part of a crucial teaching. Day by day, he grows more stoic, more malleable, and I expect soon there will be no need for discipline. I have promised to give him a woman when he is twelve and he exerts himself toward that goal. I have promised other enticements as well, criminal pleasures such as may be enjoyed in the adjoining towns. Perhaps when he is a man, he will strike me down, but he will have a sound reason for doing so and not strike prematurely, as did I. In all ways, he will act with a greater circumspection.

I tell him that the beast he frees will be more powerful than mine, that it will achieve terrible things, wonderful things. He is intrigued by the possibility, but not quite certain I have told him the truth. Last week, we were eating sundaes at the new Baskin-Robbins over in Ridgeview, a hang-out for junior high kids similar to those whom I have prepared him to dominate, and he asked for the hundredth time, at least, if I thought the beast was real.

"Of course it was real," I said.

"Do you think it was real like, you know, different from you? Separate? Or do you think it just worked your arms and legs and made you do things?"

"In here . . ." I tapped my chest. "I know it was separate. Not that it makes a difference."

"Where is it, then?"

"Somewhere around. Taking a nap in the woods, maybe. Snoring and all covered with gray hair like your old man. It's retired. Once a beast leaves you, it's done its duty."

We had placemats that depicted, against a blue background, cartoon butterflies hovering around a banana split, and my son began jabbing out the butterflies' startled round eyes with a ballpoint pen. "I don't ever want my beast to leave," he said moodily.

"It's bound to leave eventually. But if you keep up the good work . . ."

"I will!"

". . . it'll be with you a long time."

The waitress, a pretty brunette with tattooed bracelets on her wrists, refilled my coffee. He stared at her and once she was back behind the counter, I asked, "Do you like that one?"

He nodded, embarrassed. "Uh-huh!"

"Tattoos are a clear signal." I ruffled his hair, sparking a grin. "You've got a good eye."

We ate for a time, not saying much, and then he asked me to tell him about the man I'd met on the beach after my friends died.

"You don't need to hear that again," I said, but I was pleased, because that part of my story went to the core of my teaching.

"Come on, Dad!"

"Okay." I slurped my coffee. "I was at the water's edge, I'd just finished washing off the blood when this man, a big man, came along the beach. He had a fancy fishing pole and big tackle box. He was planning to do some surf casting, I guess. He stopped beside me and stared. And then he said, 'That's a lot of blood on you, son.'

"'Where you see blood?' I asked.

"'All in your hair. On the side there.'

"I touched my hair and my fingers came away gooey with blood. I knew right away I had to kill him. If I didn't, he'd call the cops. But the beast was gone, I'd thrown away my knife, and the man was immense. I was scared, I wasn't sure I had the strength or the will to do it. And then he asked whose blood it was, and I replied, 'It's mine.' I wasn't trying to lie my way out of trouble. The blood belonged to people like me, people the man wouldn't spit on if they were dying of thirst, and I was speaking for them. I wasn't telling a lie. That made me strong. I took him down and kicked him in the head until his skull broke. I had his brains on my shoes. I puked all over myself after, but I did what I had to."

He dribbled hot fudge onto his ice cream with the edge of his spoon. "I sorta don't get it."

"You get the important parts," I said. "What's that I say when you don't get all of something and you need to think about it more?"

He sat up smartly, like a little soldier, and said, "Consider it a lesson!"

Hushabye

SIMON BESTWICK

Simon Bestwick lives in the former Lancashire mining town of Swinton. His fiction has been published in a number of magazines and anthologies, including Beneath the Ground and the award-winning Acquainted with the Night. His story collection, A Hazy Shade of Winter, was published in 2004 and was nominated for the Stoker Award, and the title story was reprinted in The Year's Best Fantasy and Horror, Eighteenth Annual Collection.

Several of his radio plays were broadcast on radio in 2005 and 2006, and further scripts are in production or preparation. By day he works in an office; in the meantime, when not preparing a backlog of short stories, novellas, a novel for publication, writing new stories or scripts, or pursuing the delights of wine (well, real ale and single malt whiskey), women, and song, he tries, with limited success, to catch up on his sleep.

He has a Web site at: http://www.geocities.com/sbestwick2002/.

March started late that year, as if waiting for a cue it had missed. The conversion back to BST was scheduled for late in the month; the days stayed short, the nights dark, long, and cold. When snow fell it lay for days in a brittle crust, and every other morning all stone was patterned with frost.

I was looking unsuccessfully for paying work that didn't drive me crazy after a fortnight, and still living out of cardboard boxes in my friend Alan's spare room. Although he'd said I could stay as long as I needed when I moved in, it'd been six months now and his patience had started to fray, all our little habits scraping at one another's nerves.

So I took to going for long walks around the area. I like walking, even in the cold night on treacherous pavements.

I went down Bolton Road to the roundabout where it met Langworthy Road, then walked down Langworthy 'til I was opposite the abandoned shell of the Mecca bingo hall; I was on the corner of Brindleheath Road, which ran under a bridge, past the edge of the industrial estate and a couple of vacant lots and up onto the A6 next to Pendleton Church and near a Chinese takeaway. I decided to get some chow mein before heading back home.

As I came out from under the bridge, I heard a child call out "No."

That was followed by a noise somewhere between a gasp and a cry, then silence. My skin prickled; I ran up the road.

I saw them vanishing into the bushes at the edge of one of the vacant lots: a small girl, tiny in a red coat, and a figure that looked like a shadow walking at first, 'til I realized it was dressed in black, only the white of its face visible. Then they were gone into the dark. They hadn't seen me.

I pelted up the road and crashed through the bushes, shouting. They were white in the gloom, or at least the girl's body and the man's face were. Something silver, brighter than breath, glimmering like motes of powdered glass, was pouring from the girl's opened mouth and into his. The man looked up. His face was long, pale: a thin blade of nose, one thick eyebrow a line across the top. The eyes looked black too.

I kicked out at him, but he was already rolling away. He scrambled up and ran, vanishing into the shadows. I stood there, gasping for air; I couldn't see him and on the uneven ground all I'd do was break an ankle. And there was the girl to think about.

He'd worked fast; she lay with her clothes scattered about her, staring up at the night stars. For a moment I thought she was dead, but then I saw her breath. I took off my jacket and covered her; she flinched from my touch as if stung, whimpering like a hurt animal and curling up on her side. I couldn't tell if it was the cold or the hate that made my fingers so clumsy as I dug out my mobile and dialed 112.

The first assault on a local child had happened in Higher Broughton just before Christmas, in Albert Park. A six-year-old boy almost dead with hypothermia, his torn clothes scattered around him. There'd been more over the following months, the same pattern: police offering nothing but pleas for vigilance and information, the victims unwilling or unable to provide any leads.

They took the girl to Hope Hospital and me down to the police station on the Crescent. I was interviewed for two hours by a pair of detectives. Poole, the Detective Sergeant, was the hardest to handle, spending the first hour treating me as a suspect. In the end, the Detective Constable, Hardiman, put a hand on his arm and led him outside. They left me with a paused tape and a stony-faced policewoman; I heard raised voices through the breezeblock wall.

Hardiman took it from there. He was young, earnest, and sympathetic. Poole stayed silent, looking at the scarred desktop, light gleaming on his bald crown. He had a drinker's lined, ruddy face. Hardiman's was smooth and pale as fiberglass. I told him everything I'd seen, except whatever it was I'd seen passing from the girl's mouth to her attacker's. I didn't want dismissing as a nutter.

"You'll have to excuse DS Poole," Hardiman said later, as we watched the Identi-Kit picture take shape. "He's got a kid of his own that age. Takes it personally."

"It's okay," I told him, meaning it. Normally I'm pretty scathing about heavy-handed policing, but having seen what had been done to the girl I'd've quite happily held Poole's coat for him while he threw the offender down the stairs several times. As long as it was the right man.

"It's not," said Hardiman. "My missus wants us to have kids, but . . ." he gestured at the picture to indicate all it represented. "You shouldn't have to think of this when you're thinking of a family."

"I know."

"You're sure this is him?"

I looked at the finished picture and nodded slowly. Hardiman rubbed his eyes and pushed his fingers through his sandy hair. "Okay," he said. "Come on. I'll drive you home. And I want to thank you. This is the first clue we've had of any kind." He must've been tired, to let that one slip out.

They had my details, of course, but I didn't hear any more from them for over a fortnight. In the interim, I received bad news of a different kind: a friend of mine called Terry Browning died.

He'd choked on his own puke, sat in his armchair by the window with an empty bottle of Lone Piper beside him on the floor. It happened in his flat on Langworthy Road, a scant hundred yards from where I'd heard the little girl cry out. The funeral was at St. John's Church, in the Height, about a week later.

He'd been a priest, but had left the church with a deep loss of faith the previous year; maybe they thought it was catching, as the only dog-collar in sight was the one who read the service, which didn't mean anything to me or Terry's brother, the only other mourner, and probably wouldn't've to Terry any longer. I wasn't even sure if it meant much to the priest, but it was hard to tell. The bitter wind tore his graveside oration to shreds, like gray confetti.

Rob Browning and I went for a pint down at the Crescent afterwards, more to chase out the chill than anything else. We hardly said a dozen words to each other. He was smart and suited and had a southern accent; I knew he and Terry hadn't been close. He stayed for one drink and then left; I ordered a double Jameson's and raised the glass to the memory of a friend whose death I still felt a certain guilt for.

"Mind if I join you?"

I looked up to see DC Hardiman standing over me with a Britvic orange in his hand.

"How'd you know I was here?"

"Didn't make CID on my good looks."

I laughed. "Didn't think so."

He flipped me the bird and sat. "Sorry about your mate."

"Thanks. Looks like we're the only ones who are."

We sat in silence; I waited for him to probe about Terry but he didn't. In the end it was me who started fishing. "How's the investigation going?"

He shook his head.

"Nothing?"

"Oh no. Something. But . . . there's complications."

"How d'you mean?"

He didn't answer at first. "I looked you up on HOLMES. Quite the colorful character."

"Is that a compliment?"

"You say what you think and kick up a stink when you reckon you have to."

"Fair assessment," I had to admit.

"And you don't believe in keeping your trap shut or leaving things alone when not doing so would piss off certain people."

"People in high places, sort of thing?"

He nodded.

"Guilty, I suppose." I took a swallow of whisky. "Are you trying to tell me something?"

He studied his glass, turning it this way and that like a faceted gem. "The evidence I've got . . . it's taking me somewhere where shutting my trap and leaving things alone is pretty much what the doctor ordered."

Everything seemed to go very still. "I'm feeling on my own on this one in a big way," he said, almost to himself, then looked up. "Even Poole's not sure, and I thought he wanted that bastard more than anyone."

"Close to his pension."

"Yeah. I just thought . . . you'd understand where I'm at right now."

"I do." I studied my own drink for a minute, then looked up. "What are you going to do?"

Hardiman put his glass down on the table. "The little girl you found. Ellie Chatham, her name is. I visited her yesterday. To see if she remembered anything, or . . . I don't know. She's like an old woman. Five years old and she's like an old woman. Shuffles from place to place and just sits there. Breathing, staring. Waiting. I don't know what for. Death, maybe. Like something's just gone out of her."

I thought of the silver glittering I'd seen passing from her mouth to the attacker's. "Yeah."

"And the psychiatrist reports on the others . . . Christ, I don't think one of those kids'll ever be the same again. It's different for all of them, but . . . night terrors, rages . . . there's one, the boy they found in Albert Park, he flies into a rage every time he sees anybody black or Asian. Don't know why, there's no indication anyone nonwhite was involved. The opposite is how it looks, thanks to you. It's like he's full of hate and rage, but it's not going where it should, it's going at someone else, a scapegoat. Fuck knows why."

"I'll lend you one of my books on capitalism sometime," I said. "Might give you a few pointers."

He snorted a laugh. "That'll raise a few eyebrows in the canteen. All these kids, and he's taken something from them they'll never get back, that'll fuck them up forever. And my wife, she still wants us to try for a kid. I just . . . just want to know any child of mine is gonna be as safe as I can make it, from something like this. But I'm supposed to keep my trap shut and look the other way. Well, fuck that." He lifted his glass. "Here's to colorful characters."

I clinked my glass against it. "Amen."

Twenty-four hours after he spoke to me, Detective Constable Alec Hardiman's Ford Mondeo went off the motorway between Manchester and Bradford, on Saddleworth Moor. It was two in the morning, and no one ever knew what he'd been doing out there. His neck was broken in the crash. He left behind a wife, Sheila, but no children, actual or in the womb.

I would've gone to the funeral, but had a strong sense I wouldn't be welcome if I did. I watched it from a distance, saw a thin pale woman in black that I assumed to be Sheila Hardiman, leaning on two other women—mother and sister, at a guess. Other mourners included a gray-faced DS Poole and a lone man in his sixties, bald on top with a salt-and-pepper goatee.

It was this last mourner who turned up on my doorstep the following evening, with a brown paper parcel under his arm. My first thought on seeing him was: *Jesus, people still wear tweed?*

"Mr. Paul Hearn?" he asked.

"Yes."

"Don Hardiman." He offered his hand. "Alec's father."

"Please come in."

The parcel sat on the table, between us and our coffee cups. Don Hardiman's voice was quiet and modulated, very clear; he was a university lecturer. There was a black armband round one sleeve of his jacket.

"Alec came to me the day before he died, and put the package into my keeping, along with your name and address and a request to bring it here. We weren't particularly close, and I wasn't the first person anyone would think of coming to for any little . . . legacies of this kind. Which is why I expect Alec chose me."

My hand kept twitching toward the package, but I kept stopping it.

"My son wasn't a paranoid man, Mr. Hearn—"

"Paul."

He inclined his head. "But he was definitely afraid of something and believed he could no longer trust his colleagues. I believe I have some idea of what's in there, and I'd presume you do as well."

I nodded. "I think so."

"I suspect as well that I wasn't intended to know anything about this. Alec did love me, in his way, and would want to protect me. But I loved him in my way too. He was my son, and now he's dead. I'd like to help."

"Don—"

"Please."

"All right." I nodded. "Let's see what we've got."

Timothy was the son of Arthur Wadham, a highly successful businessman known for his generous donations to New Labour's party funds. He'd inherited his father's charm and ruthlessness, by all accounts, but neither his looks nor his business acumen. Nearly thirty, he'd launched about half-a-dozen business ventures since returning from the all-expenses-paid-by-Daddy backpacking tour following his graduation from Cambridge.

All expenses paid by Daddy, in fact, seemed to be pretty much a—even *the*—recurrent theme in Timothy Wadham's life. All half-a-dozen business ventures had ended in financial disaster, but Wadham senior was always on hand with a blank check for the next one. Hard-nosed and void of sentiment he might be, but he clearly—like most parents—had a blind spot where his offspring was concerned. Under any other circumstances, a man who could cock up running a lap-dancing club in Romford would have been filed in the do-not-touch-this-fuckwit-with-a-bargepole category and left there.

Just another rich kid bombing happily through life secure in the knowledge that pater would always be there to bail him out. What money didn't solve directly, the connections it bought most assuredly would.

I picked up the photograph of Timothy Wadham; the long face and thin sharp nose, the black eyes and the unbroken line of the eyebrow. I showed it to Don Hardiman. Wadham's address was written on the back.

"Still want to help?" I asked after he'd finished reading. He looked up with a wintry smile.

"I'm not my son's father for nothing," he said. "What do you need?"

"What in the bloody hell do you think you're doing, Paul?"

When my reflection didn't reply I opened the sock drawer and rummaged around in the back. I found what I was looking for and unwrapped the old t-shirt it was folded in.

I'd taken the Browning automatic off the body of a man called Frankie Hagen in Ordsall the month before. I hadn't killed him, any more than I'd had any idea what I thought I wanted a gun for. I began to wonder if I now knew.

I unloaded the pistol—there were eight rounds left in the magazine—and looked at myself in the bedroom mirror. I was wearing black, including a wool skully and Thinsulate gloves. I dry-fired the pistol with the gloves on. They didn't get in the way of the trigger pull; that was all I needed to know.

I took a few more deep breaths, looking at myself in the mirror, and asked myself a new question. Not *what are you doing?*, but *why are you doing it?*

For Ellie Chatham, old woman of five, and all the others naked and shivering in the cold, all leeched of parts of themselves whose absence they would never overcome. For Terry Browning, who had seen reality and refused to turn away even knowing it would destroy him, and for Alec Hardiman who had done the same. In some way perhaps it would atone for Terry, who could and should have received more from me, even if it had only been sitting up with him for a few nights. Could that have helped? It was too late to ask now.

And perhaps most of all it was for me, in my thirty-something dread of failure and the dark, so that at the withered arse-end of my life I could look back and say *this at least. Even if no one knows but me, I achieved this. Even if I started nothing, at least I ended something that needed ending; this, at least.*

Whether they were good enough or not, they were the only reasons I had, and so they'd have to do.

I pulled the curtains back and looked out of the window. Don Hardiman's Vauxhall Astra was parked outside. Fifteen minutes later he pulled up in a Volkswagen Polo. That one was for me. I reloaded the Browning and went out to meet him.

"Do you think Wadham did it?" he asked.

"Did what?"

"Alec."

I shrugged. "I suppose he could've. But more than likely it was someone looking out for him. Working for his dad, or one of his dad's connections. Don't suppose we'll ever know, will we?"

"No." He shook his head. "And it doesn't really matter, does it? The effect's the same."

"Yeah."

"Good luck, Paul." We shook hands.

"You too."

Don picked Wadham up first, coming out of his gravel drive in Sale in a BMW. We stayed in touch with mobiles, and I followed at a distance, picking up when I had to. We alternated pursuit like that for nearly an hour, until he reached Lower Broughton.

"He's pulled in," said Don. "Shit, Paul, he's getting out of the car. Heading up Broughton Road, on foot. What now?"

"Leave it with me," I said. I was surprised how calm I felt.

Wadham was heading up from the Irwell Valley campus. Broughton Road led ultimately to the Broad Street roundabout, a stone's throw from the vacant lots off Brindleheath Road. The arrogance of the bastard; so close to where he'd attacked Ellie Chatham. Of course, there were a lot of roads branching off along the way. I pulled in near the roundabout where Broughton crossed Seaford Road. He walked past, head down; I ducked so he wouldn't see me, in case he remembered too.

When he was gone, I got out of the Polo and followed at a distance, hands thrust into my pockets. He kept going up, over Lower Broughton Road, 'til he reached the lowrise blocks and estate terraces on the left-hand side of the road. Then he vanished down one of the walkways and was lost in the shadows.

I hung back, waiting by a small birch sapling someone had optimistically planted on the green apron outside the terrace. It occurred to me that, dressed in black and loitering in the shadows as I was, I might easily be mistaken for my prey, and I had to smile bitterly at the thought. Should I follow him? In the dark, the walkways were a maze, and what if Wadham knew I was trailing him? Before I could make a move, he came back out again, leading a small boy by the hand.

The boy was maybe eight, wearing tracksuit bottoms, a t-shirt, and a baseball cap, his hair almost shaved clean it was cut so close to the skull. The estate kids in Broughton are tough, they have to be, but the boy followed Wadham meekly as a lamb. Why he was out that late, or how Wadham charmed him so easily, I never knew.

Wadham and the boy crossed the road; they were heading for Broughton Park, a small zone of green surrounded by a multicolored fence. Wadham climbed the gate; the boy waited patiently to be lifted over.

I ran across the road, scaled the gate, landed in a crouch. I couldn't see them. Then there was a whimpered cry from the child, and a sound of ripping cloth. I pulled the Browning from my belt, pulled back the slide, and ran.

I floundered through the bushes; the boy lay on the open grass. He was naked except for his underpants; they came away in Wadham's hand with a final rip as I ran up. Wadham's lips were skinned back from his teeth; I couldn't tell if it was a smile or the snarl of a predator about to strike. His head turned as I reached him; our eyes met for the second time. Then I swung up the Browning and shot him in the face.

The bang was sudden and deafening; there was a flash and a brass cartridge spat out of the gun. Something warm and wet splashed my cheek. Wadham's face was black with it as he fell backwards, arms flailing, then jerked once and was still.

I turned to the boy; he was sat up, hugging his knees. "Are you all right?" I asked. He nodded. Wadham hadn't had time to do whatever it was he'd done to Ellie Chatham and the rest.

I turned and Wadham's snarling face lunged up into mine, teeth bared. One eye was gone, the socket streaming blackness down a bone white cheek. He grabbed my throat; his hand was bitter cold. I shoved the Browning into his chest and fired twice, blowing darkness out of his back; he reeled away and fell to one knee, arms windmilling, then launched himself up and came at me again.

I aimed two-handed and shot him in the forehead, then again in the temple as he fell to his knees. He rolled onto his back and I stood over him; blood-covered, his glistening face was a blackness like the rest of him. There was a noise in his throat that was either a rattle or a laugh as he began to sit up.

I shot him in the face again and again, the sulphur smell of cordite in the crisp night air, and felt sprays of blood and bone hitting me. He reached out a hand to me as the gun emptied, the trigger clicking helplessly as I pulled it, then toppled back and lay still. But I could still hear him breathing, and after a while he began moving feebly. Then the breathing stopped and his limbs went slack.

I turned back to the boy. He began fumbling in the grass for his clothes. "Come on," I said, "let's get you home."

I still have nightmares about Timothy Wadham's one-eyed corpse slithering into my bedroom by night, smashed face grinning.

About a week into April, spring was finally underway. Crocuses and daffodils were in bloom. The sky was clean and blue and the air was getting warm. I opened the windows and cleaned the house; a late spring was better than none. Then the doorbell rang. When I answered it, it was DS Poole. "I think you know why I'm here," he said.

Instead of the station, he took me down the pub; Mulligan's in town, to be precise. I've always been a sucker for Irish whiskey. Over a shot each of Black Bush, we talked.

"Worst part is," he said, "that Alec went to you, not me. He didn't trust me."

"He didn't know who he could trust," I said quietly. "It wasn't just you."

He glowered at me. "You think that helps? I was his partner. I wouldn't have let him down."

I wasn't sure which of us he was trying to convince, but I didn't press the point.

"I didn't see anything about Wadham in the papers," I said at last.

Poole grunted. "That's how it'll stay. The boy's mum called us in. No chance that one could just go away. His old man's not chasing up revenge— not through us anyway. The boy gave us a description of his rescuer. Or rather, me. No one else knows and no one else will. From that I put two and two together."

"And Wadham?"

"Up in smoke, Paul. Saw to it myself." He toyed with his drink, then looked up at me. "You know, when I saw how many times you'd shot him, I thought you must've hated him even more than I did. But when we burned the fucker, I understood why."

I waited, but I knew what was coming next.

"He was banging on his coffin lid," said Poole. "And then he was banging on the oven door. All the way through, 'til all he was was ash. And the ashes went in the river. Saw to that myself, an' all. With all the shit that's gone in the Irwell over the years, who'll notice a bit more?"

"They've just had it cleaned," I pointed out.

"Well, they'll just have to clean it all over again." We finished our whiskies; Poole looked toward the bar. "What's that bottle?"

I looked. "More whiskey. Midleton."

"Any good?"

"Supposed to be, but at a tenner a shot I wouldn't know."

Poole came back with two doubles. "To Alec," he said.

"Alec," I nodded, and touched my glass to his.

Perhaps the Last

CONRAD WILLIAMS

Conrad Williams is a past recipient of the British Fantasy Award. He is the author of three novels, Head Injuries, London Revenant, *and* The Unblemished, *as well as a collection of short stories,* Use Once, Then Destroy. *He is currently working on a novel set in the same world as his novellas* Nearly People *and* The Scalding Rooms.

Garner spent his days clock-watching in a room filled with timepieces, none of which could tell him how long was left on his shift. Hours crawled by. The first month of a job that might last him the rest of his life. Maybe one day he'd be given a more agreeable timetable and things would go better, but until then it was graveyard hours for him; in a room filled with relics from the past, Garner had never felt more dead.

He leaned over the railing and peered into the gloom. The museum's lower floor contained the paraphernalia of surgery; dozens of cabinets reproducing the gory scenarios of operations before anaesthetics were discovered or invented. There were other sections to patrol: the arcane instruments of measurement, distance, and direction; compasses and theodolites, conglomerations of brass and glass, maybe luck, maybe prayer. He always seemed to end up back in this section on the upper floor, the one dealing with time and man's efforts to capture it. He found the clocks and watches comforting.

The museum sprawled around him, a maze that he had mastered in the short time since his appointment. He knew that he would find creases of light that squeezed through the tight jambs of the fire doors along the south wall. The seventh of the twenty-nine steps leading up to the first floor exhibits was warped slightly, as if a foot that was too heavy to be borne had landed there. A soft drinks machine near the entrance might give up a can of Coca-Cola Zero if it was rapped smartly in just the right spot.

He felt it coming, a weird *swerve* of giddiness in his head, as if his brain had torn free of its moorings and intended to turn left as he went right. He began to breathe more deeply, trying to combat the inevitable surge of nausea. A disembodied voice, a truncated sentence in his head: . . . *discovered in a skip in Bayswater, minus its internal organs. The body has yet to be identified. Police are asking for any* . . .

He had learned, over the years, to live with the occasional interruptions. At least the surgeon had warned him that such invasive incidents were to be expected. Sometimes, though, he couldn't help wondering if he was making the words come himself, a quiet brain inventing a little fun for itself. His whole life was about waiting, watching. He never seemed to do anything other than spend his life in darkness, staring out at the night. Part of him believed that he had left a sliver of himself behind at the instant of his accident, his head injuries trapping him to the year 1987: his bike, a Ford Sierra Ghia, and the junction of Orford and Marsh House Lanes. He seemed to be always looking back. Remembering, or trying to. His life had altered so radically that it was a little like death, he supposed. Death, after all, was just change.

The museum, situated in South Kensington, was split into two floors and again, laterally, between east and west. The internal closed-circuit cameras were switched off at night, for economic reasons. The lighting was also reduced by 50 percent, to save 50 percent. Attendance to the museum was down on last year, a trend that didn't look like finding an upturn. The Natural History Museum and the Science Museum were nearby, and cast such large shadows that this building only ever seemed to be visited by people who stumbled upon it by accident. The expressions of its patrons coming in from the street was owlish, disappointed.

Garner was checked upon, infrequently, by Paul Frobisher, who was little more than a clipboard and three extravagantly polished pips on each shoulder. Garner had tried to initiate conversations with the younger man on the few occasions that Frobisher had dropped by, but was cut off by Frobisher's transparent disdain for lower rank guards. He spent more time studying the ball point of his Parker pen than he did Garner's face.

Garner had met the woman of his dreams here the previous day. Or had at least glimpsed her. Rita. He had named her after the Beatles song running through his head as she appeared, walking across the emptying funnel of space where the café was situated, in between the exhibits on the ground floor and the entrance hall. It was late in the day; thick bars of amber light played hopscotch with darker twins. She clutched a woolen scarf to her chest. Her shoes were silenced gunshots echoing across the marble. Like the floor, her face was slashed with bands of black hair. She marched out of the doors and into the street as the sun tumbled away from the corner of the windows.

He liked the softening of the museum as darkness came on. Hard angles were beveled by shadow. The harsh gleam of light on the glass surfaces turned to an agreeable haze. He thought he could hear, if he strained for it, the retorts of her heels continuing, either as ghosts in the museum's heights or finding him from the concrete of the Brompton Road.

The woman of his dreams. He thought about that for a while. Did the girl you fell in love with command all your sleeping attention, or was there a template for her preceding that first sighting? Had she always been a part of his thoughts, on some subtle level, only to flower into significance when he clapped eyes on her? It would be nice to ask her opinion, but as yet he had only ever conversed with her in his own mind.

Now, he whispered: "Did you enjoy your visit?"

He imagined her stopping on her way to the door, looking up at him, perhaps finally ridding her face of those blades of hair. A smile. An eyebrow arching. Her voice rising into the domed ceiling like some soft unfolding. A flower. Origami. "Yes. Yes, I did, thank you."

He strolled the aisles between the timepieces. He knew his patrol so well now; could walk it in the dark if the museum bean counters ever decided to go the whole hog and turn the lights off completely. The first few nights he had paced out the various zones like a prisoner coming to terms with his cell. Most of the display cabinets were dotted arbitrarily around the floor, others were lined neatly along the perimeter. His favorites divided time into chunks, offering it in a variety of faces, from the ingeniously simple to the shatteringly elaborate. There were Chinese water clocks, a Congreve clock powered by a stainless-steel ball that zigzagged along brass grooves. Stop-watches, pendulums, gnomons, and pallets. Pocket sundials in beautiful leather boxes. Great iron intersections incorporating cogs and springs and gears. Every kind of escapement, from deadbeat to detent to recoil to float-ing balance. Cylinder watches, verge watches, repeating watches. Velvet-lined wooden boxes. Beautiful table clocks. Oscillators, winding barrels, anchors and counterweights. The turning of circles. Touch pins that had al-lowed the pre-electricity population to read the time in darkness. Skeleton plates, repoussé cases: silver and enamel, chased or damascened. Burnished zones where the fingers of people long dead had probed.

An incremental grinding of teeth. The bruxism of time.

The clocks were on the elevated portion of the museum; this was where a break-in would occur, not down on the ground where the doors were a hundred years old and two inches thick. In this way he could justify the extra time he spent up here. Striding around glass cabinets filled with bone shears, amputation knives and hacksaws made him feel queasy. He didn't like to think how his life might be colored by that gruesome arsenal should he begin to spend more time casting his shadow over it.

He paced. He drank the coffee in his flask. He ate his ham sandwiches, his banana, his piece of fruitcake. He read the *Evening Standard*, settling for a long time on the story of the corpse discovered the previous night in a large industrial bin belonging to a hotel a mere quarter of a mile away from the museum. Police had taken the unusual measure of divulging the cause of death—the tearing out of the victim's heart—hoping it might lead to a swift arrest rather than an unlikely spate of copycat murders. He read a chapter from a novel. He paced. And another hour was measured out by countless immobile hands.

He shaped her in his mind. He gave her breath. He gave her a voice.

"You know Frank Whittle?" It wouldn't matter what she said to him. How left field, how mundane. The way she spoke, he imagined, would enliven the recitation of a library's opening times. Something deepish, something just the right side of husky.

"Not personally," he said. "But yes. Helped invent the jet engine, didn't he?"

"You know what he did when he retired?"

"Took his ear plugs out?"

"He bought a house at the end of a runway and watched planes taking off all day long."

This would be something about her that excited him. She would always be coming out with strange information. Trivia that had no bearing on anything. She would constantly be taking their conversation on jinking, unexpected routes. He could deduce this from the sparkle of her eyes, so far only ever seen from distance.

It didn't really help to pass the time, and he grew embarrassed when he thought of Frobisher walking in on him while he was doing it, but it was fun to guess, too much fun to stop. The illusion of connection was too seductive.

"Well you won't find me moving across the road from a security firm," he said. "Attractive though that might be to the ordinary man. What about you? What will you do when you retire?"

"Long time off."

"I should think so. You don't exactly look as though you're entering the autumn of your senescence."

"I'd like to live by the sea. Somewhere clean. And cold. I'd like to spend whatever time I have left looking at the stars." Her voice descended in octaves of sadness. He couldn't prevent it, despite trying to fill her mouth with different lines, different avenues of escape. She said, "There are some things we were never meant to see. Never meant to have confirmed. The skull beneath the skin. The knowledge of what we truly are, what makes us. We ought never to see that."

The darkness at four o'clock in November seems so satisfied with itself one could be forgiven for thinking that daylight might never force its way back. Garner trudged home along deserted main roads. The refuse and shadows that once conspired to upset him on his journey now interested him only peripherally. He knew the darkness well.

He had hung around at the end of his shift, reluctant to make the decision to go home and leave behind the only place where he had seen the woman. He knew she must be at home, sleeping, but the conviction remained that as soon as he turned his back, she would turn the corner onto this street.

The knowledge of what we truly are, what makes us.

Where had that come from? He ground his teeth together, frustrated with himself. Why couldn't he manufacture a simple exchange? Why did he always have to seed his imagined conversations with doubt? He wondered whether the dark slant to their discussion had come from an external source, another snatch of intercepted polemic from the airwaves, but he dismissed it. The voice had not changed. He had fed her the words.

Unusually, because of the light pollution in the center of the city, the sky was teeming with stars. He stopped for a while and stared at them. The longer he stared, the more it seemed he could see. Patches of ostensibly black sky opened up to show him dusty whorls of light. The illusion of the curved sky disintegrated. There was no shape to what he was seeing anymore. No end of depth. He reeled away when it occurred to him that his mind was too frail for what he was being shown. He thought he had seen a pattern there, for one unbearable second. Something that put him in mind of fingerprints, or the constellations of tiny muscle fibers that make up an iris. He felt cowed by the vision, such as it was, and the nearer he got to his home, the more he found himself doubting that he had seen anything. Another glance at the sky seemed to confirm this: just stars, just darkness.

He hurried past two men at a bus stop, hunkered over cigarettes and secrets. Voices not so low that he could not hear: *all 'is fuckin organs 'oovered out the poor bastard . . . 'is art . . . 'is fuckin' art gone . . .*

Back home he tried to do what most people who work shifts do: create the illusion that his working span was like any other day. So he took a bath, watched television, cooked himself some dinner, and opened a bottle of wine. By six, although it still wasn't getting light, the night had loosened somewhat. Garner headed off to bed, pausing on the way when a sudden jolt of sound—a known, frequent occurrence—drilled through his head. A film review, ostensibly, of a new picture by some European director called Guillame Angiers. He tried to find its echo on the shortwave radio by his bed but nothing remotely matched it. He fell asleep thinking of Rita, and the nature of the disease he had invented for her, all of it bracketed by words from the mysterious broadcast: *gnawed hearts . . . gnawed hearts . . .*

The sound of roadworks wakened him, or rather, the sound of the men powering the tools that tore at the tarmac. Mechanical things he had never found disruptive of his slumber, but raised voices, swearing, laughter, especially the kind of forced laughter from laborers—as if it was important it compete with the ambient sound—always roused him.

A low parallelogram of light on the wall suggested it was around midday. He lay in bed wondering about Rita. Lovely Rita. The name suited her. It was somehow exciting, but homely. Girl next door, with a bit of sass. He wished he had asked her to accompany him for coffee after work. He felt he knew her to the extent that an invitation would seem natural. He knew a great little place run by a Cuban called Paco that was open all night. He sold Turquino coffee that was so good it gave life meaning.

It felt somehow wrong, offensive, to fantasize about a woman he had never talked to, so when he felt the first twitches of an erection he rose and showered. He grabbed his novel and his digital camera, and headed for the river.

He could not shake off the feeling he had experienced the previous night. Although the stars were invisible now, he still felt able to see them. It was mildly alarming to know that they were there, against that dull carpet of pale gray, billions of them like a camouflaged army.

Garner walked down to the National Film Theatre and browsed the secondhand books beneath Waterloo Bridge. He found a film guide by Leonard Maltin and flipped through it but could find no reference to Guillame Angiers. *So what*, he thought. *Old guide, new director*. Not everything had to have a shadow. He collected a pint of lager, took a seat, tried to immerse himself in the book he was reading. The words couldn't bring him out of himself, which was what he always asked of a novel. It wasn't the author's fault. Rita, and something inexplicable, capered at the edge of his reason, fouling anything he tried to focus on. He wondered what the other might be. Something to do with the strange light, perhaps. Or the snatches of sound that fizzed through his thoughts from time to time. He felt anxious, but in an amorphous way. It was as if the anxiety existed only because he couldn't pinpoint the reason for it.

An old man with a white candyfloss beard played a violin in front of the book tables with violent panache. The river seemed hardly to move beyond him, but suggested its strength in the subtle ribboning of its surface. He surreptitiously took pictures of women who passed him by, wondering what it was that triggered attraction. It was beginning to panic him that he might never engineer a meeting between them. Soon it might be too late.

The violinist stopped playing. Nobody applauded. The musician didn't seem affected. He collected the change thrown into his violin case and walked away.

"Have you had any more transmissions lately? On Radio Garner?"

"Yes," he said, gingerly touching the back of his head. He wished he had never told Rita about his accident, and the metal plate, and the occasional rushes of static, or voices, or music, that fled through his brain like something half-remembered. "I had one last night, before I went to bed." He had seen her again, just as he arrived at the museum. There were more people around because he had turned up earlier than usual, and he had drunk a cup of tea while he watched the visitors drift toward the exit. He heard her before he saw her. The sharp, measured tattoo of her heels on the parquet. Her determined gait was in stark contrast to the meandering of the other people. It reminded him of an old film, a story dealing with escape from a prisoner of war camp. Soldiers dressing in the enemy's uniform, marching out of the open gates under the scrutiny of men with guns. She had the walk of someone with escape on her mind, hoping not to be rumbled. Her face lost its frame of black hair to reveal a pale oval filled with angles, shadows, rouge, and kohl. One hand was pressed to the center of her chest, keeping the flaps of her raincoat in position. Breathlessly, he watched as moments of what lay beneath shivered into view. Her shape seemed agonizingly available. He closed his eyes and it was there, unwrapped for him, cuppable, yielding.

"Go on."

"A film review. Well, part of one. I still get a bit of a jolt from it. Have to go and check the radio isn't on. Before I believe it's coming from me. Or coming through me, I should say."

"What was the film?"

"A new film called *Gnawed Hearts*. By some European guy. Guillaume something."

"Guillame Angiers?"

"That's it. Have you seen it?"

"No. I hardly ever get out to do stuff. Occasionally I visit the museum, soaking up a little history, you know. I spend a lot of time indoors. Just me, a glass of mineral water, a relaxing CD, and a nebulizer."

Garner winced, grateful that the dark prevented her from seeing his expression. Her health problems were clearly more acute than he'd realized. Her voice seemed happy enough though. She sounded as if she were describing something desirable. Like a holiday, or an unattainable man. He could almost believe that the echoes scattering around the museum weren't only of his making.

"Don't waste your time," she said. "Take advantage of the fact that you're mobile. That you're intelligent. Healthy. Fill each minute, because I promise you if you don't, you'll regret it."

In the dark he was aware of the minute movement of things. The slow slide of the moon's light across the wall, the epically tiny repositioning of teeth and coils, the settling of age in his bones. He had always thought of time as this linear thing, a real thing, that measured out your span for you in handy chunks as you bumbled around from day to day. In the midst of its mechanical fashioning here in the museum, he got an idea of time that was more fluid and yet less recordable than that; something that reached out in many directions beyond forwards. Something instantaneous, with a lifespan shorter than the smallest particle of its own, immense scale. He thought of something being born and dying almost instantaneously. He thought of a world 4.5 billion years old and yet never truly existing beyond the superimmediate moment.

It was strange to think of his city, his street, this museum, hosting people from different decades, different days. It must have happened—there was plenty of photographic evidence—but it still provided a mental block for him. It didn't exist anymore. It was dead time.

During the night, usually in the two hours or so before his shift ended, Garner could hear the ministrations of time more clearly: the skittling of the ball bearing in the Congreve clock, or the ticking of the newest additions to the cabinets, the Seiko Kinetic watches, design classics from just a few years previously. Garner could imagine future generations goggling at these in the same way visitors gazed at the ancient sundials while they took for granted whatever exotic technology it was that allowed them to keep their appointments. Something stitched behind the eyelid. Something bolted to the brain. Time moved on. Or maybe it didn't. Maybe time was static, and it was *us* that moved through *it*.

Garner closed his eyes against these difficult thoughts and became gradually aware of a new sound, another ticking, although this time irregular, muffled and, he could somehow tell, not from this quarter of the museum.

"Can you hear that?" he asked Rita.

"Yes," she said, equably. "What is it?"

"I thought you might be able to tell me."

"It's a clock, isn't it? Of some sort?"

"I don't know. It sounds as if it is." Garner couldn't put his finger on why the museum collected such a softness, a vagueness, at this time of night. More and more he suspected that it was him instead, relaxing, becoming more attenuated, more responsive to the sensory krill as it floated by.

He rose from his uncomfortable molded-plastic chair and strolled the usual figures of eight through the displays, in case a different position within the old building might reveal the source of the sound. It didn't. It seemed to come from all angles, and none at all. Maybe it was coming from his own body.

"It must be heating, or water in the pipes. Something like that," he said at last.

"Yes," she agreed. "It's an old building. Sometimes you just aren't aware of it, but in quiet moments it can surprise you. It doesn't matter how long you've been here. How well you think you know a place."

"You know this place well?"

She sighed, and the sound flitted around the heights like a trapped bird. "Too well," she said.

His eyes were closed. He could almost imagine the thrill of proximity, the smell of her hair, her breath. "It would be nice to get to know you better," he said, haltingly. "I could buy you a cup—"

"I don't think so," she interrupted him. "It isn't what I'm looking for."

He was confused and hurt by her instant rebuttal, and, further, the immediacy of his own dismissal. How had he misread their relationship? How could he self-destruct like this? Was he so lacking in confidence that he couldn't even fantasize successfully? They conversed easily, she laughed at his jokes, he was interested in her. What harm could a cup of coffee bring? But he knew what he was doing. He was setting up defenses against the misery of rejection. All of his life had been a scuttling back from the word *no*. He had fended off fists and stones, one time a knife, but a voice turning him down, that one found his soft underbelly every time. Rehearsing the moment, though it pained him—even in make-believe—to be unable to swing a situation toward the positive, was the only way he could combat the threat.

He resumed his patrol, walking close to the rail and looking down into the lower floor quadrant. Despite this failure, he was determined to pursue her.

He thought he saw the twin gleam of eyes turned up toward him, and the sweep of a shadow, but he knew the building was empty. Each night he had to check the toilets, the exits and entrances, trigger the alarms that protected every threshold in or out of the place. Though he had only worked here a short time, he felt he was on the way to understanding the quirks of the building as well as he did his own home. He was a good security guard. Loners often were. Something to do with being more aware of personal space invasion. Something to do with preferring one's own company.

Suddenly it seemed that the hours weren't moving as fast as they once had. There was little for him to do. The newspaper had been read, the crosswords and Sudoku completed. There was nothing left to eat in his bag and his flask of coffee had finally become tepid. His frustration had no release; what could he do but pace the same old route in his cheap serge uniform? Through the large ceiling window he again marveled at the talcum-powder stars. He thought he might have unleashed their secret; something was threatening, like the storm behind a wall of black cloud, but then it was gone; maddeningly, because the patterns remained, as well as his belief in his capacity to read them. He almost asked Rita if she could see what he was seeing, but he stubbornly stuck to his guns, no matter how much he needed some support about what was being played out far above him. He heard her voice, or his design for it, moving through his mind like a memory. He recognized the rhythms and melody of it, but not the words. It was as if he were hearing her speak through a gag. He almost asked her what was wrong, but he suspected at the last moment that her voice had come to him from a different source. His head burned with confusion; he wanted to shout out, ask what it was she wanted, but he couldn't because of course she didn't want anything. She wanted only what he decided for her.

It isn't what I'm looking for.

What *was* she looking for? Why did she come to the museum and then leave every day as if she had the devil at her heels?

At the end of his shift he stood outside for a long time, certain he could hear the pendulum beat of her shoes on the concrete, but she was nowhere; his suspicion, or need, had been infected by the soft noises occurring within the museum, those made by the wind, or the badly remembered weight of visitors on the floorboards and chairs. He tested the fire doors from the street but they did not give. Now the heels again, striking the floor as if she meant to open the ground with them. Suddenly he was convinced she *was* inside, had been all along. Somehow he had missed her during his closing time inspections. He returned to the front of the building and tried the main entrance. Locked, of course. He was a good security guard. Thorough. The museum managers, in their wisdom, had decreed after spending a lot of time and money on studies into criminal behavior, that the hours four until nine were the unlikeliest for a break-in. They were probably right, but it disgusted him that they watched the pennies where he was concerned. Topping his shift up until nine would hardly tip them into the red. But they could fall back on EU regulations, shift limits. *It's all for your good health, Mr. Garner. A fit guard is a happy guard.* Angry, he stomped to Paco's coffee shop, drank three cappuccini and scanned the previous day's newspaper that he salvaged from a bin. Another hour. He felt older. He went back to the museum and the lights were on in one of the ground floor offices. He tapped on the glass and a shape squirmed into the elaborately textured square.

"Who is it?"

Garner could tell by the voice that it was Joyce, the cleaner. He asked her to let him in.

He thanked her profusely, explaining that he had left his watch in the museum. "Funny, isn't it?" he said, ascending the stairs and looking back down at her in the reception hall. "I lose my watch. In a room full of watches."

She didn't find it amusing and, shaking her head, returned to her brushes and buckets.

Garner retraced his steps quietly until he was standing by the main doors again, checking that Joyce had shut herself in the kitchen. Now he moved quickly to the ground floor exhibition entrance. He pushed lightly at the door, but it was locked. He rubbed his face. There must be some way of getting in. He couldn't understand the force of his need. He wanted to believe that she was shut up inside the museum, that she had inadvertently become lost in the dark because she was trying to find him. And then he realized the only way he could get in, short of breaking the door down. He returned to the stairs and hurried up to the first floor. Beyond this, a STAFF ONLY sign hung from a rope barrier across a narrow set of steps leading to the museum roof. He deactivated the alarm and slammed the heel of his hand into the release bar. Outside he edged along the walkway between the railing overlooking a thirty-foot drop to the ground and the large sloping windows that hung over the timepieces. He was able to lever open one of them and slip inside. The beam of a torch yellowed the edge of one of the glass cases. What was going on? The beam did not waver. It had to be Frobisher, dropping by to do a check of the area for another superefficient clipboard report; nobody else had access to the building. Garner wondered if he should come clean to his superior, or go ahead with his plan and hope he didn't get spotted. If Frobisher was here then Garner must find the girl before he did. Frobisher would think nothing of getting her prosecuted. There was something about that beam though, something about the way it did not move.

Garner felt the first tremors of fear—minuscule, but relevant, like the tiny, shivering chip of quartz in a wristwatch. Something had happened here, in the time it had taken for him to clock off, drink a few cups of coffee, and break back in. He edged to the railing and peered into the darkness of the lower floor. Nobody walked down there, not anymore. He wondered if he had imagined her footfalls, but only for a second: he knew that he had not.

He approached the torch from the rear, hoping to find Frobisher snoozing, but his superior was not there. He retrieved the torch and switched it off. A few feet away he found Frobisher's jacket with its incandescent pips, cast on to the floor. That wasn't like him. Frobisher wouldn't hang his jacket on a hook unless there was a coat hanger to keep its shape. The complete lack of sound was distressing, occurring as it did within an environment where he usually felt so comfortable. The museum was suddenly an alien place to him. A feeling that was intensified when he vaulted the railings and dropped the ten feet into the exhibition hall on the ground floor. His unease was replaced for a short time with unalloyed excitement. If she was here, then it was the closest he had ever been to the woman that intrigued him so much.

But then: "Some of those stars up there died a thousand years before you were born," she said. "The light you can see is ancient, of a thing that no longer exists. It might be a thousand years after you die that the light will wink out. Time comes into its own where concepts like that are concerned. It puts on its best frock and flirts with the camera. Minor elements, like you for instance, trouble time hardly at all."

She was not there, but it was her voice. It wasn't his approximation either. This was not some honey-throated come-on. This was something halting and jagged, something trying to be heard in a wind tunnel. He felt it convulsing around his mind like a severed worm. He pressed his fingers against the metal plate in his head as if certain he would trace her features in it. A soft click: light flicked on upstairs. He looked around him but down here it was still too gloomy to see anything that might open Rita up to him. Nothing here but the ghosts of her footprints, the storm of her passage out of or into the museum. He didn't know what he had expected to find. By this time he was half-crippled with fear anyway. He wanted to call up to whoever was upstairs—Frobisher, he hoped, back from the toilet or the tea room—but to do that was to give himself away and he feared what consequences that might bring. Because he knew Frobisher was dead. The jacket told him that. But one of the cabinets here also spoke of things gone awry. It was some way larger than any of the others. The lid had been pushed back, which surprised him as he had never seen any of his own cabinets opened for any reason. Inside it was a nineteenth-century operating table, complete with authentic tray of sawdust beneath to absorb spillages. He reached in and touched the worn wood with its collection of nicks from the amputation blades that had sawn into it over the years. His hand came away warm and wet. His eyes snagged on a placard referring to an operation that had been attempted on a female baby suffering from a terrible condition known as *ectopia cordis*, a congenital state in which the patient is born with the heart outside the body. *The baby survived*, the placard read, *and led a relatively normal life until complications caused her eventual death, aged twenty-nine*.

Garner felt the skin on the back of his arms pucker. He knew then that Guillame Angiers did not exist, that he was a construct, a secret formed between them, a way for her to connect with the thoughts and fears in his mind. A way for her to sample the flavor of who he was.

Tentatively he climbed on to one of the display cabinets. He had to leap to catch hold of the railing surrounding the gallery above and pulled himself up as quickly as his unfit body would allow.

She said, "One man's museum is another's prison. You worry so much about your place in the world to the point where it consumes you. But you never once consider the possibility that there was never a place for you to begin with."

Frantically, Garner stalked between the display cabinets, searching for something he didn't have a name for. The clocks and watches all seemed different now that the lights were on. Up ahead he saw shadows surge across the pale carpet, then recede into the relative murk against the wall, where the pendulum clocks were aligned. He was thinking of waking each day, looking down, and seeing the thing that kept you alive, that fueled love. An obsession for life became inseparable from a fascination with the organ that drove it. You were human but you were not. Every second, every beat, was a reminder of the grave. The skin was always peeled back. You were your own horror mask.

He heard the smash of broken glass. The lid of the cabinet had been shattered. At first he thought it must be due to something having fallen from the ceiling, but even as he approached he knew this was merely wishful.

Something had been added to the collection.

It was beautiful and awful in equal measure. A silver skull watch, blood spattered and glistening. A Latin phrase was inscribed into the metal. He could just make it out despite the splashes of red: *ultima forsan*. Next to it, another kind of timepiece had been crudely mashed into the broken display cabinet. Like the others, this one had also stopped ticking, but could never be fixed to do so again.

The hole in her chest roared wetly with air as she filled her lungs. He could only glance at her, at the twitching fist of meat that clung to her chest, beating so violently he thought it must tear itself away. His panic and fear were heavy things, they dragged his gaze to the floor. Something that might once have been Frobisher lay ransacked there.

She said, "It's later than you think."

Stilled Life

PAT CADIGAN

Pat Cadigan has twice won the Arthur C. Clarke Award for best science fiction novel of the year. She lives in gritty, urban North London with her husband, the original *Chris Fowler*, and her son, *(Silent) Rob*.

Although primarily known as a science fiction writer (she's one of the original cyberpunks) she also writes fantasy and horror stories, which have been collected in Patterns, Dirty Work, *and* Home by the Sea.

Her novel, Reality Used to Be a Friend of Mine, *will appear Real Soon.*

When the weather gets warm, the human statues come out in droves. In Covent Garden, especially. As you leave the tube station, turn right to go down to the covered piazza called the Apple Market and you'll see them every ten feet on either side. Young women and men painted white or silver or gold or even black, head to foot, clothes and all, standing on a stool or a box or an overturned bucket, holding impossibly still in some marvelous pose. Besides making a little money, a lot of them are hoping to get spotted by one of those agencies that provide entertainment for corporate parties or celebrity bashes. Either could be lucrative, but Sophie was hoping more for the latter than the former. Corporate parties were good steady gigs, but even just one celebrity bash could make you a star. Sophie wanted stardom and she didn't bother hiding it.

Sophie was like that—unconditionally, sometimes brutally honest. Personally, I've always thought that excessive honesty was vastly overrated, so exactly how we became friends is a mystery to me. We had very little in common—she was London-born-and-bred, I was a U.S. ex-pat; she was in her late twenties, I was caught in the headlights of my oncoming fifties; she was a beauty, a classic English rose with fair hair, luminous eyes, and porcelain skin . . . I was caught in the headlights of my oncoming fifties—go figure. Call it a chick thing—sisterhood is powerful.

Whatever our bond was, it was strong enough that we could accept each other even if we didn't always understand each other. I mean, I wouldn't have tried the human statue thing on the street even in my early twenties, and God knows I'd tried plenty back then. But I didn't mind helping her out with her paint and her costume and props when we both had the same day off from Fresh 4 U.

That was how we met—she'd been working at the health food store for almost a year when I was hired. We bonded among the organic produce and fair-trade chocolate when we weren't standing at adjacent cash registers and ringing up the lunchtime rush of health-conscious office workers hoping that the antioxidants in the salads could counter the cumulative effects of twenty cigarettes a day. Some of them were also hoping to attract Sophie's attention, but she made it clear to all of them she wasn't interested.

"That kind of distraction would only interfere with the stillness," she told me once, as I was helping her into her alabaster goddess getup. This was a Grecian-style gown that she had bleached, starched, painted, and varnished to the point where it actually could have stood up without her. How she tolerated it next to her skin I couldn't imagine. She claimed that coating herself with several layers of greasepaint made it bearable; I didn't even like to touch the thing. The wig was even worse.

"If you say so," I replied.

She chuckled and handed me a tube of clown white so I could touch up her back. "I don't expect you to understand, Lee. You're not a statue."

Neither are you, I wanted to tell her, but I made myself shut up. Saying something like that to her just before she went into her act would screw her up completely and ruin the whole day—spoil her *stillness.* Ironic, I thought, that someone who worked as a statue could be so easily psyched out.

Besides the alabaster goddess, Sophie had two other personae: the bronze Amazon and the silver lady. The bronze Amazon wore more paint than clothing so she only came out in very warm weather, and only when Sophie was feeling particularly good about her body. The silver lady was, to my uncultured, American philistine's eye, a cross between a hood ornament and a second-place athletic trophy, which makes it sound a lot tackier than it looked. There was nothing tacky about the silver lady just as there was nothing sleazy about the bronze Amazon. I just couldn't take any of it as seriously as Sophie or her fellow statues and their helpers.

Chalk it up to my age. To me, the whole human-statue thing is the twenty-first-century version of street mimes. It was less strenuous, and it didn't involve someone in whiteface following you down the street making fun of the way you walked, which definitely counted in its favor. But anything done for pocket change was a paying-your-dues thing, not a vocational calling.

I did try talking to Sophie about her plans for the future; she was rather vague about everything. I supposed that only made sense. I mean, working as a human statue didn't suggest a specific next step, not like singing or dancing or riding a unicycle while juggling chainsaws.

"I have a pretty good singing voice," Sophie said when I finally managed to pin her down. We were restocking organic greens in the produce section. "But it's nothing special—one *of* a million, not one *in* a million, and I'm not limber enough to be a real dancer. I'm not coordinated enough to even *look* at a unicycle. Hell, it took me most of a week just to learn how to ride a regular bike. And chainsaw juggling is *so* last century."

"So you're a human statue because holding still is something you can do?" I said, examining a head of crinkly green lettuce for spots.

"It's not just *holding still*. It's the *stillness*." She was smiling dreamily, distantly. "I like the stillness. I like the way it builds from a little tiny speck deep inside. It swells, spreads all through me. When I get it to go just right, the whole world is flowing around me while I just *stay*."

"Like a rock in a stream?"

Sophie shook her head. "Better than that."

"Sounds very . . . stoic."

"Does, doesn't it?" She beamed at me. "Stoic. That's a good word, stoic. *Stoic*. Strong. We shall not be moved."

I grinned. "'Unmoved, an emperor is kneeling upon her mat.'"

She paused with a head of curly green in one hand and a softball-sized radicchio in the other. "Say again?"

"It's from a poem by Emily Dickinson. 'The soul selects her own society, then shuts the door; on her divine majority, obtrude no more.'"

"I love it," Sophie said. "'On her divine majority, obtrude no more.' That's a good mantra for stillness."

"Well, a long one, anyway." I shook my head and put a head of cos in the good pile. "Stillness is another thing I don't understand. When I was your age, I couldn't hold still for two seconds."

Sophie threw her head back and laughed. "Oh, man, what is this when-I-was-your-age shite? You make it sound like you're old enough to be my mother when I'm pretty sure you're not."

"Actually, I think I am," I said, wincing.

"Bollocks."

"Well, *technically* old enough if not really mature enough. If you know what I mean."

"Ah, right," she conceded, mirroring my wince. "Sometimes when people come in here with little kids it suddenly occurs to me that I'm old enough to be their mother." Sophie gave a small shudder. "Really weirds me out."

"What about when you're a statue? Does it weird you out then?"

"Nah. Statues can't have children." She looked down at the crate on the floor between us. "They don't have kids and they don't get older."

I gave a short laugh. "Everything that exists gets older. Statues are no exception."

Sophie tossed a wilted mass of curly-red in the bad basket. "Not the same way people do."

"Oh, *no,* honey," I said unhappily. "*Please* don't tell me you're one of those people who thinks 'age' is a dirty word."

"Oh, come on, Lee—are you saying you wouldn't stay young if you could?"

"Got it in one, girlfriend."

"*Bollocks.*"

"Why? Can you really not conceive of someone who doesn't want to stay young?"

She stared at me incredulously. "If I had the choice, I'd take it in a minute. And you'll never make me believe that you wouldn't, either."

I thought it over while we picked through some more greens. A dismaying amount of it was wilted. Stored too cold. Finally, I said, "Would you go back to high school? Pardon me, secondary school."

Sophie's lovely English Rose face took on a revolted expression. "I knew what you meant. And the answer is a resounding *hell, no, I'd rather die in a fiery car crash, thank you very much.*"

"OK, how about elementary school? That was usually a lot more fun for most people."

"Uh-uh, not there, either."

"Well, all right, then," I said. "Now you know how I feel."

Her revulsion changed to puzzlement. "About what?"

"About staying young. I'm glad I *was* young, of course. I didn't waste much time being sensible, I took full advantage of my youth—I did all kinds of reckless, crazy things, I made a shitload of mistakes and generally made a right prat of myself, as you Brits put it. *Je ne regret rien,* pardon my French."

Sophie looked pained. "I will but the French wouldn't."

"I'm also glad I was young *when* I was young," I added. "Oh, what a time it was, there were giants in those days, blah-blah-blah. But I'm over it."

I could see she was mulling it over. "Staying young and going back to school *isn't* the same thing," she said finally. "Think about it. I mean, *really* think about it. Having a young body, more flexible, without so many aches and pains? No wrinkles? No gray hair? Never getting tired, having limitless amounts of energy? What about those things?"

I started to feel more than a little defensive. "I don't think I'm all *that* wrinkled. Gray hair—" I shrugged. "There are people who pay big money to get these highlights. And as for the rest of it, well, I don't remember having limitless amounts of energy and never getting tired, but then, I wasn't actually all that flexible back then, so I wasn't wearing myself out doing gymnastics, either."

"But what about all those mistakes you claim you made?" Sophie gave me a sly grin. "You had to have a lot of energy for those, didn't you?"

I shrugged. "Sleep all day, party all night."

Her eyes widened. "Christ, what were you, a vampire?"

"Of course not. *Today* you'd have to be a vampire. Back then you only had to be a hippie. Never mind," I added in response to her puzzled look. "Different world." I tossed another wilted head of curly green into the bad pile and paused to massage the back of my neck.

"Did I mention aches and pains?" Sophie asked playfully, watching me.

"Hey, if people my age didn't have aches and pains, the ibuprofen companies might go out of business, which would lead to a worldwide economic crash and depression. You think we want that on our conscience?"

"Very funny," Sophie said, laughing. "But seriously—"

"But seriously, yourself, girlfriend. If that's what getting older means to you—aches and pains and gray hair and wrinkles, you're a lot shallower than I thought you were."

Sophie looked as if I had slapped her.

"I'm sorry, I didn't mean to call you shallow," I went on. "But that's not all there is to getting older."

"Okay," she said. "So tell me some wonderful things."

I hesitated. "That's like you asking me to tell you how wonderful it is to be me and I just can't. It's my Catholic school education—I had modesty beaten into me by a succession of husky nuns with thick rulers."

We both laughed and went on sorting lettuce while I wondered if she knew just how badly I had copped out with my modesty excuse. Tell her what's so great about getting older. Well, Sophie, honey, first of all, you're still alive. Second, you're, uh, still alive. And third, uh . . . well, you see, girlfriend, whatever else might be good about getting older, still being alive trumps them all. The whole idea is to keep breathing and last as long as you can.

Sophie quit while I was off sick for a few days. I didn't find out till I came back and met the gangly eighteen-year-old guy replacing her. He was recently out of school, friendly and polite and reasonably intelligent, and everybody had already taken a liking to him. I felt betrayed and abandoned.

When my shift ended, I headed straight over to Covent Garden. I wasn't really expecting Sophie to talk to me, about the store or anything else. I just felt the overwhelming and rather selfish need to show her my unhappy face.

It was after three when I stepped out of the tube station and headed down toward the piazza. The intermittent sun had done a disappearing act and it was misting out (never turn your back on a London sky, as I heard a customer say once) but there were still a lot of people milling about on the street. No, not milling—they were assembled, watching something.

No, not merely watching—staring, hard. Transfixed.

There was only one human statue on the walkway but, for a moment, I actually wasn't sure that it was Sophie. She was the bronze Amazon and there was no mistaking that—the spear, the helmet and wig, the torn cropped shirt, the modified swimsuit bottom, that perfect bronze-metal color coating her well-conditioned body. She stood with her feet about shoulders' width apart, just starting to raise the spear in her right hand, as if she had glimpsed some hazard that had yet to show itself clearly. Her eyes never blinked, at least not that I saw, nor could I see any sign that she was taking even the shallowest of shallow breaths. Her other arm was by her side, bent slightly at the elbow, wrist starting to flex, ready to provide counterbalance if/when she threw her spear.

Perhaps it hadn't been the weather that had driven away all the other statues. The toy soldier, the clown, the rag doll, the fox, Marilyn Monroe—I could picture them stepping down from their boxes and stools, shouldering their gym bags and retreating, defeated by Sophie's power. It was something well beyond what the word *stillness* had meant to me, well beyond what I had seen Sophie do in the past. Maybe even well beyond the motionless nature of a real statue.

Fascinated, I eased my way forward through the crowd, which was also very still and quiet—so quiet, in fact, that it felt wrong even to move, but I wanted to get up as close as possible. I was ten feet away from her when I saw something in her face change. It was barely there, not even so much as a shimmer in the heavy mist. I knew it meant that she had seen me.

Her stillness didn't crack for another ten or fifteen seconds, when I was almost within arm's reach. And that was exactly what happened: it cracked. Not visibly or audibly and yet it was, in a way—visible on the subliminal level, audible only to the subconscious. A few seconds later, her stillness flaked away and was gone, and the crowd was staring at nothing more than a scantily-clad woman in bronze body paint. The heavy mist deepened into rain.

Umbrellas went up and flapped open; voices murmured, rose, called to each other as people scattered, off to the piazza or the nearby shops and bars. I stayed where I was and watched Sophie come out of her pose like someone coming out of a dream.

"Dammit, Lee." Her shoulders slumped as she looked down at me. "This is all your fault."

"How?" I forced a laugh. "*I* didn't make it rain."

We both knew that wasn't what she meant but she let it go for the moment as she climbed down carefully from her pedestal. A real pedestal, or at least real enough. I rapped my knuckles on it.

"Where'd you get this?" I asked.

"Who ever heard of a statue on a stepladder?" Sophie said irritably.

"Good point," I said. "Does it help? With your stillness, I mean."

"Can't say, really." She eyed me darkly. "But I can tell you what *doesn't.*"

"I'm sorry I broke your concentration," I told her. "Truly, I am. I didn't mean to."

Sophie said nothing as she took off her sandals and padded barefoot to the covered space in front of a clothing store to get her duffel bag. I was surprised that she had just left it sitting there and even more surprised that Covent Garden hadn't been closed down so the bag could be removed and blown up by the bomb squad.

"I'm sorry," I said again. "I was just upset when I came into work today and found out you quit."

Sighing, she removed the helmet and the wig. "You didn't really think I was going to devote my life to organic groceries, did you? Sorting wilted lettuces and spotty apples?" She reached into the bag and pulled out a towel to dry the helmet.

"Why don't you wipe off the bronze and let me buy you a pint?" I said. "Or even an early dinner?"

She bit her lip, staring at something over my right shoulder. I turned to follow her gaze and was startled to find a man leaning against a pillar. I thought he must have just sneaked up behind me because I couldn't believe I'd walked right past someone that close without noticing. He was an inch or two shorter than I was, dressed in an assortment of things, none of which went with anything else, a bit like an extra in a production of *Oliver!,* but without the theatrical flamboyance. His smile didn't reach his eyes. "Up to you, luv."

Sophie didn't answer. She had the apprehensive look of someone afraid of saying the wrong thing.

"You know that I've nothing against you eating," he added.

I leaned in toward her and lowered my voice. "Who's that? Have you got a manager now?"

"Something like that," she said, almost too softly for me to hear. She fiddled with the drawstring on the duffel bag. "Lee's a friend from the shop," she said to the guy, then added, "Someone I know, that I used to work with," as if she were correcting herself.

He frowned at me the way people do when they're measuring something.

"She used to help me out sometimes with my costumes and paint," Sophie went on, a bit urgently. "And she covered for me at the shop, too, before I quit."

"I told you, luv, I've nothing against you eating." All at once he was nose to nose with her before I could even register that he had moved. "Here, I'll take care of your bag so you don't have to lug it around."

Sophie was slightly taller than he was but she seemed to shrink under his gaze. "I won't be long," she said, still in that urgent, pleading tone. A knot gathered in my chest. I didn't see him nod or make any other sign but apparently Sophie had. She reached into the duffel bag, took out a loose shift, and slipped it over her head. "Right. So let's go, yes?"

She was still very bronze. If she didn't mind, I didn't, either, but she seemed to have forgotten she was barefoot. I pointed at her feet. A little flustered, she pulled the sandals out of her bag, stepping into them as we walked off together.

I had been thinking in terms of sandwiches, but since her manager had gone to the trouble of saying not once but twice that he had nothing against her eating, I decided to blow the budget at a nearby brasserie. On my salary, that really was blowing the budget—I'd be living on the store's cast-offs for a while but I didn't care.

The brasserie hostess didn't even blink at Sophie's body paint, although she did look significantly toward the loo. Sophie took the hint and excused herself while the hostess showed me to a table. I ordered a large platter of potato skins as a starter and two glasses of red wine while I waited. When she returned from the ladies', less bronze but still somewhat stained, she didn't look thrilled.

"I worked up quite an appetite today," I said as she sank into her chair, "and it's been a long time since I've indulged in comfort food. Hope you don't mind too much."

"I don't mind you indulging," she said, emphasizing the *you* slightly but pointedly. "But you really should have asked before ordering wine for me."

"Hey, my treat, remember?"

"And don't think I don't appreciate it. I do. It's just that I'm off alcohol completely."

I wondered if she realized she was holding the wine glass and gazing at the shiraz with a longing that bordered on lust. "One glass of red wine with a meal is healthy," I said. "Didn't you read any of the nutritional propaganda at the store?"

She chuckled a little. "Red wine and potato skins? Very *haute cuisine*."

"This is just the appetizer. Here comes our waitress to take the rest of our order."

"No!" She didn't actually yell but she spoke loudly enough to make the people on either side of us look up to see if someone was about to make a scene. "I mean—well, it's just that I don't know if I can eat more than what we've got right now," Sophie added, slightly apologetic. "That's a whole lot of potato skins."

"Give us a little while with our appetizer," I told the waitress, grabbing Sophie's menu before she could get rid of it. "I think we just have to make up our minds."

Sophie frowned annoyance at me as the waitress moved off to take some-one else's order. "In case you've forgotten, I can't work if my stomach's too full."

"But it's the end of the day. You haven't taken to working after dark, have you?"

She sighed, put-upon. "Did it occur to you that I might have a gig this evening?"

Now I felt like a complete idiot. "Oh, shit, Sophie. No, it didn't. I'm so sorry."

Her grin was a bit mean as she pushed her wine glass over to me. "So you'll pardon me for not drinking this nice wine. And you won't try to force me to overeat now, will you?"

"No, of course not. But surely you've got to have a little something in your stomach to give you stamina—" I broke off and put my head in my hands. "Oh, Christ."

"What? What is it?" She sounded genuinely concerned.

I peeked through my fingers at her. "I sounded *exactly* like my mother just then."

Sophie burst into hearty giggles.

"I'm glad you think it's funny," I said, relieved that she still had a sense of humor. "But if you'd actually known my mother, you'd be making me crawl for forgiveness."

"That sounds ominous."

"You have no idea. But seriously, Sophie. If this—" I gestured at the po-tato skins "—is too heavy for you, what can you manage instead? A salad? Fruit? Yogurt?"

"I'm fine with a couple of these," she assured me, her expression soften-ing. "Look, I didn't mean to be pissy. I'm just kind of nervous. This is my first big evening gig."

"What is it?" I asked. "Some corporate bash? Or have you hit the big time with a celebrity?"

Her smile faded away. "I'm not supposed to talk about it."

"Top secret, huh? Then it's either politics or royalty."

Sophie laughed uneasily. "I told you, I can't talk about it."

"Okay," I said. "But that doesn't mean I can't let my imagination run away with me, right?"

"Sure, sure." She pulled one of the potato skins onto the small plate in front of her. "Knock yourself out."

My feeling that Sophie wouldn't be able to resist the appetizer proved correct. While I drank her wine and mine and then in a drunken folly ordered a third glass, Sophie ended up eating over half of the potato skins. Eating the first one seemed to loosen her up; after that, she was reaching for them casually, with no hesitation. When we got down to the last two, I helped myself to one and pushed the other one off the platter onto her plate. "That's yours," I said cheerfully.

She picked it up and then froze. "Oh, damn," she said and practically threw it down. "Oh, no—I *didn't*." She put one arm across her stomach. "Oh, Jesus, I *did*. Oh, God, I'm so *stupid*. How could I be so Goddamned *stupid?*"

"Sophie—" I started and then cut off. Tears were rolling down her cheeks. "My God, honey, don't *cry*."

"I'm *full*. No, it's worse—I'm *stuffed*."

"Sophie, don't—"

"That's what you should have said to me before, when I was stuffing my face," she said, hotly. "'Sophie, don't.' A *true* friend would have."

The people at the adjoining tables were staring at us. I ignored them. "That's an awful thing to say."

"The world weeps." She sat up straighter and took a deep breath. "Right. At least I know what to do about it." She got up.

"Wait," I said, reaching over and grabbing her wrist. "Where are you going?"

Her mouth tightened into a hard colorless line before she twisted out of my grip and headed toward the ladies room. Because I was tipsy, it took me a little time to get it. Then I went stumbling across the brasserie after her but by the time I got there, she was finishing up.

"How could you do that?" I asked her as she came out of the stall, her face all red and sweaty.

"Finger down the throat, how do you think?" she said hoarsely, splashing water on her face from the sink. "It works." She drank from her cupped hands, swished the water around in her mouth and spat it out with a grunt.

"But you're not an adolescent girl, you're—what, twenty-seven? Twenty-eight?"

"Twenty-nine next month, actually." She splashed more water on her face and then straightened up to look at herself in the mirror. Her eyes were bloodshot.

"That's way too old for bulimia, Sophie."

She shut off the faucet and patted her face dry with a paper towel. "It's way too old for a whole lot of things, Lee. I'm fighting for my survival."

"Keep doing that shit and you'll lose," I said.

"Thanks for your support." She took a deep breath and let it out, putting her arm across her stomach again. "Empty. It's all right. I never should have done this but I'm going to be all right."

"Sophie—"

"Oh, shut up, Lee," she snapped. "This soul selects her own society and it's not you. Got that? Obtrude on someone else and stay the fuck away from me." She yanked open the door and left.

I started to go after her but the hostess intercepted me politely but firmly to make sure I wasn't trying to skip out on the bill. By the time I got outside, Sophie was nowhere to be seen. I went back to where we had left her manager but there was no trace of either of them. Even the pedestal was gone.

I stayed away from Covent Garden for over a week after that. When I finally did go back, I wasn't even sure that Sophie would be there anymore. Maybe the creep had packed her duffle bag for her and taken her away. I couldn't decide whether I was afraid I'd never see her again or hoping I wouldn't. But when I came out of the tube station, I knew Sophie was still there even before I spotted the bronze Amazon. The crowd was even larger and quieter than before.

This time, there were still a few other statues trying for attention—the weather was good and the tourists were out in force, enough to support a whole flock of statues, buskers, *Big Issue* vendors, and plain old beggars. But once again, Sophie had the lion's share.

"Oi. *Oi,* you."

Something landed on my shoulder; it was Raggedy Andrew's blue ballet slipper, with his foot still in it. He was balanced on his other leg on a barrel painted to look like a very tall toy drum. It was a nice effect. No one was looking. He broke pose and sat down on the barrel. "You used to help out Miss Superstar over there." He jerked his chin in Sophie's direction.

"Not anymore."

The red yarn bobbed as he nodded his head. "Yeah, I know. You ain't been around lately so I guess the friendship's off between you two. You got no pull with her or anything, right?"

I spread my hands. "Why? Is there something you want?"

"Yeah. I want her to get the fuck outta here. We all do." He gestured at the other human statues.

I looked from him to Sophie's bronze form—even at a distance, that stillness was apparent. "I guess I can understand that."

Raggedy Andy gave a short, unpleasant laugh. "You think it's because she's getting all the money and attention. That's only part of it. But not all of it, or even most of it."

I raised my eyebrows. "So what is?"

"Stick around for a while, till she takes her break. You'll see then. *They* won't—the punters, I mean. I don't know why, but they don't. But us, we do." He waved at the other statues again. "I'm betting you will, too."

On the face of it, the idea that a grown man dressed as a rag-doll could scare me in broad daylight was laughable. But I wasn't laughing and neither was he. A chill went through me deep inside, where the warm sun couldn't reach. I turned away from him and started moving through the crowd again.

I didn't have to get that close to her to see that Sophie's body had gone from enviable to virtually perfect. Her muscle definition was better than I had ever seen on her or, for that matter, anyone else. But there was something strange about it, too. It was the kind of definition that wouldn't be apparent unless she were flexing and holding the pose like a bodybuilder, purposely displaying the muscles, and I knew she wasn't. A flexing pose would have shown off one set of muscles—arms or legs, back or stomach. Whereas Sophie's entire body was . . . well, an aerobics instructor would have wept at the sight of such an impossible ideal.

I heard the quiet *snick* of a camera shutter. The guy next to me was holding an elaborate digital SLR with an equally elaborate lens.

"Excuse me," I said, "but does that thing zoom in?"

It did. He took a close-up of Sophie and then showed me the image on the small screen on the back of the camera.

"I can't really see her face in any detail," I told him apologetically. "Would you mind terribly letting me look through the lens?"

He hesitated, then decided that I wasn't going to try to run off with it. He showed me which buttons to press and slipped the strap over my head; I put my eye to the viewfinder.

The zoom went so fast that it took a moment for the focus to catch up with it and when it did, I wasn't sure I had aimed it at the right target. It seemed to be Sophie's face but the eyes were blank. Just blank featureless bronze. Like a statue's.

Shocked, I fumbled the camera; if the owner hadn't taken the precaution of putting the strap around my neck, I would have dropped it. Not trusting myself to handle it, I motioned for him to take it back and he did so, looking more than a little bemused.

As soon as it was around his neck again, I felt like a complete ass. I had glimpsed Sophie's face for barely a second and her head had been tilted slightly forward. If I had let my own middle-aged eyes adjust, I surely would have seen there was nothing wrong with hers. Should have followed my earlier impulse and gone home, I thought as I started working my way toward the front of the crowd. I didn't need to get up close and see whether her eyes were really blank or not. I already knew I'd imagined it, and I kept going anyway.

This time, I was twenty feet away from her when her stillness cracked. I froze where I was, thinking that I had done it again. But no, this was just her taking a break, like Raggedy Andy had said.

Or rather, it was her creepy manager telling her to take a break. I could see his hand resting on the back of her left calf, signaling her as if she were a trained dog. I felt a surge of anger that he would treat her like that.

Sophie seemed to shrink and fold in on herself, practically collapsing as she climbed down from the pedestal and disappeared behind the dispersing crowd. I got more than a few dirty looks as I forced my way through the people milling around in front of me. I had the strange feeling that they had all forgotten they'd just been staring at Sophie's bronze Amazon; like they'd been released from a trance with the command to remember nothing.

When I finally reached the pedestal, I thought Sophie had left, spirited away by her manager just like the night I had taken her to the brasserie. But that was ridiculous—no one could have gotten away so quickly with so many people clogging up every available walkway. I went over to where she had left her duffel bag the last time, then to the pillar where her creepy manager had appeared out of nowhere—nothing. People bumped into me on all sides as they passed, the crowd growing thicker and everyone in it apparently in a hurry; I started to feel a little unsteady, even disoriented.

And suddenly there she was, right next to her pedestal. She was wearing a loose-fitting robe printed with abstract shapes in various metallic browns and golds that complemented her body paint in such a way that it made her seem somehow indistinct. A trick of light and color?

"Sophie," I called. "Do you have a moment?"

Shoulders sagging, she turned away from me.

"Please, wait—" I rushed over to her and then stopped short, not just because her creepy manager appeared seemingly out of nowhere but at the sight of her face, close up. "Sophie?" I asked, suddenly unsure if it really was her.

Her face had the haunted, suffering look of someone who had been enduring years of torment and was now deteriorating under the strain. "Oh, Jesus, Sophie," I said. "What *happened* to you?"

"Leave me alone," she said dully, waving me off. I grabbed her arm.

"No, Sophie, talk to me! What the hell?"

She tried to pull away but I hung on to her. Her arm felt even worse than her face looked—the muscles were soft, practically limp, as if they had atrophied, while the bone underneath was oddly light, like it might have been hollow.

"I told you, *leave me alone,*" she growled, pushing at me. I managed to get hold of her robe and tore it open.

This could not have been the body that I had seen posing on that pedestal, I thought, staring in shock. There wasn't much flesh and what there was hung in loose little folds. Her midsection was abnormally concave, as if most of it had actually been removed, while her legs were little more than sticks. This could *not* have been the body that I had seen posing on that pedestal—and more than that, this could *not* have happened to her in the space of a week.

"Sophie, what did you do to yourself?" My gaze moved from her to the creep, who was standing beside her with a ghost of a smile on his evil face. "What did you do to her?"

He put his arm around her shoulders and closed up her robe.

"Sophie, *please* talk to me." I reached for her again but somehow he slipped her around to his other side and put himself between us.

"She told you to leave her alone," he said in a low, oily voice. "And now *I'm* telling you." Before I could answer, he turned Sophie and himself away from me and in the next moment, they were just *gone,* melting into the Covent Garden crowd of tourists without a trace.

I looked around and saw that the pedestal had disappeared as well.

"Certain things are impossible," said Raggedy Andy over a pint. "You can tell yourself this. You can learn it in school or by experience or both. Then they'll happen anyway and you won't be able to do a thing about it."

The toy soldier toasted that statement with a bottle of Beck's. "Right."

They weren't Raggedy Andy and the toy soldier anymore, of course. Raggedy Andy was now a ginger-haired, green-eyed fellow named Liam who was a few years older under the whiteface than I had estimated. The toy soldier was a very tall woman named Pauline whose olive features had a strangely ageless quality; she might have been seventeen or forty. I was sitting with them in a pub near the tube station.

"Maybe that's what 'impossible' really means," Pauline added. "Impossible to do anything about."

"You think it's impossible for me to help my friend?" I asked.

Liam gave a short hard laugh. "You saw her. That's what's happened to her in a week. Can you honestly believe she's not beyond help?"

"What do you know about it?" I said. The words came out sounding defensive but at the same time, it was an honest question. "Do you know that guy she's with? Do you know anything about him?"

"No." He took a healthy gulp from the pint. "Not really." His eyes swiveled to Pauline in the chair beside him. She looked away.

I sat up straighter and grabbed his glass away from him. "Oh? What don't you really know?"

"Nothing to speak of," the other woman said, giving me an appalled look as she transferred her Beck's to the hand farther away from me. "Really. Liam doesn't know him and neither do I."

"No one does," Liam added in response to my skeptical look. "Nobody knows his name or where he comes from, who he works for if he works for anyone at all. And anyone who does know ain't talking. Like your friend." He reached for his glass; I held it away from him.

"When was the first time you saw this guy?" I asked.

"I don't know," he said irritably. "I see a few thousand people every day. After a while some faces get familiar but I couldn't tell you when I first saw most of them." He reached for the glass again but I still refused to give it to him. "And holding the last of my pint hostage isn't gonna improve my memory any. I can buy another." He started to get up; I waved him down and gave him back his glass.

"Did you ever see him do this with anyone else?" I asked.

Liam frowned thoughtfully. "No. But you hear things."

"No, *you* hear things," I corrected him. "So what have you heard?"

He looked at the woman again; she shrugged. "It was very vague. Something about a garden."

"Ah." I gave a harsh, humorless laugh. "Wait, don't tell me—could it be, oh, *Covent* Garden?"

"No, actually it wasn't," she said coolly. "Somewhere south of the river."

"Oh, yeah. That would be *New* Covent Garden, then." I made a disgusted noise. "Who do you think you're talking to, some clueless fuck of a tourist?"

They looked at each other, then got up and walked off. I slumped, resting my elbow on the table and staring at my own pint. Guinness Extra Cold; I couldn't remember whether it was my second or third. Or fourth? I was losing track and if I kept on, I was going to lose consciousness as well.

"Not New Covent Garden, either."

I jumped as the woman plopped down in the chair next to me.

"It's not any public place. A regular garden," she went on, "as in the place behind somebody's private residence."

"That's it?"

She tilted her head thoughtfully. "I got the impression it was a *big* garden. Big garden behind a big house. Posh, lots of money."

"Wouldn't it belong to someone pretty well known, then?" I asked.

Pauline blinked at me. "Why?"

"Because that's how it seems to go in this country. If you're posh, you're famous."

Now she smiled faintly. "There's posh and then there's *posh*—too posh for lower life-forms like us to know anything about. Do you know all the very high-and-mighty in America, the rarefied elite?"

"No, but this is a much smaller country. Fewer people to keep track of."

She moved my pint away from me and pushed something else into its place. "Here. You need this."

I found myself staring at a large cup of coffee. There was no milk in it but I gulped it down anyway.

"Can't hold your liquor at all, can you?"

I shrugged. "On the other hand, I have the smallest bar bill in the country."

"All that means is you drink alone. A lot."

"That may be true," I said with another sigh, "but it's rather unkind to point it out. Isn't it?" I closed my eyes and waited for her response; nothing. "Well, isn't it?"

I opened my eyes. There was no one in the chair next to me.

I pulled myself together enough to gulp down another cup of coffee, even though I knew the whole sober-up-with-lots-of-coffee thing was just a myth. If I couldn't actually get sober, I would settle for drunk and wide awake. It would save me some time and trouble if I didn't fall asleep going home on the tube. Going home was really all I was thinking about when I finally stepped out of the pub. Then I saw the crowd and headed straight down to join it.

Sophie had changed into the silver lady and the persona was a lot different than the time I had last seen it. Now she wore as little as the bronze Amazon—no, less. Her breasts were barely covered, and I wasn't sure what she was wearing on the bottom, but it looked like a modified doily, and a very small one at that.

Her body, however, had changed even more—i.e., it was better, if *better* was really the word to describe it. The impossible ideal of the bronze Amazon had somehow been surpassed. The silver lady's muscles were sleeker and better defined, her posture was so precise that she even looked *taller*. No, not just taller, but larger all the way around—

That couldn't be Sophie, I thought, goggling at her. There was a very strong resemblance but it wasn't her. This had to be someone else entirely, a bigger woman who was doing a variation on Sophie's silver lady. The creep manager's idea, no doubt. He probably had a whole stable of "clients" and made them trade off their costumes and personae all the time, just to make sure they knew who was boss.

After a bit, I realized she was moving; very, very slowly, all but imperceptibly, like the minute-hand on an old-fashioned clock, she was changing position. At the same time, I had the distinct impression of her figure *hardening,* become more statuelike rather than less. Her hands, held close together at waist level, began to descend, moving away from each other to the tops of her thighs; her head lifted, turned toward me as her weight shifted from one leg to the other.

Her eyes were blank. Smooth, featureless silver, just like a statue's.

Slowly, incredibly, painfully slowly, one arm began to rise and her weight shifted again as she reached forward. Her fingers were still curled softly inward toward her palm, so she wasn't really pointing in my direction, but for a few moments, I was sure she was going to. Instead, her arm went on rising and eventually stopped over her head, as if she meant to call down some power from heaven. Perhaps the silver lady was a goddess now.

This *was* a different woman; it was so obvious. She was several inches taller than Sophie and at least twenty pounds heavier. It couldn't have been Sophie.

Except that I knew it was.

It was practically dark by the time the silver lady broke and got down off the pedestal. In the whole time I had been watching her, I had barely moved myself. Now my legs hurt all the way up to my hips.

But at least I felt a lot more sober—sober enough to keep Sophie and the creep manager in sight despite the distance and the flow of people between me and them. I watched as the creep wrapped her up in a silver-gray robe but then carried out what seemed to be an inspection of her body. He felt her up with both hands, through the robe and then under the robe, as if she were a race horse. Sophie submitted to it with no resistance that I could discern. Whatever he discovered apparently satisfied him. He put one arm around her shoulders and herded her away, talking intently while she hung on his every word.

I didn't make a decision to follow them—I just did it. They were so wrapped up in each other that they didn't bother to watch where they were going much less look back to see me trailing several yards behind them. Some instinct seemed to be guiding them along the street, stepping up or down as necessary, while people moved aside to let them pass without actually noticing. At a quick glance, they might have passed for any newly smitten couple enjoying the high of a new relationship. But what I saw in Sophie's face was an eaten-away-from-the-inside quality similar to terminal cancer patients, while the look in her creep manager's eyes was more like gluttony than desire.

They got into a black cab outside a theater on Drury Lane; I grabbed the one behind it, unsure how the driver would react when I told him to follow that cab. He gave me an arch look but he didn't tell me to get out. I came up with a story about a sister with a large inheritance and a work-shy boyfriend I suspected was abusing her. It worked so perfectly I felt simultaneously relieved and ashamed.

I felt a lot more ashamed when we finally came to a stop in some tangle of streets whose names I'd never heard of, just around the corner from where Sophie and the creep were getting out—the fare was three and a half pounds more than I had. I asked for the cab driver's name and address so I could mail him the difference; he left me a couple of pound coins and drove away before I could even get his cab number.

From behind the low brick wall surrounding the front yard of the house on the corner, I watched Sophie waiting on the sidewalk while the creep paid the cab driver. Or argued with him—I couldn't really tell. Some kind of discussion was taking place; I didn't hear any raised voices but there was something about the way the creep was leaning in toward the driver that made me think it wasn't a friendly exchange. Maybe the creep was trying to beat *his* fare. Sophie remained motionless, not so much like a statue as just some inanimate object waiting to be picked up and carried away. Like a duffel bag. Finally, the creep stepped back and made an abrupt dismissing gesture with one hand, then turned to Sophie.

It was like he flipped a switch turning her on; she came to life and stood at attention. He put his hands on her shoulders, swiveled her around and steered her up the sidewalk in my direction.

I ducked down behind the wall quickly, almost cutting myself on the rough edge of a battered and bent metal sign screwed into the brick: FOXTAIL CLOSE. Staying low, I risked peeking around the corner again just in time to see the two of them climbing the front steps of a house almost directly across from where I was crouching.

I hadn't noticed the place before; if I had, I would have taken it for derelict. It was large and dark, set back from the row houses stretching down the block, on a patch of ground that didn't really seem to belong with the rest of the street. Sophie and the creep went inside without turning on any lights. I waited but the house stayed dark.

After a while, I pushed myself upright and shook out each leg until my knees stopped screaming. And now that I knew where she was living—or where the creep was keeping her, anyway—what did I think I was going to do next? Take down the address and send her a card?

Abruptly, a big man came out of the shadows on the right side of the house. And I mean *big,* bouncer big, the kind of guy who handles "security" at a club. At first I thought the creep had seen me after all and had sent him out to settle my hash. But the man only stood on the sidewalk in front of the house. He was wearing a headset and holding a clipboard. He really was a bouncer, I realized, and he was on the job right now.

I'd thought the creep had taken Sophie home but he'd actually taken her clubbing, at one of those secret, members-only, you've-got-to-be-invited-to-find-it places—

No, she wasn't clubbing, I realized; she was *working*. This was Sophie's major nighttime gig. The creep had her working all day and then working all night. No wonder she looked like the wreck of the Hesperus.

A cab pulled up at the curb and three people got out. The bouncer greeted them familiarly but looked them up on his clipboard all the same before directing them around the side of the house, where he had come from. The next cab arrived moments later; another was right behind it, and a third pulled up behind that one. The bouncer seemed to know everyone but made a point of checking his clipboard anyway. He sent them all around the side of the house into the shadows and they all went without hesitation. Most of them were well dressed; some were overly well dressed, and a few were more costumed than attired. I didn't recognize any of them but that didn't mean anything. Most celebrities aren't actually that recognizable in person. If the Royal Family had arrived I couldn't have been completely sure.

Eventually, the cabs came less frequently and then tapered off altogether. I waited for the bouncer to tuck his clipboard under his arm and vanish into the shadows again but he stayed where he was. Someone must have been fashionably late.

How late was it anyway? I had no idea. Late enough that I wasn't really drunk anymore. Still impaired, though—bad judgment and no cab fare. Even if I could find a tube station, it would be closed by now.

"Well? Are you just going to lurk there all night?"

I looked over at the bouncer to see who he was talking to, already know-ing that he was calling to me.

"Come on, now. You came this far. Might as well come the rest of the way, yes?"

I made myself move forward, stopping at the corner. "How long have you known I was here?"

The bouncer laughed. "All along, luv. What do you think, we wouldn't have good security?"

I could run, I thought. Then I stepped off the curb and went over to him.

"This way." He tucked the clipboard under his arm.

"Aren't you going to check if I'm on the list?" I asked.

"Don't have to. Come along, now."

The party in the backyard had apparently been going on for some time. I sat in the chair where the big man had left me; it was next to the swimming pool, one of those silly, kidney-bean-shaped things, good only for getting your bathing suit wet rather than real swimming. It seemed to be much deeper than normal, however—even under the bright lights, I couldn't make out the bottom. Or maybe the water was tinted dark. To discourage guests from getting rowdy and pushing each other in, perhaps? It didn't seem to be that kind of crowd, I thought, watching the well-dressed people drift around chatting to each other and helping themselves to refreshments from a large round table.

A nondescript man in a nondescript waiter outfit materialized in front of me with a plate of hors d'oeuvres. He held it out with a faint smile. I pushed myself up out of the chair and walked away. The food smelled impossibly good, the way it does when you suddenly realize you haven't eaten all day, but I didn't want to accept anything. I had it in my mind that if I did, it would be like accepting what had happened to Sophie, approving of it. They might have had my name on their list but I wasn't *at* this party. Not the way all the rest of these people were. Whoever they were. The nameless posh, perhaps, what the toy soldier had called the rarefied elite, and this was how they lived, one party after another, day after day, night after night. Wasn't there some old joke about people who would go to the opening of an enve-lope? I didn't see any envelopes here. Maybe they were in the house.

Or out in the garden.

Something about a garden. Big house, big garden.

I looked around but the lights were so bright and every one of them seemed to be shining right in my eyes.

"Not lost, are you?"

I knocked the creep's hand off my shoulder. "Where's the garden?"

He smiled. "You think that's where she is?"

"If she isn't, where is she? I want to talk to her."

"Okay, you got me." A phony sheepish smile. "In the garden. But she won't talk to you. She's busy."

"When's her break?"

Now the creep acted surprised, as if I had asked him something completely absurd. "Her *break?* She doesn't take one."

"You've got her working without a break?"

"I said she was *busy.* I didn't say she was *working.*"

I wasn't about to let him draw me into a word game. "Just tell me how to find her. If she's too busy to talk to me, I want to hear it from her. To my face."

"Yeah. Your face." He beckoned. "This way."

He led me around the pool and down some stone steps to another patio where even more people were sitting around eating finger foods and talking in low murmurs about who knows what. This area was bounded on one side by a tall hedge with a wooden door in it. He stopped in front of the door, turned around and started to say something. Ignoring him, I reached for the handle; he pushed me back with a strength I hadn't suspected.

"Ladies and gentlemen," he said, raising his voice to address everyone there. "This is a little bit earlier than I had originally planned but I apparently underestimated the eagerness of some people—" he glanced at me "—to see what we've done with the reclaimed land. So without further delay, please follow me for your first look at the finished—"

I ducked around him and pushed through the door.

More bright lights hit me in the eyes along with the overpowering aroma of fresh flowers in massive quantities. The utter intense beauty of the smell was like being assaulted with bouquets.

Behind me, people were ooh-ing and aah-ing and I could hear the creep telling them to watch out for patches of uneven ground.

"Sophie?" I called hopefully.

". . . statues are *perfect,*" a man said, going past on my left.

I looked up. Yes, they were. And there were so many of them.

Every ten feet, there was a different figure standing on a pedestal about five feet off the ground. Men and women, gold, silver, bronze, black, alabaster, even marble. Warriors, kings and queens, fairies, gods and goddesses, shamans, witches, aliens and animal hybrids—dog people, cat people, lion people, lizard-, snake-, and bird-people. Some nude, some nearly but not quite. All of them deeply still, completely wrapped in stillness.

"*Sophie*!" I ran along the row of statues on my right, looking up at each female. "*Sophie, answer me*!" I was expecting the bouncer to tackle me at any moment but no one tried to stop me. No one even came near me—when I looked over my shoulder, I saw that the creep and his party guests were staying up near the entrance. Giving the crazy woman a wide berth.

I slowed to a stop next to a woman made up like Marie Antoinette in marble. "Sophie, dammit, answer me or I'll start tearing things up! I swear I will, I'll rip all these flowers up by their roots!"

Nothing. I turned to see how the creep was taking this; he didn't look too worried.

"Sophie?" I started walking again, looking significantly at the flower beds on either side. This section was all tulips, every variety and color. "Sophie, I'm not kidding. I'll tear this place apart, I really will."

I went another twenty feet before I stopped again. Just how big was this Goddamned yard anyway? Shading my eyes from the bright overhead lights, I tried to see where it ended. "Sophie?"

The rest of the people at the party looked ridiculously far away now, as if I were seeing them through the wrong end of a telescope. I couldn't hear the murmur of their voices or the music. I listened for traffic noises, the rustle of trees, any ambient night sounds, but there was nothing. It was completely still.

"*Sophie!*" I bellowed her name at the top of my lungs. Still nothing.

I turned to look at the nearest statue. A young man who might have been either Robin Hood or Peter Pan. "You, in the jaunty hat," I called up to him. "Come down and help me out here or I'll pull you down."

He didn't twitch. I reached up and grabbed his ankles, intending to yank him off his perch. My hands closed around cold, hard stone. I let go with a yelp and staggered back, wiping my hands on my jeans. Great. I couldn't tell the difference between a human statue and a real statue. The creep and his party guests were probably very impressed. I moved to the next statue: Zorro. I didn't bother even touching him—the swirl of the whip was suspended in midair, like the lasso of the cowboy next to him.

I crossed over to the other side of the garden where a bronze-colored matador stood with his face turned haughtily away from me. He held his cape low, the hem touching his feet. I put a hand on the cape. It was hard, cold, unyielding. Yet something about the set of his shoulders suggested he was human, not stone or metal. If only I could see his eyes, I thought.

I looked back over my shoulder at the other statues.

They had all moved, the matador, the cowboy, Zorro. Not much—barely noticeably—but I could tell.

"Sophie?" Dread rose inside me like cold water as I moved farther down the row of statues, away from the house. "Sophie, I really need you to answer me now. *Please*."

A blank-eyed marble Cleopatra holding a snake to her breast stared through me.

"Where is she?" I demanded.

Next to her a chimney sweep was staring off to my right. I followed his gaze past a Victorian lady, past Oscar Wilde, a cricket player, a Madonna, a town crier, a jester, all the way down to the end of the garden.

The bronze Amazon stood on a pedestal in front of another hedge with a door in it.

She looked larger than life now, much larger—if I hadn't known better, I would have sworn she was seven feet tall, her perfectly sculpted muscles in flawless proportion.

"In metal, it would weigh several hundred pounds," said the creep, following me over to her.

" 'It?' "

He ambled around me to stand in front of the pedestal, planting one elbow next to Sophie's foot. "And *it's* almost ready for the next garden," he added, glancing at the door.

"Sophie, come down," I begged.

"She doesn't hear you," he said cheerfully. "Once they're in the next garden, none of them hear anyone like you."

"But she's not in the next garden yet," I said, moving closer to her. "Sophie, you hear me, I know you do. Please, come down and let me take you out of here."

"Why should she? What can you offer her? Friendship in the monotony of a nothing job in a world where things ripen and then rot, to be discarded and forgotten." He laughed nastily. "You can go now, she doesn't care to listen to anything you have to say."

"That's not true, is it, Sophie?" I put a hand on her cold leg. "Please come down. I'll help you."

"Help her *what*?" The creep gave me a shove that sent me back a few steps. "Help her rot and convince herself she's happy about it? She's a star, now, she's my masterpiece and she'll stand in the next garden forever, unmoved and perfect. Take your spoiled meat out of my sight. You're not even mildly amusing anymore." He went to shove me again but I dodged around him and threw my arms around Sophie's pedestal.

I don't know whether it was the sight of the creep getting physical with me or just that the activity itself was a distraction, but she lost it.

This time, the cracking was quite audible. It came from deep inside of her and it was the sound of pure breakage, what you hear when something shatters that cannot be mended. Her body shuddered and began to collapse inward like a deflating balloon. Except her skin didn't hang on her now—there wasn't enough substance for that. This was what a living mummy would look like: wizened, dried up, little more than a husk. She wavered, trying to lift her torso and pull her rounding shoulders back but the cracking grew louder and more intense,

Suddenly the pedestal broke apart, dumping her down on the grass on her hands and knees in front of the creep.

"*What did you do*?!" His voice was as inhumanly shrill as a siren. I wasn't sure whether he was yelling at Sophie or me. "*What the hell is this, you were better than that, you told me you were better than that, what did you do*?!"

Sophie reached one hand toward him; he stepped back, revolted.

"Now you have to start all over!" he squealed.

Sophie was nodding her head, trying to speak. I wanted to sweep her up in my arms and rush her away from him but I was afraid to touch her, afraid that she would crumble to dust in my hands.

"Only I don't *have* another pedestal, you stupid cow!" he went on. "Every spot is taken! You'll have to wait! You'll have to wait and you'll never last that long!"

Sophie was gasping and wheezing as she tried to crawl toward him. Evading her, he turned to me with fury in his creep face. "This is your fault, you bitch! You had to come here and spoil everything! She was the best I'd ever had! I'll never get anyone else that good, *ever!* Get out of my garden before you spoil them all, get out of my garden *right now!*"

The bouncer and another equally burly man materialized on either side of me. I tried to twist away but one of them dug a fist into my hair and held on. I had one last, quick glance of Sophie flattened on the ground with the creep screaming at her before they rushed me out of the garden and into the darkness.

The sky was just getting light when the police woke me in Leicester Square. I was lying on a park bench in the garden, right next to a statue of the Little Tramp.

I tried to get him to tell me what had happened to Sophie but he wouldn't even twitch. I thought it was because the police were there but Chaplin was just as mute and still when I came back by myself later. All the statues are like that, everywhere I go—Leicester Square, Covent Garden, the West End, the South Bank. It doesn't matter what I say or how loud I yell, they're all unmoved. Like stone.

The Janus Tree

GLEN HIRSHBERG

Glen Hirshberg's most recent collection, American Morons, *was published in 2006.* The Two Sams, *his first collection, won the International Horror Guild Award, and was selected by* Publishers Weekly *and* Locus *as one of the best books of 2003. Hirshberg is also the author of a novel,* The Snowman's Children.

With Dennis Etchison and Peter Atkins, he cofounded the Rolling Darkness Revue, a traveling ghost story performance troupe that tours the west coast of the United States each October. His fiction has appeared in numerous magazines and anthologies, including multiple appearances in The Year's Best Fantasy and Horror *and* The Mammoth Book of Best New Horror, The Dark, Trampoline, Cemetery Dance, *and* Dark Terrors 6, *as well as online at* SCI FICTION. *He lives in the Los Angeles area with his wife and children.*

So much about your life depends on when you fight. And whom. I learned this growing up in Silver City, Montana, which someone proclaimed the richest ruined mountain on earth half a century ago, and where the ghosts are still waiting two generations later for the last dazed living to leave so they can set up permanent shop in the abandoned mansions and collapsing mine shafts.

You do have a choice. You can take on the Company grinding you into debt, or the Chinese next door trying to lowball you out of your job. Take your stand against the Communists coming for your freedom, or the copper barons coming for your last unclaimed dime. You can fight for the town you hate, or the earth that dried up underneath you. For mining safety regulations, or the Apex Law that lets you follow a vein off your underground claim right into the tunnels of someone else's, and you can fight that one in court with lawyers or underground with dynamite and high-powered hoses. Up to you.

At the moment it happened, I really believed I was fighting Matt Janus for Robert Wysocki, whom I couldn't help anymore, and Mr. Valway, who may not have cared, and Jill Redround, who didn't love me. But I was doing it for myself. In a way, I guess I won.

What I remember is walking with Robert one night during the summer after sixth grade, all the way across Aluminum Street past the hunched, dark taverns with their decades-old, hand-lettered signs proclaiming NO MINERS still posted in the windows. Just in case Company employees from some other town with enough miners left to matter decided to come by on a road trip, we guessed. We walked under a ridiculous, blazing moon, down rows of tightly packed, boxy Company houses, their yards full of rusting bikes and truck parts and swingless swing sets, into a wind that pummeled our faces or horse-kicked us in the back, depending on whether we were coming or going. We were bouncing a red rubber ball we'd found somewhere. Robert had his black cloak billowing around his peach polo shirt and yellow shorts. And he had his backpack, of course.

"The Dark Lord appeared at my window at dawn," he said.

"Again?" I asked.

"He's never been at my window."

We cleared the houses, and the wind half lifted us off our feet, but we punched forward. To our right, the gouged mountains loomed black and treeless. The moonlight pooling in the biggest of the abandoned blast pits up there made it look more like an eye than a wound. To the east and below us, the plains stretched out, running free of the mountains. Robert took a cigarillo from his shorts pocket and pretended to snap an imaginary match to life on his thumb. He made puffing motions with his mouth, and the cigarillo popped out. Robert picked it off the pavement and plugged it back in his lips.

"Where'd you get that?" I asked.

"Elven Trading Post."

This meant the 7-Eleven the Welsh women owned on Magnesium Street, in Robert-speak. It also meant he'd been shoplifting again. At age eleven, he'd already been caught three times. The last time, his parents had avoided reform school for him by agreeing to a weekly 110-mile trip to Missoula for a kid-shrink Robert called the Delphic.

We came to the place where the sidewalk gave out like a tapped ore vein and just kept walking, past the last houses, to the rocky overlook over Snake Lake. Robert pointed down the slaggy hillside to the surface, which reflected the moon, all right, but in the hard, flat way tin roofs do.

"New ones," he said.

He was right. A whole family, it seemed. Every year, some hopeless set of ducks who'd somehow missed the memo alighted to fish and nest down there. Calling the place a lake was a local in-joke. Once, it had been the biggest open-pit mine in North America. Lately, it had started filling with a red-streaked, metallic liquid that almost *looked* like water. At least to the dumbest ducks. We usually found the ones that hadn't sunk bill-down on what passed for a beach, dead-necked, like unfolded paper boats.

Dropping to his knees, Robert scooped up a fistful of pebble-sized slag, whispered one of his spells over it, and pitched his first toss of the night toward the lake. One pebble actually dropped close enough to a dead duck to splash muck onto it. A rare occurrence, as most of Robert's throws never got near the water.

"One night," he said happily, "when the moon is full, and my aim is true . . . ducks will rise from the dead."

I threw some pebbles of my own, pegged one bird right on its flappy foot, and barely moved it. Then I bent down to scoop more rocks.

"What'd the Dark Lord want?"

"He summoned me to the Janus Tree."

Halting midthrow, I turned and looked at Robert. He just stood there, toeing the backpack at his feet.

"Matt Janus came to your window?"

"He said to come tonight. At the stroke of twelve."

"Your parents will never let you out."

"My parents are offering libations."

It was the first I'd known that Robert's mother had started drinking again, too. "I'm coming," I told him.

"The Dark Lord said to come alone."

"Don't go, Robert. I mean it, don't go."

"Young Ted, don't be a jackanapes. It's Matt."

"He's . . ." But I stopped, having no idea what to say. I hadn't actually spoken to Matt Janus in close to a year. Not since his partyfreak dad bolted for South America or somewhere, and Matt had stopped hanging around the basketball courts with me or climbing into the old quarries to have minia-tures battles with Robert. I only saw him at school, where he mostly lurked by his locker or hunched over his desk in the black leather jacket his dad had given him as a going away present while his legs just kept sprouting under-neath him, longer and longer. The way he always seemed to be leaning for-ward made him look like a praying mantis.

"He's not the same kid," I finally mumbled.

"Nor am I," Robert said. Turning my way, he squared his shoulders and huffed out his practically concave chest at me.

I snorted. "Yeah, okay, Warlock."

"Sorcerer."

"I don't think you should go. I mean it. Didn't his dad just come home? I hear he's super-sick, and he never . . ." *Liked you*, I was going to say, and didn't.

Robert wasn't listening anyway. He stared up the butte overlooking Sil-ver City, squinting at The Virgin of the Great Divide, all lit and glowing white in the moonlight. For the thousandth time, I wondered who had de-cided to build a giant statue of Mary up there, right as everyone who had the means was fleeing town. It was as though all those soon-to-be-former inhabitants from all those faraway places, sharing virtually nothing except their devastating plunge into poverty, had built themselves a collective mom to wave good-bye to.

Eventually, Robert said, "I'll take the backpack."

Did Robert Wysocki really believe his backpack was magic? He never once let on either way, even to me, which is probably why kids liked him or left him alone. It also may be why I let him go. Robert just seemed to have this bubble around him. Aura, he might have called it. Or level three shield or something. Whatever it was, I think I believed in that.

Two evenings later—moon gone, thunderheads looming way out on the prairie but riding the wind clear of town—Robert and I biked to a Silver City Copper Barons game at Anaconda Stadium, recently proclaimed the worst facility in minor league baseball by some magazine or other. We sat in the backless, splintering bleachers out past third base, several rows closer than we used to sit to the high school girls in their short skirts and pink lipstick, all of them whispering together and catching the eye of every uniformed player jogging back to the dugout.

In the fourth inning, Robert stood up, knocking my half-eaten hot dog out of my hands, lifted his backpack, unzipped it, and turned it upside down. A roll of cherry Chapstick and a single, black Darth Vader minifigure spilled onto the cement at our feet. Before I could even react, Robert threw the backpack onto the field, where no one paid any attention to it, climbed over the three-foot wall separating the stands from the parking lot, made his way to the heap of slag beyond the left-field fence where little kids chase home run balls, and started climbing it. No one except me even looked at him until he started taking off his clothes. The cloak went last. Then he sat down stark naked on the rocks, put his face in his bone-white hands, and started weeping.

It took maybe ninety seconds for paramedics to show up and scoop him off there. The Wysocki family fled town that night for Missoula, then Seattle, and then they disappeared into Canada somewhere. I left the backpack where Robert had dropped it, which I've always regretted. And I never saw him again.

I didn't see Matt Janus either, or anyone else much for a while after that. That fall, in my first month of seventh grade, I started yelling at teachers in the middle of class for any reason I could think of or sometimes no reason. On my fourth or fifth trip to the principal's office, I shoved her, and that was that.

My parents came to get me, but when I saw their car pull into the lot, I bolted off campus, through the neighborhoods, hopping fences, dodging broken bikes and yapping little black dogs I desperately wanted to kick and would have if I'd had time, and lost everybody on my weaving way back to Snake Lake. I think my plan was to dive in there, take a giant swallow, fill my mouth and lungs with metal. But the humped, furry dead thing splayed on the rocks nearby—could have been a crow, a baby coyote, or even a cat—stopped me. In the hard September sun, it looked gray-red, oxidized, more like a discarded mining tool than anything formerly living. Even at twelve, I understood that that's what all the residents of Silver City were, even with the Company long gone: discarded mining tools. I sat down in the slag and thought about Robert and kicked stones in the lake and stared up the mountains at the Virgin and then to the left, where the easternmost roofs of the Janus mansion could just be seen, tucked among the ledges, red and complicated, like an aerie. At some point, I broke down. After that, I just sat for more than twenty-four hours, until I was good and sick. Then I went back to my house.

My parents decided to homeschool me, and somewhere in that first month I must have made some kind of decision, because I stopped battling them. All morning, I forced myself through the math and geology I hated (although I liked the bits about exactly what the Anaconda Company had done to my hometown). It was fun explaining to my parents exactly why we had to drink bottled water, and why our sheets came out of the laundry pocked with permanent orange spots that looked like bloodstains and terrified the two motels' occasional out-of-town guests, most of whom had only come to examine the business prospects in the malls my dad spent his working life developing.

Afternoons, I went to the library. There, for my English and history work, I started rooting through the dust-caked shelves full of decades-old books and periodicals. I taught myself to research. On the Friday of each week, I came home with a paper I'd written—annotated in proper footnote format—about fights my parents had never heard of despite living in Silver City all their lives, like the 1889 boxing match at a roadhouse outside the town limits, where some miner named Groeninger broke his left arm and hand in the forty-eighth round against some carpenter named Broad and went on fighting until he knocked Broad out in the 105th. Broad died the next day, and Groeninger disappeared out of the newspapers, off the registry, completely out of history.

As surprised as my parents were by the way I hurled myself into my schoolwork, I think they were more surprised by the sheer number of kids I somehow surrounded myself with. This wasn't so much through any conscious plan as the discovery of the one thing Robert had missed, or didn't care to know: that just plain smiling, acting interested, and not expecting much can earn you a whole lot of friends.

So I came out of the library and rode skateboards (badly) down the banister rails on the front steps and got chased out of the lot with the buzz-haired skateboys and girls. From one of the infamous picked-over junkshops in Uptown, stocked half a century ago with the belongings the mining families and their bosses could no longer afford to own or carry, I bought a set of congas. One drumhead was complete, though the other had a jagged rip down the center, like a mouth with teeth. I took my new congas to Kenny Tripton's house when he and his fledgling cowpunk band had their Thursday night rehearsals in the basement, and if I never exactly became a band member, they did get me a stool and a microphone after a while, and I got to beat my one good conga and scream *"Hey F OFF!"* when the choruses called for it, which they generally did. One of the conditions of rehearsing at the Tripton's was that we were only allowed to say "F." It became a band trademark.

I didn't join the junior high chess class at the library on Tuesday afternoons, but I lurked in the doorway, and there were seven class members, so they needed an eighth come game time, and eventually I became friends with most of those people, too. I snuck onto Anaconda Stadium field with the football team one sleety night and came home soaked and bloody-mouthed. In May, my parents applied to Mrs. Morbey, the principal, for my reinstatement, and were welcomed enthusiastically.

"We've taken note of Teddy's progress," Mrs. Morbey bubbled as we squirmed in the cracked green vinyl chairs across the desk from her. "It's a hard thing to lose a pal like that. We all understand."

Lose a pal. I wanted to jump on her desk. Kick the lamps over. But I didn't really want to shove her anymore. The truth was, Robert already felt like years ago. That weirdo with the backpack I'd hung around with in grade school. And anyway, as soon as that meeting was over, I was going walking with Jill Redround.

I honestly don't remember exactly how that started. At the Spring Pow-wow, probably. Watching Matt Janus, come to think of it. His dad and Mr. Redround, the local Blackfeet chief, had been business partners for years on casino and nightclub projects on the reservation and off, and Matt had known Jill since birth and also had the softest outside jumpshot in Butte, which is why he'd been the only white kid welcomed to play in the reservation games. Seeing him now, it was like his spine had just popped up on him like an expanding tent pole. His blond, spiky head loomed too far over his absurdly elongated body, and his legs had stretched even taller and thinner. Also, weird muscles bulged out the sides of his shoulders, all knobby and asymmetrical, as though he'd stuffed his skin with slag. He'd always been pale enough to verge on albino, but now his cheeks had ugly, blotchy patches, and little pits, too, as though he'd been mined.

He dominated the basketball game. Not only could he still shoot from outside, but everyone just ducked out of his way as though fleeing a bear when he barged through the paint for rebounds. Twice, he caught Jill's eyes and waved. Once, near the end, he saw me, stopped in middribble, and got called for traveling. Shrugging, he tossed the ball to the ref and retreated to the other end of the gravel court.

At some point, Jill wound up next to me. She had on some open-sleeved, beaded dress with fringes everywhere for the Powwow, I remember that, and she wasn't wearing shoes—she rarely did, except when forced—and her boundless black hair streamed over her strong shoulder blades and back.

"You're the only person everyone I know knows," she said. "Know that?"

I smiled—the smile I'd practiced all year long—and earned myself an answering grin. "You, too," I told her.

"And Matt, of course."

Glancing toward the court, I saw him sink a jumpshot, flash an unreadable look our way. Or maybe just our direction.

"And Matt," I agreed.

That night, at her invitation, I watched her dance the dance to Old Napi, and then we took our first boulder-scramble up the buttes. After that, we did it at least once a weekend and usually more for the rest of the summer.

I got my first shock on the morning I returned to regular school before I even left my house. "Listen, Teddy," my dad told me, over the warmed Grape-Nuts he ate every morning, their smell rolling through our bright, window-jeweled, hardwood house like new soil imported from somewhere cleaner. "Mom and I put you in Valway's English class."

Tomato juice halfway to my mouth, I froze, staring at my father. Until that moment, I'd been thinking how different school was about to feel. Friends in every class. Basketball at recess without Robert darting onto the court to bless the ball. Boulder-scramble with Jill as soon as the bell rang; we'd arranged to meet by the Copper Miner fountain in the front hallway.

My dad had some blueprints half-unrolled at the table and was studying them self-consciously. This was his traditional method whenever he lost whatever straws he drew with my mother and so had to break news to me: casual, as though it were nothing.

"You know about him," I said slowly. "Right?"

"I know exactly as much as you do. Which is a few stories. Nothing."

"He keeps rat traps in his wastebasket. Makes kids reach in there and get pens he's dropped on purpose. Just to see what happens."

"You ever actually see anyone with a broken finger?"

"He wears a gas mask."

"He has emphysema."

"Dad, he's supposed to be the worst teacher in Silver City, why would you do that?"

"He saw you researching at the library this summer, apparently. Went to Mrs. Morbey and begged her to let him have you. And we believe in second chances around here, don't we?" He gave me what passed, on my tanned, health-crazed father's permanently smiling face, as a severe look. "In case you failed to notice, Ted, he wrote half the articles and at least a few of the books in that Silver City history corner you spent most of last school year buried in."

Had I noticed that? I must have, but it had never occurred to me that I'd one day have to deal with him personally. I'd never actually met him, barely even seen him. He'd written Bloody Fisted Dublin Gulch, *come to think of it; my favorite. And the one about the prostitutes the copper barons used to send to single mining men some Saturday nights, when the employees hadn't been spending enough at the Company stores or their wives were starting to get active about new labor laws or something. I'd kept that article to myself, never written about it for my parents.*

"Okay," I murmured.

"Just an experiment. You don't like it, you're out of there, that's the deal we made with Mrs. Morbey. No questions, no delay."

The second shock came ten minutes later, as I was strapping on the bike helmet I would shed as soon as I got out of sight of our front door.

"Don't make plans for Saturday," my father said. "Matt Janus Senior has invited all of us to some giant game-barbecue up at his place."

This time, I actually fumbled the bike helmet and dropped it. It landed hard-side down. Staring into it was like looking into the hollowed-out rind of a melon, or a skull. I thought of Robert naked and howling on the slag heap, and I missed him, hard, for the first time in months. Last I'd heard, Matt Janus's father was all but dead.

"Not that you'd be able to make plans." My father's voice was jokey, chipper. "Sounds like everyone you've ever met, and me, too, for that matter, is going to be there. Invitation was weird, for Janus Senior, anyway. No booze bottles, no half-naked women. Just this gold-embossed card with balloons and a pick-shovel on it, I'll show it to you: *Welcome Back Matt Party. Come Celebrate My Resurrection.* That's what it said. Odd duck, Mr. Janus. Should be something."

The third and final shock came as I stood in a tightly packed row of fellow eighth-graders before the skinny standing lockers we'd just been assigned. The lockers were dull green, the combination locks clunky and rusted. Every now and then, there'd be a *snick* and a laugh as another student got his lock popped open, hopped into his locker and hopped out, just to prove you really could fit a whole kid inside. Every now and then came a *clang* as someone banged the metal door with his head or a backpack in gleeful frustration. We'd been waiting years for this moment, after all. The lockers in the back hallway with the windows facing directly onto the hill that had once been the black, beating heart of Silver City were the great prizes Lower Magnesium Middle School had to offer for getting to the final year before high school. Our rewards.

I'd finally found the sweet spot on my own lock, clicked it open, and swung my door wide when it slammed shut almost right on my elbow. I fell back, startled, and stared up at Matt Janus breaking into his own locker with a single twist-and-yank. Opened all the way, his door completely blocked access to my locker.

But I'd learned about people, that year I'd been gone. I truly believed I had. I stepped forward, left his door where it was, and waited for him to dump the entire contents of his blue backpack into his locker. The backpack sat ridiculously high on his immense shoulders because the straps were way too small. It looked like a beetle climbing the scaly trunk of an oak.

"Hey, Matt," I said. "Long time."

His whole torso swayed to the left, as though a wind had blown through him. Then he turned on me. His pupils looked weirdly wide in his eyes, which were shot through with red. That blotchiness I had noticed this summer was all over his forehead now, creeping down his neck into the tight collar of his black shirt like moss.

"Don't talk to me," he said, kicked his door shut, and left.

That afternoon, I followed the instructions on my schedule card all the way back past the green lockers, down a staircase I hadn't known was there, along a windowless, tiled corridor that reeked of chlorine and reminded me of the bottom of an emptied pool, and arrived for the first time at Mr. Valway's room. The door was green, thick, and closed. I was about to knock when it flew open, and a startlingly tan girl I'd never seen before stuck her poodle-nose right in mine and said, "Boo."

The girl's grin was too wide, her plaid skirt disconcertingly short, her curly brown hair bouncing around her ears as though she were hopping on a trampoline instead of standing in front of me. She didn't move back far enough as I slid into the room, and my chest grazed her elbow and then the tip of one of her breasts. My first feel.

"Whitney," she said, and did a drum roll on her thighs, her hands hitting half skirt, half skin. "Drum. New here."

I'd noticed her eyes by then. Very brown, pretty enough. Also very red around the irises. Stoned enough. I gave her my practiced people-smile, anyway. "Teddy. Ted."

"Teddy-ted?"

I blushed, started to protest, saw Jill Redround grinning at the back table, and hurried toward her.

"Hi, Teddy-ted," Jill said.

"Shut up." I dropped my books. The sound echoed off the bare cement walls.

"Teddy and Reddy," said Jill, gesturing to herself, then glancing around, pulling her black hair back into a ponytail and shivering a little. "Ready, Teddy? Not sure I am."

Sitting, I took in the room. Once, clearly, it had been a science lab. Instead of desks, we sat at long black tables, each of which had a chemical sink with one of those pointy nozzles on the faucets. The school had newer science labs now, thanks to a grant from the Janus family. Judging by the rust on the pointy nozzles and the rotting rubber hoses dangling from a few of them like dried skin from some unimaginable mine reptile, this particular lab was probably from two grants ago.

"Surprised to see you here," I murmured to Jill as Whitney Drum flung open the door to greet two ghost-pale, glassy-eyed blond girls I'd never seen before. "Your dad can place you pretty much anywhere, right?"

"Matt Janus got dumped here. His dad asked my dad if I'd keep him company."

"Mr. Janus—" I started, and Matt strode into the room. He caught sight of Jill, then me.

Something flittered over his lips. Possibly a smile. Jill started to wave him toward the stool on the other side of her and stopped when Whitney said, "Ooh, my favorite boy at LMMS." I think Jill realized at the same moment I did where Whitney must have scored her weed. Matt followed her toward the row in front of ours, and sat down fast in her stool when she started to settle, so that she wound up on his lap. I found my eyes flicking toward the hem of her skirt against his hip. She wriggled once against him before slapping his jeans and sliding off.

In the front of the room, where the fluorescents had either burned out or been turned off, something stirred. Finally, as a group, the nine of us in Mr. Valway's last English class turned toward his desk.

The whole of it was occupied by one of those gigantic blue jugs of water that usually sit upside down in dispensers. This one rested on its rounded bottom, top open to the stale air. When Mr. Valway, grunting through his green oxygen mask, somehow shoved the thing sideways far enough to lean around the side of it and face us, the water in the jug sloshed, and some of it flew out the top and slapped across Mr. Valway's cheeks and onto the desktop. Even Whitney Drum stopped talking.

Most of Mr. Valway's face was green mask and dirt gray eyebrow. With the wetness dripping down it, it looked like cave wall. To speak, he lifted only the bottom of the mask, so that I never got a good look at his nose or mouth. We sat for what seemed minutes and listened to him wheeze. What we could see of his body looked lumpy, immense.

Then he grunted again. *Was that a laugh?* "Well," he said, his voice surprisingly strong, not exactly friendly but clearer than expected. "We still supply the water. Course . . . no bathroom within a hundred yards. So you bring your own bottles to piss in." More grunting, after that. A lot of it.

Very slowly, over the next forty-five minutes, Mr. Valway explained procedure. No lessons; those involved too much useless talking. We'd read what he told us to read. We'd write papers on topics he and we agreed upon. When the papers were finished, we'd bring them individually to his desk. He'd tell us what he thought. We'd do what he instructed. If we tried hard, we'd learn more about writing than any other students in Silver City. If we didn't, we wouldn't. If we bothered him, he'd invite us to go fishing in his trash can. Questions?

There were none. We still had ten minutes left of class. Two minutes before the bell, when I think every one of us had figured out that Mr. Valway really had closed his eyes and that his breathing through the mask had gone even and slow, Matt Janus climbed carefully onto a table and knelt next to one of the sinks.

Mr. Valway didn't move. So Matt took the rotten rubber hose hanging from the nozzle next to him and pointed it at the teacher's desk and made a soft, shooting sound. Mr. Valway didn't move. So Matt stood all the way up, his spiky blond head brushing the ceiling. He offered Whitney Drum a hand, and she hopped up beside him, laughing. I watched Jill's frowning face, and every now and then glanced toward the roundness at the top of Whitney's tanned, swaying legs. The bell rang, and we all fled.

It was already getting dark by the time Jill and I made it to the foot of the butte, and we only climbed half an hour or so before turning back. I realized we'd be doing this more rarely, now. If ever. Jill had tribal duties on weekends, and basketball, and a thousand friends, and I had a thousand friends, too, these days. And both of us worked hard. And within a month it would be winter.

She was turning up the hill toward her father's when I asked if she wanted to grab a snack at the Elven Trading Post.

"The where?"

Grinning, I said, "7-Eleven. Sorry."

"Can't. Promised Matt I'd help him get started with bio. He's really bad at bio."

"Matt," I mumbled.

I don't know what she saw in my face, but she snapped at me for the first time in our lives. "That a problem for you? He's probably my oldest friend."

"He's . . ." I was waving my hands. Of all the people I now knew, Jill was the last I wanted mad at me. "He used to be my friend, too."

We didn't say anything for a few minutes. But she didn't leave. Eventually, she said, "He's really mixed up, Teddy. He really needs me."

With that, she went to him.

That Saturday, along with half the town, I got my first look at what was left of Matt Janus's father. In the morning, as though to remind anyone who'd somehow forgotten that we lived in Montana, a freak storm blew over the top of the buttes and dumped six inches of snow. By noon, the temperature had soared back up to fifty-five, and the new gray drifts came sliding off the rocks and rooftops. My family arrived spot on time, but well after most of the other guests. As we got out, my father told my mother, "Apparently, he caught whatever it is that's made him so sick while he was in Chile. Guess he finally found a party even *he* couldn't handle."

After that, my parents grabbed crystal champagne flutes off one of the dozens of circulating trays and disappeared amongst the grown-ups, and I floated into the terraced yards. The Janus estate was laid out like a layer cake, with descending sculpted meadows interspersed with layers of wrecked, red rock that looked almost earthy, close to beautiful with the snow melting on it and the sun shooting everywhere and the giant stone house with its red roofs looming overhead. Armies of serving girls circled among us, passing out skewers of barbecued white meat that tasted peppery and wild. I couldn't get enough of it. Neither could anyone else.

I spent part of the time among some skateboys trying to negotiate the drainage ditch that dove from the easternmost corner of the house down the terraces of rock and lawn to empty against a cyclone fence, but I didn't skate. I was looking for Jill, but spotted only Chief Redround, in jeans and a black Grateful Dead sweatshirt, holding court with some business people in shirt-sleeves and ties, one of whom I recognized vaguely as the mayor.

Finally, a good couple hours after we'd come, I spotted Jill and Matt way up the hillside above the house, sitting together in the mouth of the old mining shaft, right at the foot of the Janus Tree. I felt the expected stab of jealousy and then—unexpectedly—a little gush of nostalgia. In third grade, Matt and Robert and I had had our greatest-ever miniatures battle right there. It had ended with Matt's evil dwarves trying to storm their way out of the mine behind a balrog, and Robert and me bringing the balrog down with arrows made of pine sticks. For dramatic effect, Matt had spun when his balrog got hit, swept up the little metallic monster, and tossed him over the sheer edge of the cliff behind him, where it tumbled from our lives in absolute silence.

Either Jill and Matt had been watching me, or they'd sensed me watching them, because Jill stuck up her hand and beckoned. I started to obey, and Matt lifted his hand, too. *To stop me, or invite me?* I couldn't tell. Didn't care. I was passing the patio and the murmuring adults clustered among the scatter of lounge chairs there when I stopped. Slowly, my head swung around.

I *did* recognize him. By his teeth. Despite whatever had happened, his smile still radiated a blinding whiteness that no snow in Silver City ever did. His skin—what there was of it—hung more tan and taut than ever on his cheeks. But where once Matt Janus Senior had looked round-cheeked, wide-eyed, and relentlessly cheerful—the self-proclaimed "party-pumpkin" of western Montana—he now looked like a Tinkertoy with hide barely stretched across it. Bones poked every which way from him, instead of the startling muscles I remembered. His massive chest had deflated completely. He had no hair on his head. No brows. Nothing.

All the murmuring, I realized, had been coming from him; no one else was talking at all. He went right on murmuring as his eyes alighted on mine. "That's the great myth," he was saying. "The story everybody likes to tell. The Incas, well, they just . . ." he snapped his fingers, the bones clacking together like drumsticks. "*Vanished.* You're telling me we can find full skeletons of 350-million-year-old trilobites—probably right here on this hillside—but we can't locate a single dead Indian in the ruins of his own village? You know that's what they call the town where Anaconda relocated down there, don't you? *Indio Muerto.*" This last he said slowly, rounding his lips around the *o's* as though blowing a smoke ring. "Dead Indian."

Abruptly, he blinked, and recognition flared in his face. "Hey, now. Young Ted. Long time. You ever hear from that poor boy? That Robert?" Then his head jerked up the hill, and he saw Jill and Matt. The white teeth flashed. I hadn't liked his smile even when there'd been flesh attached to it. "*Matt,*" he called, and a hundred feet above, his son twitched, looked at Jill, and stood. Around Matt Senior, the adults huddled closer, some of them starting to talk amongst themselves, most just glancing about like squirrels storing gossip-nuggets for later.

Matt arrived at his father's side, towering over him. His everpresent leather jacket hung open, revealing a black button-down shirt with polished buttons. "That beautiful native's monopolizing a bit too much of your time," Mr. Janus told him. "You've got fun to spread. To all your guests."

That's when I understood where Matt got the weed he was selling all over school. It shouldn't have surprised me. Mr. Janus had given Robert, Matt, and me big bottles of Moose Drool beer in the basement when we were nine.

Jill stayed by the tree, and she didn't come down for a long time. I slid to the side of the house and watched her.

That tree. Long before, when I'd been a regular guest at the Janus house, I'd asked my father about it, and he said it was an alligator juniper. So I looked that up, but the book in the library said it couldn't grow where we lived. Whatever it was, it stuck almost sideways out of the rock, a stumpy pine with a scaly black trunk that looked like an arrow buried in the side of the mountain. The only tree on that entire butte. On the uphill side of it, the branches had curled in on each other, gnarled together, and died. But on the downhill side, the same branches sprouted clusters of brilliant green leaves whose shadows slid over the rock and Jill's crossed arms and bare feet.

When she finally came down, I moved toward her, but her father steered her away to say hello to the town dignitaries. Eventually, Matt Senior drew her down beside him in his lounge chair. He made her take sips of champagne from his own glass, and slid one skeletal arm around her shoulders to caress her skin where it poured out of her dress and play with her hair while her father stood over them, laughing. For one moment, glancing up, I caught Matt Junior's eyes across the patio. The fact that I probably wore the same expression he did unnerved me badly.

That night, over chicken that seemed utterly tasteless and flaccid compared to the meat at the Janus house, I asked why Mr. Janus had gone to South America in the first place. My mother just shrugged.

"It happens to people when they don't have to work and their wives die," she said, as if she had all kinds of acquaintances in similar situations. "I think he wanted to see who his grandparents and parents raped to make all their money. So he traveled halfway down the world to find another ruined mountain and more big poison holes in the ground."

"Then there was that whole Ponce de Leon thing, that was funky," my dad said, pushing away his chicken barely eaten.

"Ponce de Leon went to Chile?" I asked. "I thought he was in Florida or somewhere."

My mother shook her head. "The things some people will try, just to avoid growing up."

"He seemed a little . . ." My father paused, considering. "Wiser, maybe? More resigned? Something."

My mother stretched her lips into a smile that looked exactly like Mr. Janus's. "*You have to get old,*" she hissed, imitating his new, shredded voice a little too perfectly. "*Everyone has to get old.*"

"Christ, you're a little too good at that," my father said. "Funky guy."

"He was funky when he was just a cokehead," I said.

"That's not nice," my mother snapped.

"'Went to see who his parents . . . *raped?*' Was that the nice word your mother used, Ted?"

Even my mother laughed.

I thought about Jill and Matt up the hill, under the juniper shadows in the mouth of the balrog cave, then of Matt Senior's shrinking body. "So he's better now?" I asked. "Mr. Janus, I mean?"

Now my mother sounded tired. Sad and tired. "He's dying," she said. "Couldn't you tell?"

The weather got cold, and school days dropped into their school-day rhythm. Most often, I got to my locker long before Matt, and didn't see him until Valway's class at the end of the afternoon. But every time he did arrive at his locker while I was still at mine, he threw open his door right in my face, dumped his books, and stood a few extra seconds as though daring me to say something. Then he slammed his locker and sauntered off. He never so much as glanced at me, and we never spoke.

School really had gotten better, though. Without Robert to take care of, and with the range of friends I'd made, I had people to laugh with in every class, and every class was easy. I ate lunch at a different table each day, and was welcomed at all of them. The person I most wanted to eat with was Jill, but as Student Council President, she ran meetings every day but Friday, when she mostly stayed in the library and did work.

The first kid Matt Janus brutalized was a hulking, stupid linebacker who strolled up to him on the athletic fields at the end of P.E. one day as all of us shivered in our shorts and the nearly winter wind roared down off the rocks. He said, "Think you're tough, Mr. All-in-Black Fagboy?" The linebacker wound up in the emergency room with three broken ribs and a shattered jaw, and Matt got suspended for a week.

The second kid might have been an accident. It happened in the middle of a lunch-break basketball game. The kid had been pouring in jump shots, but Matt's team was still winning, and as far as I knew, the kid—little seventh grader, big glasses, elephant ears that seemed to flap when the wind caught them—had never even spoken to Matt. But he pump-faked the shit out of his defender late in the game, drove the lane, and went hard to the hoop. Matt's elbow caught him under the Adam's apple and seemed to drive it all the way up into the back of his mouth. The kid hurtled into the basket pole and collapsed, face smashed, mouth gulping as though trying to work the Adam's apple back down so he could swallow some air.

Matt was the first one on his knees at the kid's side, and he was kind of crying as the paramedics carried the kid off. No one claimed it had been anything but unintentional. But no one played basketball with Matt anymore, or anything else, either. He ate alone, and then he went out to the court, rain or snow or whatever, and stood underneath the rim in his open leather jacket, tossing a ball up and through, up and through, until someone came to buy from him. Then he'd go back to shooting baskets by himself until the bell rang and the rest of us went inside.

In Valway's class, I sat in the hissing, echoing half-light and worked alternately on papers for Valway and notes for Jill. The notes I passed had jokes in them, and funny things I'd heard other kids say, and random Butte facts I pulled off my library notecards from the year before, and invitations to go walking. Jill smiled occasionally at the jokes, topped my amusing quotations with better ones from the girls she knew, parried my Montana facts with Blackfeet lore (her personal medicine, she revealed, was an eagle-bone whistle that she carried around her neck in a beaded pouch), and rejected every one of my invitations by writing *"Can't,"* then drawing a frowny-face next to the word. Occasionally, passing the paper back, she'd brush or even squeeze my hand.

While Matt snoozed at his desk or thumb-wrestled with Whitney, and the other kids did the rest of their homework or threw spitwads at each other, Jill and I raced one another to finish papers. In late October, I got into a long one about the lynching of Wobblies on the railroad bridge out the east end of town. When I finally finished a draft and took it to Mr. Valway's desk, he twitched in his chair as though I'd woken him—which I very well might have—and half turned his bulbous, veiny face toward me so that I could see the perpetual dampness reflecting the fluorescent light. Without lifting his oxygen mask, and with no audible shift in his slow, measured breathing, he started reading.

With every previous paper I'd shown him, he'd reached the end, spat out three or four concise, disinterested suggestions, and told me to try again. But this time, a couple paragraphs in, he abruptly tilted forward in his chair. His breathing didn't alter, but he looked up after a bit, and then he lifted his mask. Horrible, stupid thoughts flashed across my brain—I think I actually believed he might shoot out a tongue and lick me—and then he said, "Get me a pen."

From the flick of his hand, I thought he meant in the trash can, glanced toward it, and shuddered slightly. The thing was just a metal canister, but it had an oversized green bag stuffed in it, so that there was no way to see what your hand might be reaching for. But he thumped the desktop with his fist, and I realized he meant the drawer. I opened it and gave him a fine-tipped black marker.

For the next half an hour, he bent over my paper, scratching relentlessly at it with the pen. By the time he'd finished, the bell had rung, and everyone but Jill had gone. Eventually, he dropped the marker to the desktop, shoved the paper across at me, lifted the mask one more time, and said, "Well, now."

In the hallway outside, I thanked Jill for waiting for me, and she poked me in the ribs with her finger, kicked her tennis shoes off because no one cared after the last bell, and gave me the brightest smile I'd had from her in ages. "The score after two months," she said. "Teddy: one 'well now.' Red-round, nothing. The crowd goes wild." I asked her to go walking, she said, "Let's go to the Elven Trading Post," and once there, she bought us a bag of Funyuns and we stood in the doorway while yet another late-fall thunder-cloud crawled over the Virgin of the Great Divide.

On the Wednesday before Thanksgiving, my mom stopped me on my way out the door and told me I should seek out Matt and check on him. When I told her I never spoke to Matt anymore, she shrugged and said, "His father's gotten worse. He's about to die."

Walking through a slanting, stinging rain, I thought maybe I *would* check on Matt. I passed the corner where I used to meet Robert, and I thought of his cloak and backpack, and Matt's leather jacket and scowl. Not so much difference, really.

But he wasn't at his locker when I got there, and he wasn't on the basket-ball court at lunch, and he wasn't in Valway's room when the bell rang. Al-most no one was in Valway's room that day. Jill's family had gone north to Alberta to see cousins, and three of the other six students had been resched-uled by furious parents into other classes, leaving only the blond girls, Whit-ney Drum, Valway, and me.

Valway looked particularly ghastly, leaning sideways in his chair with his head tipped so far back it seemed halfway chopped off, eyes closed, green mask clamped to his face like a feeding spider. Every few seconds, the mask seemed to lift slightly, and it hissed.

For the first fifteen minutes, I forced my way through some of Valway's latest suggestions on my Wobblies paper, which had ballooned to more than twenty pages. But with Jill gone and the whole school sagging toward the holiday, what little work energy I had bled away. The only consistent move-ment in the room came from the blondes, who kept passing tired notes back and forth. Whitney Drum had her head down on the table, her arms—still miraculously tan, darker even than Jill's—stretched out straight, once-bouncy curls flat against her scalp. Her white sweater was too short, unravel-ing some, and I watched strands from the hem of it trailing down the small of her bare back where it curved into her jeans.

The first bombardment of fists-on-door shook us like bombs dropping, and set the blondes crumpling notes and scurrying off their seats. Whitney dragged her head up, turning more toward me than the door, and I saw the redness in her irises and knew Matt Janus must have been at school that day after all. Valway never even stirred.

Another flurry, longer, louder. We all knew who it was. By now, Whitney was grinning, the other girls gawping, and even Valway opened his eyes, squinting under that massive brow. Then he lifted his mask. As always, the clarity and off-hand *loudness* he could still generate startled me. "You. Ted. Better let him in. Or else I'm going to castrate him."

Whitney giggled. I got up and let Matt in. I started to say something to him, "Hello" or "Sorry about your dad," but before I'd formed a single word he was past me, sliding into place next to Whitney and dropping his huge white hand on her thigh and leaving it there.

The room reasserted itself. Valway went back to sleep. The blondes crept back to their stools and, after a few seconds of staring—along with me—at Matt's hand high on Whitney's leg, returned to note-writing. I tapped my paper with my pencil and tried revising a little more. And Whitney, after a few seconds, snuggled in against Matt and put her head down on his leather-jacketed arm.

We all stayed like that a while. Every sixty seconds, the clock on the wall lurched another drunken step toward 3:30.

I didn't see it happen. I think I might have been asleep. For a few indefinite moments—the thought disturbs me even now, for reasons I will never be able to explain—Matt Janus may have been the only person awake in that room. Then the reek flooded my nostrils, and I jerked my head up to find Whitney bolt upright in her chair, eyes hurtling back and forth between Valway slumped at his desk and Matt with the bong lit and bubbling in his cupped palms.

"Sssh," he said—to all of us, maybe—and grinned. The thing looked grimy, hideous, very possibly assembled out of a stolen chemistry beaker and some rotten rubber tubing from this room. Sucking in a huge drag, Matt held the smoke in his teeth, then blew it in a rush toward Valway's desk. The girls in the corner had gone completely still. Matt glanced that way, held up the bong, and offered it to them. They swept their notepads into their backpacks in a single collective rush and fled the room.

Shrugging, Matt lifted the bong toward Whitney, and she took it and Matt's long white finger into her mouth at the same time. He stiffened in his chair. She was laughing so hard she could barely get the smoke to her lips.

Almost as an afterthought, Matt turned to me. His eyes had no redness in them, were almost frighteningly clear, and I *saw*, or for just one second thought I saw . . .

Both of us looked away at the same moment, Matt toward the floor, me toward Jill's seat. Eventually, Matt noticed the direction of my gaze and snorted.

"What?" he said, waving the tube of the bong. "You think she never has?"

More because of the way he said that than anything else—casual, right on the edge of cruel—I passed on his offer with a wave of my hand. Whitney snatched the tube from him and took another hit. The clock lurched, the bell rang, we all stood, and Valway opened his eyes.

"Mr. Janus," he said quietly. "I seem to have dropped my tie-clip in my trash can. Could you come get it for me?"

Whitney and I had frozen the second Valway started speaking. Now we just stood, transfixed, as Matt lifted the bong away from Whitney, dragged on it while staring right back at Mr. Valway, and then moved slowly around the table toward the front of the room.

"What is it you dropped?" he said. "Old man." His legs, I noticed, no longer looked stick-thin. The muscles that had bulged out of proportion on his arms early in the year had spread through his body now. From the back, he looked twice his age, powerful as hell.

"Tie clip," Valway told him. "Little metal heart."

Matt never took his eyes off him. Bending at the waist, he placed the bong gently on the corner of Valway's desk, as though it were an apple he was offering, then slid his hand into the green folds of the trash bag, which folded around it like an anemone's mouth. Whitney and I strained forward, watching Matt's hand disappear up to the wrist, past it. Valway leaned back again, closed his eyes. There was a soft *smack*.

Matt's legs straightened, and then he held still for a long moment. Finally, he stood. Clamped on his middle and ring fingers was a small, rubber-guarded mousetrap attached to a blocky wooden base. With the rubber sheathing on its jaws, the snap of that trap probably wouldn't have killed a housefly, let alone hurt Matt. In slow motion, almost thoughtfully, Matt pried the trap off his fingers and dropped it in Valway's lap. Valway barely glanced at him. Matt was grinning as we left the room.

Mr. Janus's funeral was held that Sunday. The rain had stirred the dredged earth and set it sliding in filthy glaciers down the hillsides. Caked, coppery clods checkered the lawn of the First Saints Cemetery, where the preceding generation of Januses, Clarks, Heinzes, and other copper lords had been returned to the ground they'd ravaged. Jill's father gave the eulogy. At the end, he held up a fringed hide bag filled, he said, with "magic dust. Good medicine." They buried the bag with Mr. Janus. On the way home, my parents had a big fight trying to decide whether he'd been joking. Neither of them had any doubt what the bag contained.

Jill came back on Tuesday, but she barely spoke to me. On Wednesday, I wrote her a note asking what was up, and she scowled at Matt's back and then gave it the finger. But when I started to laugh, she gave me the finger, too, and moved several stools away to the next table. On my way out of the schoolyard that afternoon, I saw Matt Janus pass an elementary school kid and shove him down in the mud, then rip off the kid's shoes and hurl them forty feet onto the puddle-soaked grass.

The Monday before winter vacation, I lurked at the top of the stairs leading down to Valway's room until Jill came, then stopped her. She had her black hair tied in a tight braid and tucked into her heavy gray sweater, and her eyes looked so empty that I found myself thinking about Matt on the day of the bong. *You think she never has?*

"Let's go walking," I told her.

I half-expected her to ignore me completely, slip right past into the classroom and to her new seat a table removed from all of us. Then she sighed. "It's going to snow."

"So we'll get wet."

"I was thinking more about rocks being slippery."

"So we'll fall down."

Abruptly, she smiled. Tight-lipped, fleeting, but a smile all the same. "Soon, okay? Please?"

As in, please, let's go walking? Please leave it alone? I left it alone. But when I followed her downstairs and inside the classroom a minute or so later, I found her papers piled at her old seat next to mine, and Jill back on her accustomed stool. Five minutes into the period, she passed me a note. It had a gallows with a noose drawn on it, and a row of twelve dashes underneath. Immediately, I wrote 'S' and passed the paper back, and she sketched a head into the noose. No S. I tried other letters, began filling in the word. I'd just figured it out, gotten to m o t _ e _ f _ _ k e _ , and Jill had a neck and trunk and one arm on the stick figure she meant to hang before I got the other blanks, when the classroom door swung open. Glancing over, we were astonished to see Mrs. Morbey, in pink business suit, framed in the grim light creeping down that hall from the stairwell.

My gaze slipped toward Matt, who tapped his closed notebook and played with Whitney's fingers, and then toward Valway, who made no move to straighten in his chair but did open his eyes.

"Albert, could I see you outside a minute?" Mrs. Morbey said.

Obviously, we knew Valway could move. He got to the classroom every day, didn't he? Nevertheless, the sight stunned us, the way he just hopped to his feet and shambled around the desk, tugging the green oxygen tank on its wheels as though pulling grandkids in a wagon. Passing our tables, he caught Matt's eye—or maybe mine—and winked. We watched his huge gut sway under his yellow-check leisure suit jacket as he left the room.

Had Matt been planning for such a moment? Was it impulse? I've always wondered. Never known.

All at once, he was on his feet and hoisting Whitney Drum by her hips onto the table in front of him. She giggled in her stoned, happy way, swatted his shoulders, and then kicked her legs around him. Her knee-length, plaid skirt had slid all the way up her thighs when Matt spun her to face him. Now he kissed her so hard her head snapped back, and I swear the *crack* of their teeth colliding rattled the legs of my stool. I had my mouth open, and one of the girls in the corner started laughing—in sheer panic, I think—and then came a ripping sound, and a shred of Whitney's heart-dotted panties appeared in Matt Janus's fist as he dropped it behind him. On Jill's backpack.

Most of the rest of the time, I watched Jill. But she never took her eyes off what was happening in front of her: Matt's pants dropping to his knees; Whitney's navy-blue espadrilles curled around his waist. She'd stopped laughing now. I could hear Jill's breathing, hard and hitched between her clenched teeth, could see her shoulders stiffen with each thrust of Matt's body. Whitney gave a single, strangled gurgle, then started crying. When I let myself look at her, I found her eyes locked on Jill's.

When he'd finished, Matt pulled his pants up, picked another ripped shred of Whitney's panties off the table, and mopped some of the blood off her legs. Then he kissed her cheek, eased her gently down onto her stool, and held tight to her hand. Valway never came back, and when the bell rang, Whitney shook free of Matt's grip and fled. Jill raced after her, and I ducked out fast and slipped through a back door of the school building and walked all the way to Snake Lake with no books except my English notebook and no jacket—everything else was in my locker—and sat where I had when I'd broken down eighteen months before. Just as before, I stayed there rocking on my heels and ducking my face against the cat-o'-nine-tail whips of the barbed winter wind.

That night, I tried calling the Redround house for the first time in my life. Why had I never done so before? I'd just had this sense that I wouldn't be welcome. And Jill had never asked me to. When the Chief himself answered, I almost hung up. But in my ears, I heard the hard hitch in Jill's breathing as she'd watched Matt and Whitney—*what Matt had done to Whitney?*—and also her voice.

Soon. Please?

"Chief Redround, this is Jill's friend Ted. From—"

"Gone to Albuquerque," he said. I recognized the slur instantly, from years of incoherent phone conversations with Robert's parents.

Gone. "When . . . do you know when she'll be back?"

"Mother says never," Chief Redround said.

"Will you tell her . . ." But I let the sentence trail off and hung up and went to my room and locked the door.

Fifteen minutes before the bell for winter break—Whitney had not returned to school either, and it was only the blond girls, Matt Janus, and me in the classroom—Matt stood up and took a single sheet of paper to Valway's desk. Even Valway opened his eyes and sat forward in his chair. Unless I'd missed it, this was the first time the entire semester that Matt had given Valway anything to read.

Valway glanced at the paper, breathed through his mask. He handed the paper back without looking up. "Go back to your desk," he said, at half his usual volume. "Matter of fact, Matt, get out of my room."

Sometime that afternoon, in the hours between the moment the school emptied for vacation and the moment the janitors finally made it downstairs to that hidden hallway for the year's final mopping of the floors, Mr. Valway died at his desk.

The Tuesday after New Year's dawned freezing, snowless and gray. I sat in the silence I'd cocooned myself in the entire vacation, poking a bowl of Kix with my spoon, watching the pebble-sized bits bump against each other and thinking of the slag outside, the empty streets of uptown with the wind walking where once Welsh miners and local senators and German-born copper kings and Chinese dancing girls and whole armies of mixed-blood kids had whirled from bar to keno parlor to restaurant to dance hall, shouting and shopping and kissing and fighting. Once, wandering around there—Robert liked to sneak up the hill, even though his parents forbade it; he treated the whole place like one giant Dungeons & Dragons set—we'd followed this faint ringing sound all the way through the maze of streets before finding ourselves at the foot of a flagpole. We'd found no flag, just the rope, which was pinging against the pole and making the sound. On the way back, we'd passed a homeless woman staggering from one sidewalk to the other, muttering, "Somebody slapped me. Somebody slapped me."

Those were the thoughts I was having when my mother brought me the phone. As she held it out, she touched my hair gently. They hadn't asked, even once, where all my new friends had gone during this vacation. For that, I was profoundly grateful.

"Hello?" I said.

"My dad said you called," said Jill, and I dropped the spoon and glanced up at my mother. The hopefulness in her answering smile almost set me crying.

"Jill? It's great to hear your voice, where are you?"

"Home."

"Here?"

"Here, yeah, home, what'd I just say?"

I stood, spun from my mother toward the hall for my winter boots and heavy jacket. "Let's go walking. Right after school, I'll meet you by the Copper Miner fountain. We'll get good and frostbitten."

"Tomorrow, okay?" Her voice, suddenly, was the one she'd used when I'd seen her last. And her breathing had that hitch again. "I think I'm coming back tomorrow."

"You heard about Valway, right? What English class did they put you in?"

Silence, except for her clipped, hiccoughing breath. Then, "Hey. Teddy?"

I waited, listening to her breath, holding my own.

"Thanks for calling," she said, and hung up.

Walking to school, I replayed the whole conversation in my head, sifting it. The day had proved strangely windless for Silver City, and lead-colored clouds hung over everything, smothering the mountains and suffocating the whole town. I was running late, saw almost no cars or kids until I hustled through the front doors. The bell had just rung, and the hallways filled with banging and chatter as locker doors shut and kids dragged themselves toward their first classes of the new year.

I made it to my own spot and fumbled the door open just as Matt Janus emerged from the restroom. He came up beside me, flung open his locker directly in my path as usual, and started riffling through his books. Impossibly, he looked even bigger. His black jeans barely contained him, and when he swung off the leather jacket and hung it on its hook, his arms looked positively cartoonish, almost childlike despite their size, like clubs from a *Flintstones* cartoon. They were also covered in purple-red blotches. *Bruises*?

Elbowing me even farther back without so much as turning his head, he slammed his door and started off. To either side, kids ducked away and then closed behind him. He never looked around or back, and so never noticed that one of his jacket sleeves had caught in the locker door, and that the door had not shut.

Later—much later, when I talked about it at all—I told people the decision wasn't conscious. But that was a lie. It was immediate, but I thought about it every step of the way.

I stared at the locker. At Matt's retreating back. I pulled his locker door the rest of the way open. I wasn't seeing Robert's weeping face, or hearing Jill's breathing. I was thinking of that basketball kid's shoes tipped sideways in the puddle where Matt had hurled them, half-sunk, like the dead ducks beside Snake Lake. And also Mr. Valway's damp, dour smirk.

Matt's jacket felt heavy and huge as I pulled it off the hook, more like a dog carcass than clothing. It smelled bad, too, like caked liniment oil. Turning, I dropped my backpack and started with the jacket down the hall toward the front of the school. Toward the Copper Miner fountain.

The most immediate effect was the spreading silence. Every step I took, another group of kids glanced over, saw what I had in my hands, and stopped talking.

I didn't rush. I looked around. Saw three of the skateboys I knew, and nodded. Saw the bass player from Kenny Tripton's band, held the coat out to him. He recoiled as though I'd offered him a dripping wolf hide. If the leather had been any less heavy or smelled better, I might have slipped the thing on, like Hercules donning the skin of the lion of Nemea. That's what I felt like. Giddy. Almost invincible.

I walked straight to the fountain, gurgling stupidly in its toilet-shaped porcelain pool. In the center of the pool stood a bronzed, bearded miner, copper shovel poised over the water. Folding Matt's coat neatly—sleeves first, zipper up—I held it outstretched in my arms a few more seconds. Then I plunged it into the lukewarm water, laying it right under that copper shovel, and held it hard on the bottom as though drowning puppies in a sack.

Without drying my own arms and without looking back, I left the jacket where it was, walked back up the row of dead-quiet kids, collected my books, and went to math.

The news that I would soon be dead reached me during milk break. Whitney Drum, of all people, came scurrying up as I emerged from second period bio and dragged me around a corner into an empty chem lab. Her eyes, for the first time since I'd known her, were all the way clear, and her skin glowed a little paler than I remembered. She looked hosed clean, and somehow more frail.

"He's going to fucking kill you," she said.

The weird thing was that until right then, I'd felt no fear whatsoever. In fact, I'd half-forgotten what I'd done, wandered through the morning in a daze. The fountain felt like months ago, and the only thing echoing in my head was that homeless woman's voice. *Somebody slapped me.*

"Beat me, maybe," I told Whitney, and tried to smile. "Break my fingers."

"End your life," Whitney said. "Stop your breathing. That's what he told me."

Just like that, my legs went, as though the bones had been pulled from them. I sat on the floor, staring at my knees.

"Get out of here," Whitney murmured. "Go home, Teddy. Jesus Christ, go home." She was sobbing as she darted from the room.

The whole rest of the snack break, I was thinking I would do exactly that, wait until the next class bell and then slip out amidst the bustle. I'd have gone right away, except I had no idea where Matt Janus went on his break. In fact, now that Valway was dead, I had no idea where his schedule took him at any point in his day.

So I waited. Once, four minutes before time, I heard heavy boots clump down the hall toward the room where Whitney had steered me. I glanced around the lab, thought about breaking a beaker and wielding it in front of me. But if Matt came, and I cut him, I'd only enrage him more. There wasn't anywhere to hide. I ducked to the side of the window carved into the door, so at least no one could see me through that. Whoever it was went past without slowing. The bell rang.

It was all I could do, the whole way down the hall, to keep from running. I kept jerking my head to both sides, waiting for that telltale parting in the crowd, that towering figure bearing down. The double doors of the gym stood half open, and as I passed one of them banged back and a giant roared out, but it was only Mr. Kellaway, the basketball coach, chasing a ball. He saw me leap back, knocking over two girls behind me, stared at me a few seconds, and started to laugh. Ignoring the girls—who'd realized who I was, and crab-walked away before getting to their feet—I kept moving.

Thirty feet ahead, I saw the stony gray light through the front doors. Behind me, sounds were thinning as students split off into classes, all of them watching me, most of them whispering. I could hear individual footsteps, now. Some of them heavy. I didn't look back. I kept walking. Fifteen feet. I thought of the crawl space in our empty house. I'd take a salami sandwich and a flashlight down there, stay until mom got back from work or dad from whatever construction site he was on. I had my hand outstretched for the door when I thought of Jill, wondered what crawl space she'd slipped into in her house. Without thinking about it, I veered right, half-sprinted down the front hallway, and went to Spanish after all.

I don't remember any of the next two periods. I'm not sure I even got my name on the pop World Civ quiz. No one spoke to me. No one even looked at me, though they all glanced in my general direction periodically, as though I were already a ghost, something they could *feel* but no longer see. When I came out of Spanish, Matt Janus was standing by the fountain, and he was looking straight down the hall toward me. He waited until he was sure I was looking. Then he lifted out his folded coat from under the copper shovel, held it up, and wordlessly, expressionlessly, slid it on. He stood there dripping and staring. I ducked down a side hall and went all the way around the school to reach the cafeteria.

Once there, I hurried to get a place in the middle of the line, surrounded by as many other people as possible, but I'd been too long arriving and wound up at the end. Frantically, I scanned the huge, echoing hall, the students huddled around the squat, rectangular wooden tables, their chairs screeching horribly in the ruts in the scarred and cracked linoleum floor.

No Matt.

I scanned again. The line inched forward. The room echoed, and chairs screeched. I'd reached the edge of the actual food displays, picked a pudding and placed it on my tray, when the silence bloomed behind me.

It came like a wave of radiation, spreading from the door of the hall outward in all directions. Matt didn't waste any time. If I'd made any calculations at all, I realized right then they were wrong. Whatever Matt was doing, it wasn't for effect, or for sending a message. He didn't wait for the silence to become total. He didn't stroll in slow motion. He just came for me.

Don't turn, I was murmuring inside my head. Stupid, really. A completely inappropriate climber's thought. As if not looking, in this particular case, was going to help. *Don't turn.*

Would he do it with his hands?

It was that thought, mostly, that triggered my reaction. My hands were already gripping the food tray so hard it seemed I could feel my fingertips touching through the plastic. When I whipped it off the countertop, sending the pudding goblet flying to the side to shatter, the tray felt light, so pathetically light. Whirling, swinging wildly, I caught Matt Janus on the point of his chin and dropped him to his knees like a felled tree.

Around us, the silence exploded. Everyone was shouting, though I couldn't make out a single word over the buzz in my ears. I also couldn't blink, couldn't even look away from Matt where he knelt, chin split and bleeding, gorilla-hands at his sides. After a few seconds, he glanced up. The look on his face wasn't quelled-bully, and it wasn't amazement, and it sure as hell wasn't fear. I bolted, hurtling to the side as his hands shot out for me, and this time I kept going, through the school's front door, down the hill, off the street into the trees, and home.

From the garage, I grabbed one of the ceremonial silver shovels bankers always gave my father when he broke ground on some new project. Instead of going into the crawl space, I crouched on the couch by the front window, then later went outside so I could breathe better and hid in the pine tree in our yard, watching the road. Of course, the air out there was Silver City air, probably had less oxygen in it than what was in our house, and as the gray light turned darker gray, then black, the cold got inside my jacket, then my skin, then my organs, so that each new pump of my heart sent a fresh shock of iciness down my veins. Finally, I went back indoors.

I'd had the whole afternoon to think of something to say to my parents. In the end, I told them I felt sick, might not be able to go in tomorrow. I didn't specify what kind of sick, and they didn't ask. They turned the heat up high, though—my mother's habitual response to anyone's illness—and in the sweating small hours I lurched awake, believing I'd heard a scratch at my window. *What time had Robert said the Dark Lord had come?*

Dawn. He'd come for Robert at dawn.

The only thing that came for me was the light. I curled deep into my sheets, rolled around, twisted them up, tried a practice moan or two. I didn't usually play sick, and didn't think my parents would ask, but I wanted them to believe it. Somehow, I tricked myself back to sleep, and awoke with my mother placing the phone at my ear.

"How're you feeling?" she asked.

"Not so—" I started, and Jill's voice poured through the receiver.

"Teddy?"

"Hey." I sat up.

"Walk today?"

"You're coming in today?"

"Meet you by your locker right after last class? Wherever I have that now?"

"Okay."

Dazed, wordless, I handed the phone to my mother, ignored her questioning look, and got dressed.

I considered taking the ceremonial shovel. During breakfast, I actually pocketed the knife my mom always laid on the margarine container. So that if Matt maybe brought some toast, we could butter it before he dismembered me. I'd left my books, my backpack, even my winter coat on the school cafeteria floor. Maybe someone had collected them.

In the end, I just put on a second sweatshirt, kissed my baffled parents, and set off into a surprising, dazzling winter sun. The light carried no heat, but it caught the shards of uncollected copper and useless ore refuse in the rocks, turned the buttes blue and maroon and orange like stained glass. Shattered stained glass, but still. I came through the front door of LMMS right on time, moved steadily through my classmates, who parted before me and went quiet yet again. I glanced around for Jill, didn't see her.

Matt Janus was leaning against my locker in his leather jacket.

I could have run. I could have gone to Mrs. Morbey's and gotten myself suspended for vandalizing Matt's locker and also decking him with the food tray. I could have demanded that the police come and search Matt's locker and his pockets for the drugs he almost certainly had stashed there.

I walked straight up to him instead. *It's going to hurt*, I thought. *And then, one way or another, it's going to be over.* I thought of Robert weeping. And, yet again, of Valway's masked face. And his, *"Well, now."*

I reached Matt and stood before him. There were probably two hundred kids watching. I couldn't hear them, could barely make myself believe they were there.

"I don't suppose sorry's going to do it," I said, staring at his collarbone, the masses of muscle crowding in on his neck. Then, finally, I made myself look at his face.

His expression was utterly unreadable. But his eyes . . .

I couldn't make sense of it. Not quite yet. I can only say what I thought: *The only thing in Matt's eyes, right that moment, was Matt.*

He didn't move for a while. At no point did he grin. What he did do, finally, was step back and tap my locker with his long, white fingers.

"What?" I whispered, barely breathing. "Open it?"

Matt tapped again. I twirled the combination, fumbled it twice, finally got the door unlatched. Inside, my backpack and coat and books lay neatly re-stowed. Elbowing me—not hard—to one side, Matt ducked in, pulled everything out in a single pile, and dropped it on the floor beside him. Then he stuck out his hand in a slow, graceful movement—if not for his coat, and his muscles, and the fact that he was Matt Janus, he could have passed for a butler—and gestured me inside.

For a long moment, we just looked at each other. Me, and the balrog of the abandoned mineshaft. My friend from years ago.

I stepped into the locker. Matt shut the door, shoved it until it the click told him it was locked. The bell rang, and a buzz roared through the halls. From the breathing just outside, and the weight I could sense when I pushed my hands against the inside of the door, I could feel that Matt was still out there. Soon, there was silence.

At one point, ten minutes or so into first period, with Matt still leaning on my locker, it occurred to me that nothing was over. That he was going to rip the door open now that we were alone and tear me to pieces.

Except that he didn't know the combination. Had put me—intentionally, or otherwise—in the one place in Silver City where he really couldn't get at me.

Somewhere in that whirl of thoughts, I realized I couldn't hear his breathing anymore. That there was no one outside. I waited another few minutes, heard footsteps, shouted out. It took Mr. Kellaway four tries, with me repeating that he had to bump it after the "38," to get the door open.

When I stepped out, blinking, he exploded into laughter, shook his head, and walked away.

There were terrified, stunned stares when I walked into bio a few minutes later. But there were cheers when I got to Spanish. I was shuttled to the front of the lunch line. I kept waiting for that blooming silence, the heavy footfall that would tell me the real consequences had come. But they didn't come. If Matt was in the cafeteria, I never saw him.

Somehow, slowly, P.E. and English crawled by. Fifteen minutes from the bell, I realized I was about to go walking, for the first time in two months, with Jill Redround. When we were good and high on the buttes, I was going to kiss her.

The second the bell rang, I sprinted for my locker. I knew Matt might be waiting for me there. I no longer cared. I just wanted to be waiting when Jill showed up. I didn't even notice the note taped to my door at first, because I was too busy scanning every passing face.

The note was handwritten, on the yellow legal paper Jill always used.

Gone to the Janus Tree. Matt begged me. I told him it was the last time. Call me tonight? Can't wait to see you, Teddy. RoundRed.

Dawn, I thought, my hands shaking so hard I tore the note in half. "*The Dark Lord summoned me to the Janus Tree.*" That's what Robert had said. Pretty much the last thing he'd said, when he was my friend. *The night he'd gone up the hill. Seen what he'd seen.*

Then I was hurling students aside, flying for the front door and out, cutting through the yards toward uptown and the road up the rocks to the Janus house.

The sun still shone, but snow was flurrying in gray, gust-driven balls like tumbleweeds. Overhead, I could see the Virgin of the Great Divide through the drifts, blank and mysterious as a sphinx, some other culture's monument. I was thinking of the vanished Incas, the village Mr. Janus had told us about. *Indio Muerto.* I could hear his voice. *You're telling me we can't locate a single dead Indian, in their own village?* Most of all, I was thinking of his crooked, decaying fingers stroking Jill Redround's upper arm, inches from the swell of her breast.

Everyone has to get old, he'd said. *Everyone has to get old.*

Vanished. Where had they gone?

When Robert had received his summons, Mr. Janus had barely got back from Chile. He must have hardly begun testing out what he'd learned in the village of dead Indians. He might not even have been positive it was working. Or what anyone else would make of the changes, if there'd even been any. Had he picked Robert because he was wacky, vulnerable, the kind of kid bullies always chose? Or because he thought—hoped—Robert was sensitive, and might confirm that something was indeed happening. To himself. To his son. . . .

I understood long before I got there.

Inside the Janus house, nothing moved. Nothing would, of course. *Why had NO ONE asked whom Matt would be staying with, now that his father and mother were both gone? Because somehow, subconsciously, everyone else already knew, too. Not that anyone would say. And it was too much even to admit.*

Through the snow, in the red-yellow sun, I could see them on the hillside. Matt right under the tree, so that it seemed an extension of his spine, the dead branches to the right and the live ones on the left fanning open on either side of him like wings, the scaly bark so closely resembling his own blotchy, shedding skin. And Jill on her knees in front of him. Screaming.

I'd gotten within ten feet before I realized even Matt hadn't gotten *that* tall, couldn't have, and finally noticed the wheelbarrow he was standing in.

"What the *fuck*?" I screamed. And then, *"Jill!"*

Matt kicked the wheelbarrow out from under himself so hard that it swung up and smacked Jill in the forehead. She fell back flat, still screaming, hands at her face and blood spurting into her eyes. So only I saw.

I saw legs kicking. Not dancing, kicking. Not at the air, but at each other. I saw Matt's right hand yanking at the noose, his left hand wrenching at the right, all but pulling it off its wrist. Then something in the rope slipped, Matt dropped another six inches, and the snap of his neck exploded off the rocks like gunshot.

The ambulance and the hearse arrived together. I knew, even as I kissed her bloody forehead, that Jill was gone from me, too. Her mother moved her to Albuquerque for good three days later. I wrote her there. Sometimes, she wrote back. She never returned, and she never invited me down, and I've never gone.

I can't. Because every time I think of her or see her face, I see Matt's face. In the noose, kicking and fighting for his life with his father, who'd slipped inside him. Or by my locker, at the moment he directed me into it, when he was just Matt, who'd flung a balrog off a cliff, having lost a battle to a boy who stored magic in a plastic light-saber in his backpack.

The Bedroom Light

JEFFREY FORD

Jeffrey Ford's most recent novel, The Girl in the Glass, *won the Edgar Allan Poe Award. His short novel,* The Cosmology of the Wider World, *was published in 2005 and his second collection of short stories,* The Empire of Ice Cream, *was published in 2006. He has recently had stories published in the anthology* The Coyote Road: Trickster Tales *and in the Datlow-edited issue of* Subterranean *magazine. He will also have a story in the forthcoming anthology* The Starry Rift. *Two of his stories were reprinted in* The Year's Best Fantasy and Horror, Nineteenth Annual Collection.

Ford lives in New Jersey with his wife and two sons. He teaches Literature and Writing at Brookdale Community College.

They each decided, separately, that they wouldn't discuss it that night. The autumn breeze sounded in the tree outside the open kitchen window and traveled all through the second-story apartment of the old Victorian house. It twirled the hanging plant over the sink, flapped the ancient magazine photo of Veronica Lake tacked to his office door, spun the clown mobile in the empty bedroom, and, beneath it, set the wicker rocker to life. In their bedroom it tilted the fabric shade of the antique floor lamp that stood in the corner by the front window. Allison looked at the reflection of them lying beneath the covers in the mirror set into the top of the armoire while Bill looked at their reflection in the glass of the hand-colored print, "Moon Over Miami," that hung on the wall above her. The huge gray cat, Mama, her belly skimming the floor, padded quietly into the room and snuck through the partially open door of the armoire.

Bill rolled over to face Allison and ran his hand softly down the length of her arm. "Today, while I was writing," he said, "I heard, coming up through the grate beneath my desk, Tana, getting yelled at by her mother."

"Demon seed?" said Allison.

He laughed quietly. "Yeah." He stopped rubbing her arm. "I got out of my chair, got down on the floor, and turned my ear to the grate."

She smiled.

"So the mom's telling Tana, 'You'll listen to me, I'm the mother. I'm in charge and you'll do what I say.' Then there was a pause, and I hear this voice. Man, this was like no kid's voice, but it *was* Tana, and she says, 'No, Mommy, I'm in charge and you will listen to me.'"

"Get outa here," Allison said and pushed him gently in the chest.

"God's honest truth. So then Cindy makes a feeble attempt to get back in power. 'I'm the Mommy,' she yells, but I could tell she meant to say it with more force, and it came out cracked and weak. And then there's a pause, and Tana comes back with, 'You're wrong, Mommy. I am in charge and you will listen to me.'"

"Creep show," Allison said.

"It got really quiet then, so I put my ear down closer. My head was on the damn floor. That's when I heard Cindy weeping."

Allison gave a shiver, half fake, and handed Bill one of her pillows. He put it behind his head with the rest of his stack. "Did I tell you what Phil told me?" she said.

"No," he said.

"He told me that when he's walking down the street and he sees her on one side of the road, he crosses over to the opposite side."

"I don't blame him," he said, laughing.

"He told you about the dog, right?" she said, pulling the covers up over her shoulder.

Bill shook his head.

"He said the people who live in the apartment on the second floor next door—the young guy with the limp and his wife, Rhoda—they used to have a beagle that they kept on their porch all day while they were at work."

"Over here," he said and pointed at the wall.

"Yeah. They gave it water and food, the whole thing, and had a long leash attached to its collar. Anyway, one day Phil's walking down to the Busy Bee to get coffee and cigarettes and he sees Tana standing under the porch, looking up at the dog. She was talking to it. Phil said that the dog was getting worked up, so he told Tana to leave it alone. She shot him a 'don't fuck with me' stare. He was worried how it might look, him talking to the kid, so he went on his way. That afternoon the dog was discovered strangled, hanging by the leash off the second-story porch."

"He never told me that. Shit. And come to think about it, I never told *you* this. . . . I was sitting in my office just the other day, writing, and all of a sudden I feel something on my back, like it's tingling. I turn around, and there she is, standing in the doorway to the office, holding Mama like a baby doll, just staring at me. I jumped out of my chair, and I said, like, 'I didn't hear you knock.' I was a little scared, actually, so I asked her if she wanted a cookie. At first she didn't say anything, but just looked at me with that . . . if I was writing a story about her I'd describe her face as *dour*—an old lady face minus the wrinkles. . . . Then, get this, she says in that low, flat voice, 'Do you Lambada?'"

"What the fuck?" Allison said and laughed. "She didn't say that."

"No," he said, "that's what she said, she asked me if I *Lambada*. What the hell is it anyway? I told her no, and then she turned and split."

"Lambada, I think . . ." she said and broke out laughing again, "I think it's some kind of South American Dance."

"What would have happened if I said yes?" he asked.

"Lambada," she whispered, shaking her head.

"Phil's got the right strategy with her," he said.

"But I don't like her coming up here in the middle of the day uninvited," said Allison.

"I'll have to start locking the door after you go to work," said Bill.

"This place . . . there's something very . . . I don't know." She sighed. "Like you ever lean against a wall? It kind of gives like flesh," she said.

"That's just the lathing . . . it's separating away from the Sheetrock cause the place is so old. I know what you mean, though, with that egg shell smoothness and the pliancy when you touch it—spongy-weird."

"I'm talking there's a sinister factor to this place. The oriental carpets, the lion's paw tub, the old heavy furniture—the gravity of the past that was here when we moved in. I can't put my finger on it. At first I thought it was quaint, but then I realized it didn't stop there."

"Like melancholy?" he asked.

"Yeah, exactly—a sadness."

"Just think about it. You've got Corky and Cindy down there, hitting the sauce and each other almost every night. They must have had to buy a whole new set of dishes after last weekend. Then you got the kid . . . nuff said there. What about next door, over here on this side, the guy who washes his underwear on the fucking clothesline with the hose? That guy's also classically deranged."

"I forgot about him," she said.

"Well," he said, "let's not forget about him. I watch him from the kitchen window. I can see right down through the tree branches and across the yard into his dining room. He sits there every night for hours, reading that big fat book."

"I've seen him down there," she said. "Sometimes when I wake up at three a.m. and go into the kitchen for a glass of water, I notice him down there reading. Is it the Bible?"

"Could be the fucking phone book for all I know."

"Cindy told me that when they got Tana that yippie little dog . . . Shotzy, Potzy . . . whatever, the kid was walking on that side of the house over by the old guy's property, and he came out his back door, and yelled at her, 'If I find your dog in my yard, I'll kill it.' Now, I know Tana's demon seed and all, but she's still a little kid. . . . Cindy didn't tell Corky because she was afraid he'd cork off and kick the crap out of the old guy."

"What, instead of her for once? Hey, you never know, maybe the old man's just trying to protect himself from Tana's . . . *animal magic*." said Bill.

"You know, Cindy swears the kid brought a dead bird back to life. She just kind of slips that in in the middle of a 'hey, the weather's nice' kind of conversation."

"Yeah, I've caught that tale," said Allison. There was a pause. "But do you get my overall point here?" She opened her hands to illustrate the broadness of the concept. "Like we're talking some kind of hovering, negative funk."

"Amorphous and pungent," he said.

"I've felt it ever since the first week we moved in here," she said.

"Does it have anything to do with the old woman who answered the door with her pants around her ankles?"

"Olive Harker?" she said, "Corky's illustrious mom?"

"Remember, Olive hadda get shipped out for us to move in. Maybe she cursed the joint . . . you, know, put the Lambada on it."

"It wasn't her so much," said Allison. "I first felt it the day the cat pissed in the sugar bowl."

He stopped rubbing her forehead. "Right in front of me—between bites of French toast," he said. "That cat sucks."

"Don't talk about Mama that way," she said.

"It baahhhs like a lamb and eats flies. I hate it," he said.

"She's good. Three whole weeks gone and she still came back, didn't she? You shouldn't have thrown her out."

"I didn't throw her, I drop-kicked her. She made a perfect arc, right over the back fence. But the question is, or at least the point is, if I follow you, is how strange is it that she pissed right in the sugar bowl—jumped up on the table, made a beeline for it, parked right over it, and pissed like there was no tomorrow?"

"That's what I'm getting at," said Allison. "It fulfills no evolutionary need. It's just grim."

"Maybe it's us," he said. "Maybe we're haunting ourselves."

"I saw Corky digging a big hole out in the yard the other day," she said. "His back's full of ink—an angel being torn apart by demons. . . . I was more interested in the hole he was digging 'cause I haven't heard any yipping out of Potzy for a few days."

"Don't worry," he said. "I'm ready for him."

"How?" she asked.

"Last Thursday, when I went out garbage-picking and found Veronica's picture, I brought back a busted-off rake handle. I wound duct tape around one end for a grip. It's in the kitchen behind the door for when Corky gets shit-faced and starts up the stairs. Then I'm gonna grab that thing and beat his ass."

"Hey, do you remember that guy Keith back in college?" she asked.

"McCurly, yeah," he said. "He did the apple dance. What made you think of him?"

She nodded. "Every time he flapped his arms the apple rolled off his head, remember?"

"He danced to Steve Miller's 'Fly Like an Eagle,'" Bill said. "What a fuckin' fruitcake. I remember Oshea telling me that he ended up working for the government."

"Well, remember that time he was telling us he was reading *The Amityville Horror*?"

"Yeah," he said.

"McCurly said that one of the pieces of proof that the author used in the book to nail down his case that the house was really haunted was that they found an evil shit in the toilet bowl. Remember that?"

"Yeah."

"You said to him, 'What do you mean by an *evil* shit?' And McCurley looked like he didn't get your question."

"But what he eventually said was, 'It was heinous.' I asked him if he could explain that and he said, 'Really gross.'"

They laughed.

She touched his face as if to make him quiet, and said, "That's the point. We paint the unknown with the Devil's shit to make it make sense."

"Heavy," said Bill. A few seconds passed in silence.

"Right? . . ." she said.

"That Amityville House was only like two towns over from where I grew up," he told her. "New people were in there and it was all fixed up. I'd go out drinking with my friends all night. You know, the Callahans, and Wolfy, and Angelo, and Benny the Bear, and at the end of the night we'd have these cases of empty beer bottles in the car. So around that time the movie of the Amityville Horror came out. We went to see it and laughed our asses off—come on, Brolin? Steiger we're talking. One of the things that cracked us up big time was the voice saying, 'Get out. For god's sake get the hell out.' I don't want to get into it now but Steiger and the flies . . . baby, well worth the price of admission. So we decided we're gonna drive to the Amityville Horror House and scream, 'Get the hell out,' and throw our empties on the lawn."

"That's retarded," she said.

"We did it, but then we kept doing it, and not just to the Amityville Horror House. Every time we did it, I'd crack like hell. It was so fucking stupid it made me laugh. Plus we were high as kites. We did it to people we knew and didn't know and we did it a lot to the high school coaches we'd had for different sports. There was this one guy, though, we did it to the most—Coach

Pinhead. Crew cut, face as smooth as an ass, goggly eyes, and his favorite joke was to say "How Long is a Chinaman." He was a soccer coach, a real douche bag, but we swung by his house every weekend night for like three months, dropped the empties and yelled 'Pinhead!!!' before peeling out on his lawn. We called the whole thing a 'Piercing Pinhead.'"

"Could you imagine how pissed off you'd be today if some kids did that to you," she said.

"Yeah," he said, "I know. But get this. I was talking to Mike Callahan about five years later. When he was working selling furniture and married to that rich girl. I saw him at my mother's funeral. He told me that he found out later on that Pinhead died of pancreatic cancer. All that time we were doing the Piercing Pinheads, screaming in the middle of the night outside his house, tormenting him, the poor guy was in there, in his bedroom, dying by inches."

"That's haunted," said Allison.

"Tell me about it," he said and then rolled closer to kiss her.

They kissed and then lay quiet, both listening to the sound of the leaves blowing outside. She began to doze off, but before her eyes closed all the way, she said, "Who's getting the light?"

"You," said Bill.

"Come on," she said, "I've got an early shift tomorrow."

"Come on? I've gotten the damn light every night for the past two weeks."

"That's 'cause it's your job," she said.

"Fuck that," he said but started to get up. Just then the light went out.

She opened her eyes slightly, grinning. "Sometimes it pays to be haunted," she said.

Bill looked around the darkened room and said, as if to everywhere at once, "Thank you."

The light blinked on and then off.

"Maybe the bulb's loose," he said.

The light blinked repeatedly on and off and then died again.

"That's freaky," she said, but freaky wasn't going to stop her from falling asleep. Her eyes slowly closed and before he could kiss her again on the forehead, she was lightly snoring.

Bill lay there in the dark, wide awake, thinking about their conversation and about the lamp. He thought about ghosts in Miami, beneath swaying palm trees, doing the Lambada by moonlight. Finally, he whispered, "Light, are you really haunted?"

Nothing.

A long time passed, and then he asked, "Are you Olive?"

The light stayed off.

"Are you Pinhead?"

Just darkness.

"Are you Tana?" he said. He waited for a sign, but nothing. Eventually he closed his eyes and thought about work. He worked at Nescron, a book store housed in the bottom floor of a block-long, four-story warehouse—timbers and stone—built in the 1800s. All used books. The owner, Stan, had started, decades earlier, in the scrap paper business and over time had amassed tons of old books. The upper three floors of the warehouse were packed with unopened boxes and crates from everywhere in the world. Bill's job was to crawl in amid the piles of boxes, slit them open, and mine their cargo, picking out volumes for the Literature section in the store downstairs. Days would pass at work and he'd see no one. He'd penetrated so deeply into the morass of the third floor that sometimes he'd get scared, having the same feeling he'd had when he and Allison had gone to Montana three months earlier to recuperate and they were way up in the mountains and came upon a freshly killed and half-eaten antelope beside a water hole. Amidst the piles of books, he felt for the second time in his life that he was really "out there."

"I expect some day to find a pine box up on the third floor holding the corpse of Henry Miller," he'd told Allison at dinner one night.

"Who's Henry Miller?" she'd asked.

He'd found troves of classics and first editions and even signed volumes for the store down below, and Stan had praised his efforts at excavating the upper floors. As the months went on, Bill was making a neat little stack of goodies for himself, planning to shove them in a paper sack and spirit them home with him when he closed up some Monday night. An early edition of Longfellow's translation of Dante; an actual illuminated manuscript with gold leaf; a signed, first edition of *Call of the Wild*; an 1885 edition of *The Scarlet Letter*, were just some of the treasures.

Recently at work he'd begun to get an odd feeling when he was deep within the wilderness of books, not the usual fear of loneliness, but the opposite, that he was not alone. Twice in the last week, he'd thought he'd heard whispering, and once, the sudden quiet tumult of a distant avalanche of books. He'd asked down below in the store if anyone else was working the third floor, and he was told that he was the only one. Then, only the previous day, he couldn't locate his cache of hoarded books. It was possible that he was disoriented, but in the very spot he'd thought they'd be, he instead found one tall slim volume. It was a book of fairy tales illustrated by an artist named Segur. The animals depicted in the illustrations walked upright with personality, and the children, in powder-blue snowscapes surrounded by Christmas mice, were pale, staring zombies. The colors were odd, slightly washed out, and the sizes of the creatures and people were haphazard.

Without realizing it, Bill fell asleep and his thoughts of work melted into a dream of the writer Henry Miller. He woke suddenly a little while later to the sound of Allison's voice, the room still in darkness. "Bill," she said again and pushed his shoulder, "you awake?"

"Yeah," he said.

"I had a dream," said Allison. "Oh my god . . ."

"Sounds like a good one," he said.

"Maybe, maybe," she said.

He could tell she was waiting for him to ask what it was about. Finally he asked her, "So what happened?"

She drew close to him and he put his arm around her. She whispered, "Lothianne."

"Lothianne?" said Bill.

"A woman with three arms," said Allison. "She had an arm coming out of the upper part of her back, and the hand on it had two thumbs instead of a pinky and a thumb, so it wouldn't be either righty or lefty. The elbow only bent up and down, not side to side."

"Yow," said Bill.

"Her complexion was light blue, and her hair was dark and wild, but not long. And she wore this dress with an extra arm hole in the back. This dress was plain, like something out of the Dust Bowl, gray, and reached to the ankles, and I remembered my fifth grade teacher, Mrs. Donnelly, the mean old bitch, having worn the exact one back in grade school when we spent a whole year reading *The Last Days of Pompeii*."

"Did the three-arm woman look like your teacher?" asked Bill.

"No, but she was stupid and mean like her. She had a dour face, familiar and frightening. Anyway, Lothianne wandered the woods with a pet jay that flew above her and sometimes perched in that tangled hair. I think she might have been a cannibal. She lived underground in like a woman-size rabbit warren."

"Charming," he said.

"I was a little girl and my sister and I were running hard toward this house in the distance, away from the woods, just in front of a wave of nighttime. I knew we had to reach the house before the darkness swept over us. The blue jay swooped down and, as I tried to catch my breath, it spit into my mouth. It tasted like fire and spread to my arms and legs. My running went dream slow, my legs dream heavy. My sister screamed toward the house. Then, like a rusty engine, I seized altogether and fell over."

"You know, in China, they eat Bird Spit Soup . . ." he said.

"Shut up," she said. "The next thing I know, I come to and Lothianne and me are on a raft, in a swiftly moving stream, tethered to a giant willow tree that's growing right in the middle of the flow. Lothianne has a lantern in one hand, and in the other she's holding the end of a long vine that's tied in a noose around my neck. The moon's out, shining through the willow whips and reflecting off the running water, and I'm so scared.

"She says, 'Time to practice drowning' and kicks me in the back. I fall into the water. Under the surface I'm looking up and the moonlight allows me to see the stones and plants around me. There are speckled fish swimming by. Just before I'm out of air, she reels me in. This happens three times, and on the last time, when she reels me in, she vanishes, and I'm flying above the stream and surrounding hills and woods, and I'm watching things growing—huge plants like asparagus, sprouting leaves and twining and twirling and growing in the moonlight. Even in night, it was so perfectly clear."

"Jeez," said Bill.

Allison was silent for a while. Eventually she propped herself up on her elbow and said, "It was frightening but it struck me as a 'creative' dream 'cause of the end."

"A three-armed woman," said Bill. "Rembrandt once did an etching of a three-armed woman having sex with a guy."

"I was wondering if the noose around my neck was symbolic of an umbilical cord. . . ."

He stared at her. "Why?" he finally said.

She was about to answer but the bedroom light blinked on and off, on and off, on and off, without stopping, like a strobe light, and from somewhere or everywhere in the room came the sound of low moaning.

Bill threw the covers off, sat straight up, and said, "What the fuck?"

Allison, wide-eyed, her glance darting here and there, said, "Bill . . ."

The light show finally ended in darkness, but the sound grew louder, more strange, like a high-pitched growling that seemed to make the glass of the windows vibrate. She grabbed his shoulder and pointed to the armoire. He turned, and as he did, Mama the cat came bursting out of the standing closet, the door swinging wildly. She screeched and spun in incredibly fast circles on the rug next to the bed.

"Jesus Christ," yelled Bill, and lifted his feet, afraid the cat might claw him. "Get the fuck outta here!" he yelled at it.

Mama took off out of the bedroom, still screeching. Allison jumped out of the bed and took off after the cat. Bill cautiously brought up the rear. They found Mama in the bathroom, on the floor next to the lion paw tub, writhing.

"Look," said Bill, peering over Allison's shoulder, "she's attacking her own ass. What the hell . . ."

"Oh, man," said Allison. "Check it out." She pointed as Mama pulled this long furry lump out of herself with her teeth."

"That's it for me," he said, backing away from the bathroom doorway.

"Bill, here comes another. It's alive."

"Alive?" he said, sitting down on a chair in the kitchen. "I thought it was a mohair turd."

"No, you ass, she's having a kitten. I never realized she was pregnant. Must be from the time you kicked her out."

Bill sat there staring at Allison's figure illuminated by the bulb she'd switched on in the bathroom.

"This is amazing, you should come see it," she called over her shoulder to him.

"I'll pass," he said. He turned then and looked through the open kitchen window, down across the yard toward the old man's house. For the first time he could remember, his neighbor wasn't there, reading the big book. The usual rectangle of light was now a dark empty space.

Later, he found Allison sitting in the wicker rocker, beneath the clown mobile, in the otherwise empty bedroom. The light was on, and she rocked, slowly, a rolled up towel cradled in her arms. "Come see," she said to him, smiling. "The first was stillborn, and this is the only other one, but it lived. It's a little girl."

He didn't want to, but she seemed so pleased. He took a step closer. She pulled back a corner of the towel, and there was a small, wet face with blue eyes.

"We have to think of a name," she said.

The Suits at Auderlene

TERRY DOWLING

Terry Dowling is one of Australia's most awarded, acclaimed, and best-known writers of science fiction, fantasy, and horror. His short stories have been published in the anthologies Dreaming Down Under, Centaurus, Gathering the Bones, *and* The Dark, *and reprinted in several* Year's Best *volumes. They are collected in* Rynosseros, Blue Tyson, Twilight Beach, Wormwood, An Intimate Knowledge of the Night, Blackwater Days, The Man Who Lost Red, Antique Futures: The Best of Terry Dowling, *and, most recently,* Basic Black: Tales of Appropriate Fear.

Dowling edited Mortal Fire: Best Australian SF, The Essential Ellison, *and* The Jack Vance Treasury. *He is a musician, songwriter, and communications instructor with a doctorate in creative writing, and has been genre reviewer for* The Weekend Australian *for the past seventeen years.*

One hour with Gilly Nescombe in the bar of the Summerton Arms confirmed everything the truck driver had said about the meteorite. My article for *Cosmos* seemed more a reality than ever.

Tracking it back, waxing lyrical and gesturing like a fool, I kept trying to impress on her the scale of it all.

"You know how these things go, Gilly," I said. "They just get larger and larger." And off I went, telling her yet again how I would never have heard about Auderlene at all if it hadn't been for a meteorite called the Pratican Star and a talkative truck driver who had insisted on an extra beer one evening at the Three Weeds Hotel in Rozelle and had mentioned it. And pushing it back still further, if I hadn't been freelancing again and looking for a suitable follow-up article for *Cosmos*, I'd never have made the connection, seen the seed of a story when that long-hauler started telling *me* over drinks how a drunken farmer in Summerton out in the state's southwest had told *him* about the old Auderlene place and the iron suits and that part of the town's little secret.

Sitting across from me in the bar, Gilly just smiled her engaging, lopsided smile and took it all in her stride. She was more than just one of those life-hardened rural women whose life seems forever at angles to your own. Close to my own age, late thirties, early forties, looking easy with herself in white blouse, denim skirt, white deck shoes, with hazel eyes and a smile that was too Ellen Barkin for my own good and kept growing wider as I tried, yet again, to convey the scale of what had brought me here.

I managed to save it. This time I stopped midsentence, laughed out loud, and shook my head in wonder at it all. Trying the main town pub had been the obvious thing to do—but meeting Gilly like this! I wished her only sunny days.

Yes, a sizeable nickel-iron meteorite *had* fallen to ground on the Pratican estate in Summerton one summer night back in 1904. No, it had never been displayed, never examined or written up, just as the truck driver had said his own Summerton local had insisted. Now here was this very personable barmaid confirming that, yes, *if* it still existed, *if* it hadn't been thrown away or melted down, there was a good chance it was still somewhere at the old Pratican place outside of town.

Driving down from Sydney, the question had been whether it was worth the trouble of checking out at all. Science journalism, like any journalism, gets to be a subtle trap. So often you put together the article in your head long before the substance of it is in place, and sometimes the angle and *how* it catches the popular imagination is more important than the actual content.

More specifically, in a world where science readers expected to be flooded with the latest word on bosons and the Higgs Field, the bone morphology of dinosaurs, or asteroid-strike extinction events, there was still room for a bit of scientific romance, a human interest piece with a regional twist. Whatever I wrote, the Pratican Star would be the heart of it—one of the largest unlogged meteorites ever to come down in Australia since European settlement.

I'd done all the relevant searches. Most meteorites are octahedrites. From what Gilly had said, the Practican Star was the nickel-iron variety—an ataxite, with extremely high traces of those two nickel-iron minerals kamacite and taenite. But more importantly, meteors large enough to survive impact and receive a name rarely dropped out of the picture like this. Short of being nonexistent or outright fakes, named meteorites in themselves were always newsworthy in one form or other, even when the name had been lost to all but local lore.

That had done it. But now it was more than just having my byline under a two-thousand-word regional piece. Now, with any luck, it would be an intriguing small-town story of lost opportunities and a truth waiting to come out, full of hard facts rather than just hearsay with a bit of local color for padding.

Which brought up questions of access, of course; but, again, Gilly was making that easy.

"So, Nev, you can either stay here at the Arms or I can put you up at Sallen. Your choice and no offense taken."

"I don't want to impose."

"Don't be silly. One: there's plenty of room. Sallen often doubles as a guest house. Two: it's close to Auderlene, next property over. Three: I'm one of the custodians of the place. Keeper of the keys. I can get you in, help you find the thing if it's still there to be found."

I couldn't believe it and yet, after landing regular freelance work for *The Weekend Australian*, then meeting a truck driver who'd met a farmer who knew about a forgotten meteorite, it was clearly a world where anything was possible.

"And four?" I shouldn't have said it. I was just too happy, too relieved to think twice.

Gilly pretended outrage. "Now, now! I'd have to know you a lot better before there was any talk of a number four!"

She gave me a wink that was playfully ambiguous, then went on as businesslike as you please.

"A few house rules up front, Nev. No one gets to spend the night at Auderlene, so put that out of your head right away. You want to look for a meteor, we do it during the day. The old girl was insistent before she died. She had a special document drawn up back in 1968, had meetings with the local council. She lost her only boy in 1912. Very tragic. An outing with other kids went wrong. Some said murder, others manslaughter. Most said too much skylarking down at the weir one day. Anyway there was no other family. Jeanette Pratican left the house and grounds to the local community of Summerton for 'its recreation and general well-being' on the sole condition that three stipulations were met. I can quote them pretty much as they're written. There had to be 'no fewer than seven horses kept on the grounds at all times, allowed free run and given proper care.' The house was to remain 'untenanted, uninhabited, and unimproved beyond the reasonable maintenance of all existing structures.' Last of all, while it was 'to serve as a museum for the common good during daylight hours,' under no circumstances could anyone 'remain between seven in the evening and six in the morning.' Mrs. Pratican was very specific."

"Did she give reasons?"

"Not that I know of. It was take it or leave it. Enough of the Pratican fortune remained at interest to ensure it went the way she said. So you'll still find the horses, still find Harry Barrowman and his boys doing odd jobs, and the historical society reps—that's Harry, Chris Goodlan and me—making sure the doors and gates are always locked at sundown."

"There are rooms the public doesn't get to see?"

"Eighteen of the twenty-two are open. The rest are for archives, office space, that sort of thing. There's no meteorite in plain view, Nev. None that we've seen. We've been through her stuff lots of times."

"But there are vitrines? Display cases?"

"There are."

"Gilly, with something like this, the angle you take on a story is almost as important as the story itself—"

The grin was there. "You did mention that."

I grinned back. "Reckon I did. It's just people aren't that interested in rocks from space. They *are* interested in rocks from space that seem to have been hushed up and have a story attached. Please, let me know up front. What are the chances of this meteorite business being a local beat-up?"

Gilly hopped off the bar stool, smoothed her denim skirt, and took her car keys from her shoulder bag. "You're the one who has to decide that. Let me show you the place. And the suits. Wait till you see them. Wonderful or awful, depending on your taste. You follow me out in your car. I've got to get back and work here till four. Chris Goodlan will show you round."

Five minutes out of town, Gilly honked the horn of her Land Rover and did a bent-arm pointing gesture at the big house on her left. The sign above the front gate said SALLEN. It looked fine.

Another thirty seconds along the road and we were at Auderlene.

Everything Gilly, the truck driver, and his farmer had led me to expect was true. The property was the kind of enclave of transplanted Englishness that was such a cultural signature during the heyday of the British Empire and had endured as cherished benchmarks of Britishness even more vividly during the long afternoon of its decline. You found similar estates, similar enclaves in the once fashionable surrounds of Capetown at Stellenbosch and Franschoek, close by Ottawa's Rockcliffe Park or Ontario's Almonte, in the exclusive parts of Christchurch, yes, and all over the Indian subcontinent as abandoned touchpoints of what was once the British Raj: a stylish, modest Warwickshire mansion set in spacious grounds, but imposed—like one map intercut with another, leaving oaks dislocating into eucalypts, hedges into scrub, like something out of one of those forever restless colonial paintings by John Glover. In fact, strip away the town and the estuarine harbor from Glover's 1832 painting, *Hobart Town, taken from the Garden where I lived*, leaving Stanwell Hall, and you pretty well had Auderlene: an elegant, two-storied mansion set among fields and well-tamed bushland.

And, as Gilly had said, there were horses. All seven came trotting over to the gate as she unlocked the padlock and chain. She gave each one a sugar cube from the pocket of her skirt.

"Chris is up at the house, Nev. You drive on over and he'll show you round. I'll lock the gate behind you. Come back to the pub when you're done and let me know what you've decided about Sallen."

There wasn't a wink this time, but she did give that all-conquering smile.

A short amiable-looking man in his midsixties was waiting for me as I pulled in. When I'd parked the car, he greeted me warmly by the front steps.

"Chris Goodlan," he said, shaking hands.

"Neville Reid, Chris. Nev."

"Come on in, Nev. Gilly phoned on the way over and said to give you the tour. Said you're doing an article or something."

"Hoping to, Chris. Depends on what I turn up."

"Well, let me do the honors."

The long front hall opened onto large sunny rooms to the left and right, then led us into what had once been a formal ballroom as wide as the house. It was sparsely furnished now, with just a few chairs against the side walls and a chaise longue positioned in front of a large Persian rug laid out in the middle of the floor. Impressive identical staircases to either side led to upstairs bedrooms; a central door beyond the rug continued through to what were no doubt the kitchen and service rooms.

But what immediately caught the eye were the five suits of medieval armor standing in raised alcoves in the wall between those flanking staircases, three to the left of the main axial door, two to the right; the second alcove of the right-hand three was empty. Each niche was set a foot above the polished timber floor, and just large enough and deep enough—with the one exception—to accommodate its iron suit.

Though they weren't really suits of armor, I quickly saw, or even convincing replicas for that matter. I'd done a project on medieval armor back in high school, and had seen museum exhibitions of Kunz Lochner suits from Nuremberg and some fine fifteenth-century Italian suits from Milan. More than a cursory glance showed that each suit here was clearly a single rigid whole, a hollow welded iron statue painted a drab matt black that further ruined any chance of their being taken for the real thing. The pauldrons across the shoulders were curved iron segments clamped and welded onto the breastplates and identical on each one, as if the same template had been used over and over for convenience sake. The groin tassets were flat functional plates, angled and fixed in place as if their creator had been following a simplistic illustration in some old picture book. What would have been the vambraces and rerebraces on the arms and the cuishes and greaves on the legs were not shaped to protect human limbs at all, but rather were completely sealed stovepipe tubes tapered appropriately. Their joint guards—the couters at the elbows and poleyns at the knees—were token fixtures as well, cut and folded, then welded in place, while the gauntlets were locked fists, never to be opened. The feet in their iron sollerets were planted together at the heels, but turned outwards in the same duck-footed stance.

It was the full-face helmets that gave them their greatest semblance of authenticity. They looked like true early medieval casques and basinets for the most part, complete with fearsome eye-slits and breathing and vision perforations at the front. Left to right, suits one, three, and five had great helms in the distinctive, thirteenth- and fourteenth-century "bucket" style, like the headpieces of antique robots. Suits two and four had the pointed "pig-faced" visor style from the mid-1400s that had always struck me as so bestial and disturbing.

Love them or hate them, it was quite a display. Comical yet dramatic.

And there were contradictions. While they were clearly homemade constructs, the joins and seals that I could see were all full welds. There was no spot welding anywhere.

"Quite something, eh?" Chris Goodlan said. "You see why the bus tours get a kick out of coming out here."

"Very striking," I said, though I thought they looked awful. Who would give over a feature room like this to such an overpowering display? "They're more like statues really. Hollow iron statues. You can't take them apart."

"You can't, no," Chris said, as if he feared I might try.

"Off the record, what do you think of them?"

"Well, they're part of the place, aren't they? Old Nettie Pratican—"

"*Off* the record, Chris. Just between us."

Chris Goodlan chuckled. "Bloody eyesores, if you ask me. But Mrs. Pratican loved 'em well enough."

"Loved them? Really?"

"Well, she had 'em made, didn't she? Set 'em up like this. I mean, she had Myron Birch and his boys turn 'em out back in 1914."

"Any of the Birches still around?"

"Killed on the Somme in September 1916, all of 'em, if you can believe it. Father *and* sons. Bloody tragedy. The mother had already died. They made these for Mrs. P. before they went away."

"Where's the sixth one?"

"There were only ever the five, Nev."

"There are six alcoves."

"Lots of folks ask about that. But only five suits were made. Maybe there was meant to be a sixth and it was never finished. The Birches never said, but then again they were none of 'em much for writing stuff down."

"Did Mrs. Pratican leave any specs? Invoices? Diary entries?"

"Nothing we've found. No meteor either, Nev. Sorry."

"Chris, I have to ask. You've probably lived here quite a while."

"All my life, man and boy."

"Any chance that meteorite they talk about was melted down and included in this lot?"

Someone else might have showed surprise at such a notion or expressed curiosity as to why someone would do such a thing. Not Chris Goodlan. "Gilly said you might be doing a piece on the Star. Well, I've got to tell you, Nev. From what I heard growing up, that meteor wouldn't have been much larger than my fist. It wouldn't be enough to do much good. Those suits are mostly just fourteen or sixteen gauge sheet iron reworked, as far as I can tell, but that's still a lot of metal. You can climb up and take a look yourself if you want. Grab a chair from out back. You'll see they're hollow sheet iron."

"But it *could* have been included? If a metallurgical analysis was ever done, say?"

Again Chris Goodlan looked worried. "Couldn't allow anythin' like that, Nev. Things have got to be left."

"Of course. But hypothetically?"

"Well, sure. Anything's possible. Could've been melted right in when the Birches got working."

"Where did they have their workshop?"

"The foundry was in town. But if you look round back through the trees, you'll see some old work sheds just off the estate. They set up a small furnace there and brought out what they needed."

"For secrecy?"

Now Chris did look puzzled. "Convenience, I would've thought. Just large enough for the cutting and welding. And Mrs. P. could check on the progress."

It all sounded reasonable enough. The angles for my article seemed to be growing fewer by the minute.

"So what's with the curfew, Chris? No one being allowed to stay over?"

"Beats me, Nev. One of the rules though. Doors are locked by five or six most days. It's how she wanted it."

"But why?"

"Why indeed?" Chris said. "She was a weird old bird. Got weirder when Andrew died." Then he sighed and slapped his thighs as if he had decided it best to change the subject. "But she did leave us Auderlene. Let me show you the rest of the place."

Chris Goodlan was patient and very helpful. He waited while I checked in cupboards and cabinets, shifted smaller items of furniture, even moved things on shelves to look at what might be concealed behind. He reassured me five or six times that he had nothing better to do, that he was supposed to be keeping an eye on things. "Nothing personal, mind," he kept saying. It was in the rules.

There were indeed the vitrines and display cases Gilly had mentioned, things that clearly served as the sort of cabinets of curiosities that would probably have housed an unusual found object like a meteorite. There was nothing that looked remotely like it might be the Pratican Star.

I examined anything that could have been fashioned out of meteoric iron just in case: metal statues and figurines, lamp stands, decorative buckles, finials and locks. They all turned out to be bronze, brass, or pewter as far as I could tell, many with conspicuous craftsmen's marks stamped into them.

But it gave us lots to talk about, mostly about how such items fitted into the town's history. Things became so easy between us in fact that, over a cup of instant coffee Chris fetched us from the kitchen, I was able to bring up Gilly Nescombe's role in the whole thing.

"Chris, what's Gilly's place in this? She doesn't seem like a history buff. She's not a relative."

"Just someone who values what we have," he said, willingly enough it seemed. "But you go easy on her, Nev. She's had a hard time of it, what with the miscarriage and the divorce four years back. Other things."

"Other things?" I couldn't help myself.

Chris cooled a little. He'd said too much. "She'll bring it up if she wants to. I'm saying it in a neighborly way, you understand, but you just go easy."

I did end up staying at Sallen. Gilly put me up in a large airy room on the northern side of the house, and I met her other two guest house regulars, Lorna Gillard and Jim Camberson, over a fine roast chicken dinner around seven o'clock that evening.

If her "number four" quip from the morning had been any kind of come-on, there was no sign of it. Which was probably just as well; I couldn't remember the last time I'd been so taken with someone. But in view of Chris Goodlan's advice, I made sure that I remained appropriately interested yet suitably gentle and respectful.

Still, the possibility of alienating Gilly was soon to be much more of a reality. I'd decided that I had to see Auderlene again, had to go inside on my own and—yes—after dark. It wasn't just that the old mansion had been calling to me through my bedroom window while I was unpacking, nothing so simple or melodramatic. As much as I wanted to look around without being watched, it was more a case of getting the feel of the place in *all* its phases, grabbing some genuine atmosphere, even angles on future pieces I might try. My vacation was almost over and I'd come all this way. I was having an adventure. It would be wrong, a breach of trust certainly, but what real harm could it do? I'd just play dumb, be the too-eager outtatowner who never for a moment thought it was such a big deal.

Dinner was followed by two hours of cards and some rounds of *Pictionary* that were more fun than I ever thought such things could be.

At 10 P.M. I excused myself and made a strategic withdrawal, trying my best to follow Chris Goodlan's advice.

Back in my room, I stretched out on the bed fully clothed and waited for the household to settle.

Now Auderlene did seem to call to me across the fields of dry grass and eucalypts, no more than ten minutes away in the fragrant spring evening. I *had* to see the place at night. It was starting to feel like a compulsion.

After an hour or so of doors closing and the house growing quiet, the time seemed right. It was 11:20. If Gilly caught me going out, I'd say I needed some air, that my mind was racing with ideas and possibilities, that I had to relax myself a little.

No one noticed me as far as I could tell. The faint sound of a television came from one of the other guest rooms, otherwise nobody stirred.

The keys marked AUDERLENE 2 were on a hook by the back door. Within minutes I had them in my pocket, had my torch from the car, and was crossing Gilly's property toward Auderlene's southern boundary.

More than ever I was keenly aware of failing these new friends in a fundamental way. With every step I kept trying to justify it to myself, going over the excuses I'd give if Gilly *had* heard me go and confronted me later. Like that I'd noticed something at the old mansion earlier that day that I hadn't asked Chris about and it was bothering me, wouldn't let me rest. Like that I hadn't believed the curfew business was meant to be taken seriously, not really; I'd meant no harm. Or perhaps telling it like it was, that this had become something all its own, vitally important in an odd way. I had to see the Pratican place alone and during curfew. Just did.

No excuses seemed to cover it, but the fact that I kept trying to come up with them said everything about how I felt about being in Summerton. At Sallen.

But soon I was at the front steps of the old house and there were other things to think about. There had been no alarm fittings that I had seen, no security keypads or warning signs. Auderlene wasn't set up that way yet. There were just dead bolts on the access doors and the ground-floor windows, a padlock on the gate out by the road.

I would have rather used the back door under the circumstances, but, while the front door faced the highway at the end of the drive, that was the approach I knew.

There were six keys on the AUDERLENE 2 ring and I began trying them. The fourth turned smoothly in the lock; the main door opened without so much as a squeak.

The house was quiet but for the ticking of the big grandfather clock in the hall. I moved past the large front rooms, grateful that the curtains had been left open and that enough moonlight found its way in to show doorways and hall fixtures. More than ever I was certain that no silent alarm was registering on a far-off security desk. Five years from now maybe, but not yet.

Soon I was at the ballroom and relieved to find that the curtains had been left open there as well. Later in the year they would probably be closed to protect the furnishings from the harsh summer sun.

Getting my bearings, I crossed to the chaise longue in front of the carpet and sat while considering how best to proceed. Switching on the house lights was out of the question, and using the torch to explore the upstairs rooms would make passing motorists think there were burglars on the premises.

Which meant that there was very little I *could* do other than soak in the atmosphere. At Sallen that had seemed reason enough. Now I was left wondering why I had risked so much by insisting on a nocturnal visit. I could hardly believe it had seemed so important. But here I was, and there was no need to hurry. I had time to get the feel of the place without watching eyes.

Human eyes at least. The suits were right there, darker shapes in the gloom, so many streaks of coal-cellar midnight flanking the blackness of the central doorway.

I settled back and listened. The clock was ticking in the hall. The sound of crickets came from the dry grass and modest gardens beyond the locked windows, otherwise nothing. No traffic on the road from town that I could hear. None of the big city white noise sounds I had become so used to.

The sense of being watched by the suits was inevitable under the circumstances, but, oddly enough, it was that silence that bothered me most of all. It was *too* quiet. Which, I told myself, smiling wryly, was precisely one of those touches of atmosphere and local color I'd been looking for. But all things considered, Auderlene was just a large empty house, like a deserted theater or a school gymnasium after dark, any other large open space.

That silence soon took its toll. Apart from the clock, possibly the drip of a tap way off in the kitchen, all sound came from out there, from the world beyond, and it lulled me. I'd only meant to sit a while, to listen and consider options, then head back. But without meaning to, without even knowing I did so, I drowsed. I was at the end of a long drive and a busy day and the adrenaline rush of sneaking away from Sallen. I just slipped into a reverie that quickly became something else.

Till something woke me. I activated my watch display, saw it was 2:23 A.M. So much time had passed.

Crazy thoughts were there then. What if Gilly had decided to check on me? What if she had come by, found me gone, and realized where I'd be? Crazy thoughts.

I couldn't be sure I'd heard anything, of course, but the shock of believing I had was there to deal with. Real or imagined, something had woken me.

I kept as still as I could and listened. There was nothing, just the clock ticking and night bird and insect song beyond the windows. Just the conviction that something had stirred in the quiet house and gone silent again.

But what? What?

Then it was there: first as a sense of sound, more felt than actually heard, like a low-level tinnitus, something you shook your head to be free of. But within seconds, minutes—however long it was—it crossed that border between unreal and unmistakably real, became a low keening in the darkness, building toward a distinct and eerie moaning.

One of the suits was sounding!

I was sure of it. Suit four or five, there was no knowing for certain, but from one of the alcoves to the right.

I swung my legs off the divan, set my feet firmly, silently, on the floor.

The keening continued, kept growing if anything, and, strangely, was easier to take than the do-I-hear-it? do-I-not? uncertainty.

I grinned in the darkness. Of course. Gilly was off somewhere playing tricks, goosing the outtatowner, what I deserved for breaking faith as I had. She'd waited and she'd followed.

But then a suit to the left of the display began sounding as well, making a distinct harmonic to the first, impossible for one person—a single voice—to manage. It, too, grew in the darkness, clear and separate.

She had friends helping. That was it. The other custodians. Reliable old Chris Goodlan. Or Lorna, and Jim Camberson. Or there were hidden speakers. They'd done this before. It was their usual strategy for curfew breakers.

Messing with my mind, Gilly. In more ways than one.

I smiled and stood. Using the new sounding to orient myself toward suit one, I switched on my torch. Let the locals see torchlight flickering. Who'd be out at this hour anyway? And more rationalizations covered it: I'd been out walking and heard a noise inside the old house. Chris mustn't have shut the front door properly. I just came in . . .

The weak cone of light caught suit one in its glow. The iron helmet glowered back, eye-slit fierce in the meager light. It was so easy to imagine the glitter of eyes in the narrow slot, too easy to imagine a poor soul trapped within, crying in the night. One of five.

I crossed the ballroom as quietly as I could, keeping the torch beam on the eye-slit in the narrow bucket-shaped helm.

The song kept swelling. It seemed that three, possibly four suits were sounding now, but how could I be sure? The harmonics were too diffuse, the actual source points too difficult to judge in such a large space. I kept shaking my head to make sure I was actually hearing it. Was it me? Could it be me?

When suit one was within reach, I stretched out a hand, placed my fingers on the black metal chest.

It was vibrating. It was! There was a resonance in the old iron, a deep thrumming.

I felt such relief. Not *me* then. Not something in my mind. Something *in* the world, *of* the world.

I fought down the dread, the panic waiting right there. There were answers. There had to be. I just needed daylight to check for audio leads and concealed speakers. Short of switching on the house lights, there was no way of doing that now.

Go or stay: they were the only choices.

I made myself move along the row, shining my torch on the eye-slit of suit two as I reached it, then doing the same with suit three, touching each iron shape as I passed and feeling the same deep thrumming in the metal.

So far so good.

The open space of the central doorway was there then—a sudden maw of black in black—and I was at suit four, reaching out to touch the breastplate. The vibration was there as well, deep and constant, resonating so powerfully that I snatched my hand away.

Keep moving! Keep moving! One to go!

The empty niche was so welcome with its silence, but I didn't linger. Couldn't. I was nearly done.

I moved on to suit five, placed my fingers on the iron chest. Again, the nightsong was there, adding its harsh edge to the whole.

All five were sounding.

I'd done it, made myself finish, but mainly because I kept picturing Gilly hiding close by, stage-managing all this. That was what stopped me from fleeing the house, rushing back to Sallen, back to town, back to Sydney. There was a prankishness, an absurdity to the whole thing and it kept the panic at bay, brought cautious fascination instead of fear, a determination to grasp what was happening and how it was being done.

I had managed, was managing.

Provided I didn't look at the eyes-slits too long, didn't imagine the whites of eyes trapped behind the midnight slots and perforations, following every move.

It had to be Gilly and the others. Had to be.

And I had to stay rational, in control.

I made myself start back along the row, this time on a "science-and-logic" run—how I thought of it—an attempt to learn how these effects were being achieved.

I was at the empty alcove when the keening stopped.

Just like that. The suits were silent.

Such a simple thing, but all that was needed. More than ever I *knew* there were eyes peering out, staring in the silence.

In the world, *of* the world!

Which was more than I could bear.

I scrambled across the ballroom, rushed along the dark hall to the front door and out into the night, imagining those fierce unblinking eyes on me all the way back to Sallen.

Gilly seemed not to have noticed my absence. She said nothing about it over breakfast the next morning and I detected no signs that things had changed between us.

She had another 10 A.M. shift at the Arms, she told me, but said that Chris would be happy to show me through Auderlene again if I thought it would help. I thanked her, and almost called her on the night's "entertainment" with an oblique challenge: "First round to the Summerton crew, I guess," but decided against it. What if I was wrong?

After chatting in the kitchen a while, she gave me a tour of Sallen in daylight. It ended with us sitting in the lounge room, rarely used these days, she explained, but a large sunny formal space from days when ushering neighbors into parlors and serving them Devonshire tea vied with taking them straight through to the kitchen for an informal, no-frills cuppa.

I sat on a sofa by the large front windows, with Gilly close by in an armchair beside a display cabinet filled with Nescombe heirlooms: trays of old coins, war medals, a collection of vintage perfume bottles, the body of a headless china doll.

"Been in the family forever," Gilly said, indicating the display. "Funny how we keep things because we've kept them for so long. How real reasons are lost."

It gave me my cue. "Gilly, what happened to Mrs. Pratican's son back in 1912? You know, down at the weir?"

Gilly's eyes flashed with an odd mix of emotion. Surprise? Anger? Relief? Whatever the rush of feeling was, she had it under control just as quickly. "No one's really sure. Andrew was down there with some kids from town. They were skylarking around, you know, like kids do, throwing rocks, pushing and shoving. Andrew was out on the old skiff they kept down there. Someone threw a rock and hit him on the head. He went over the side. They found his body the next day."

"And don't tell me. There were five other kids with Andrew that day."

The flash of emotion was there again, showing mainly in a tightening of the eyes. She quickly looked off through the nearest open window. "Four or five. Something like that."

"Or six."

She looked back at once. "What are you saying, Nev?"

"There are six alcoves at Auderlene, Gilly."

"You're not seriously suggesting—"

"Just seriously asking. What happened to those five or six other kids?"

She tried to put me off. "How the hell would I know? They grew up. Moved away. Died. They could be anywhere. You think they took your meteorite, is that it?"

More deflection, but it didn't stop me. "Not at all. But you would've tracked it back surely. You know the local families. You've had access to the district records. You would've found the names, tracked it back."

"Nev, what's with all this? Why the private eye stuff all of a sudden?"

I didn't hesitate. "I heard the suits, Gilly. I went out to Auderlene last night and I heard them."

Gilly feigned outrage pretty well. She stood, even put her hands on her hips. "And that's the thanks I get for trying to help. Listen, Nev—"

"You knew I would, Gilly. You wanted me to. You left the keys out."

"I what?"

"You know the suits start sounding at night."

"Lots of folks round here do."

"No they don't. That sort of thing would get out, especially if there's a quick buck in it. There'd be ghost tours, souvenir hunters, the lot. I might be wrong, but I'm thinking that you and Chris and Harry Barrowman and the rest keep this pretty quiet."

"As if we could."

"As if you haven't. The question is why. You knew I'd want to go out there alone, that I'd probably want to see the place at night. You wouldn't tell me about the suits, but you wanted me to know about them. That's why you picked me, why the come-on at the Arms yesterday. You wanted me here at Sallen."

"What a bloody nerve! Who the hell do you think—?"

"Gilly, it's okay! I accept that there are rules here. Promises being kept; things you can't share. But since we're coming clean, let me ask if there really was a meteorite?"

Gilly seemed caught between genuine relief and maintaining a proper indignation. "Of course there was. Letters mention it. It came down on twenty-four January 1904. Mrs. P. had Myron Birch dig it out and bring it over to the house in his wagon. The local newspaper wrote it up; you can check the edition for the following week, if you want. It was probably kept somewhere in the house originally."

"But not displayed. People don't record seeing it when they visited."

The emotion still translated as anger. "It didn't go away, if that's what you mean. People still talked about it. But it was just a local thing. No big deal. There's so much meteorite activity in the skies out here. Tektites. Austrolites. You do things differently when you live on the land."

"But it was never seen after 1912? After what happened to Andrew?"

She sat in the armchair again, but didn't settle back in it, as if ready to leap up at any moment. "What are you driving at, Nev? Look, I did do a bit of a beat-up on the thing yesterday—"

"Though you won't say why."

"Can't say why. You were here. You'd heard about the Pratican Star. You made it easy."

So much for item number four, I didn't say. Gilly was frowning, clearly troubled by something.

"So you *can't* tell me why. Listen, Gilly—"

But she cut me off, as if something had just occurred to her. "Nev, do you really think the meteorite could be in those suits? Melted down and mixed in? You asked Chris about it."

Why does it matter? I wanted to ask, but went with the deflection, needing to keep Gilly this side of shutting down altogether and kicking me out. She wanted me to know things she couldn't talk about directly, whatever the reasons.

"If the Birches worked with existing plate, just cut and bent scrap they had on hand, then maybe not. If they actually melted the iron ore themselves at their foundry in town, then sure. It would be a lot more work, a very different scale of work, and there'd be a very small distribution given the size of the Star."

"Like that 'memory of water' thing in homeopathy."

"I guess." This was my chance. "And correct me if I'm wrong, Gilly, but I'm guessing you're a descendant of one of the six responsible for Andrew Pratican's death back then."

Gilly looked out the window again before returning her gaze to me. "You keep saying six."

"There are six alcoves. Mrs. Pratican had the suits made for a reason. Yes, I believe there's a sixth suit somewhere."

"But where?" Gilly said, and seemed encouraged by my certainty.

No, not encouraged. Encouraging!

She already knew where it was!

I dared not say so, dared not ask. Not yet. "Come and help me look for it. Take the day off."

"I can't, Nev. I can't set foot on the property. Why do you think I never gave you the tour myself?"

"Tell me."

"Something will—hurt me."

I didn't know how to take that. Literally? Metaphorically? "Something?"

"Just trust me. Look, I have to get to work. We can talk about this later."

"Gilly, I have to know. We're very close to something here. Why can't you go inside Auderlene?"

"It's not just the house. I said I can't set foot *on the property*!"

"All right. You can't set foot on the property. Something hurts you. Tell me the rest. Please."

Gilly didn't speak. She just grabbed my hand, pulled me up from the sofa, then led me out of the lounge room and along the hallway to her bedroom. My thoughts went every which way in an instant. It was so easy to misread the signals and take this as some impulsive reprise of our modest flirtation at the Summerton Arms. Even more so when she'd closed the door behind us, because in moments she was unbuttoning and removing her blouse, reaching round and unbuttoning and unzipping her skirt and stepping out of it so she stood before me in bra and panties. It was all done so quickly that I nearly said something stupid before the real reason registered.

Gilly's body was covered with scars. Healed ones, a myriad tiny wounds like punctures and slashes on her breasts, belly, and groin, on her back too when she turned to show me. Nothing above the neckline or that extended to the arms and legs. A very selective maiming, like stigmata, but all healed over, laid like dozens of silky threads against her skin.

"Gilly, how on earth—?"

"Don't ask. Please. Just know that I didn't do it, okay? That no husband or boyfriend or neighborhood sicko did it. No one passing through."

Don't blame you if you'd rather pass, Nev, she didn't say, didn't have to say because her eyes did, quickly and eloquently. It was there in the way she reached for her blouse and skirt.

"Gilly—" I just stepped forward and held her.

She clung to me. It was the sort of simple, desperately human act we get to experience maybe two or three times in our lives if we're truly lucky, one we all need to know—as giver *and* receiver—to complete our full equation of humanity. Without it we are creatures forever lacking.

Her sobbing lasted barely moments. Gilly had the habit of being strong in the world and she rallied quickly, though she didn't break the embrace.

"If I say too much, it'll start again," she murmured into my shoulder, burying the words in my shirt. Auderlene was ten minutes away, listening, watching.

"It's a haunting," I said, because *I* could.

"I've said too much, Nev."

"I have to go back, Gilly," I said. "I have to go back tonight."

Her answer chilled me with its simplicity. "Yes."

It was strange spending the day at Auderlene knowing that I'd be there again that night, so strange to see the suits looking so makeshift and ordinary, robbed of any trace of their nighttime power. This time I did grab a chair from the kitchen as Chris had suggested, and stood on it to check every suit. There were no speakers that I could find, no hidden wires unless they had been threaded up through the soles of the iron feet, an elaborate and unlikely prospect without public ghost tours to justify the effort and expense.

Everything was different now, though Chris and I acted as if nothing had changed. I wasn't sure how much he knew, whether Gilly had told him of my visit the previous night, so I said nothing about it.

During the morning we searched the wine cellar and various outbuildings for any sign of the Pratican Star and he was as patient and helpful as ever. We did the attic in the afternoon, and spent two hours hauling boxes this way and that, doing a thorough search of the contents of each one. There was nothing that resembled a meteorite.

We left off around four o'clock and climbed down, cramped, dusty, and exhausted from our efforts. After Chris had fed the horses, we spent the final hour till lockdown sitting on the front steps of the old house drinking a bottle of respectable red from the Auderlene cellar. We didn't talk all that much, just watched the occasional cars that passed on the highway and how the light went from the land toward sunset and the great silence came up, how the lights came on at Sallen across the way. The article for *Cosmos* seemed a forgotten dream, part of another reality, another ordering of the world. Now I could only think of the silky scars on Gilly's skin and her clinging to me, and how, even as the rooms behind us were falling into darkness, the iron suits in the ballroom were already crammed full of night.

I was glad when Chris checked his watch, pushed the cork back in the bottle, and stood. "Let's go, Nev. Time to lock up."

As we moved toward the front gate, a pair of new headlights appeared on the highway and Gilly's Land Rover turned in at Sallen.

———

This time she saw me off. At 11:30 P.M., with Lorna Gillard and Jim Camberson safely tucked away in their rooms, Gilly stood on the northern turn of the verandah and watched me cross into Auderlene.

There had been a kiss on the mouth from her—full, firm, and brief, as dry and smoky as the evening had been—but no more words. What could you say? Be careful? Don't let the boogeyman get you? There was often so much comedy in terror when you looked for it. It was the way of the world.

What followed was very much a repeat of the previous evening, but without the self-recrimination and guilt. This time I had the permission of a custodian—all the custodians when I thought about it, given how much they seemed to share of this.

This time I also had one of Gilly's powerful household torches to light my way. Fifteen minutes after leaving her on the verandah, I was stepping through the front door at Auderlene and shining its light down the front hall. It banished the gloom so much better than mine had.

As I entered the ballroom and took my position on the chaise longue, the strong beam of light emphasized the homemade quality of the suits, the sheer ordinariness. Only the eye-slits—five razor-cuts of night—kept their power. It was a relief when I switched off the torch and returned everything to an even darkness.

Too even. Too complete. The curtains had been closed!

Chris could have done it. Must have. It was getting to be that time of year. But it meant that the suits were no longer deeper strokes of blackness in the gloom. The windows themselves still had ghostly outlines, but the iron shapes were lost to me.

Which made it so much worse. It had become like the child's game where you crept up on someone while they weren't looking. There was the awful sense that the suits were moving toward me in the darkness, would suddenly be there, frozen but closing in, the moment I switched on my torch. Then they'd come on again on unbending, stovepipe legs, iron hands reaching—

I forced down the panic, amazed that things were getting to me this way. First the compulsion to visit after nightfall, now this ongoing dread.

Still, as difficult as it was, I resolved to leave things as they were. The curtains could be opened easily enough, and Gilly's torch was right there.

I made myself stretch out on the chaise longue and listen to the house. This time I *wanted* to drowse but it was impossible. The ticking of the clock came from the hall behind, the sound of crickets and night birds still worked their way in, but these things all seemed just that much further off now. The sense of being stranded, no longer connected, was stronger than ever.

I kept going over the events of the day, thinking of that single hurried kiss, of Gilly's scars and what could have caused them, of a sixth suit hidden from view, one that couldn't be mentioned because something would hear and respond. Couldn't be talked about; couldn't be *thought* about. Where did it end?

Given my earlier funk, I tried not to think too much about the suits here either. When they started sounding—*if* they did—I would repeat my "inspection" of the previous night, but with one important difference. This time I wouldn't simply pass the empty alcove. This time I would lean in and listen. Such an obvious thing, but I hadn't done it. I would give the missing suit its chance.

The waiting became a special kind of hell. My imagination kept playing tricks, providing things. Not just the suits creeping forward in darkness, creaking and sighing, not just house sounds—doors opening, things shifting—but doubts as well. What were the chances of Gilly and the others setting me up, *serving* me up to whatever lay at the heart of Nettie Pratican's estate? It was crazy, but suddenly so real.

Maybe the sixth suit was out there somewhere, moving through the darkness. Maybe *it* was the one heading this way. It would suddenly be in the alcove when I next switched on the torch!

Worse yet, maybe that sixth suit was for me. I'd find myself the one peering through the slits and perforations, unable to move, unable to cry out!

Completing the array. That was what the keening was: a summons!

It changed everything. I imagined the other suits watching through their narrow edges of darkness. *Yes! Yes! Join us!*

A special hell indeed, made for a solitary watcher on a quiet spring night.

I was actually relieved when the song started at 1:39. Again, it came as the barest sense of something, just as it had before. Then, across seconds, minutes, a suit near the center of the display had definitely begun to sound.

I switched on the torch and moved the powerful beam along the row, saw the suits watching in their ones and twos, always with the sense of eye glitter as I moved the torch beam on. All tricks of shadowplay and a shifting light source, of course, but an alarming optical effect: eyeslits empty and unmoving until *you* looked away, then the sense of eyes rolling back at you.

I win! I win!

I found myself actually switching the torch beam back and forth, trying to catch the whites of those imagined eyes, then considered the shock such a discovery would bring and stopped at once. The thought of it was enough.

Yes, imagination was the real enemy here. Imagination and uncertainty.

Gilly's scars were real, *looked* real. Yet could it all be a hoax? The possibility was there.

But in the torchlit darkness, with the suits keening as they had the night before, I chose to believe in Gilly and the others. It went against so much, but it was what I decided.

Keeping the torch beam as steady as I could, I crossed to suit one and touched the breastplate. The metal was thrumming, jarring my fingertips even more than I remembered.

I moved on to suit two, then to three, touching each one the same way. They were both sounding, adding their fierce harmonics to the whole. Such angry iron.

Then there was the doorway, a gaping darkness with suit four beyond.

I dared not hesitate. I crossed the gulf, reached for the breastplate, lighting only what was needed, not daring to look for eyes peering down.

Singing. It was singing.

The fifth alcove was still empty, thank God. No new arrival.

Not far now. I continued on, reached out, and pressed my fingers to the final metal chest. It was thrumming, jarring like the rest.

All five were sounding, keening.

Screaming. That's how it seemed.

Time to finish it. I turned back to the empty niche, moved the few steps needed and leant forward into the opening.

Angle of the head, angle of reality, it was enough. A single word filled the space, came again and again in a voice that was a rasp and a curse, a cry of despair and an accusation all in one, that—like a whisper gallery to infinity— seemed to cross a great gulf and yet was right there, intimate and close.

Yes.

That single word.

One way or another it answered every question I needed answered.

Is there a sixth suit?

Yes.

Can it be found?

Yes.

Is it close by?

Yes.

Can I save her?

Yes.

Then, while still straining to catch the forlorn, achingly desperate voice and its single word, the keening stopped.

And the torch went out.

There *were* eyes in the helmet slits now, I was certain. Fixed and staring.

I fumbled with the switch, tried again and again. Nothing.

Panic came like iron hands, closing hard. I threw the torch aside and went scrambling across the carpet, found the hall, the door and blessed night beyond. In moments, precious seconds, I was deep in that other darkness and running toward Sallen with a smile on my face. It was relief and reprieve. We had our answer. We truly did.

I was left to work out for myself where the sixth Pratican suit would be. It wasn't so difficult once I accepted that they knew, all of them, but couldn't tell, couldn't speak of it directly. Once I remembered the clues they'd been trying to give me all along.

Chris Goodlan and I had checked the official outbuildings maintained in the Auderlene Charter, but, as he had told me that first day, there were some old work sheds off the estate proper, back through the trees; buildings the Birches had used for the cutting, shaping, and final suit assembly.

Off the estate.

What were the chances?

Gilly nodded when I told her what I intended doing, and surprised me by wanting to come along, but she said very little when she parked her Land Rover off the highway beyond the Auderlene estate and we started walking the northern fence line toward the northwestern corner.

There were three structures in among the gum trees, one large and two small, all ramshackle and badly run-down, all made of the same weather-worn gray timber and sheets of rusted iron. Without Gilly telling me, I knew it would be the farthest one out, just did, and led us to its sagging wooden door.

"I can't go in, Nev," she said.

"But it's off the estate."

"That suit is *from* the estate. It *is* the estate. What Auderlene exists for. You go in."

"You're talking about it now, Gilly. I thought you couldn't."

"Depends on whether you find something."

"How so?"

"It happens at night, Nev. If you're wrong, then I may not survive the night."

"Your—visitor—will come calling?"

"Let's just say that coming out here again, I've broken the rules."

Again. Gilly said again. She *had* been out here before.

"Gilly—"

"Please, Nev. I'm sick of this, after all these years. It's the other part of the story. Go and see."

I said no more, just hauled back the old door and stepped inside. The interior was cluttered with lengths of timber, rusted irrigation pipes, pieces of old farm machinery. Once it would have been a gloomy space, but no longer. The roof was sprung, sagging where fallen tree branches had struck. The walls bowed under the weight of the remaining roof beams. Hot sunlight streamed in.

It didn't take long to find. The suit was lying on its back, one more half-rusted shape near the shed's far wall, almost indistinguishable amid abandoned farm machinery. Hidden in plain sight really.

And not complete—or rather not intact, which had further helped conceal it. The helm had been sawn away and left to one side, a cylindrical casque like a discarded bucket.

I crouched next to the broken figure and peered into the chest cavity. It was a cave with stalactites and stalagmites! The hollow space was filled with them, spines pointing in from front, back, and sides. They were probably in the groin and legs as well.

I hauled the helmet around and peered within. More spikes. The whole suit was like the inside of an iron maiden, that engine of torture and death from crueller times.

Not crueller, no. Nothing was crueller than this: a hollow but sealed prison, impossible to escape yet impossible to inhabit because of those knives.

Special knives. Each one tipped with its tiny bit of the Pratican Star, I was sure of it. Restless iron from out there. Metal from somewhere else.

Trap them and never let them rest.

But there had to be more to it. The meteoric tips were the avenger's *pièce de résistance*, a bereaved mother's ultimate reward for those who had been present at the death of her son. Perpetrators or innocent bystanders, it hadn't mattered to Nettie Pratican, hadn't been an issue in that inconsolable mother's plans. A look at the town records would probably show nothing either, no sudden accidents or disappearances. Nettie Pratican had been patient. This was a revenge taken *after* their deaths, quite likely after her own. And one of Gilly's ancestors—great uncle, great aunt, great cousin, someone in her family's past—had been one of those bystanders, witnesses, accomplices. Privy to a game gone wrong, to teasing taken too far.

More questions for Gilly when questions could be answered again.

But there had to be something else she couldn't mention, possibly didn't even know herself: *how* Mrs. Pratican had trapped them inside!

The shed still had lifting tackle on one of the roof beams, chains and pulleys from back when these materials were moved on a fairly regular basis. It was no coincidence that the rig was positioned *above* the suit, from when it had last been used, though then the suit must have been lifted at the shoulders so the helmet could be sawn off.

So what had been trapped inside could be released!

I had to know. Getting the chain around the ankles and hooked in place was easier than I first expected because of the tapered jambs and the flattened spur-butts on the iron feet.

The block and tackle was old and rusty; the supporting roof beam less than completely sound, but the chains moved in the double pulley system easily enough and the surrounding beams held. The legs rose off the earthen floor, tipping the chest at an angle.

It wasn't enough. If something was trapped inside, it had to get through the forest of spines. I doubted the roof could take the weight of a full lift, but all I needed was a steep enough angle. I hauled on the chain, hoisted the legs higher.

Just when I thought I might have misjudged the whole thing, something rattled down over the spikes and appeared in the neck opening.

The head of a doll, battered and hairless. Something that had belonged to Gilly's great-aunt, great-cousin, whatever, but the other part of the broken doll I'd seen in the heirloom cabinet at Sallen.

I lowered the suit to the ground and went out to where Gilly was waiting.

When she saw what I was holding, tears sprang to her eyes. She took the tiny head from me, gripped it hard between her hands and turned away.

I waited till she turned back.

"Who did you get to saw off the helmet, Gilly?"

"That truck driver who told you about Summerton and the meteor. Three years ago. He was passing through and I told him the story, asked him to help. I thought opening the suit would do it. He helped me bring it out here."

Part of me wanted to ask if he'd inquired about a "number four" option as well, but I didn't. None of my business, yet completely my business, both.

Gilly understood that. "He was just trying to help, Nev. Sending someone else along. Looking out for me. He never saw the scars."

The weight sank away. "You both saw the spikes?"

"We did. But we thought that was it. That we'd released it. We never thought that there'd be—" Gilly searched for the right term.

"Something keeping it there," I said.

"Right. This bloody doll's head!"

"And the spikes, Gilly. I think you'll find they were tipped with metal from the Pratican Star."

Gilly frowned, saw the connection, and nodded. "But why was it angry with me? I'm kin. Why me?"

"The old story of the genie trapped in the bottle. For the first thousand years he swears to reward whoever frees him. For the next thousand he swears to destroy whoever does it. Maybe your family *became* the reason it was trapped in there. Maybe communication just becomes messed up—"

"When you're dead."

"When you're dead. The prison was open but it still couldn't get free. Not completely. Imagine the agony, the fury. How did you know which suit to open?"

"Whenever I heard them sounding at night, whenever I passed close by, that one suit called out a word. In my mind."

"What word?"

"Just the one. You."

"Gilly, I'm guessing that Harry Barrowman and others you can name are descendants of those kids at the weir that day. I'm pretty sure they've heard the same word in front of a particular suit too, yes?"

The barest hint of the smile was there. She could talk about it now. They couldn't, but she could. "They didn't dare open the other suits after what happened to me. They've got families to think of. You're good at this, Nev."

"I'm outside of it—*was* outside. It helped. So you tell them what has to be done. They open the suits and remove whatever objects were used as lures."

"We're imposing our sense of justice on someone else's here, aren't we?"

"That's the operative word, Gilly. Justice. Nettie Pratican went beyond justice the moment she had the suits made, the moment she decided on the spikes and what to tip them with."

Gilly Nescombe held up the doll's head as if reading a crystal ball or considering a piece of fruit from the Garden of Eden. "The spiteful old bitch. Even God doesn't get to be that vindictive anymore."

For Tammy Vance

About the Editor

ELLEN DATLOW has been editing science fiction, fantasy, and horror short fiction for over twenty-five years. She was fiction editor of *Omni* magazine for seventeen years and the award-winning *Sci Fiction* for six years, and has edited more than fifty anthologies, including the horror half of the long-running *The Year's Best Fantasy and Horror, The Del Rey Book of Science Fiction and Fantasy, The Dark, Vanishing Acts, Troll's Eye View: A Book of Villainous Tales, The Coyote Road: Trickster Tales,* and *Salon Fantastique,* (the latter three with Terri Windling). She continues to edit anthologies for adults, young adults, and children. Datlow has won eight World Fantasy Awards, two Bram Stoker Awards, three Hugo Awards, four Locus Awards, the British Fantasy Award, and the International Horror Guild Award for her editing. She lives in New York City. For more information and lots of photos, see www.datlow.com.